WHERE DREAMS ARE BORN

A PIKE PLACE MARKET SEATTLE ROMANCE

M. L. BUCHMAN

Buchman Bookworks

PRAISE FOR M. L. BUCHMAN

3x "Top 10 Romance of the Year"

— BOOKLIST

13 times "Top Pick of the Month"

— NIGHT OWL REVIEWS

I became completely immersed in this story and it had me at page one. Entertaining and full of emotion.

— FRESH FICTION, *WHERE DREAMS ARE BORN*

A favorite author of mine. I'll read anything that carries his name, no questions asked. Meet your new favorite author!

— THE SASSY BOOKSTER, FLASH OF FIRE

M.L. Buchman is guaranteed to get me lost in a good story.

— THE READING CAFE, WAY OF THE WARRIOR: NSDQ

I love Buchman's writing. His vivid descriptions bring everything to life in an unforgettable way.

— PURE JONEL, HOT POINT

Buchman has catapulted his way to the top tier of my favorite authors.

The only thing you'll ask yourself is, "When does the next one come out?"

Superb! Miranda is utterly compelling!

Miranda Chase continues to astound and charm.

Escape Rating: A. Five Stars! OMG just start with *Drone* and be prepared for a fantastic binge-read!

Other works by M. L. Buchman: *(* - also in audio)*

Other works by M. L. Buchman:

Contemporary Romance (cont)

Love Abroad
Heart of the Cotswolds: England
Path of Love: Cinque Terre, Italy

Where Dreams
Where Dreams are Born
Where Dreams Reside
Where Dreams Are of Christmas*
Where Dreams Unfold
Where Dreams Are Written
Where Dreams Continue

Science Fiction / Fantasy

Deities Anonymous
Cookbook from Hell: Reheated
Saviors 101

Single Titles
The Nara Reaction
Monk's Maze
the Me and Elsie Chronicles

Non-Fiction

Strategies for Success
Managing Your Inner Artist/Writer
Estate Planning for Authors*
Character Voice
Narrate and Record Your Own
Audiobook*

Short Story Series by M. L. Buchman:

Romantic Suspense

Antarctic Ice Fliers

Delta Force
Th Delta Force Shooters
The Delta Force Warriors

Firehawks
The Firehawks Lookouts
The Firehawks Hotshots
The Firebirds

The Night Stalkers
The Night Stalkers 5D Stories
The Night Stalkers 5E Stories
The Night Stalkers CSAR
The Night Stalkers Wedding Stories

US Coast Guard

White House Protection Force

Contemporary Romance

Eagle Cove

Henderson's Ranch*

Where Dreams

Action-Adventure Thrillers

Dead Chef

Miranda Chase Origin Stories

Science Fiction / Fantasy

Deities Anonymous

Other
The Future Night Stalkers
Single Titles

ABOUT THIS TITLE

One calendar. Twelve lighthouses. Two hearts.

Cassidy Knowles, *the nation's fastest rising food-and-wine writer, receives a gift. A calendar of lighthouses surrounding Seattle. And a dozen letters revealing a past she never knew.*

Russell Morgan, *born to a fortune, went out and made one of his own. With a calendar of lighthouses as a chart, he steps aboard a sailboat, seeking a new heading for his future.*

Where their courses collide? That is Where Dreams Are Born.

To my Lady Fair:
My thanks for the calendar,
And the journeys we shared
to explore the settings of this tale.

And to my sister:
A tintypist.
Who taught me the love of photography
in the darkroom we shared as teens.

A BEGINNING

*R*ussell leaned his back against the studio door after he locked it behind the last of the staff. He barely managed the energy to turn off his camera.

He knew it was good. The images were there; he'd really captured them.

But something was missing.

The groove ran so clean when he slid into it. First his Manhattan high-ceilinged loft would fade into the background, then the strobe lights, reflector umbrellas, and green-screen backdrops all became texture and tone.

Image, camera, and man then became one and nothing else mattered—a single flow of light, beginning before time was counted, and ending its journey in the printed image. One ray of primordial light traveling forever to glisten off the BMW roadster still parked in one corner of the rough-planked wood floor worn smooth by generations of use. Another ray lost in the dark blackness of the finest leather bucket seats. A hundred more picking out the supermodel's perfect hand dangling a single shining and golden key—the image shot just slow enough that the key blurred as it spun, but the logo remained clear.

He couldn't quite put his finger on it...

It would be another great ad by Russell Morgan, Inc. The client would be knocked dead—the ad leaving all others standing still as it roared down the passing lane. This one might get him another Clio, or even a second Mobius.

But...

There wasn't usually a "but."

And there definitely wasn't supposed to be one.

The groove had definitely been there, but he hadn't been in it.

That was the problem. It had slid along, sweeping his staff into their own orchestrated perfection, but he'd remained untouched. That ideal, seamless flow hadn't included him at all.

"Be honest, boyo, that session sucked," he told the empty studio. Everything had come together so perfectly for yet another ad for yet another high-end glossy. *Man, the Magazine* would launch spectacularly in a few weeks, a high-profile mid-December launch, and it would include a never before seen twelve-page spread by the great Russell Morgan. The rag would probably never pay off the lavish launch party of hope, ice sculptures, and chilled magnums of champagne before disappearing like a thousand before it.

"Morose much?"

The studio kept its thoughts to itself—the first reliable sign that he wasn't totally losing his shit.

He stowed the last camera with the others piled by his computer. At the breaker box he shut off the umbrellas, spots, scoops, and washes. The studio shifted from a stark landscape in hard-edged relief to a nest of curious shadows and rounded forms. The tang of hot metal and deodorant were the only lasting result of the day's efforts.

"Get your shit together, Russell." His reflection in the darkened window, stories above the streetlights of West 10th, was unimpressed and proved it was wise enough to not answer back. There was never a "down" after a shoot; there was always an "up."

Not tonight.

He'd kept everyone late—even though it was Thanksgiving eve—hoping for that smooth slide of image-camera-man. It was only when he saw the power of the images he captured that he knew he wasn't a part of the chain anymore and decided he'd paid enough triple-time expenses.

The next to last two-page spread would be the killer—shot with the door open against a background as black as the sports car's finish, the model's single perfect leg wrapped in thigh-high red-leather boots all that was visible in the driver's seat. The sensual juxtaposition of woman and sleek machine served as an irresistible focus. It was an ad designed to wrap every person with even a hint of a Y-chromosome around its little finger. And those with only X-chromosomes would simply want to be her. He'd shot a perfect combo of sex for the guys and power for the women.

Even the final one-page image, a close-up of driver's seat from exactly the same angle, revealing not the model but instead a single rose of precisely the same hue as the leather boot, hadn't moved him despite its perfection.

Without him noticing, Russell had become no more than the observer, merely a technician behind the camera. Now that he faced it, months, maybe even a year had passed since he'd been yanked all the way into the light-image-camera-man slipstream. Tonight was a wakeup call and he didn't like it one bit. Wakeup calls happened to others, not him. But tonight he could no longer ignore it, he hadn't even trailed along in the churned-up wake.

"You're just a creative cog in the advertising machine." Ouch! That one stung, but it didn't turn aside the relentless steamroller of his thoughts speeding down some empty, godforsaken autobahn.

His career was roaring ahead, his business' growth running fast and smooth. But, now that he considered it, he really didn't give a damn.

His life looked perfect, but—"Don't think it!"—his autobahn mind finished despite the command, *it wasn't.*

Russell left his silent reflection to its own thoughts and went through the back door that led to his apartment—closing it tightly on the perfect BMW, the perfect rose, and somewhere, lost among a hundred other props from dozens of other shoots, the long pair of perfect red-leather Chanel boots that had been wrapped around the most expensive legs in Manhattan. He didn't care if he never walked back through that door again. He'd been doing his art by rote; how god-awful sad was that?

And just to rub salt in the wound, he shot *commercial* art.

He'd never had the patience to do art for art's sake. Delayed gratification was his idea of no fun at all. He left the apartment dark with only the city's soft glow through the blind-covered windows revealing the vaguest outlines of the framed art on the wall. Even that almost overwhelmed him tonight.

He didn't want to see the huge prints by the *art* artists: autographed Goldsworthy, Liebowitz, and Joseph Francis' photomosaics for the moderns. A hundred and fifty rare, even one-of-a-kind prints adorned his walls—all the way back through Bourke-White to Russell's prize, an original Daguerre. The Museum of Modern Art kept begging to borrow his collection for a show...and at the moment he was half tempted to dump the whole lot in their Dumpster if they didn't want it.

Crossing the one-room loft apartment—as spacious as the studio—he bypassed the circle of avant-garde chairs that were almost as uncomfortable as they looked and avoided the lush black-leather wrap-around sectional sofa of such ludicrous scale that it could be a playpen for two or host a party for twenty. He cracked the fridge in the stainless-steel-and-black corner kitchen searching for something other than his usual beer.

A bottle of Krug.

Maybe he was just being grouchy after a long day's work.

Juice.

No. He'd run his enthusiasm into the ground but good.

Milk even.

Would he miss the camera if he never picked it up again?

No reaction.

Nothing.

Not even an itch in his palm.

That was an emptiness he did not want to face. Especially not alone, in his apartment, in the middle of the world's most vibrant city.

Russell turned away, and just as the door swung closed, the last sliver of light—the relentless chilly blue-white of the refrigerator bulb—shone across his bed. A quick grab snagged the edge of the door and left the narrow beam illuminating a long pale form on his black-silk bedspread.

The Chanel boots weren't in the studio after all. They were still wrapped around those three thousand dollar-an-hour legs: the only clothing on a perfect body. Five foot-eleven of intensely toned female anatomy right down to an exquisitely stair-mastered behind. Her long, white-blonde hair lay as a perfect Godiva over her tanned breasts—except for their too exact symmetry, even the closest inspection didn't reveal the work done there. She lay with one leg raised just ever so slightly to hide what was meant to be revealed later.

Melanie.

By the steady rise and fall of her flat stomach, he knew she'd fallen asleep while waiting for him to finish in the studio.

How long had they been an item? Two months? Three?

She'd made him feel alive...at least when he was actually with her. Melanie was the super-model in his bed or on his arm at yet another SoHo gallery opening. Together they journeyed to sharp parties and trendy three-star restaurants where she dazzled and wooed yet another gathering of New York's finest with her ever so soft, so sensual, and so studied French accent. Together they were wired into the heart of the in-crowd.

But that wasn't him, was it? It didn't sound like the Russell he once knew.

Perhaps "they" were about how *he* looked on *her* arm?

Did she know tomorrow was the annual Thanksgiving ordeal at his parents? The grand holiday gathering that he'd rather die than attend? Any number of eligible woman would be floating about his parents' house out in Greenwich; anyone able to finagle an invitation would attend in hopes of snaring one of *People Magazine's* "100 Most Eligible." They all wanted to land the heir to a billion or some such; though he was wealthy enough on his own, by his own sweat, to draw anyone's attention. He ranked number twenty-four on the list this year—up from forty-seven the year before despite Tom Cruise being available yet again.

But not Melanie. He knew that it wasn't the money that drew her. Yes, she wanted him. But even more, she wanted the life that came with him—wrapped in the man-package. She wanted The Life. The one that *People Magazine* readers dreamed about between glossy pages.

His fingertips were growing cold where they held the refrigerator door cracked open.

If he woke her there'd be amazing sex. Or a great party to go to. Or...

Did he want "Or"? What more did he want from her?

Sex. Companionship. An energy, a vivacity, a thirst he feared that he lacked. Yes.

But where was that smooth synchronicity hiding, like the light-image-camera-man of photography that he'd lost? Where lurked that perfect flow from one person to another? Did she feel it? Could he ever feel it? Did it even exist?

"More?" he whispered into the darkness to test the sound. He knew all about wanting more.

The refrigerator door slid shut—escaping from his numbed fingers—which plunged the apartment back into darkness, taking Melanie along with it.

His breath echoed in the vast darkness. Proof that he was alive if nothing more.

It was time to close the studio—time to be done with Russell Incorporated.

Then what?

Maybe Angelo would know what to do. He always claimed that he did. Maybe this time Russell would actually listen to his almost-brother, though he knew from the experience of being himself for the last thirty years that was unlikely.

Seattle.

Damn! He'd have to go to bloody Seattle to find his best friend. There was a possible upside to such a trip—maybe there'd be a flight out before tomorrow's mess at his parents'. He slapped his pocket, but once again he'd set his phone down in some unknown corner of the studio and it would take forever to find. He really needed two—one chained down so that he could always find it to call the other.

Russell considered the darkness. He could guarantee that Seattle wouldn't be a big hit with Melanie.

Now if he only knew whether that was a good thing or bad.

WEST POINT LIGHTHOUSE

Discovery Park, Seattle
First lit: 1881
Automated: 1985
47.6617 -122.43499

$\mathcal{C}$hief Boatswain's Mate Christian Fritz served as the lighthouse keeper for many years in the early 1900s. One of the reasons he chose the West Point Lighthouse posting was that the terrain from the keeper's cottage to the lighthouse was relatively level. This allowed his blind wife to freely stroll the station's grounds accompanied by her guide dog, a boxer named Cookie.

In 1985, it was the last lighthouse in Washington State to be automated despite its close proximity to Seattle.

"If you were still alive, you'd pay for this one, Daddy."

The moment the words escaped her lips, Cassidy Knowles slapped a hand over her mouth to negate them, but it was too late.

The sharp wind took her words and threw them back into the pines, guilt and all. It might have stopped her, if it didn't make this the hundredth time she'd cursed him this morning.

She leaned in and forged her way downhill until the muddy path broke free from the mossy smell of the forest. Her Stuart Weitzman boots were long since soaked through, and now her feet were freezing. In a last gasp effort before the chill trees would let her go, a root snagged their two-inch heels once again in an attempt to flip her into the mud.

Free of the pernicious wood at last, Cassidy stared at the lighthouse. It perched upon a point of rock: tall and white, with its red roof as straight and snug as a prim bonnet. A narrow trail traced along the top of the breakwater leading to the lighthouse. The parking lot, much to her chagrin, was empty; six, beautiful, empty spaces.

"Sorry, ma'am," park rangers were always polite when telling you what you couldn't do. "The parking lot by the light is for physically-challenged visitors only. You'll have to park here. It *is* just a short walk to the lighthouse."

The fact that she was dressed for an afternoon lunch at Pike Place Market safe in Seattle's downtown rather than a blustery mile-long trek on the first day of the year didn't phase the ranger in the slightest.

Cassidy should have gone home, would have if it hadn't been for the letter stuffed deep in her pocket. So, instead of a tasty treat in a cozy deli, she'd buttoned the top button of her suede Bernardo jacket and headed out onto the trail. At least the promised rain had yet to arrive, so the jacket was only cold, not wet.

Finally free of the trees, a new problem arose. Beyond the lighthouse ranged a vast expanse of Puget Sound and it was being whipped into a frenzy like someone desperate to make a towering meringue rather than a smooth zabaglione custard. White caps tore off the tops of waves, dark clouds the color of month-old bread scudded low over the water, and the far shore might as well have been the North Pole rather than Bainbridge Island for how inviting it looked. The towering heights of the Olympic Mountains scraped at the clouds with glacier-clad peaks and made her spine feel like fingernails were scrubbing a chalkboard the size of the sky.

Her jacket's stylish cut had never been intended to fight off these bajillion mile-an-hour gusts that snapped it painfully against her hips. Her black leggings ranged about five layers short of tolerable and a far, far cry from warm.

Approaching the lighthouse across the exposed—and still utterly vacant—parking lot, any part of her that had been merely numb slipped right over to quick frozen. Leaning into the wind to stay upright, tears streaming from her eyes, she could think of a thing or two to tell her father despite his recent demise and her general feelings about the usefulness of upbraiding a dead man.

"What a stupid present!" Her shout was torn word-by-word, syllable-by-syllable and sent flying back toward her nice warm car and the ever-so-polite park ranger.

A calendar. Her dad had given her a stupid calendar of stupid lighthouses and a stupid letter to open at each stupid one. He'd been very insistent, made her promise. The one kind of promise she couldn't ignore—a deathbed one.

Cassidy leaned grimly forward to walk through the onslaught only to have the wind abruptly cease. She staggered, avoiding a brutal faceplant on the pavement only because another gust sent her crabbing sideways. With resolute force, she planted one foot before another until she'd crossed the open pavement. Not only were the handicapped too intelligent to come to the West Point Lighthouse, so was everyone else. There was just her and the wind.

The empty lot and the lighthouse were separated by a short path along the top of a rocky breakwater. Boulders the size of her car had been piled up to resist the pounding of the sea. The top had been made into a solid path, so her footing was sure even if the wind continued to buffet her wildly.

The building's wall was concrete, worn smooth by a thousand storms and a hundred coats of brilliant white paint. With the wind practically pinning her to the wall, she peeked into one of the windows. Her hair blew about so that it beat on her eyes and mouth trying to simultaneously blind and choke her. With one hand, she smashed the unruly mass mostly to one side. With the other she shaded the salt-crusted window.

The cobwebbed glass revealed an equally unkempt interior: no lightkeeper sitting in his rocking chair before a merry fire with his smoking pipe and a lighthouse cat curled in his lap. There was some sort of a rusty engine not attached to anything. A bucket of old tools. A couple of paint cans.

A high wave crashed into the rocks with a thundering shudder that ran up through the heels of her boots and whipped a chill spray into the wind. Salt water on suede—Daddy now owed her a new coat as well.

Cassidy edged along the foundation until she found a calmer spot, a little wind shadow behind the lighthouse where the wind chill ranked merely miserable rather than horrific on the suck-o-meter. Squatting down behind one of the breakwater's boulders helped a tiny bit more. She peeled off her thin leather gloves and blew against her fingertips to warm them enough to function. Once she'd regained some modicum of feeling, she pulled out the letter.

She couldn't feel his actual writing, though she ran her fingertips over it again and again. His Christmas present: a five-dollar calendar of Washington lighthouses from the hospital gift store and a dozen thin envelopes wrapped in an old x-ray folder with no ribbon, no paper.

In the end he'd foiled her final Christmas hunt. It had been her great yearly quest—the ultimate grail of childhood—finding the key present before Christmas morning. There was no present he could hide that she couldn't find. Not the Cabbage Patch Kid when she was six; the one she'd had to hold with her arm in a cast after falling off the kitchen stool she'd dragged into her father's closet to aid the search. Not the used VW Rabbit he'd hidden out in the wine shed thinking that she never went there anymore. And she didn't, except for some reason that day before her eighteenth Christmas.

A part of her wanted to crumple the letter up and throw it into the sea. It was too soon. She didn't want to face the pain again.

Too soon.

She looked out at the crashing waves. With a sudden roar of wind, a slash of spray slashed the air mere feet from her face, barely averted by the staunch tower of the lighthouse. Clearly someone wasn't happy about her desire to avoid the task at hand.

The rest of her body did what it supposed to do. The dutiful daughter opened the envelope and pinned the letter against her thigh so that she could read the slashing scrawl that was her father's. Even as weak with sickness as he must have been, it looked scribed in stone. His bold-stroke writing gave the words a force and strength just as his deep voice had once sounded strong enough to keep the world at bay for a little girl.

Dearest Ice Sweet,

He'd always called her that. Icewine. The grapes for icewine were traditionally harvested on her birthday, December twenty-first. "The sweetest wine of all, my little ice sweet girl." By the age of five she knew about the sugar content of icewine, Riesling, Chardonnay, and a dozen others. By eight she could identify scores of vintages just by the scent of the cork and hundreds by their logos though she'd yet to taste more than thimblefuls of watered wine at any one time.

Cassidy stared at the waves digging angrily at the rocks not far below her feet. The wind dragged tears from her eyes even as she struggled to blink them dry. She hadn't cried in a long time and she was damned if she was going to start now simply because she was cold and there was a hole in her heart.

Just seven days. She'd looked away for one single wretched moment seven days ago—and he was gone. Christmas morning. He'd hung on long enough to tell her of his last present, hidden in plain sight in the used x-ray folder on the bedside table. A lengthy list of crossed-out names had shuttled films back and forth across Northwest Hospital.

I bought this calendar the day you moved back to Seattle. Marked in all the "dates." Now I know that I won't get to go with you. I'm sorry to leave you so young.

"I'm twenty-nine, Daddy." But it felt young. Her birthday

gone unremarked because he'd never woken that day so close to his last.

The hole in her heart was so broad that it would never be filled. He'd only been gone a week. Cremated, waked, and ashes spread on his beloved vineyard by the permission of the new owners. They'd owned his vineyard for five years, but still, they were the new ones. It wasn't right—them living in the place where her father belonged. She could picture him so easily striding among the vines, rubbing the soil in his palm, showing his only child the wonders of the changing seasons, the lifecycle of a grapevine, and the nurturing of honeybees.

For our first "date" I will just tell you how proud I am of you. My daughter took a vintner's education and turned herself into the best food-and-wine columnist ever.

He always believed in her. Always rooted for her. Her number one fan, he'd always cheered her on. He'd been the same way with her boyfriends: welcoming them when they arrived, consoling her when they were gone, and offering no harsh judgment—not even about the boys she should have avoided like a bottle of rotgut Thunderbird.

The wind rattled the paper, drawing her attention back to the letter.

You are so like me. You figure out what feels right and you just go do it, damn the consequences. I could never fault you for leaving. I always did what I wanted, too. Saw it and went right for it, no discussion needed, always wearing perfect blinders that blocked out everything else. You got that from me. You come by your whimsical stubbornness honestly, Ice Sweet.

But he was wrong, she wasn't stubborn. It had taken years of careful planning for her to reach this far. Even her move to Seattle to be with him had been calculated, though she never told him about that. She shifted on the hard rock that was in imminent danger of freezing her butt.

Her father kept apologizing for all the wrong things. Seattle had ended up being an exceptional career move, or was finally becoming one as she'd hoped. In New York, she worked as one of a thousand food-and-wine reviewers. Okay one in fifty—maybe even one in twenty-five, she was damn good—but there were only three women at that level. The other twenty-two were members of longstanding in the old boys' club.

"We're looking for someone with a more refined palate." Read that as someone who was "male."

She'd let go of her sublet in Manhattan when she'd found out her father was sick. Bought a condo in Seattle to be near, but not too near him on Bainbridge Island. Helped him move into the eldercare by Northgate when he couldn't care for himself any longer and from there to Northwest Hospital where she'd lived out his last two weeks in the chair by his bed.

The Village Voice dropped her the day she left Manhattan. That had hurt as they'd run her first-ever review, a short piece on Jim and Charlie's Punk-and-Wine Bistro. Jim and Charlie's was still there, partly thanks to that review that was still framed and hung in the center of bar's mirror.

But in Seattle she was rapidly rising to the very upper crust of the apple pie. Her reviews ran in every local paper. The *San Francisco Chronicle* had picked her up for their Travel section the next week making it difficult to stay grumpy about the loss of *The Voice.* Then AAA took her national with a regular column for their magazines. From there, it hadn't been a big step to national syndication. Six more months in New York and she'd have still been grinding her way up from the twentieth spot to the nineteenth. She was going to bypass the lot of them by skipping right past the "required seats" and sitting at the head table herself.

Her father's cancer had brought at least that much good.

Now if only it hadn't taken him with it.

And she wasn't whimsical no matter what he thought. Her dad had always described her mother as the organized one. And

17

Cassidy had done her best to be just like her. You didn't become a top columnist by following the wind all willy-nilly.

But *this* wind would freeze her in place if she didn't hurry. She chafed at her legs with one hand and then the other, but it didn't help. She was cold past any cure less than a piping hot tub bath. She peeked ahead in the letter, just two and a bit more pages. She turned to the second sheet, barely managing not to lose the first to the wind.

I started the vineyard after my tour in Vietnam. Got signed off the base and walked out of San Francisco right across the Golden Gate. No home, no job, and no one to go back to. I headed up into the hills; didn't even know why or where I was. I walked and hitched 'til dark, slept, woke with the light, and kept moving.

One morning, I woke up in a field close to a rotting, wooden fence-post, looking at the saddest little vineyard you could imagine. Poor vines dying of thirst. I found an old bucket and started watering them from a nearby stream. An old man came out to lean on the fence. Watched me quite a while, a couple hours maybe. I didn't care about him. Those vines were the first thing I'd cared about in a long, long time.

"You want 'em?" the old guy asked. "Five hundred bucks and they're yours."

I don't even remember how it happened. One minute my final pay was in my pocket, then in his. Later on, other vets drifted in. I charged them fifty bucks to join. Five of us worked the land and recovered those vines. That was the start of the thirty acres of Knowles Valley Vineyard.

She'd never heard how his first vineyard started. Didn't even really know where it was, somewhere in the hills of northern California. Though he might have ambled all the way to Oregon for how much she knew.

Walk the year with me. Let's take our time. My past is mine, but your future is not. That's only up to you. That I leave you to walk alone, though I'll warn you that it's a rough trail often over rocky soil. But keep your head high and you'll go far.

Whatever happens, know that I love you. I'm so proud of you.

Love you Ice Sweet,

Vic

Vic. He always signed his letters "Vic." Never what she'd always called him. "Daddy."

I could never fault you for leaving.

Yet between the lines that's just what he did. Nothing on the backs of any of the pages. She worked to refold the pages in the wind. The damp chill was now worse inside than outside her skin. The wind's chill was a nasty, temperamental thing, clawing to reach her; the pain she felt right down to her core.

"No, you're imagining things, Cass. You think too much. Get your head out of your own butt." And she mostly did. One of the many gifts Vic Knowles had given her, the ability to be clear about her own actions and reactions.

He'd financed her dream of getting away from the rain capital of the Pacific Northwest. He'd paid for her college in full and cooking school as well. It was only while cleaning up his papers this last week that she saw how close it had come to breaking him. He'd just made it a natural assumption that she'd go to college and he'd pay. She'd gone to Vassar College back East, just like her mom. He'd always talked about how smart Cassidy's mother was.

"Look in the mirror, Ice Sweet, and you'll see she was the most beautiful woman you can imagine. I miss her every day."

She tried to see, but all she ever saw was herself. She did better without the mirror. Even now, looking north along the steep, conifer-clad shore and over the heavy waves she could imagine her father happy. A woman at his side with soft brown hair who did and didn't look like Cassidy.

He hadn't gone to college himself, not even high school. His past was little more than a few facts she'd winnowed over the years. His own dad had left before he could remember. He'd dropped out of third grade to help his mother run the grocery store. They were desperately poor when she died. Then he'd gone to Vietnam at eighteen as the only way to make a living wage. And afterwards had walked to a vineyard. But he gave Cassidy that gift of education as if it was no hardship to him.

Did he now begrudge her that past? The future he never had.

No. That didn't make any sense. He hadn't thought about the money, he'd invested in his dreams for her. She was just going nuts from missing him so much and angry at him for being dead.

"Useful, Cass, real useful."

To prove her sanity, she forced the rumpled letter back into the envelope, as neatly as possible in the midst of the maelstrom, and she forced that back into her leather pack.

Her father, the self-educated man, also the most well-read man she'd ever met. But she'd learned early on to do her math and science homework before he came home from the fields. His frustration at being unable to help her there had always been a strain.

Cassidy's mother was a single solitary memory. It had been a night as foul-tempered as this day. Mama had been standing in the open doorway of the house, leaving to answer a call to the hospital. Odd, Daddy had never mentioned her nursing school days, but talking about her had always hurt him, so Cassidy had learned not to ask.

The wind at the door had blown her mother's long hair across her face as she leaned on Daddy's arm. That was Cassidy's only memory of Adrianne Knowles, a woman with no face. Then Bea Clark had rushed in from next door to sit with her.

She and Daddy did talk about the many books though. He had sharpened her mind as they puzzled them out together. Ayn Rand piled next to Shakespeare, Heinlein beside Hugo, and

Dickens leaning against a biography of Jimi Hendrix. Their house was always awash in books. And the massive collection of wine books, thumbed again and again by both of them, the only books to have a proper bookcase, had sat in the place of honor in the living room. Everything else jumbled into stacked wooden crates, mounded on tops of dressers, and enough on the dining table to make it a nightly battle to find room for their two plates.

The chill spray of a particularly large wave spattered her with a few drops, and the next with a few more. The tide must be coming in.

She scrambled from her hiding place and rose back into the wind which threatened to topple her off the breakwater and down into the roaring waves. She forged her way back to the parking lot. The wind tore at her backpack and thumped it against her spine. The camera. Right.

She squatted to get out of the wind and pulled out her trusty point-and-shoot. The wind nearly blinded her when she turned back into it. Her hair swirled about her head, completely in the way.

A sailboat. Two lunatics in a sailboat were off the point of land. A cobalt-blue hull climbed out of one wave, pointing its bow to the sky, and then plunged down and buried its nose in the front of the next wave before rising again in a great arc of spray and green water. Huge, maroon sails snapped in the wind, loud enough to sound like gunshots above the roaring surf.

Whoever the captain was, he and his buddy were crazy. They must both be male because no woman in her right mind would ever go out into a storm like this. But if they wanted to sail right into her picture, she wasn't going to complain; it was a beautiful boat. At the perfect moment she snapped the photo then turned for the woods and the long trail home.

"HEY ANGELO. TAKE THE HELM." Russell had to shout to be heard above the sharp crack of the dark-red mainsail.

"Got it, Captain." His friend grinned at him as he grabbed the tiller and they slid across the waves off the West Point lighthouse.

Russell let out a whoop as they rode high over a crest, paused, and went briefly weightless before they plunged into the next trough. The *Lady Amalthea* had been built for weather like this. At first Russell had been afraid of such heavy weather. His parents' boat, *Julia*—a twenty-eight-footer they kept at the summer place on Fire Island—would have had a very tough time in this sea. At fifty feet long, the *Lady* just ate it up; she practically flew over the wavetops.

He ducked below and grabbed his camera.

Belowdecks would definitely need some work. Okay, a lot of work. The only decent thing in the old gal was the forward stateroom. Russell could hardly wait. The marine surveyor had pronounced both the hull and mast sound. That was all he cared about because fixing either was a little too scary.

The interior he could deal with. It just needed to be torn out and redone from the ballast up. He'd have to figure out a better system for diesel than that old beer keg strapped to the engine room wall. Get her plumbed for fresh water and wired with more than an old car battery charger. But she really had potential. Most importantly, the *Lady* sailed like there was no tomorrow.

He scrambled back on deck and started snapping pictures. Angelo posed in his foul weather gear, the yellow slicks and orange float jacket making him look as much like a clown as a sailor. He made some foolish faces to go with it and Russell captured them for posterity. He'd send the most ridiculous one to Angelo's mother, Maria, just to shame him on his next visit home.

Then he aimed at the lighthouse and snapped off a couple

dozen images. He didn't even bother to check the LCD, they'd be good. The lighthouse perched on the rocky edge of Discovery Park was too photogenic a place for bad pictures. He bracketed the exposure and focus just to be sure. It was perfect. Steep, wooded cliff rising up behind the pristine white and red of the squat lighthouse. He'd crop the image to avoid the sprawl of the treatment plant just around the rocks to the north.

He tried to get the rhythm of the lighthouse's flash: alternating white and red every ten seconds. He got them both then stowed the camera away.

"Ready about?" Angelo called from above.

Russell scrambled back on deck, checked the lines, and preset the port jib sheet next to the winch. The line felt oversized but solid in his hand, the rope was a half-inch thick just to handle the sail, the same size as the blasted anchor line on his parents' *Julia.*

"Ready."

"Helm's a lee!" Angelo threw over the tiller and the *Lady* lifted up her bow and spun like a dancer.

Russell waited until the very last second before releasing the starboard line and heaving in on the port one. Moments later the line snapped taught and would have flipped him overboard if he hadn't let go, a rope burn creased his palms with searing heat.

Angelo was laughing his head off. "And you, Mister Great Sailor, are going to solo around the world?"

"Shaddup, Angelo. It was your idea."

"I gave you a hundred ideas on Thanksgiving Day, I figured you wouldn't listen to any of them like usual, especially not this one. What about being a scuba instructor off Fiji with all of the cute tourists?"

The boat slammed over another wave like she was skating on glass.

"Nah! Not for me. Don't like getting my hair wet."

He saw Angelo twitch the tiller, but he didn't move fast enough. A wave plowed into his face, freezing rivulets of seawater running right past the tight collar of his float jacket and down his back underneath. He lost the line for the jib sheet again and the line whipped away. The jib sail luffing with sharp slaps and cracks.

He sputtered and spat as Angelo pointed the boat's bow back into the wind.

Russell retrieved the sheet and hauled it back in, and leery of Angelo, passed it several times around the winch as he did so. Russell grabbed the winch handle and ratcheted in the last few feet of line.

"She's bigger than Dad's *Julia*." Russell liked one-upping Dad on that.

"Duh! That jib—a sail that's so much smarter than you, by the way—has more area than both of hers."

True. He'd bought a big boat. But she flew so sweet that he knew he'd made the right choice. And only a nut would try crossing an ocean in a twenty-eight-footer. He'd looked at a sixty-five-footer, but it was more boat than he wanted to wrestle with. That really would need two people and heaven knows you couldn't count on finding a compatible first mate.

Melanie had been some serious kind of pissed. And that was before he'd decided to stay in Seattle past a few days to visit Angelo. Now she wasn't even speaking to him; at least he didn't think she was. He'd chucked his phone overboard after their last conversation and hadn't gotten around to replacing it yet.

Russell looked back at the lighthouse.

"You know they wanted to automate her in 1979. The light-house keeper begged them to let him keep running it, at least until her hundredth birthday. On her centenary in 1981, the keeper climbed up to the outside of the light and sprayed a bottle of champagne over her. Legend has it he also danced a hornpipe up there."

"A good choice for the January lighthouse." Angelo pointed ahead. "Where are we going?"

Russell ducked low to peek under the sail. The western shore of the Sound was a half-dozen miles off. Some rain was moving in, but they were dressed for that. It was too perfect a day to turn back for the marina yet. He waved ahead.

"Thatta way. The isle of Tortuga."

"Aye, *Mon Capitaine.*" They both laughed. Nothing like a good pirate movie quote when you were off sailing. The crazed French accent made as much sense from his short, Italian friend as it had from a tall, English Basil Rathbone.

Russell let the main sail out a bit to get better air flow across the upper third of the sail and then headed forward to inspect the boat under way. The tail end of the jib halyard had slipped free and was snaked all over the deck. He checked aloft. The halyard ran clean up to the top of the mast, over a pulley at the top and down to the top of the jib sail. Damn that was a tall mast. Sixty-five feet from water to masthead, sixty from where he stood on the cabin roof. He looped the line into a neat hank and hung it back over the cleat. The lines would have to be routed back to the cockpit so that he could single-hand her in rougher weather. That meant longer lines. He glanced aloft again.

"Well, I'm gonna have to climb you someday. Just like a six-story walkup back in Manhattan, so I should be okay." He didn't feel so certain as he watched it whipping back and forth across the sky each time she leapt over the next wave.

He made an inventory as he walked forward. New hatches, these were old and leaking despite their layers of duct tape. Most of the rope rigging would have to go. Some of the wire too.

His heel found another of the squishy spots in the decking. He'd have to rip off the bubbled fiberglass covering from the whole deck and deal with any rot under there. And the bowsprit definitely needed safety lines—the sprit, no more that a nine-inch round stick of wood, stuck six feet over the emptiness of heaving waves. That would take some thinking.

A thirty-five-pound anchor rested in the split and worn mahogany of a deck chock. The *Julia's* anchor weighed fifteen. When he'd unearthed the *Lady's* sixty-pound storm anchor under the forward bunk with another twenty-five pounds of chain, he felt a little humbled. Hauling that up from depth would be a beast.

Leaning against the taut jib sail for support, he edged out onto the slender bowsprit. He grabbed hold of the wire forestay that rose from the tip of the sprit and soared to the top of the mainmast—fine for Puget Sound, not up for an ocean crossing. He added, "make it a double stay," to his mental list.

Then he got his face into the air ahead of the sail. The wind roared in his ears. The bow sliced the waves below his feet laying twin white curls of water to either side. The air was so fresh and so clean it was impossible that it was the same stuff that he'd breathed every day in New York. Here it was in his face, in his hair—in his soul.

"Sorry, Melanie." *This* was the most alive he'd ever felt, and he never wanted it to end.

IT HAD REQUIRED A VERY LONG, very hot bath and most of an afternoon curled up in front of the gas fire before Cassidy had felt even halfway normal yesterday. The drenching rain had caught her halfway back to the car. Her suede jacket was a ruin and her leggings had defended her for thirty seconds, at most.

This, at least, she knew how to solve. REI may have expanded into a national brand, but their flagship store was just a few blocks from the *Seattle Times* where Jack was an editor. She should have set up a lunch date, they hadn't seen each other in a week, but she couldn't find the energy. Not the best of signs, but she'd think about that later.

The underground parking garage was a collection of small, ratty cars that should never have seen the light of day and a fleet of Toyota and Honda hybrids. She parked her dad's five-year-old Jetta and glanced around for the inevitable parking level reminders. "Evergreen." She wasn't on level "2," she was parked in a tree.

The small exit sign indicated that the garage in no way connected to the store.

She clambered up the outdoor walkways and bridges over an artificial waterfall that was actually quite impressive. It roared and splashed, even had spray. She could smell the damp mist on the morning air as she unearthed the concrete stairs spiraling through the trees.

The elevator, when she finally found it, was outdoors as well and wholly unused. Apparently everyone who came here was so ecstatically outdoorsy that they took the stairs everywhere. She stepped in and stabbed the button for the top level. Rapped it twice more for good measure.

The glass elevator stopped on a wide concrete veranda that afforded a view out over downtown Seattle and the older buildings of the Denny Regrade. It was a magnificent view of the city. Though Puget Sound would soon be hidden as Seattle continued its grow, Queen Anne Hill would be visible for decades to come.

A latte vendor tended his outdoor stall and a crowd clustered about pretending it wasn't thirty-six degrees and drizzling on the second of January. They were clearly all certifiable. Being born and raised locally had not provided her with the die-hard, outdoorsman independent spirit that was still *de rigueur* in Seattle.

She raced through the foyer doors. A greeter smiled and asked if she needed any help. Cassidy assured her she was okay.

It was warm inside and buying clothes was one thing she could handle.

A shout drew her attention upward. A twisted rock some forty feet high soared upward at the end of the entry lobby. A woman was falling—Cassidy let out a scream to match the climber's just as a safety rope jerked tight and the climber swung brutally against the stone.

Then Cassidy heard the woman's laughter over the pounding of her own heart.

A man clung to another face. "Quit goofing around, Teri. You fall on El Capitan and we're going to let you go."

"Gimme a break, Tom. I slipped is all."

Cassidy hurried through the main door, resisting the hesitancy about grabbing the nasty ice axes that served as door handles.

Maybe she did need help, like help packing a moving van and getting back to New York. Or at least with the vast arrays of equipment that spread before her in every direction. To her left was a vast rack of backpacks big enough for her to climb into, each with a thousand straps. To her right were more sleeping bags than she'd seen since her one Girl Scouts' camp-out.

"Keep moving, Cass." Books, energy bars, silvery packets marked "stroganoff" and another "ice cream." Even as she watched, someone selected a half dozen packets and put them in a basket. She moved on and entered a world of kayaks, with nothing but canoes and bicycles beyond. To her right, skis and snowboards. A bit farther, boots.

Boots!

She needed boots, good start. She'd work from the bottom up. A plan of attack, excellent. It still required some exploring to discover these were all ski boots and that walking boots were up on the massive mezzanine level.

Once there, she moved across the plank flooring and entered the racks of boots, but it didn't smell like it should.

There was no canvas and fine leather of Nordstrom or Saks nor the mellower tang of Gucci, not even the smooth sweetness of Armani. There was a heaviness like saddles that had hung too long in a tack room. Manly boots doing manly things.

Reaching the end of the boot aisle, she faced the wall of individual boots waiting for their mates. There wasn't a single manufacturer she recognized. Neither Anne Klein nor Kenneth Cole walked here. These all had tough, outdoorsy names: Vasque, Montrail, Ugg. Even the women's boots were from companies marinated in testosterone.

"Can I help you?" Cassidy turned. An incredibly fit girl who looked no more than nineteen confronted her in a little green vest and a white turtleneck. This time she'd take the assistance.

"I need some new boots." Her three-hundred-dollar Weitzman's had dissolved on the trail back to the car. She'd lost a heel when it got stuck between two rocks. As she prowled about in the driving rain, seeking the right parking lot lost in the park's forest, the leather had actually separated from the sole. She'd done the last hundred yards with the broken boot in her hand, her sock-covered foot squishing with freezing mud, and the other leg two inches longer at the heel. It was amazing she hadn't gotten frostbite or something.

"Do you know what kind you want?"

Again she faced the wall. They all looked the same, with brown tops and black rubber soles. But she knew how to handle that as well.

"The best."

"What kind of hiking are you doing?"

"That matters?"

The girl was really polite. Not at a Nordstrom personal shopper level, but she managed to hide any disdain she was feeling from her perfect, teenage face.

"Oh, yes." She pointed at the one pair with a four-hundred-dollar price tag. "We just sold eight pairs of those to a women's team who are taking on the seven summits challenge."

"The seven summits?" Cassidy had entered not only another world, but they spoke a different language here.

"Kilimanjaro, Denali, Elbrus, Aconcagua, Carstensz Pyramid, and Everest. I'm forgetting one. Hold on. Don't tell me."

As if Cassidy might have a clue what she was talking about.

Her blue eyes searched about. "Oh. And Vinson. I always forget Vinson."

"Vinson?" Kilimanjaro, Denali, and Everest were the only ones she'd ever heard of but she finally got the idea. The highest peaks on each continent. And a team of women were going to climb them in those boots. The ones perched smugly right there on the wall glaring down at her for daring to enter their presence.

"Antarctica. Nearly five thousand meters. I like to read about it, but I'd never be crazy enough to try it." The girl was terribly cheerful, which would be irritating if it weren't so genuine.

"I, uh, won't be climbing Vinson."

The girl laughed, "Everest either?"

"Nope." She joined in the laugh and it felt good.

"Heavy backpack?" The girl inspected her from the black leather jacket down to her Josef Seibel heeled, leather loafers, but was nice enough to keep her thoughts to herself as Cassidy was demoted another level.

"Nope."

"Walks around Green Lake?"

"A bit tougher than that." Slogging uphill through the mud and the moss, definitely a bit tougher than the three-mile, paved jogging path.

"Light hiking, but the best?"

"Yes, that sounds good."

The girl reached out and unerringly grabbed a boot that looked just like all the others. She excitedly launched into a long description, but after Cassidy heard the word "waterproof," she tuned out the rest. That would teach the stupid mud to mess with a veteran shopper.

Most of the other items fell to similar tactics. She became better at it as item after item filled her basket. On the second floor "light hiking" linked with "cold weather" had gotten her a lecture about skipping polar fleece and going with the traditional layering of silk socks under wool. Including "year-round" had added long underwear of Merino wool. "All weather" had added waterproof yet breathable pants from some company founded by aliens, Arc'Teryx. Or maybe dinosaurs. But the price was the highest, over two hundred dollars, so they must be the best.

She threw in a black PolarTec fleece jacket with no one's help at all. But the waterproof jackets were impossible. Even asking for help didn't clarify the mess. The selection was larger than Saks designer racks and apparently each jacket had a different feature that made it particularly wonderful. She finally walked away when she learned that they all stopped at the waist.

Cassidy wanted something longer and warmer. Thankfully, she knew right where to get that. Michael Kors had a beautiful, knee-length, down-filled coat in this year's line. He didn't make it in black, but there was a brilliant red one that would look great. That would make it easier to tolerate the massive damage she was doing to her shopping budget with clothing she'd wear only twelve times in her life. Eleven, she'd already been to the January lighthouse.

The basket was getting heavy. This was nuts. There was over a thousand dollars in there. Of course her agent had just e-mailed her about the *London Times* picking up her column in their Travel section with a query about a wine-only column in the Sunday edition; she was going international. Cassidy would justify this splurge as a sort of psychotic celebration.

Back on the ground floor, she passed close to a counter

covered in a nest of electronics. She was nearly attacked by an overeager boy who looked so healthy he'd probably climbed Vinson before his fifteenth birthday. With his eyes closed. Backwards.

"I see you're going out in the weather," she followed his glance to her basket. On the top were the red fleece watch cap that she'd chosen because it would match the Kors coat and the heavy gloves that she'd reluctantly chosen over the nice pair of sheepskin ones. "All weather" and "waterproof" had combined for the win there.

"Yes, I am."

"Going off the beaten path at all?"

The two hours she'd spent slogging through the muddy forest of Discovery Park answered that clearly for her.

At her nod, the boy nearly exploded with joy.

"You've just gotta have one of these!" He waved something at her too quickly to focus on.

"What is it?" As soon as he stopped waving it about she saw the price tag of three hundred dollars and prepared to walk away.

"GPSs." At her blank expression, he launched ahead. "Global Positioning System. These toys tell you exactly where you are. See?" He punched a couple buttons and a pair of numbers appeared. Numbers a lot like the ones she'd been unable to decipher on the outside of her dad's lighthouse envelopes.

"Then you can key in your destination, latitude, then longitude. We're west so we're minus."

So that was what the numbers on the envelope were, latitude and longitude. She felt stupid for not figuring that out, not that there was any reason she should have. She'd never seen coordinates in decimal form before—she'd been raised on degrees, minutes, and seconds. This whole REI experience echoed with Hansel-and-Gretel breadcrumbs, always searching behind herself to see just where she'd dropped all of those IQ points she'd had before she walked through the doors. But hey, now she knew where Mount Vinson was. Or was it Vinson Mountain? Massif? She looked behind her, but didn't see any of the lost IQ points she'd scattered there.

He continued stabbing at the keys like a pro then turned it to her. "And there you go."

The tiny screen connected a green dot to a red one by a thin wandering line of red.

"The nearest Starbucks coffee. That's your route. How you get there. Someday everyone will have one of these in their pockets."

She inspected it more carefully and could see that the line followed the streets of a tiny map. He tapped it and it zoomed in. A bright arrow pointed toward the front door.

"Do you have one of those that would show," she clamped down on her tongue for a moment, "parks and other such places?"

He waved it at her again. "This is it. Look. I've loaded in Washington State detail and the National Parks and the Blue chart. This is really cool. Look." More button pushing and he turned it back to her.

It showed a map in tan and white with tiny numbers on the white.

At her blank look, he rambled on. "Blue chart. Water. The blue stuff. It has all the coastline info."

"Like lighthouses?" It slipped out before she could stop it.

"You bet!"

She'd clearly been labeled as a tourist.

"Did you know we have one right here in Seattle city limits? Here it is over in Discovery Park. Shows the water depth." He aimed at some numbers with a ragged fingernail—probably broken while wrestling a grizzly bear for food. "There's the lighthouse and how often her light flashes. Then you just toggle it like this and, bang, there's the park and most of the trails. The maps are surprisingly good even down at that level. Hit this button and you get the topo overlay so you can see which trails go up and which ones down. It's just the best."

That last did it for her.

———

CASSIDY DIDN'T glance toward the last covered bottle of wine. It was best to let a wine speak for itself. She had little respect for judges who looked ahead, setting their expectations before they had discovered what was really in the wine.

But this was different.

She'd been invited to a blind-tasting challenge. Ten bottles of wine lined up on an immaculate white tablecloth. An okay ambience with a modern motif, the restaurant had been around six months or so.

They should have decanted the wines into identical carafes for a truly blind tasting, but at least the foil had been stripped away and the brown paper presentation was always more popular with the crowd.

The final wine's color was splendid. A ruby red so opaque it was almost black. The initial nose was a bit closed, but the wine had been properly served at sixty degrees, nicely below room temperature. Another point to the event's sponsor. A quick swirl revealed abundant tears running down the inside of the glass. And the wine opened a bit. She swirled again. Dark fruit. Brown spice. Tarragon. Even... No, she wasn't going to jump to conclusions. A bad habit on one hand. And on the other, she had an audience.

The restaurant owner had done a respectable job of marketing his "Ten on January Tenth" challenge, pulling more than just the usual crowd of oenophiles out of the woodwork. He'd promised some fine wines in the collection, both U.S. and European. The nice spread of free appetizers hadn't hurt either, though they needed to be further from the tasting table. Twice she'd had to cross to the far side of the dining room to make sure the scent was the wine and not his Italian herbs. The second time the owner noticed, and in moments the waiters had shifted the more aromatic foods to the farther end of the buffet. Good service.

The sip and quick intake of breath over the wine as it still swam on her tongue gave the expected results. Lemony, and a confirmation of the anise on the nose rode into the finish. She spat into the bucket and nosed the wine again.

There was something more. She didn't have it yet.

Another swirl and sip. More air. Another spit. Exactly the same dark richness.

Ah, there it was: not something there, but something missing. Almost no tannins at all. A wine this dark, yet so clean; it definitely wasn't mainstream. It was a true challenge wine to set apart the real tasters.

She opened her eyes and realized that the restaurant was completely silent. Every face was turned in her direction, even the early diners had stopped eating to watch her. Mr. Terence, that obnoxious cookbook chef who coyly avoided any request for his first name—it probably said "Mister" on his birth certificate—had peeked at the wine label and then crumpled his bit of notepaper. The restaurant owner had noticed and was scowling. There was someone who had just lost his next invitation here.

Cassidy didn't need to look.

It took her several moments to come back to the wine, the taste still rolling across her tongue. To come back and realize that she really had done something; she had moved out of the crowd of being but one of many in the New York tastings. Here, in Seattle, the many were waiting to hear her verdict.

Hers.

The temptation to dismiss the phenomenon as a big frog in a small pond was there. But Josh was here from *Gourmet Week* as well, which had made her nervous through the first four wines. He'd actually trained under Parker. He too wore a look of anticipation. He held up a piece of notepaper, carefully folded to show he was ready, and nodded for her to go ahead. Well, there was no avoiding it, and she didn't need to on this one.

"Italian. Apulia." Some of the diners' faces blanked. "That's the region. The boot-heel of Italy."

Josh was grinning when she turned to face Mister Terence who was making a show of hiding the bottle.

"Taurino from the Negroamaro grape. The Notarpanaro Salento Rosso. Either the '97 or the '01, but I'd bet on the former."

Terence's face fell and Josh flipped open his slip of paper and turned it for her to see. He'd written just a number on it, "97." The restaurant owner clapped his hands together and laughed, his teeth bright in his dark, Italian face.

"An exquisite final choice, Mr. Parrano. It truly stands clear, even after the other wines. Even a rearrangement of your last name. An elegant touch."

He bowed deeply before taking her shoulders and kissing each cheek.

"Angelo." He had one of those Italian accents that was designed to make a woman melt and it wasn't hard to give in to it. "Please call me, Angelo, Ms. Knowles. Always Angelo."

"Cassidy then." She let herself melt a bit farther, her wine columnist attitude slipping off a little more.

He took her hand and raised it. "Ten wines and not a miss." Josh had missed one, but a totally understandable mix up unless you'd specifically studied the Loire Valley Vouvrays. He'd gotten the region and grape, but not the winery. Mister Terence had missed the Vouvray placing it as an Oregon Pinot of all silliness, the Taurino, and three others, two of them quite obvious mistakes. Two of the three amateurs had bested his score though they both missed the Vouvray, a tricky wine because of its gentle voice, and the Taurino, probably because of its high price. She'd had it only a few times herself.

"A meal on the house. No, you don't get to order, I will make the menu specially for you."

Everyone applauded as he conducted her to a table set for two. Angelo looked around and waved for Josh to take the other seat; Josh might be happily married but he was an old friend and a lively dinner companion. Angelo left Terrence out in the cold with the three amateurs to browse the free appetizer table.

"If you give me the meal, I can't write it up. Conflict of interest."

"Some other time, you come back and I charge you double. Not tonight." He lowered his voice. "I've been waiting for an excuse to chase that hoity-toity Mr. Terence out of here, but you have taken care of that for me. He won't dare show his face for quite a while to come. For this I am eternally grateful. And you are eternally welcome in my restaurant."

She nodded, not minding being used to that end in the least, and then glanced at Josh. "Perhaps I could make one request about the menu."

She raised an eyebrow and Josh laughed, then flipped open his slip of paper again. Angelo tried to look angry but he couldn't hold it for more than a moment. He stepped back to the tasting table and, securing the Taurino from Terence with a slight tug, he placed it at their table.

"The meal shall match this perfectly."

"Damn, you're good!" Russell took another piece of garlic bread and mashed it around in the red sauce to soak up all he could.

Dinner service roared through Angelo's kitchen with a crash of pans, calls back and forth across the cook line, and ballet-like orchestration. Russell had grabbed some pasta and retreated to the sidelines to watch the mayhem. The kitchen ran with a smooth perfection that should happen only in movies.

"You should see what I sent out on the floor tonight. Exquisite. The Cingale with Truffle Sauce." Angelo kissed his fingertips and threw the kiss to the kitchen's ceiling. "Outdid myself even if I'm the one who says so."

He slapped Russell on top of the head.

"That's grilled boar meat to you, you peasant."

"I know what *cingale* is," he cuffed Angelo back somewhat harder. "And your food is always awesome, buddy." Russell kissed his own fingers and then made a show of licking them clean of the garlic butter.

"Yeah, you need to clean up. You're messing up my kitchen, man. Just by breathing." Angelo peeked into an oven and closed it again. He returned to mincing chives at an impossible rate for some garnish.

Russell looked down to inspect himself. His jeans were smeared with white fiberglass resin from the seals on the new decking. It had hardened into crackling streaks that wouldn't let go of the cloth even when he picked at them. His shirt was clean, just a couple tears from where he'd caught it on the old decking he'd been tearing off the boat. Maybe he was a bit disreputable for the stainless-steel-and-white-tile kitchen.

Just because Angelo was right, Russell wasn't about to admit it.

"Wait until I start the woodwork. Then I can offer you a healthy dose of sawdust on your tile floor to make it look properly lived in. You could eat off the damn thing now."

"Thanks, but no thanks. I think a health inspector would rather see a rat in my kitchen than you." Angelo danced around a half-dozen desserts with a squirt bottle adding little swirls of reduced pomegranate sauce even as the waiters put them on their trays. A moment later his sous chef dumped a steaming cauldron of homemade pasta into a colander. Angelo attacked it with quick tongs and a bit of oil before plating it next to an Eggplant Parmigiana that still bubbled from the oven.

Russell licked another dribble of butter off the back of his hand.

He smelled her before he saw her. Like warm wood and something else he couldn't identify but could never forget.

He turned to look and wasn't disappointed. Trim and chic in a black pantsuit over a black turtleneck. The cut was perfect for her figure which was pleasantly womanly in its curves. It suited her five foot ten very nicely, making her look even taller and more slender than she was. He checked her shoes, okay, five foot eight without the heels, which fit her even better. Her face was so subtly made up it looked as if she wore no makeup at all. Her russet hair pulled back into a tight chignon from which not a single strand strayed. The shape of jawline to neck, of ear to cheek, was like a flash from the past.

For the first time in the month and a half since he'd closed the studio, he wished for lights and a camera. But she was everything he was leaving behind. Everything that had been wrong with his former life. He could imagine Melanie on his boat much easier than this one, even Melanie let her hair down on occasion—she actually made a trademark of doing just that.

Where Melanie's voice was affected French, to cover her New York accent, this woman's voice was throaty and warm as she did the "thank you so much" thing with Angelo. She glanced at him twice with intensely hazel eyes that were deeper than the ocean. A glance he could easily read. "What was this slob doing dirtying up Angelo's pristine kitchen?"

Then she was gone and Angelo just stood there beaming.

"Hey, Buddy-boy." Russell poked his fork into his pasta. He had to do it a couple times before he finally landed some. "She's got you bad."

"Oh yeah." Angelo sounded a little dreamy. "You weren't

here. She's just the nation's hottest food-and-wine columnist. It took me six months to tempt her here."

He shook himself and then punched Russell's arm hard.

"And she loves my food and my restaurant!"

"Hey! Ow already!" He knocked Angelo's hat to the floor just as Angelo kicked Russell's stool over backward. He landed hard against the refrigerator. Once he had his balance, he prepared to lunge forward.

Angelo moved faster and aimed his weapon at Russell's chest.

"More garlic bread?"

Russell kicked the stool back into place and took another steaming slice from the wicker basket. He easily matching his friend's grin.

"THE WHAT OF JANUARY?"

"Just grab a bottle, cheese and crackers if you have 'em and come along."

Russell dug around in the cooler, found a couple of beers. The cardboard box that was his pantry had some Ritz crackers, his absolute weakness. He slapped the package against his thigh to dislodge the worst of the wood dust from the box.

Closing up his sailboat, he followed Dave down onto the floating slipway. They turned toward the far end of "D" dock. The thousand masts of Shilshole Marina cluttered the night sky. To the east, brightly lit houses looked down on them from atop the high cliff. To the west, Puget Sound stretched to the moonlit peaks of the Olympics. It was clear and cold enough to freeze a sailboat's tail, or at least his own.

"The what of January?" He repeated, his breath puffing a white cloud into the night air. He had to trot down the dock to catch up with Dave even though the man had to be in his fifties.

"The ides."

"I thought only March had ides. The day Brutus stabbed his buddy Caesar in the behind."

"The ides is lands on the fifteenth of March, May, July, and October, I think. The thirteenth of all the others. And today's the thirteenth. Sounds like a good reason for a party."

Russell didn't need any more prompting than that.

"Lead on, Brutus. Just be careful of any desires to do some stabbing."

"Don't worry. We start small in January, plastic spoons. It's December that's dangerous when we haul out our broadswords."

"You don't stab with a broadsword, you hack."

Dave laughed, "Yes, you'll fit in here fine." They arrived at Dave and Betsy's forty-four-foot catamaran.

Russell had been sorely tempted to buy one of these; they were fast, spacious, and stable as could be. Unless you got flipped. In something nasty, like a hurricane, a monohull would roll under and usually self right, sometimes without its mast, but at least it would right. A catamaran was more stable upside down than right side up. A little too wild for him. It would also be a hell of a lot of boat to single-hand in a storm.

He'd befriended Dave just to get a look inside and they'd spent hours talking about ocean crossings and ports of call. Russell had helped a buddy do the New York-Bahamas run on his friend's J/boat—never more than a day or so from land—a long step from crossing one of the oceans. Dave and Betsy had taken the *Lark* on a four-year tour that included both capes, Good Hope and Horn, Antarctica, and all of the seven seas.

"Ponds," Betsy had corrected him. "Not seas. We talk about crossing the ponds, not so scary that way."

Still worried him either way, even if that was part of his master plan.

He clambered aboard and joined the crowd of "D" dock liveaboards. Teri and Tom were curled up on one of the settees, a bottle of cheap white wine in front of them. He'd been here barely two weeks and he already knew of their reputation. It had been hard to miss actually.

They had terrible fights when running in the local races, and screamingly good, or at least loud sex when at dock. Few secrets could be kept through a few millimeters of fiberglass hull. Even his *Lady's* double-plank oak hull wasn't going to muffle all that much if he ever had a flesh-and-blood lady aboard. Most sailors were discrete, Teri obviously didn't care or didn't think to. He eyed the incredibly tight sweater on the shapely dishwater blonde. Or maybe she liked bragging.

Russell slid in next to Perry. The old man had a bottle of decent whiskey capped beside him, a small tumbler in his massive fist. He rarely spoke, but Betsy had told Russell that the old-timer had been born on a tugboat off Vashon Island. Had worked boats, mostly log tugs and fishing tenders, for the eighty years since. He lived on a 1904 Arrow tug, one of only four built that year, that he was restoring a little way down the dock.

Dave and Betsy had made their money *then* moved to the boat and the seas. He drank Heineken and she had a glass of red wine in a short, wide glass that wouldn't tip easily at sea.

Others he didn't know drifted in behind him, each arriving with a wintry blast of the chill January air and a muttered curse from those closest to the hatch. As the crowd grew, he refused to be nudged from the small table with Perry and Dave. Soon, people were perched on counters or squatting by the windows.

"What do you do to keep yourself busy?" Dave grabbed a couple of his Ritz crackers.

"Other than my boat, you mean?"

"Other than your boat."

"I take pictures. Used to." Russell thought of the images of Angelo and the lighthouse still in his camera. "Still do."

"Any good?"

Dave had asked the question, but it was Perry who inspected him with blue eyes shaded by a black Greek sailor's hat, the rest of his face mostly lost in a white beard and mustache that would have put Santa Claus to shame.

"Used to make a pretty decent living at it."

Perry nodded and sipped his whiskey.

"Good," Dave agreed. "Need something to give purpose to your wanderings. Betsy there is a marine botanist. Must've logged five thousand samples over the last decade. She has this little rig that lets her grab water at surface, then one, two, five, and ten meters all at once. Keeps her moving ahead. She catalogs the whole mess and ships the data to the Scripps Institute. They love her for it, though I'd hate to be the staff grad student when she sends in a case of vials. Me, I'm a writer. Spent thirty years doing technical writing. Now I'm doing the travel narrative thing and might do a fiction book set in the seaports of the world. What are you gonna do?"

"You mean about 'moving ahead'?" Russell munched on a couple of crackers and opened another bottle of beer. "Hadn't really thought about it."

Hadn't thought at all really. Back at Thanksgiving—when he'd made a joke to match every one of Angelo's ideas about what to do with his life—Angelo had finally pulled a next-year's calendar off the wall and heaved it at him.

"Here, you big idiot. Buy a sailboat. On the first of each month, you sail to each one on the calendar. By the end of the year you'll be good enough to sail outta my life and let me get some peace." It had been a calendar of lighthouses. Two days later he'd found the *Lady* and bought her before her hull was even wet after the boat appraiser's inspection.

Angelo had laughed when Russell told him of his purchase. "Getting pretty sick of you moping on my couch, when can you move?" Three weeks of slavery, but he'd got her watertight and moved aboard just yesterday afternoon.

Hadn't thought about what it meant to buy a big boat; he simply did it.

And now he hadn't thought about what it meant to be a live-aboard; he simply did it.

Russell glanced about the crowded cabin. Liveaboards came in two main varieties: couples and single men. Not a single woman in the whole crowd. Teri had gathered a small court, all of whom she flirted with shamelessly. Tom was approaching meltdown, even though she was snuggled back against him while she flirted with the others.

"We know what those two will be doing."

Perry and Dave glanced over and answered in unison. "Fighting." Perry's first word of the evening.

"Can't imagine them making it out of the Sound, never mind anywhere further."

"She's a handful, that one." Dave took another cracker. "They've been married and living on that thirty-two-footer for two years now. Trying to pay off the boat so they can go offshore. Don't think they're any closer to it than when they started. Besides, his passion is rock climbing."

Russell would rather go solo any day of the week. Then he looked at Betsy. She and a couple he didn't know were lounging together against the galley counters, sharing gentle conversation and easy laughs. Both women were healthy and attractive. Any lack in the raw sexual appeal that Teri radiated was more than balanced by... What was the word to describe the tableau of friends? Comfortable. They were comfortable together, with those around them, with this setting, this boat.

It just took the right kind of woman. Maybe he'd find one. If not, he'd go and trust to his journey. He'd know the right one when she showed up.

Funny to have a boat now. As a kid he'd always dreamed of sailing around the world. The streetlights that had shown up through his Upper West Side Manhattan bedroom windows had painted a map of shadow and light on his ceiling that he had peopled with pirates and discovery.

In all his boyhood dreams, he'd never pictured a woman on the boat. Of course he hadn't hit puberty then either. At first, he'd imagined he and his grandfather sailing together. After he'd died, Russell had always pictured himself solo without really thinking about it. Once puberty hit, he'd thought about women and not sailboats. He hadn't remembered the boats until Angelo heaved the calendar at his head. He tried to mentally place Melanie aboard, but it wouldn't stick. And that was far more likely than Angelo's wine lady. There was a laugh.

Solo. Why had he always pictured himself sailing solo?

"Careful what you wish for, buddy, you're gonna get it," he muttered under his breath.

Maybe he could wish for this. A couple dozen people all crowded together. Nothing more important to do than spend some time with each other. Thank all the gods, no one sidling up to discuss the next shoot, no one after marrying into his parent's money. He definitely wouldn't miss someone barfing on his floor while they held themselves up with a palm in the middle of a ten-thousand-dollar photograph.

He'd given his whole damn art-photo collection to MOMA on permanent loan. Pete, the head of the art handling team who'd come to cart it off, had practically cried on his shoulder. His diminutive wife actually had—oddly enough at a tiny tintype self-portrait by a young Bourke-White.

Russell was already closer to Dave and Perry than he'd been to most of the people at the final studio party. The people here from Perry to Dave and even Teri were more real than any of his former...associates—except perhaps Melanie.

He looked back at Perry and Dave with a shrug, "I'm just gonna sail."

Dave looked a bit unsure but didn't say anything.

Perry poured another short whiskey and rolled the tumbler

back and forth between his callused palms. The surface rippled with golden light in the deep-cut glass.

"Pictures."

He and Dave faced the old salt who continued to study his drink.

"Pictures? I dunno. Boats and port towns?" Russell offered. A real yawn once spoken aloud.

"Quiet streets and pretty women?" Dave added. That was a little better.

Perry slid back into his silence, but Russell would swear there was a smile going on somewhere behind that bushy mustache.

"What?"

The old man just shook his head and sipped his whiskey. With a wink, he snagged a couple of Russell's Ritz crackers.

RUSSELL WOKE when his boat shifted. Someone was aboard— without knocking on the hull first. Someone was breaking the first rule of boat etiquette.

Teri. Crap. Teri was coming on board. She'd been eyeing him toward the end of the party last night. Did she have a late-night welcome ritual for any new single man on the dock? Certain parts of his body were indicating they wouldn't complain about that sort of welcome. But no way.

He scrabbled about for his pants, knocked his head sharply on a deck support he'd been meaning to wrap in foam rubber. He was going to give himself a permanent crease in his skull pretty soon.

"Don't be stupid, Russ. It's just been too long since you've had sex." Not since Melanie had jumped him Thanksgiving morning before he'd had a chance to tell her that he was leaving for Seattle in a few hours.

She hadn't stayed after the studio closing party that he'd flown back for a week later and he couldn't blame her. Others had offered to stay, but he wasn't that crass. Or, now that he thought about it, that interested. It hadn't been a cheerful bash though it had all of the catering and blues band trappings of a good go.

The bright flashes before his eyes eased and he struggled into his pants as the boat rocked again. Then there was a step thudding back down onto the dock. He tried to think if there was anything to steal up on deck.

The forward porthole showed no one crossing past the bow toward land. Who'd be up in the middle of the night prowling around the marina? He'd better stop them before they hit a boat that had something to lose.

He ran down the short companionway, the wood shavings and sawdust were prickly against his bare feet, and threw open the rear hatch. The cold hit his bare chest like a slap. He looked along the dock and could just make out a broad figure in a dark coat with white hair.

"Perry?" he half-whispered sending a puff of steamy breath out into night.

The old man waved a hand over his head, but didn't turn around. He continued toward his battered old tug.

That's when Russell heard it, the faintest sound at his feet.

He looked down.

Perry had left a cardboard box.

Russell shivered as the chill air wrapped around his body.

The box moved. There was something inside.

And then the box mewed.

ALKI LIGHTHOUSE

Alki Point, West Seattle
First lit: 1868
Automated: 1970
47.5762 -122.4206

*A*lki, the Washington State motto, means "by-and-by" in Chinook, a local Native American language. In 1851 the first white settlers in the area landed at the present-day location of the lighthouse. They named the settlement New York-Alki.

A few years later a young entrepreneur named Doc Maynard was made unwelcome there and moved on to found another settlement a few miles from the inhospitable point. It is one of the ironies of his life that in his last years, a near destitute Maynard lived close to the lighthouse where New York-Alki had long since succumbed to Doc's city, which he'd named Seattle.

*C*assidy parked the car and pounded a fist against the steering wheel. The horn blared and she'd have jumped out of the seat if it hadn't been for the seat belt.

Once again she stared at the GPS. The "current position" and "destination" coordinates were superimposed. The coordinates matched the numbers on the envelope sitting beside the stick shift. She looked out her windshield. No question, that was it. The Alki Point lighthouse stood barely a dozen yards off the main beach road. She'd even found a parking spot directly in front of the gate. Over two thousand dollars of hiking gear and hour upon hour learning how to use the GPS so that she'd never get lost again.

And there was the stupid lighthouse in plain view down a little garden path.

She tossed her stupid alien-manufactured rain pants over the stupid GPS and climbed out of the car. Maybe if she left it unlocked, someone would steal all of the crap and she could pretend this was just a bad dream. Deep breath, Cass. Take a deep breath. She pressed the button and the car sealed everything safely inside with a contented chirp.

She pushed on the gate and the lock rattled, but it didn't open. A bronze plaque was bolted onto the fence.

"Winter hours: Sat-Sun 12-3. Mon-Fri closed."

Today was Saturday, the first of February. But it was nine in the morning which meant three hours to wait.

She kicked the gate.

Hard.

Well, that was one advantage to her new light-hiking, all-weather, waterproof boots by Vasque, which sounded like a plaque rinse more than a boot. They gave her the ability to kick a solid iron gate and not break her foot.

She couldn't even get a decent snapshot from the road, too many trees had grown up in the gardens. The expensive houses were packed side-by-side and she couldn't see any passage through.

She returned to the driver's seat and glared out at the neighborhood. Pounding her feet on the floormat made her feel a little better. She started the car and popped the clutch badly enough to stall the engine.

"Okay, Cassidy, you can do this. You know how to drive a goddamn car." She hadn't needed one in New York, so it had been something of an adventure to drive one when she returned to Seattle. She'd learned on a stick, but after a decade in the city, it hadn't come back as quickly as she'd expected.

She was glad she hadn't invited Jack James along; she was no mood for a date. At least not if she wanted it to go well. And Jack's everlasting calm would just irritate her more. He never engaged his emotions in anything. Not in anything at all, now that she thought about it. Including her.

Once again: start the engine, in gear, ease out the clutch. She rolled out of the parking spot and down the street looking for a place to turn around. Fifty feet farther on, a little sign was posted on a rusted fence.

Two words.

"Beach Access."

"Yes!" Lighthouses were on beaches.

She checked the rearview mirror. Someone was pulling into her spot.

"That was mine, mister."

The next one she could find was halfway around the bay over a quarter mile away according to her stupid GPS. She considered taking the instrument with her to throw in the ocean but resisted in the end. With the way her luck was running, the moment she heaved it overboard, the technologically ecstatic clerk from REI would just happen by. Then he'd give her a sad puppy-dog look and she definitely couldn't deal with that today.

The wind was at her back as she returned to the little flight of gritty concrete steps down to the sand-and-rock beach. With no park ranger to refuse her a parking pass, she'd have an effortless walk along the water's edge on a bright blue winter's day.

At the bottom of the steps she turned right along the sandy verge and was confronted by a much bigger sign.

"Residents only beyond this point."

Well, her car was parked in the neighborhood, sort of, so she was resident here at the moment. Besides, she formed the argument in her head, the sign was faded and was badly broken in one corner. "Broken sign, rule no longer valid."

Finally she rationalized that no one would be out on a day like this to give a damn anyway. It was blowing stiffly, though not like last month, and the air was definitely cold enough to snow. Thankfully, the sky was sparkling blue, not a white, puffy cloud in sight—truly little danger of a soaking rain today.

She strode past the sign all warm in her red watch cap, her knee-length Michael Kors parka, and her Vasque hiking boots that could definitely climb this beach, which was much less steep than any of those seven peaks.

The view was once again spectacular. Seattle was out of sight around the point commanded by the lighthouse. The bay curved away to the left, the tall hills of West Seattle towered behind, dotted with beautiful houses and massive pine trees. In front of her, almost too vivid to be real, floated Vashon and Maury Island. Beyond them, soaring up into the sky were the Olympic Mountains; the Bothers peaks postured—each striving to raise his rugged, white-capped shoulders higher than the other.

The sand disappeared and she was forced to clamber over huge rocks that had been piled up in front of the houses as a breakwater. In addition to the breakwater each house had a massive seawall of concrete. She could see over the top of one to the array of kayaks and children's toys in the narrow back yard. The next house had a crane with a dock actually dangling from the end of it. It must be able to swing out and drop into the water on calmer, warmer days.

The third house had a tall tree that blocked her view of the house and looked as if it blocked the owner's view of the Sound. Well, that certainly made no sense. This view was so valuable that the land here was probably sold by the square foot.

Then there was the lighthouse.

The same angle as it appeared on the calendar. Maybe the photographer had come on a day when the front entrance was closed as well. A small yard of perfect grass surrounded the old keeper's house, set back among the gardens.

The lighthouse itself was perched on the edge of the massive boulders, just feet above the sea. All around its base were small white stones, as if the building were afloat in its own little white-foam sea. The Alki light lacked the rigid stoutness of the West Point lighthouse. Rather than squat and powerful, its red-capped light soared three stories into the blue sky. The white paint shone so brilliantly in the sunlight that it was painful to look at. Maybe she should have bought a pair of those polarized, glacier-expedition sun goggles.

She tugged out her camera and snapped a couple of photos. Only after the last shot did she notice that a sailboat had sailed into the picture on the far side of the lighthouse.

Cobalt blue hull...red sails?

If there hadn't been a photo of the first lighthouse with that same boat framed on her condo wall, she'd think she was losing her mind.

She took another picture just so that she could prove later that it was real. Maybe this was a trademark in Seattle and lots of sailboats looked like that. Though she couldn't imagine why. It was as if the last month hadn't really happened. Or was happening again.

Sitting down on a moderately flat rock, she watched the waves for a while, without the slashing spray this time. She tugged the Michael Kors jacket over her knees and almost down to her ankles. The watch cap pulled down over her ears kept her head reasonably warm.

"Becoming quite the adventuress, aren't we, Cass?" She felt strangely light, as if the breeze that was making her nose and cheeks sting with the cold could lift her up and she'd just fly away. Unfettered. Bound to no one.

Except a couple kajillion readers. That slammed her back to earth and she could feel the cold rock against her butt despite the jacket, her leggings, and the woolen underwear that she just might start wearing year-round it was so warm.

She pulled off her heavy gloves and dug out her father's letter. Nothing new on the outside of the envelope. Just a destination point for this month's crazy journey.

Dearest Ice Sweet,

His voice sounded in her head. He wrote the same way he spoke. Warm, friendly, his letters were always an intimate conversation.

We made it to the second lighthouse. Alki, by-and-by. That's what it means. Maybe you remember that from school; it is the state motto after all. I always sat on the south side of the ferry just to watch for this lighthouse.

"I remember, Daddy." He must have pointed it out to her on every single trip to Seattle, both directions. He'd said it so many times that it had lost all meaning, just words that were a part of the day like, "Good morning." or "How was school?" Ignored, forgotten.

Suddenly she was a child in the big ferry boat once again, hundreds of people milling about, trying to find a way to be comfortable on the rigid plastic seats for the half-hour crossing. Children racing up and down the aisles waving their Gameboys or Walkmans. Tourists snapping photos through the salt-stained glass that would never come out the way they pictured them; the journey a blur of half-forgotten images of a place they'd never been and would barely remember.

Things really do happen by-and-by, especially the good things. We were working the California vineyard. A couple of the guys had drifted off, and one had slashed his leg so badly with a rototiller that he'd gone into the VA hospital after coming out of the war unharmed. Strange, I can't remember his name. Don't even know what happened to him.

We made some of the worst wine you can imagine those first years. But we got better, figured it out the hard way. It was still a brutal amount of work, but it was drinkable by the time your mother first came by.

She was a tourist, vacationing in California after getting out of school. Came to the coast to check out Berkeley for graduate work. She and a carload of girlfriends were doing the vineyard circuit. I opened a bottle of our Merlot for them to taste. Our absolute best. Hadn't meant to do that, but your mother always had the ability to turn me into a bumbling fool, right from the first time I saw her. She came back the next weekend with one friend, the week after alone. Soon she was helping in the fields. The rest, as they say, is history.

"Pretty slick, Daddy. Hitting on a college girl on vacation." She remembered the story. Daddy always told it exactly the same way, as if the tracks of it had been burned forever upon his heart. Unchanging, unchangeable over the years.

This lighthouse always made me think about the strange course my life has taken. The wanderings that took me to a place I'd never been or imagined going. That gave me a family, a wife and daughter, and a place to be in the world. Looking back, everything happened as if there were some great master plan. From the past looking forward, it was the most haphazard series of choices and chance.

Remember, Cass, pursue your dreams, but don't expect them to follow that straight and narrow path that you see so clearly in your head.

Life happens in its own fashion. At its own pace. I learned not to second-guess it. All that is good in my life came to me "by-and-by."

Vic

"Ha!" There was another memory she'd lost track of. That's what he'd said every single time he saw the lighthouse. "It'll come to me by-and-by." She glanced back over her shoulder.

The lighthouse stood there looking down at her.

"By-and-by, huh?"

It didn't answer.

"Good thing I didn't wait for by-and-by, Daddy. I'd never have gotten here."

Or would she? Mama went to Vassar in economics. Cassidy attended her mother's alma mater and got her degree in marketing, most of it done as an independent study.

While other students were partying, she was taking courses at the CIA. The Culinary Institute of America was less than a dozen miles up the road after all and it was too good a chance to pass up. No major surprise, what with being her father's daughter, that she had an exceptionally well-trained palate. By the time she'd graduated from high school, she'd read a hundred books about wine. She'd graduated from both Vassar and the CIA at the same time. Columbia School of Journalism had occurred more by chance than conscious choice. The class assignment to write a review of the Punk and Wine Bistro had led to her major first sale and she'd never looked back.

Daddy was wrong, it certainly hadn't been by chance. She'd planned and she'd worked so hard and given up so much. She was out here alone wasn't she?

"Given up a hell of a lot, Daddy." She brushed at a tear raised by the icy wind.

Her fingers were frozen, even colder than her cheeks. Blowing into her curled hands warmed them little. She pulled the gloves back on, forming fists with her hands, leaving the chilly fingers of the gloves empty.

The lighthouse stood high above. The sailboat was disappearing southward, continuing its own chilly journey. A container ship sliced northward, but there were few other craft on so bitter a day.

She'd planned to get as far away from Seattle and Bainbridge Island as she could. Marketing had started out as a degree in business. A thousand times she'd pictured herself smashing through the glass ceiling at some huge corporation. Of being like Carly Fiorina, then a top AT&T exec. She'd gone on to be president of Hewlett-Packard. Cassidy had written her a piece of teen fan mail, the only she'd ever written, but no answer came. One thing Cassidy knew, though, a woman could do anything.

"If Carly can do it, so can I."

"Absolutely!" Her father would agree. "Anything but food or wine. The reviewers are such an old boys' club." His voice was a whisper in her memory, as warm as the wind was cold. He'd warned her of that so many times that she'd taken on the challenge.

"But I found a way through. You know, Daddy, I did an end run on them."

"Right," she waved her arms about to make her point and then waved them some more to get a decent blood flow. "I ignored that old boy's club completely and forged my own path to the tables." She'd cut quite a swath, stepping on a number of toes, but success forgave many sins.

"I knew what I was doing." Even as she said it, the words went sour. Her path that had been so clear, was only so in retrospect. Maybe that part of Daddy's letter was true.

"But I'm in control now. The rest of your letter is plain silly. I know where I'm going." And she did. A year maybe two more on the west coast, a couple in Europe, and she'd swing back into New York at the very top. Let the *New York Times* beg her to come aboard. They were the only major metro newspaper that didn't syndicate her column. Well, other than the *Washington Post*, but that was such an inside-the-Beltway paper that it didn't bother her nearly as much.

"I know what I'm doing. My path is clear, Daddy."

The roar of the wind and the crash of the waves against the beach were her only answers.

"Crystal clear." Again the sour taste. Her path wasn't that all that clear. The only thing that was had to be that she was losing her mind.

She was sitting on the windiest point of Seattle in a below-freezing day on the first of February. Sitting here with icicles where most people had fingers, holding a conversation with her dead father about career choices he'd be the first to argue were hers to make.

That was a laugh. Actually, it was. It bubbled up from somewhere deep inside her. It started small but it built and built until it burst forth and she could barely catch her breath.

"Totally and completely nutso!" she shouted at the wind and

her words drifted away, wrapping around the lighthouse on their way landward.

"It will all make sense by-and-by, my ice sweet girl."

She spun around, but there was no one near. No one but memory to whisper to her with her father's voice.

⸻

ANGELO LAY back on one of the cockpit benches of the sailboat, his back against the cabin wall. His hood raised against the wind. He clutched a silver travel mug in his gloved hands.

Russell imagined that someday he'd be able to feel his cheeks again, but not anytime soon—damn but it was cold.

"Hey Angelo." His friend had been quiet for the whole trip.

"What?" A one-word answer. His friend was Italian and never gave one-word answers.

"It's Saturday. How can you afford to be out here with me? Thought you did a Saturday lunch. Not that I don't appreciate it and all." He pointed the boat up a few points tighter to the wind. Even with the reef in the main and the small jib up forward, she still skidded over the wave tops at better than seven knots.

"We do a lunch." Angelo's voice was so quiet Russell could barely make out his answer over the wind.

"Well?"

"Well, what?" It wasn't like him to be obtuse.

Angelo took a long pull of his coffee. Seriously long.

"Well?"

"No traffic, my man. Saturday lunch is so slow, the sous chef can handle it. With one arm behind his back." More coffee. "And his head in a sack."

"But you're the best cook there is, Angelo."

"Don't let my mother hear you say that."

He still had his sense of humor, that at least was a good sign. Russell had been planning to scamper back to the marina just across the span of Elliot Bay, but instead he kept them headed down the Sound. Maybe they'd duck over to Vashon Island before turning back.

"What about your wonderful wine reviewer? Didn't she make it all better?"

Angelo shook his head. "A complimentary article about the tasting, business picked up a little, but people don't come to restaurants to drink hundred-dollar bottles of wine. They come for food. I still haven't really paid off the tasting and that was three weeks ago."

"How much did you spend?"

"Publicity, a couple of ads in the right places, I picked up the hotel for the guy from *Gourmet Week*, all the appetizers. The wines alone cost a grand. Wholesale."

"Shit!" Russell eased out the sails a bit so that he could pay less attention to the boat and more to his friend.

"How close are you to failing?"

Angelo shrugged and he didn't look up.

"Look. You need money, it's not an issue. You know that."

Angelo nodded. He'd never taken money from the Morgans, except for the college expenses Russell's dad had insisted on giving him. Not even pocket change from the Morgan millions.

"What's your hook?"

Angelo squinted up at him. "My hook?"

"Sure, every ad has a hook. Every business has one too. My hook as an ad photographer was, 'Highest quality, spare no expenses.' And I didn't. If I needed an elephant in the distant background, I hired the elephant, handlers, and whatever. My clients paid, man did they pay. And they got the best damn quality that could be achieved in return. What do you have?"

Angelo looked puzzled for a moment, shifted on the cockpit seat.

"Authentic Italian cooking."

"Tony's pizza by the slice claims that in every mall store across the whole freaking country."

Angelo's glare was intense enough that Russell decided to back off rather than push harder. He really didn't want to go for a swim in February. But he'd definitely need more time than a downwind run back to his Shilshole dock to crack this nut. He tacked to take them down the western side. The wind was dead astern, perfect to run south down the narrower Colvos Passage. On the return they'd have room to tack back upwind along the wider East Passage. It would be his longest sail yet, and it might give them some time to work something out.

"Other than your mother, you're the best damn cook. Right?"

"Damn straight." Angelo was still pissed about the mall store crack.

"And still you aren't a big success."

The pissed look eased back toward sad, such an unusual expression on his friend's face that it took Russell several moments to identify it.

"So we need to come up with a hook. Something to get you noticed—other than a thousand dollars of wine."

"Damn good Italian food should be enough."

"That's better."

"What is?"

"Damn Good Italian Food. It's a good pitch."

"My mother would slap us both and wash out our mouths with soap." But there was a shadow of a smile. Better.

"Your mother gonna slap you even worse if you give up."

Angelo nodded and for the first time on the trip, took some interest in the sailboat. He pulled a winch handle out of the pocket mounted inside the cockpit and cranked a couple of turns on the jib sheet. A little too far, but Russell decided that the better part of valor was to keep his mouth shut. Sailing with the wind was warmer and quieter, but also less demanding. If

Angelo was still sulking when they rounded the south end of Vashon, his mother wasn't the only one who'd be slapping him.

"What part of Italy do you know better than any other?"

Angelo shrugged, "You know that. Liguria. Mama's from Liguria; Pop was from Tuscany. Mama and I went back every year. You came with me for the whole summer after senior year in high school. Why you ask such a stupido question?"

"I knew the answer. Wanted to make sure you did, dummy."

Angelo's glare finally had a bit of energy behind it.

"How much of your menu is Ligurian, even northern Italian?"

Angelo gazed off the side of the boat at the big ferry boat passing off the stern.

"Maybe half. Maybe less. Sicilian is a big draw. So is the far north, up in the Piedmont."

"So you've got to stock ingredients for everywhere from Sicily to Venice to Milan. And all those fancy wines you served to the Madonna wine lady?" About the right image with her perfect coif and hard-iced poise.

He blinked this time. "Why...uh...none. Only two were even Italian."

"*Mi amico.* I, the great Russell Morgan, have found your problem and your answer. The best damn Ligurian food in the Western Hemisphere. Okay, the title sucks. No one knows nothing from Liguria anyway. Best Damn Tuscan Food in the West. Still sucks. We'll work on that. First thing, you sell off or drink any wine not from northern Italy. Eat the out-of-region ingredients on your days off."

He pinched Angelo's cheek and pulled on it like a matron auntie.

"Then I make-a you an ad spread," he blew a kiss in the air off his fingertips, "that will-a make you mama proud."

"You? I thought you were done with that, man."

Russell had thought he was as well, but Angelo needed help. His kind of help.

"That's okay, I'm gonna make you pay, brother. Through the nose."

Angelo lost some of his happiness. "You know I don't have that kind of money."

"No. But you make the best damn pasta sauce on the planet."

Angelo perked up. "I do, don't I."

His punch thudded into Russell's shoulder hard enough to hurt. He'd let his friend get away with that...for now.

"You left New York for this?" Melanie stood on the pitching dock barely wide enough to walk on and clutched tightly onto Russell's arm for stability.

"Yep! Isn't she beautiful?" Melanie made a career of being called beautiful. But if it meant that she was similar to this boat, a shudder rippled up her spine, she'd give it up.

The boat, which was moving with a life of its own that had nothing to do with the dock, lay spread out before her. In the late afternoon light she could see the blue paint on the side was peeling. The white masts were doing the same. There was a great expanse of red material wrapped about the horizontal piece—the boom, Russell called it. It looked like a virulent growth that one should spray immediately with Lysol. A lot of it. Before burning it in the bathtub. The floor was all torn up, great strips of gray and black canvas had been peeled up to reveal rough wood that looked even worse.

"Want to come aboard?"

"No!" But Russell was already stepping up onto the boat and her tight grip on his arm dragged her along. The boat was so small that it rolled back and forth just from their weight. The only boat she'd ever been on was the New York Circle Line, a massive ferry filled with thousands of tourists. And that had been for a fashion shoot, so she hadn't paid much attention to anything but the photographer. That had been her second spread and first cover for *Elle*. Even for that she might not have climbed aboard this boat.

"See, over here I've been replacing the deck."

Deck, not floor. She repeated the word a couple of times to herself.

He had ducked under the virulent boom thing and was pointing at a place she couldn't see along the cabin. She took a breath and leaned over to see. If felt as if she was going to be flung headfirst into the inky depths between Russell's boat and the ragged old powerboat parked next door.

The deck looked better on this side. More like the parquet of her kitchen floor though not nearly as pretty.

"It's so," narrow, she wanted to shout. The water was right there. "Nice." She checked Russell's face and he beamed like a newborn's father. The right answer. Perhaps it was okay to relax a little.

"Down below is still a mess." She hadn't really thought about the inside of the boat. The cabin was barely as tall as her knees. There was a tiny door that might do for the White Rabbit, but she was no Alice in Wonderland to go crawling on her hands and knees, especially not in her cashmere coat.

He opened the door and then slid a part of the roof back. A little ladder went much farther down than she thought. Down far enough to stand in. Down until, she glanced over the side and then back down the ladder, until she'd be standing under-water to her knees.

"Make sure to hold on as you come down." Russell clambered down into the cabin like he was born to it, facing forward as he dropped down the ladder holding onto nothing at all. She knew from experience that men lived in a world of their own.

Russell had always been a cut above: more civilized, more polite, and usually more thoughtful.

At the moment, she could kill him.

But if she wanted him, she was going to have to do this stupid male test. One of thousands men threw at women. At least with Russell it didn't have a backing of cruelty behind it, just his own version of naiveté. And she did want him. Why else had she cancelled two shoots on short notice when he'd called with a Valentine's Day invitation to come to Seattle? Even at her level, those cancellations would have ripples across her career for months to come.

"Get a grip, girl." She took hold of either side of the doorway, thankful for her leather gloves. Though they didn't stop the cold, at least she didn't have to risk a splinter. There was no way to descend the ladder as Russell had. She turned and went down it backwards. Even one at a time, the steps were steep and difficult. The boat kept shifting, little jerks in unexpected directions. This is how clumsy people must feel. She hated it. Hated it so much she wanted to cry. She clamped down on that hard, careful not to bite her lip.

The floor was a surprise when she ran out of steps. Then she turned. There was just enough room to stand upright, but her instincts wanted to hunch down like a troll.

The ceiling was high in the middle, but sloped down to either side. The floor was a narrow strip running all the way to the front. The walls sloped outward from the floor. Seating was perched part way up the wall, making more use of the wider space. God, it was even smaller than her father's trailer—may the old bastard rot in hell.

"I'm going to put the galley here," he pointed to a couple of cardboard boxes of groceries, an ice chest, and a small camping stove.

"Pilot's berth there." A bed no bigger than a coffin, across the narrow walkway from the galley. How could you even climb into the thing? The deck was just two or three feet above the narrow bench.

"A settee that can be a dining table or collapse into a comfortable double bed right here across from this little wood-stove." He continued forward oblivious of the fact that all this meant nothing to her. Whatever he was calling a settee was now a card table and two folding chairs. And how that became a bed for two was beyond her and a place she'd certainly never be found.

A section of the flooring was pulled up and she half expected to see the ocean beneath it. Instead, about six inches down, was concrete and, she swallowed hard, a wash of blackish water sloshing back and forth with each motion of the boat.

A loud buzz below her right foot made her jump. There were splashing noises and slowly the skin of water disappeared. The buzzing stopped with a sigh and a gurgle.

"That's just the bilge pump."

The smell of fresh cut wood and paint added to the queasiness in her stomach. The bilge pump, she resumed her quest to catalog all of the strange words he kept using. Booms and tillers and hulls. Even something called a fang or a vang that he wanted to replace for reasons she'd never understand.

Again she focused on the curve of the hull. It was even narrower inside. She peeked out one of the round windows and could just see the water. The floor was deeper than she'd thought, she was in the ocean up to her waist.

The "head" was next on the tour.

She blinked twice but it didn't go away. A porcelain toilet. With handles and levers that would make a dentist chair look safe. Sitting right there in the open on the floor. It was a good thing that he'd promised her a hotel room or she'd be on the red-eye back to New York.

He waved at a blank section of hull, "Books, maybe a bench seat that could double as another bunk. Don't really know yet."

The last of the tour was the forward stateroom. A fancy name for a double bed jammed into the pointy end of the boat. He was dreaming if he thought they were going to make love there. The place wasn't as cold as a meat locker, by maybe five degrees but not by ten. She hadn't roughed it since she and her mother had escaped the trailer park and she wasn't about to start again now.

Tools were piled everywhere. Cans of paint and who knew what. They smelled—it all smelled—nasty.

He was waiting for her to join him at the far end.

Deep breath. Deep breath.

He was so damn handsome. And he'd never looked better. Standing with his legs spread like a sea pirate atop his well-buried treasure. The work on the boat had flattened his stomach even more and his arms had a power that was stronger, safer than she'd imagined possible when they'd hugged at the airport.

Keeping her attention on his eyes, and where the hole in the floor was, she headed in his direction. When the boat shifted, she reached up and a small rail was in just the right place to grab. She could do this.

She was halfway there when something shot between her legs. She gasped and hung on to the too-thin rail with both hands.

Russell casually reached down with one hand and scooped up...a kitten. A black kitten with shaggy hair and outrageously long whiskers.

"This is Nutcase. She has absolutely no fear. She sticks her little nose in the strangest of places. One day she fiberglassed her tail and it took me an hour to trim it off because she wouldn't hold still." It climbed up his chest to perch on his shoulder.

"You can see where it hasn't grown back yet." He pulled the

long tail from around his throat and one side was indeed shaved.

A cat.

When she was just starting out, her career was almost aborted by a cat. Right before a shoot when she was ten, she'd tried to pet the photographer's cat. It had swiped her with its claws and left a long red scratch down the side of her finger. They had to get another hand model.

Her mother had been furious.

Melanie didn't sleep for four days as she watched it to make sure it healed. Skipped school and rubbed in salves and moisturizers to make sure there was no unsightly puckering. Finally wept herself to sleep with relief when she could no longer find exactly where it had been. She turned down every shoot with a cat since then.

There was no way she was going to pet Russell's cat.

"She's really quite sweet. She likes being scritched under the chin like this." He demonstrated and Nutcase purred loudly.

How badly did she want this? How badly did she want him? She'd never told him of her failure with the cat. Never told anyone that she could still feel the outline of her mother's slap on her face that had shone as livid a red as the cat's mark for days— the mark that still burned though her mother was long dead.

"She won't hurt you."

How many tests did she have to pass? Clearly there would always be another. But she hadn't reached her limit yet. She'd manage this one.

Melanie extended her finger until the cat had to lean forward to sniff the black leather. After a careful inspection, its pink and black nose wiggling like a tiny bumblebee, another of her morbid fears, the cat leaned even farther out and rubbed its chin along her finger. Russell was right. She was gentle.

But there was no way she was taking off her gloves.

"No, it cannot be." Jo Thompson insisted in her best lawyer voice.

Before Cassidy could add her own protest, Perrin continued on, excitement rippling off her in high-energy waves.

"Uh-huh! Way! Could I make something like this up? Well, I could, I guess, if I wanted to but I'm not." Perrin spoke loudly enough that half-a-dozen heads turned in their direction despite the noise level in Cutters.

The lounge was hopping and it was barely six o'clock. Another hour and it would really be rolling. The décor was simple and modern in a plush-chairs-around-knee-high-glass-tables motif. The air smelled of exquisite seafood being served in the restaurant beyond the tinted glass wall. The wrap-around windows revealed the tail end of an awesome winter sunset over Puget Sound.

This had been their "spot" since forever, since they'd been broke college kids with fake IDs. Every time she'd come home since college—at a minimum Daddy's birthday, July Fourth, and Christmas—the three of them had met here.

And from long practice, Cassidy had learned that it wasn't worth the effort to quiet her friend. Perrin didn't mind being shushed, but ten seconds later she'd be bound to forget and her volume would climb once again.

Everything about Perrin Williams was loud. She'd dyed her hair half chrome-blue and half the black of India ink. And not side-to-side or front-to-back, but in diagonal stripes three-inches wide spiraling down from the high part. The stripes followed the line of the sloping haircut that started at her right jaw and was cut longer and longer before it brushed her left shoulder. The clothes following the line of the hair from a high collar to a bare shoulder on the other side. It was quite striking once you got past the strangeness of it.

Cassidy hoped that maybe it was wig, but it was always hard to tell with Perrin because she did her fashion statements so perfectly.

Her clothes matched the shocking blue and her accessories the black. Fashion was her life, her shop was as much gallery as boutique, but there was a streak in her that had never left sixteen behind. She giggled merrily at the effect of her news.

"Pamela and Janice? But I thought they each had long-term boyfriends."

Perrin nodded and took a gulp of her Cosmo.

"I kinda set them up, though I didn't know at the time I was setting them up, I just kinda did it because I did. Separately I sold them those cute blouses. The ones that were mirror images of each other. You know the ones. Anyway, I showed them to you the last time you were in the shop. The green velour with blue silk sleeves and the other blue velour with the green silk sleeves. Isn't there a song about that somewhere?"

Jo nodded and Cassidy followed suit even though she didn't remember the blouses or the song. They'd both learned long ago to never stop Perrin in the middle of a story or she'd sidetrack and the ending of the tale would be lost forever.

"Well, two best friends dating two guys who were also best friends. You know, the mirror twins on a double date. Totally cute and sure to make the guys' eyes pop. That's what I thought. How was I supposed to know they'd decide they were a set and they'd take a trip down the other side of the street? They came in a couple days later to buy the matching mirrored pantsuits."

Cassidy could remember those. Everything switched, which side of the jacket buttoned over, which lapel had been cut on a different slant, which breast had the pocket kerchief, opposite swirls of the slanted pinstripe. She could picture Pamela and Janice, the Swedish-pale and the Jamaican-dark, both very tall, both very curved, an unlikely pair. They probably looked amazing together.

Jo was laughing and Cassidy joined in just a moment late, a moment off beat, but neither of the others noticed. No one else in the lounge noticed—neither the fashionable women nor any of the business-suited men. Thankfully, most of her little social ineptitudes were invisible; she'd gotten good enough to hide them even from her closest friends.

"How about you, Jo? What adventures in the wondrous world of law? Huh? Huh? Come on, something juicy," Perrin begged like a puppy dog eager for a new toy. "Don't let Perrin be the only one with good gossip. I hate that I always have the best gossip."

She cocked her head sideways and her hair swirled back and forth in a hypnotic spiral.

"No, actually, I don't mind. I kinda like knowing more than everyone about everything. So give me some juicy law stuff to add to my collection."

Jo brushed back the long, black hair that her half Alaskan-native heritage had made as naturally dark as Perrin's dyed locks. That half-heritage had also granted her a scholarship from the state. Law undergrad followed by corporate law grad.

Her heritage had also given her a broad face that always looked as if it had a nice tan, and round brown eyes that welcomed you in. She brushed some imaginary dust off the navy-blue pantsuit that made her look terribly professional and immensely sexy at the same time. There wasn't a male judge who didn't smile when she entered their courtroom; nor an opposition lawyer who didn't groan.

"I made partner, does that count?"

Perrin screamed loudly enough to turn every head in the place and then raised her Cosmo in a toast. Cassidy's merlot and Jo's Irish Coffee followed.

"That's great! Why didn't you tell us sooner?" Cassidy sipped her wine, they really needed a better house red than Ste. Michelle. Nice enough at the price, but limited. Overly fruity.

She flagged a passing pretty-boy waiter, "Could we have three flutes and a bottle of Moet and Chandon? The Brut Imperial '99 if you have it."

He scribbled a note and left without saying a word. Clearly he had no idea what it was.

"Ooo, Cassie's ordering. This should be good." Perrin knocked back her Cosmo and then rubbed her hands together in excitement.

Jo set aside her Irish Coffee and nibbled on one of the crackers. Being Cassidy's roommate in college for four years had taught her about clearing her palate. Perrin had been the wild girl across the hall who had taken Jo and Cassidy under her wing to make sure they didn't stay too focused on their studies through all those years together. They hadn't.

"I found out just a few hours ago."

"Tell us. Tell us." Perrin's hair swung about as she bounced in her seat.

The bottle arrived and he presented the label. She nodded, exactly right.

The sommelier was going to be pissed when he found out that a hundred-dollar bottle of champagne—at retail—had been opened from his collection without his being present. Opened as casually as a ten-dollar Cook's.

He uncorked it well, with a restrained pop beneath his cupped hand. He just dropped the cork on the table and she picked it up for a sniff. Warm and bright with just the hint of wood she remembered. Never much in a champagne cork, but she liked them for not needing to brag.

Three baseless flutes that looked like picked flowers were resting at a tilt in a tall, curved vase. Before she could stop him, he began pouring. The flutes were colored, making it impossible to see the wine's hue. Then she noticed Jo and Perrin's reactions to the glasses. They were oo'ing and ah'ing about how much they looked like flowers.

She let it go.

Perrin laughed after she sipped, "It tickles."

Jo took her taste and blinked as if she'd just woken up.

"Cassidy, that's wonderful. Thank you."

She took a sip herself. The wine effervesced strongly, releasing its flavors. Pear and citrus. Balanced. She couldn't detect any real shift. She swallowed...almond. She waited for the hint of toast, but the aroma of garlic bread and steamed clam appetizers arriving at their table made her miss it.

"You earned it. So, how did it happen?"

"You are aware that I recently beat that Class Action suit against the Alaskan fisheries? The partners called me in, all three of them so serious." Jo drew her face down into a frown. " 'Well, Ms. Thompson. We, with our most recent victory in Alaska, are now the most sought-after environmental law firm in the Pacific Northwest. So, we're going to have to make a change.' He pulled a blank piece of letterhead out of his portfolio and pushed it across the table toward me."

Jo brushed her hair back over her shoulders.

"First of all it was not their win, it was mine. And second, if they thought I was going to write my own letter of resignation, they could go..."

"Fuck themselves!" Perrin filled in. Gave her a thumbs up. "You go, girl!"

Jo tipped her flute in Perrin's direction, "Exactly my thoughts, though I was preparing to express them differently. Then I looked at the letterhead. You look at something like that a hundred times a day and it just disappears. But there was a change. It didn't take me long to discover the alteration. My name had been added to the letterhead."

"Super extra double *cool!*" Perrin reached out to high-five Jo and almost upset the whole table.

"To our Jo." Cassidy raised her glass and clicked it with the other two. They all knocked it back and she refilled their flutes.

Leave it to Jo to make partner two years ahead of any normal schedule.

"It gets better."

"Better?" The second flute had lost a bit of the effervescence but none of the brightness. This time she caught the toast in the smooth finish.

"By the time I left the boardroom, my name was gold-leafed onto a corner-office door and everything moved in for me. When I left this afternoon, parked right where my old Toyota should be, sat one of those new BMW roadsters I've been lusting after. The one I showed you in that ad. Right down to the red rose on the front seat."

Cassidy remembered the ad, it wasn't one that you could miss. Something about it leapt out and grabbed you by the... well, clearly she'd had too much to drink already.

"I get first ride," Perrin giggled and topped off all of their glasses. "Let's get smashed tonight. Tomorrow you can take me for a drive."

"I'll take seconds...I guess." Long time since she'd done that. Funny thing about being back with them. It was almost like being in college. Perrin always so loud and wild, attracting all the worst boyfriends of course. Which were the ones Perrin always fell for: wild flings, roaring breakups, and a heart that was permanently broken...until the next one. She remained that way still.

But Perrin also attracted the best, though she never kept those. Cassidy had learned to wait for the ones who recovered quickly from Perrin's dazzle. Some of them had been quite interesting and she'd never have had a chance at them if they hadn't flocked first to her friend's light.

Jo dated the same guy for all four years of college. Where Perrin was long and elegant, Jo was voluptuous and sure of herself in a way that an unsure, freshman Cassidy had done her best to copy. Jo so quiet and studious, college valedictorian, *summa cum laude.* Cassidy had always been second, even finishing as the salutatorian.

Cassidy had some good boyfriends, but none who were four years steady nor even near worth that. She'd forgotten all that, right until this moment.

She'd had enough seconds to last her a lifetime. That was one of the few good things about having left New York. There, she'd been relegated to the second tier of reviewers by the very nature of the old boys' club. She was so done with that, too.

She'd been casually watching the people parade through the door when one caught her full attention. A tall blonde of such perfection that she looked right out of a magazine. The noise in the bar dropped by a third as every man, as if on some hidden cue, turned to watch her walk down the side of the lounge toward the restaurant.

Had her companion been any less striking, he would have been invisible in her presence. He wasn't all that handsome. Okay, she had to admit to herself, not as handsome as Jack James for example, but he made up for it in a breadth of shoulder, a confidence of motion, and an easy smile making him impossible to ignore.

Cassidy recognized him from somewhere. A *nouveau riche* software guy on the news or some such.

Perrin stuck her pinkies in her mouth and let out a wolf whistle. The bar broke into self-conscious laughter. The woman smiled and moved past the tinted glass partition. The man faced their table directly for a moment.

A jolt of recognition pounded against her champagne-befuddled memory.

Where had she seen him?

Recently.

Close, very close.

It was the eyes; she remembered his nice eyes. Okay, screw that. She remembered his unbelievably amazing eyes.

Jo tapped her on the shoulder. "Cassidy. Earth to Cassidy."

"Um, yeah?" He was gone and she sipped her champagne but didn't notice anything except that it was wet in her suddenly dry throat.

" 'Yeah,' she says. Erudite. Articulate." Jo waved her flute toward the entrance. "Didn't know you had a penchant for women."

"I don't. What woman?"

"Miss should have been a *Playboy* centerfold. Miss Cover of *Vogue*, *Elle*, multiple *Sports Illustrated Swimsuit* editions, and practically every other magazine out there," Perrin supplied.

"Oh."

"Oh?"

"I was noticing her companion."

Perrin craned her neck around but they were out of sight. "Boy or girl?"

"Boy. Man." Definitely man.

Perrin looked again. "I missed him. I don't usually miss the guys."

"Then why did you whistle?"

"Every guy here wanted to whistle at Ms. Supermodel but was too inhibited. So I did it for them. It's just the kinda helpful person I am."

THEY HAD ORDERED dinner and the first hors d'oeuvre had arrived, seared bay scallops with a brandy glaze, before Russell noticed that Melanie was unusually quiet. When had she changed? She'd been a little tentative on his boat, but she'd opened up to Nutcase. Silly pest did have its uses.

When they'd arrived at the restaurant, she gone quiet. He hadn't planned to make quite such an entrance.

"You okay, Melanie? You want to get somewhere else where they don't whistle at you?"

She sipped her diet Coke and shrugged. "I get that everywhere."

"Huh. Guess you would."

"Though that's the first time it was by a woman punker."

"Punker?" Russell hadn't noticed a punker.

"Sitting at that table, three dykes all together, all so buddy-buddy."

All he'd noticed was that wine reviewer Angelo was so hyped up on. Now that Melanie mentioned it, there were two other women at the table. He could see them as clearly as a photograph in his mind's-eye. Not punk and he doubted the dyke remark. They weren't dressed for each other, they were dressed to be looked at; all three very high-end, very city—no, two high-end and one as exotic as a scarlet macaw. Her companions were both attractive, but neither matched the russet-haired reviewer once again in a tight turtleneck, moss green this time, and a top designer's take on a lightweight bomber jacket. The woman had a clear sense of what looked good on her. Her hair, back in a ponytail as tight as her earlier chignon, was rich as a pine forest at sunset.

He brought his attention back to Melanie.

"Well, I guess I'm just not used to it is all."

"That's because you're where you don't belong. Back in our crowd they know me. They knew you. Beauty isn't as big a deal there as it is out here in the sticks. Don't you miss it?"

He dipped another scallop in the mango-pineapple sauce and popped it in his mouth. Other than Angelo's, this was rapidly becoming one of his favorite places to eat. He didn't usually face the Friday night crowd; late Wednesday lunches were more his speed. Sometimes there were less than a dozen diners and those were businesspeople. He always brought a good book, but spent most of the time watching the amazing view, the ever-busy Seattle waterfront bustling with ferries and freighters and sailboats, and the shifting light on the permanent snowfields atop the Olympic Mountains. All that was lost now in the winter evening's darkness.

"No. I'm sorry, Melanie. I really don't miss that life. I miss you." Far more than he'd expected. Flying her out for Valentine's Day was about more than the great sex they'd have tonight at the Sorrento. It was more than that. But he hadn't given much thought to what more.

"I don't miss the city or the studio at all." That last was a surprise. He stabbed the last scallop while he thought about it. He *really* didn't miss it.

The waiter showed up and slid a petite filet mignon in front of Melanie and a platter with a matching filet and a large Australian lobster tail before him. He put his nose down to the plate and inhaled the heady mix of beef and seafood. The almond butter tickled his nose and the dollop of horseradish nearly made him sneeze it was so fresh.

"And I certainly don't miss the food." He cut into the steak. "You'll see, Melanie. I've got Dave and Betsy all lined up to take us out on a daysail tomorrow afternoon. Their boat is in a lot better shape than mine. You'll like it. Tomorrow night we'll dine at the top of the Space Needle and have a nightcap at the Alexis —very old world, very traditional. Sunday I've got a pilot to fly us around Rainier and St. Helens. They're amazing from the air. I'm thinking of taking lessons."

He'd intended to let the itinerary be a surprise as they went, but she looked so down that he'd spilled the beans. She seemed to perk up a bit and take a bite of her steak.

Wait until she saw the city from the rooftop, outdoor hot tub perched outside the penthouse at the Sorrento with its awesome night view of the city.

BY THE TIME they'd finished dissecting Jo's promotion, the lawsuit that had done it for her, and who she was going to tackle next, they'd worked their way through most of the bottle of champagne, the clams, a Dungeness Crab Seafood Cocktail, some Coconut Tiger Prawns, and a mountainous pile of onion rings that none of their waistlines would appreciate in the morning.

Cassidy decided she'd left the point of no return already and took a big piece of the focaccia bread. For good measure, she dipped it in the olive oil and garlic.

"What 'bout you, Cassidy? Tell us the wonders of your week." Jo's voice had slipped out of power lawyer, back into Vassar casual. It took a lot of wine to do that.

"Yeah, what 'bout you? Something more exciting than the man with two first names, puh-lease. He is just such a total drip." Perrin mocked Jo's slip but everyone was too tipsy to care.

Jack James, the man with two first names. He was handsome, polite, sometimes lover, and a useless jerk.

"Seconds."

"What's that?"

"Sick of 'em."

"She's shhick of 'em." Perrin was now mocking her.

Her mind wasn't connecting the bits and pieces together. But somewhere or other the thought did have sense of purpose even if she was too drunk to see it.

"No more sad second-raters for this girl."

Jo grew quiet. One very drunken night in their dorm room, Cassidy had confessed to how much she hated being second to both of them. Perrin with all her flash and confidence, Jo with her perfect grades and steady boyfriend.

"No more thankless thirds either, huh?" Perrin purred pleasantly.

Cassidy started to giggle at the alliteration in her head. Perrin purring pleasantly through a pursed pucker.

"Thankfully through with the, uh, thoughtless thirds," Cassidy acknowledged.

Jo cracked a smile but suppressed it quickly, but not before Cassidy caught her.

"And those sad, sad sloppy seconds." Perrin started nodding, then kept doing so as if she'd forgotten she'd started. Her hair swooshed back and forth in a mesmerizing pattern of diagonal stripes.

It sounded even worse put that way. Cassidy glanced at Jo, but she shook her head ever so slightly. She'd never told her about Cassidy's complaint, Perrin was just on a roll.

"And those fucking fourths. Even I don't want those," Perrin continued.

"I'm done with them all," Cassidy declared. "I'm better than that."

Perrin jutted out her chin, "Damn straight, girlfriend. So what now? Fancy frolicsome firsts?"

"Damn straight!" she shot back. "Nothing but the best for Cassidy Knowles from now on."

Jo raised her flute and Perrin her third Cosmo.

"To Cassidy's fun firsts."

"To Cassidy." Jo nodded to her so she'd know that Jo had meant to end it there.

Perrin slowly scanned about the room, then abruptly turned and leaned in so close that Cassidy could smell the Triple Sec, lime, and cranberry on her breath.

"So, what's the news? What are we drinking to again?" Her eyes were squinted as she tried to remember.

"No sad seconds," Jo reminded her quietly.

"That's not news. That's just about fucking time. I want the news."

Cassidy considered as well as the champagne would allow her. News. News. News. There must be something. She still

81

hadn't told them about the lighthouses. But she didn't want to, not yet anyway. It was still too close to losing her father.

What was the topic?

No settling anymore—that was it.

"I broke it off with Mr. Jack James."

"Thank God above and Satan below," Perrin clapped her hands together and looked to the ceiling. "He was such a waste of your time."

Jo was waiting. Waiting and watching.

"When?" Jo's soft question barely penetrated Cassidy's whirling thoughts.

It took her three tries to finally slip her flute back into the vase. It kept moving around the table.

"Um," she laughed and it partly came out as a sob. She covered her face with her hands for a moment feeling the burning flush on her cheeks. A quick wipe at her eyes and she sat up straight, slapped her hands down on her thighs.

"About a dozen seconds ago." That laughing sob came out again. She tried to refill the flute and her hands were so unsteady she ended up pouring the champagne into the vase instead. She set the bottle down hard enough that for a moment she was afraid she'd broken the glass table.

Jo handed her own flute over and Cassidy knocked it back. The bubbles burning the back of her throat.

"Why now?"

"What's today?" She waved her hand at them, at the restaurant.

"The fourteenth," Jo blinked hard to focus on her watch. "Still."

"Valentine's Day," Perrin offered, oddly the most romantic of the three of them.

"Right. And where is the man with two first names? Where is Jack James?"

"Where?" Perrin asked caught up in the question.

"I don't know. But he certainly isn't here. Probably doesn't know what day it is. Handsome, pleasant, and totally lost in his own world."

"Bor-ring!" Perrin declared around a hiccup. She tucked the long side of her hair behind one ear. She took one of Cassidy's hands and held it tightly. In that instant, the flashy designer was gone and one of her best friends sat beside her.

"Cass. He was never even a flatu-, 'scuse me, flatulent fifth. You are so much better than hi-im." That hiccup launched her hair from behind her ear and over half her face again.

Cassidy nodded. She knew she was better. She just didn't feel that way whenever she was with him. She always felt... grateful. Whether it was his doing or hers, it didn't matter; it was too sad for words.

Tears started to flow and she couldn't stop them. It wasn't sadness, not for casting off the man with two first names. A bit of it was for thinking so little of herself in the first place. A big chunk of it was plain and simple relief.

"I am so done with sec-onds." Now she had the hiccups.

Perrin answered with a another hic-nod-hair swirl.

Jo burst out laughing. A rare event in itself.

And totally infectious.

They leaned together as the tears, laughter, and hiccups flowed between them.

"See." Melanie waved a negligent flick of her fingers toward the lounge as they left the restaurant.

Russell glanced over the heads of the dozens of little groups in the lounge. One of the top "meat markets" in town. The best place to meet the other fast-rising singles of Seattle's finest, Cutters' bar, if he'd cared for such things. Once he had, which was weird.

Then he spotted them and his mind froze the scenario. The perfect image. The image that passed by when the camera had missed the moment. The image that could never be recreated no matter what was done in the studio.

Angelo's wine reviewer, still perfectly put together, not a hair astray, dressed so perfectly understated, laughing or maybe crying on her friend's bare shoulder. Blue and black, matching and contrasting. The third, serious, reserved, her clothes as light as her hair dark. A single arm extended forward to rest a hand palm-down between the shoulder blades of her grieving friend.

Three women. They were so close. Clearly they knew each other the way new friends couldn't and even lovers rarely did.

"Traveled Road...partway." That's what he'd call the shot if he had it. Or perhaps that carefully reserved and rarely bequeathed "Untitled" for when no mere title could possibly add more.

It was easy to picture them together in a couple of decades, hair gray, surface beauty faded, and all three still close. Still radiant.

LIME KILN LIGHTHOUSE

San Juan Island
First lit: 1914
Automated: 1962
48.5159 -123.1524

*T*he last major lighthouse established in Washington State, it faces Canada and still watches over the entrance to Haro Strait. It was also the last to receive electricity, not until after WWII.

It is one of the best-known lighthouses in the state, known far and wide as a whale observatory. Pods of orcas and gray whales frequently pass close in front of the lighthouse's craggy doorstep.

MARCH 1

"*I*t sounds like someone is screaming and laughing at the same time."

The technician, who wore his own set of headphones, nodded. "J-pod. That's their dialect, Ms. Knowles."

"Cassidy. What's J-pod and they have dialects?" The two of them sat shoulder-to-shoulder on the first floor of the Lime Kiln lighthouse. Through the narrow window she could see the Georgia Straits. No whales anywhere in sight.

"The J-pod is one of our local groups of orcas. They wander up and down Puget Sound nattering away like a bunch of old-timers. And then," he paused as a particularly quick set of chirps rattled through her headphones.

"There, hear that? That's a group of youngsters. Sound like they're maybe a mile offshore. The main pod is two or three miles out."

"This is incredible." She was listening to passing whales swimming somewhere out of sight below the surface.

Jeff was typing madly on his laptop.

"What are you doing there?"

"Just recording the time of passage and how many voices I hear, fourteen so far."

She inspected him more carefully. Mid-twenties, nice face, at least what she could see above the heavy beard, with his brown hair back in a ponytail. He sat in front of a console with switches and plug-ins, though clearly most of it occurred in the laptop where wiggling lines mimicked the sound in a series of waves too fast to follow.

"We can only hear about a third of what they say. Most of the rest is ultrasonic to our hearing."

"Ultrasonic, like the planes?" Whale-sized sonic booms?

"That's supersonic. 'Ultra' means too high for us to hear. We had to develop special microphones to hear their full vocal range. See, our hearing stops here," he pointed at a line near the lower part of the wiggles on the screen. Even as he did so, one of the lines shot well above his finger and she didn't hear a thing on the headphones except a creepy sensation of fingernails running up her spine.

"What are they saying?"

He turned to face her, his neutral brown eyes wrinkled with a bit of a smile.

"Not a clue, yet. We think a lot of the high stuff is echolocation so they can find food and one another. Same things bats do. But what they chat about all day is a complete mystery. Their vocabulary is huge whatever it is. Not just squeaks and squawks. There are patterns, thousands of them as far as we can tell. Perhaps a fully evolved and complex language."

Jeff's specialty was as narrow as hers, and as highly trained: nuance, common themes, major notes, and minor notes. Hers were color and smell and taste, and his was sound, but they had far more in common than she'd have guessed.

They sat in companionable silence as the whales sang to each other. She tried to separate their voices. Did one always have a deep, dropping pattern? Heee-whaaa. What would it be like to learn more about another species? To study something with such passion?

Well, she *had* actually, since birth she'd been exposed to the details of wine and food.

Of course her passion didn't require sitting in a concrete lighthouse with peeling white paint.

Maybe Jeff's passion wasn't so charming once she thought about it. The concrete room certainly wasn't very warm despite the heater under the desk. She couldn't smell the ocean just a dozen feet away. Instead it smelled of mold and decaying paint. It smelled of heated metal and sounded of the squeaky fan that was barely keeping her legs above freezing.

Out the slender window, an impossible vision appeared; not a whale breeching nor a row of tall fins skimming the water.

It was a blue sailboat with maroon sails. The same number of sails as the two pictures on her wall. One big one in front of the mast and reaching all the way to the deck. The other one, from the mast back until it reached past the where the captain stood in the back. It hung so low that it looked as if it might hit him when it swung.

"Thanks, Jeff." She dropped the headphones and rushed out as he stammered a call after her. She ran over the rocks, digging for her camera in her leather backpack. She managed the picture barely in time before he sailed out of the frame with the lighthouse.

She took another photo just of the boat just in case the first one didn't come out.

He must have the same calendar because this was past coincidence. They'd met three months in a row. Too bad there was no way to signal him. It would be a good laugh to meet in a bar somewhere, maybe see if he had a set of letters too.

No, that would be too weird. Two lost people having their lives shaped by a calendar. She raised a hand in salute, but he was facing away, looking forward. He'd have no conceivable way of knowing why she was waving. It wasn't as if she wore a huge red sail.

This is what her father had told her. In his letter he'd confirmed that she wasn't unique. She tucked a hand into the pocket of her Kors coat and held the letter as she moved back to the cliff edge beside the lighthouse and looked out at the shining water. In the distance, Vancouver Island lay across the horizon, where she could see some tiny shapes at the limit of visibility, the buildings of the city of Victoria.

Farther south, the Olympic Mountains were still white. She could smell the snow and the sea salt. She could imagine the light, cold breeze starting as a whisper on the distant polar seas, a wave splash pushing the air ahead. The small swirl building along the Aleutians and sweeping down the coast. Threading among the Canadian Gulf Islands on its way to here, the wind's first contact with the continental U.S. And she was the first to breathe it, to take in the salt spray thrown into the air three thousand miles away.

I had no direction. I was out of the Vietnam War, out of the army, and unexpectedly still alive.

Cassidy could hear her dad's voice from the letter, soft and warm on the cold breeze. Not rough with throat cancer. She heard his voice from when she was a teenager, a sound she could wrap safely around herself when she grew scared. She didn't turn to him, didn't want to break the illusion.

Your mama never made it to grad school, I always felt bad about that. After a month we were living together. After six months she'd turned our vineyard into a business, not a big one, but a business. It was the real birth of the Napa Valley and there we were on the ground floor.

"Napa Valley? I certainly didn't grow up in the Napa Valley."

The big surprise came along, you. So we had a wedding in the fields right before the harvest.

September wedding in the vineyards, it must have been

beautiful. He'd never told her they'd gotten married because Mama was pregnant. She'd always assumed it was the other way round. Not that it bothered her much.

Not much of a reception. I spent our wedding night out in the fields watching for an early frost. A real freak cold snap slid down from Canada and we weren't big enough to survive the loss of even a single crop. We dodged that one, but then we were into the harvest. Never did have a honeymoon. Too much work to do.

But it didn't matter. Your mama and I were just plain right for each other. From that very first moment when she'd tumbled out of that VW van. Her hair the same dark red as grape leaves in autumn.

You'll find the right man, Ice Sweet.

That was a laugh. She was thirty now and the "right man" was a myth. She did require at least "compatible" though, and Jack James hadn't even been that.

I know you don't believe me, but you will. Until then, don't worry if it doesn't make sense. My life never did.

Love you, Ice Sweet.

"Love you, Daddy."

"DAMN YOU, ANGELO."

His friend didn't answer. Probably because he wasn't there, but that was a lousy excuse.

"Too busy redesigning your damn restaurant to take four days off to go sailing." Russell grabbed for the jib sheet as he came about, but missed it. And he hadn't tied a knot in the bitter end. The line shot out of the cockpit, nearly snagged Nutcase as it whipped past the cat, making her jump straight up like a furry fireworks, ran out the pulley block, and was over the side trailing in the water.

He brought the boat up into the wind, forcing the sail back over the boat. Then he sprinted forward, snagged the line dripping with freezing water, and ran back for the cockpit letting the rope slip through his fingers. He added a cold rope burn to his list of complaints against Angelo.

The boat fell off the wind again before he could run the line through the block. He whipped a couple turns around the winch and let it draw all wrong while he got control of the tiller again.

The line burned in his sore hand as he got the boat moving again. Once he had some speed up, he brought her into the wind again to take the pressure off the line. This time he got it through the block and around the winch. With the tiller between his knees, he tied a quick figure-eight knot in the end of the line so it couldn't go overboard again. He wouldn't make that mistake again.

He was almost back to the lighthouse by the time he had it under control.

He'd gone out twice now with Angelo along just for the ride while he practiced single-handing the big boat. Angelo had kept up a running commentary that amused himself no end as Russell scrambled about the boat. But he'd done it.

Then he'd set off alone for the Lime Kiln lighthouse on San Juan Island. On the first morning out, he'd thought it was fun plunging through the steep wake of a big tanker. The *Lady* had driven her bow deep into the third wave and water had come running down the deck and sluiced out the scuppers he'd only cut in a week before. So sweet.

It wasn't until he'd anchored and tried to bunk down last night that he'd discovered his mistake. He hadn't latched the forehatch. The hinged wood must have floated up when the wave came aboard and a two-foot square chunk of wave had poured into the center of the stateroom bed. Everything was sopping. He'd now spent two extremely uncomfortable nights trying to sleep on the main cabin floor underneath a spare sail. One foot kept slipping through the missing floorboard and thudding down onto the concrete bilge.

Nutcase had curled up on his chest and been perfectly content to snore her way through the night with occasional flails of her tail across his nose during particularly good dreams.

She also hadn't minded Russell's mistake of anchoring that first night right next to a bell buoy. Each tiny swell that ran under the boat made every line slap against the mast with a sharp clack. And then it would reach the buoy and a piercing ring would echo through the boat. Nutcase had snored on.

It was a good thing Melanie wasn't along, roughing it on the floor wouldn't have made her happy.

As a matter of fact, he wasn't sure what would. She'd liked the penthouse suite at the Sorrento well enough, and the sex had been pretty spectacular. She'd appeared to enjoy the sail with Dave and Betsy, even the scenic plane flight. The pilot had let him take the controls for a few minutes, he definitely had to learn to fly someday. Such a feeling of freedom. It didn't have the peace of sailing before the world's winds, but it was a close second.

Russell managed to jibe the boat without losing any lines overboard and ran out from shore a ways before turning back to find a good angle for his photo of the lighthouse.

All through Valentine's Day weekend he'd thought everything was great...right until he'd found Melanie on their last morning together. She was sitting on the shower's floor crying. He'd almost closed the door quietly and let her be, but there was too much between them for that.

Instead, he climbed in beside her and sat down with his back on the opposite wall. She tried to push him out, but he wasn't going to leave that easily. She kept her arms wrapped tightly over her breasts. He reached out to stroke her wet hair, but she slapped his hand aside.

"*Merde!* You do *non* get it, do you?" Her voice was sharp with accusation.

Despite the steam and pounding hot water, he could see the

running tears and snot. He tried to think of what he'd missed. They'd had fine meals, tickets to the ballet, and some good fun.

"You don't?" she was shaking her head. She looked up into the pounding spray for a moment as if seeking God. One of those perfect hands reached out and she stroked her thumb down his cheek. He turned his head to place a kiss in her palm, but she pulled back before he could.

She sat up straighter.

"You really don't. Oh, Russell." Her soft accent gone, replaced by the flat slap of New York. She wiped at her eyes, gray eyes filled with infinite sadness.

"I'm sorry for me, but I'm more sorry for you." She rose from the floor, rinsed her face for a moment under the hot spray and stepped from the shower. He'd watched her through the glass door. Sat under the spray while she dried off that gorgeous body. Applied moisturizers. Baby powder. Added makeup. Dried her hair in a roar of blow dryer that didn't penetrate the shower's patter but sent forth long billows of blonde.

Even now, two weeks later, he could feel the power of her parting kiss at the airport. She pressed her body to his so that every curve fit—her hold so tight it almost knocked the breath from his body.

Then she was gone, a head of blonde sunlight sailing through the crowds at security. Never once turning to see if he was still watching.

He blinked and turned the boat sharply. If he didn't pay more attention, he'd play moth to the lighthouse and ram himself right up on her rocks. Once he had his heading settled, he grabbed his camera and snapped a few quick shots off the stern.

A loud splash sounded beside the boat, and he spun about looking for Nutcase. The cat stood with its nose pressed against the safety netting he'd added to the lifelines, staring down into the water off the starboard side. As he leaned over to follow her gaze, a massive wall of black-and-white whale shot out of the water then splashed down beside him. He shouted in surprise as the orca crashed back into the water less than twenty feet away.

A wave of spray showered onto the boat. Nutcase howled and scrambled below, her coat dripping with seawater.

Russell caught half a dozen photos of the orca before it sounded and disappeared.

Damn!

Angelo was going to be so jealous.

Excellent!

RUSSELL SHOOK any errant sawdust off the paper towel and wrapped it around his sandwich. He grabbed a beer from the cooler and a box of crackers. He set his lunch on the table he'd just finished making. Once more he lifted the top to admire the chart drawer built right into the tabletop. Room for four around the settee or drop the table down level with the benches and it could sleep two. Especially if they were feeling cuddly.

He pulled out his laptop and set it beside his dinner just as Nutcase crawled out from behind a pile of books. He plugged in a mouse and booted the machine while she ambled over to check out his roast beef sandwich. When he flapped a hand at her, she just moved to the other side of his beer and plopped her butt down on the table. Then she started on the impossible task of bringing order to her fur.

Russell took a bite of the sandwich and shoved a Springsteen CD into the car stereo mounted in its little cubby. He flicked a switch to turn off the speakers in the cockpit so that he didn't disturb anyone else in the marina.

Once the laptop was up, he wiped the mustard from his fingers, and plugged in the chip from his camera. It started transferring the pictures automatically. Almost three hundred. Shit! He hadn't done this in a while.

While the copy bar chugged along, he started sorting them out. Lighthouses. Boat remodel. Nutcase. Angelo. More Nutcase. Melanie. Flying. Melanie.

Then one stopped him. It was a shot of just Melanie's face— her watching him as she lounged in the rooftop hot tub with the steam rising into the chill Valentine's Night. A vase of a dozen long-stem roses floated nearly rim deep beside her. A glass of wine perched on the edge of the tub behind her. But it was her eyes he couldn't get away from.

She was right.

There was something he didn't get.

The computer dinged that it was done and he went back to his filing. The last was a series of shots he'd taken of Angelo cooking, plating, greeting customers, visiting tables. And close-ups of many of his dishes.

That's when the idea caught up with him. He did a quick Internet search—there it was. The Bite of Seattle. Twenty-five years old, now one of the major trademark festivals of the city. A Seattle institution. It was perfect.

He popped up his layout software and began tinkering. The first ad came together so fast it worried him a bit, but the first draft was good. It had sharpness. It had edge. He'd have to run the comps past Angelo, but it was the right answer. Seattle, Tuscany, great food, all in one pitch. *Angelo's —a bite of Tuscany.*

No, not homey enough. Angelo's remodel had turned his Pike Place Market address from the American cliché of a modern Italian restaurant into a cozy Tuscan family room.

When Russell was there the worries of the world felt far away. It was safe…comfortable. He tried to picture a lady just beside him. He'd be content. As if sitting with his feet stretched toward—

Angelo's Tuscan Hearth.

Bloody perfect! Damn he was good.

He e-mailed it off to a print shop to run a full-size for Angelo.

Another bite of his sandwich and he cranked up the Bruce a bit before turning back to sorting the images, an automatic action with the years of practice. Contact sheets were a thing of the past, which he didn't miss at all, but he did miss the dark-room work. Now it was all load 'em up, apply effects, and crank 'em out.

Nutcase's folder grew faster than he expected. The kitten afraid to leave its box that first night. The kitten discovering that there were things worse than crawling into the bilge, like being washed with soap afterward to remove the muck. Sleeping on the boom was her latest trick. Russell had almost catapulted her overboard when he came about one day. Now he knew to check the boom and Nutcase had learned to dive for the deck when he shouted, "Helms a-lee!"

Nutcase was about halfway through her preening. He reached over and mussed her fur as thoroughly as he could until the cat batted at his hand, rolled over on her back, and started to wrestle.

He recovered his hand with only a few scratches and knocked back the rest of his beer.

He created subfolders for each lighthouse. There. That was the shot he'd print out to give to Angelo's mom. Lighthouse blurry with its distance off the stern. Angelo sitting with the tiller in one hand and a stainless-steel travel mug of cocoa in the other. Rain hood blown back off his dark, curly hair, a smile of sheer bliss on his Mediterranean-dark face.

Russell started marking the best images for printing. He'd ship them to Arnie in New York. No one else could do what she did with digital-to-paper; the woman was a magician.

West Point lighthouse was easy. His favorite shot of the Alki light had a red blemish in one corner. It distracted the eye from the lighthouse and ruined the balance of steadfast lighthouse and transitory, upscale homes clustered about it.

Maybe he should check his camera.

The next image had the same red mark. But it wasn't in the same spot in the frame. He flipped through half a dozen before he found one where the mark was a different shape.

He zoomed in. The mark wasn't a blemish, it was a person. They wore a bright red coat, but he didn't have enough resolution. The blemish might have brown hair, or maybe red, or maybe neither. A head made up of three pixels wasn't enough information for any detail.

"Well, man or woman, you're messing up my picture."

Nutcase stuck her nose around the corner of the screen to peer at it intently. As Russell pulled the mouse to select the more recent Lime Kiln lighthouse photos, she pounced on the mouse's wire. He almost picked up the camera, but he already must have a dozen shots of her doing just this.

He opened everything in the Lime Kiln folder. Not many shots of the lighthouse, about as many as of the whale. There were far more of the stupid cat.

He reached for his beer, but his hand never made it there.

"Red coat."

Nutcase ignored him, watching the mouse intently and waiting for movement.

Again no close-ups, though better than Alki, brown hair, rich russet-brown and long. And a guy wouldn't wear a calf-length red coat.

The hair.

Long enough to reach well past her shoulders if it weren't being blown about. He zoomed in, but her face was just a tiny cluster of tan pixels in a sea of russet.

Lime Kiln in March and Alki lighthouse in February.

He pulled the mouse back from Nutcase's grasp and pulled up the West Point photos from January.

No red coat. No one at the lighthouse. That would be too much of a coincidence. He pulled up the spoiled images from the trashcan.

Nothing.

Nothing.

Nothing.

Then the one where he'd misjudged a wave and snapped more of the north shore than he intended. He'd discarded the shot because mostly he'd caught the wastewater treatment plant.

Huddled among the lee-side rocks there was a banner of dusky red hair caught in the wind. She wore a tan coat and black pants, but it was definitely the same hair. And she was very slender.

Someone had the same calendar he did. He double-checked the file dates; the first of every month which proved he wasn't losing what little remained of his mind.

He pulled Angelo's calendar off the bulkhead and flipped to April. Slip Point lay out on the Olympic Peninsula, and most of the way down the straits of San Juan de Fuca. Treacherous water there, but it would be good practice, especially if he was going to go deep sea by year end.

He buzzed through the calendar and looked at the last lighthouse. He dug around until he found a pen and put a note on December first.

Wow! He was really going to do this. He was going to unplug from society and sail into a dream that his thirteen-year-old brain had painted across a New York City bedroom ceiling. Russell reached for the beer, but it was empty.

He'd go to each lighthouse first—by then both he and the boat would be ready. It was taking longer than he'd expected. But there was no real hurry anyway and he wanted to be around until Angelo was really up and rolling. Then who knew where his next port of call would be.

He checked the December note once more before he closed the calendar.

"Leave."

<hr>

"I'M TELLING YOU, Angelo. It sucks out there."

"What does?"

"This." Russell turned around his bottle of Birra Morena aiming the label in Angelo's direction. The beautiful Italian girl on the label was impossibly beautiful: black hair, blue eyes, perfect skin.

"*Vecchio mio.* You are so sad. You know this. That's my sister."

"You don't have a sister." Russell considered heaving some of the tiramisu at Angelo, but his kitchen staff was mostly done with cleaning up for the night, so he ate it instead.

"You worry too much. She is a pretty Italian and probably a very nice girl. Nice like your Melanie and almost as pretty."

Melanie. Shit! He still couldn't figure out how he'd screwed that up. He dug at the edge of the label with the rough edge of his thumbnail.

Angelo stopped clowning and pulled up a stool next to his.

"Russell, my old friend. What's up? This is me, Angelo. Every time I mention her since you bring her here two weeks ago, you clam up like an oyster. Come on, buddy. Give."

"I don't think she had much fun here."

"Duh!" Angelo took a sip of Russell's beer and set it on the stainless-steel prep table.

"What do you mean?" Russell grabbed his bottle back and took a deep pull that did nothing to slake his thirst.

"Please tell me that you didn't show her the boat?"

Of course he had. Why wouldn't he? He shrugged and finished the bottle.

"Shit, man! You've never been dumb about a girl before. Think, *amico*. Think about Melanie."

Every time he did that he saw her eyes watching him from across the hot tub. Eyes filled not with lust, nor was it playfulness, though that was there…

"That boat is what you want. What do you think she wants?"

He planted the bottle back on the table with a crash and started to get off his stool. Angelo grabbed his arm and jerked him back down to his seat before he could turn away.

He pushed his face so close to his that Russell wanted to pound a fist into it.

"I know what she wants. Even if you're too damn stupid."

He let fly and caught Angelo on the point of his jaw. Angelo flew backwards off his stool and crashed against a rack of storage shelves.

Seconds later a dozen hands had grabbed him and shoved him down on the wet, tile floor. He tried to fight back but they had him pinned until all he could do was scream out his frustration.

They let go of him so abruptly that he didn't move for a moment. He regained his feet to face Angelo who was rubbing his chin. A circle of dishwashers and cooks stood to either side of him.; all ready to tackle the bull who'd wandered into their fucking china shop.

"Good thing you're half drunk or that wussy-ass excuse for a punch might have hurt."

"Shit!" The heat roared to his face. He hadn't taken a real stab at Angelo since junior high. He sat back down on his stool. "Great! Just fucking great! Now I'm damn stupid and a wussy-ass."

Angelo moved forward and clapped him hard on his shoulder. One by one the cooks and dishwashers faded back to their cleanup tasks.

"You are always both of those. In spades."

"Fuck you."

"Man, it just makes you sick that I'm smarter than you, and better looking too. We Italians, no one as good as us."

"Yeah? Well, it's your chin that's hurting, not mine."

Angelo opened a fresh pair of beers and sat back down across from him.

"Okay. I'll give you that much credit. Now, you gonna shut up and you gonna listen to your best buddy Angelo."

Russell sipped his beer and nodded. He could still feel the heat on his cheeks.

"How do ya feel about Melanie?"

"She's a lot of fun. We're good together."

His friend waited but Russell couldn't think of what else to say.

Angelo slapped his forehead with his palm. *"Figlio di puttana."*

"Calling me a son of a bitch really isn't helping my mood. Remember who taught me to cuss in Italian." He aimed a finger at his friend's white-smocked chest.

"And don't think Mama didn't give me hell for that when you paraded it all through the house." Angelo pushed off his stool then walked to the far end of the kitchen and back.

"Okay, Russell. We a-gonna talk 'bout sometin' else. Hokay?"

"Hokay, if you lose the stupid accent."

"Hokay. I'm making a meal. I think about how I want the diner to enjoy it. Do I start with a light pesto pasta, go to a lemon chicken, and a plate of Santa Lucia cookies with decaf coffee? Or do I start with the same pasta, but with veal meatballs. Then I follow with Rabbit alla Campagnola, a tiramisu, and an aged port. Light and fluffy—Serious and solid. You with me?"

"I have no idea where you going with this, but I'm not stupid."

Angelo slapped him upside the head. "You're an idiot. Now shut up and listen to Angelo, your only friend in the world."

"Hokay. But I might have to pay you back for that."

Angelo rubbed a hand across his jaw and Russell shut up.

"Now. I tell you about another meal. Then you tell me 'light and fluffy' or 'serious and solid.' Deal?"

"Deal." One of the burlier cooks swung by and stared at Russell to make sure he wasn't getting out of line.

"My boyfriend invites me across the country for a holiday. Not any holiday. Valentine's Day. You probably greeted her with roses."

"A dozen reds. Prickly bastards."

"Shut up. I didn't give you permission to talk."

Russell closed his mouth.

"Takes me to nice restaurants. Has enough damn brains to bring me to the best restaurant in town where his best friend cooks like he never cooked before."

"It was good."

"It was a fuck of a lot better than good. Then a fancy hotel."

"The Sorrento. Penthouse."

"Damn fancy hotel. More roses?"

"More roses. Champagne. Strawberries."

"Shut up."

Russell shut up.

"Now, my boyfriend does all that for me, what am I thinking?"

"I don't want a boyfriend."

"Shit, Russell. I'm trying to help you out here." For a moment he thought Angelo might return the favor by massaging Russell's chin with a fist.

"Okay. Okay." So, if he were Melanie, he'd be wearing a little — *Yeah. Shaddup, Russell.* If he were Melanie, who had just received first class tickets, roses, scenic flights, penthouse suite...

"Oh shit!"

Angelo raised his hands to the sky. "There but by the grace of god go I."

"I proposed to her."

"But you didn't."

He closed his eyes. But he hadn't.

He'd wanted her to come out Seattle and have a good time. To see that there was life beyond the city and maybe she'd want to go sailing with him. They'd have a hell of a lot of fun.

But they wouldn't.

He would have the fun and she'd be miserable every single day.

He could see her eyes. Finally understood how she'd looked at him in the shower—with pity.

He lay his head down on the cool stainless steel of the counter. It burned against his flushed face.

Russell also finally understood the expression in the photograph as she soaked in the hot tub.

Angelo rested his hand on Russell's shoulder for a moment before going to finish closing his restaurant.

Of course he hadn't recognized it.

He'd never photographed love before.

THERE WAS no way to apologize. No way to say how sorry he was. He considered flying back to the city, but to what end? He didn't want New York any more than Melanie wanted a sailboat. He wrote her a long letter, doing his damnedest to explain what had happened and how much of an idiot he'd been. Then threw himself into fixing the boat.

He skipped the Ides of March party. Stabbing his lover in the back was a moment he'd rather not remember. It was three weeks since he'd punched Angelo and he was still trying to finish the head. He lay on his right side next to the toilet trying to cut the fiberglass cloth to wrap properly around the base for the shower floor. Nutcase was perched on his left shoulder watching everything he did, insisting on sniffing each tool he picked up to certify it as inedible.

The boat shifted as someone came aboard, but he sure wasn't crawling out from under when he was this close to done.

Nutcase launched toward the entry leaving permanent claw marks burning on his upper arm. Her bright meow signaled that she knew whoever it was.

"Come on in," he shouted loud enough to be heard which made his ears ring in the enclosed space.

"Thanks."

"Angelo." Russell swung upright and banged his head sharply on the counter for the small sink he'd installed. Which he shouldn't have done until he'd finished the floor.

"Crap." He crawled out into the companionway.

"You avoiding me, buddy?" Angelo looked some kind of pissed.

"No." He rubbed where he'd banged his head. "Avoiding myself more like."

Angelo mellowed instantly. "Well, I'd avoid you too if I had the choice."

"Shithead."

"Back at you."

Angelo tossed a couple of white, folded-paper containers on the table. "You eat anything better than crap since I last saw you?"

"No, mother." Then he smelled the food as Angelo started popping lids. He snagged a couple of Cokes and some forks.

He took a forkful of Egg Foo Yung right out of the box. Pork. It burned the roof of his mouth and tasted wonderful.

Angelo pointed at the various containers. "Shrimp Chow Mien, Twice-Cooked Beef with Snow Peas, Fried Rice, and I sat on the fortune cookies. Sorry about that."

Russell stabbed a shrimp for the cat. "Forgiven."

Nutcase took her piece of shrimp and they ate in silence for a bit, at least until the worst of his hunger was gone.

"So, what are you gonna do?"

"You won't leave it alone."

"I'm Italian. Sue me."

Russell shrugged. "Can't do squat. I've thought about it a lot, but I'm so done with New York and all that. If I never go there again, it won't break my heart. And Melanie sure isn't one to go cruising."

"And…" Angelo waved his fork over the chow mien for him to continue.

"You shit. You *are* Italian." He took a deep breath and felt about half as strong when he let it out. "And whatever I feel for her, which is a lot, it isn't what she feels for me. So, I'm a total heel, like she wasn't good enough for me or something, which isn't true. It's just not there. And she doesn't deserve that, whether she wants it or not."

Angelo offered another shrimp to Nutcase who took it with all the daintiness of a six-inch-tall savannah lion.

"You ain't so dumb after all, buddy."

"Worse," Russell rubbed his hand over his face. "But I'll get over it."

"And who should come to your rescue, once again I might add, but the wonderful, magnificent, handsome Angelo."

"And world-class shithead."

Angelo aimed a forkful of snow peas at him. "Keep that up and I won't be helping you."

"Helping me how?"

"Tuesday, April fourth, six days from now, you are having dinner at my place at seven o'clock. And you are going to be on your absolute best behavior."

"This is my best behavior." He brushed all of Nutcase's fur backwards to prove his point, not that you could really tell the difference on the little fluff ball. She batted at him but was assuaged with a scrap of twice-cooked beef.

"Christ Almighty you really are sad. You screw this up and I really will stop talking to you. Just be there. And dress in clean clothes."

"Why, what's up?" Russell dug the last piece of Egg Foo Yung out of the container and ate it with relish. But didn't have time to swallow it.

"You have a blind date."

He choked and spat it back up on Angelo.

SLIP POINT LIGHTHOUSE

Clallam Bay
First lit: 1905
Automated: 1977
48.2645 -124.251

*C*lallam Bay is a small fishing village located halfway between the Cape Flattery and the Ediz Hook lighthouses. Named for a distinctive landslip on the face of the point's rocky bluff, the U.S. Congress appropriated $12,500 dollars in 1900 to build the lighthouse, fog signal, and the keeper's dwelling.

The dwelling was well back from the point. A long, elevated catwalk of wood plank was installed along the face of the cliff permitting the keeper to walk just above the waves' fury to service the light.

"*I*'ve been robbed!" Russell pushed the tiller over and shouted, "Helm's a-lee!" even though Nutcase was sensibly down below already, out of the heavy winds that were buffeting the boat. He'd rigged for rough weather before leaving Port Townsend this morning, reefing down the main to about half its normal size and trading out the big jib for the working foresail.

For what must be the tenth time, he cruised along the sun-bright shore as near as he dared. There were rocks close in and the seas were vicious but he held his course. The *Lady* repeatedly dug her bow into the waves and threw great sheets of water skyward as she rose free. The sharp cliffs of Slip Point plunged down into the mad surf that threw itself against the rocks with the anger of a pissed-off rodeo bull.

He checked the chart again, but there was no question about this being Clallam Bay. The chart didn't report a lighthouse, a fact he'd overlooked on his way here. Instead, it had a marker for a bell buoy named "G" and sure enough, there it was. He'd sailed right up to the thing to check the designation, having to cover his ears against the frantic clang as it bobbed and pitched in the waves. It had almost whacked the boat in a surprise bob and weave.

But the calendar's picture of a long, narrow catwalk snaking along the dramatic cliffs was nowhere to be seen. The lighthouse, a distant, narrow, white tower in the photo, should be right at the end of the point. Right...he scanned the shore carefully as the bow plunged and the stern lifted him high in the air...there.

The angry waves pulled back for a moment and the gray regularity of concrete foundations showed wetly for a moment against the dark slickness of the rock. Somewhere between the photograph for the calendar and now, the lighthouse had been taken down and the walkway ripped from the cliffside without any hint of where it had been. He continued northwest, scanning the cliffs for any sign of the catwalk.

The shore altered abruptly from sheer, soaring crags to the narrow flatlands of the bay. A large, white house stood there; it must have been the keeper's house—it had the trademark whitewashed shine topped with a red roof.

His breath caught.

He was in the right place.

At the right time.

Because standing just back from where beach met cliff and wave, was a woman in a red coat. He'd put his longest zoom on his camera just for this moment and snapped a quick succession of a dozen or so frames. Then another wave caught the *Lady* and threw his bow to one side. He came about unexpectedly, the main boom nearly cracking him on the skull as it slammed from one side of the boat to the other. The camera would have gone overboard if habit hadn't wrapped the strap around his forearm. He plunged it back into its case that was strapped by the tiller, slapped down the waterproof cover, and scrambled to bring the storm sail about.

Even with so little sail, he rocketed most of the way to the next point on the far side of Clallam Bay before he had her fully under control. He brought her about and shot back down the wind.

"Please be there. Please be there."

With the wind and the waves behind him, the *Lady* surged along incredibly quickly. The knotmeter's needle pegged against the stop several times, which was probably eleven knots, well above the theoretical limits of her hull. Rather than her normal top speed of nine miles an hour, he was crossing thirteen.

Full keel boats weren't designed to surf, but that's what she was doing. A wave would lift her stern and she'd fly down the face, the wave moving fast enough that they stayed together in long bursts of exhilarating speed. That was immediately followed by terrifying plunges as she dug her bowsprit and her bow completely into the next wave face. But then she'd soar clear, shedding green water off either side—ready to surf once more.

"I love this boat!" His shout blew ahead, flying past the masts and the bow, reaching ahead and clearing the way.

The ride was less rough going with the wind, so he pulled out the camera early. It took a moment to spot her, she was trudging back toward the parking lot which boasted only three cars. He snapped photos of her and the vehicles. One more pass and he'd get a picture of the lot with one car missing, then he'd know what she drove. Not that it would mean anything. But he'd know.

The wind whipped her hair. It caught at her bulky coat and pushed at her, but she moved with strength and grace.

Then she was gone. He flew downwind looking for her to no avail; she'd stepped behind the white keeper's house with its red roof and simply disappeared.

Coming about—into the teeth of the wind—he fought his way back to Slip Point. Maybe he could slip in close enough and get her attention. Then he could wave her toward the town and the small bay itself. There was a fisherman's marina marked on the chart at the west end of the bay. Unless they'd taken that down too.

They could meet in town. There was bound to be a small café, if he could figure out how to bring the boat in by himself in such weather.

But she was gone.

Two more passes and still no sign of her.

And three vehicles were still there.

A sudden twist of the wind kept him too busy to check the camera's display for proof that he hadn't imagined her.

CASSIDY PEELED off her gloves and wrapped her hands around a cup of hot cocoa. The receptionist at the Coast Guard station looked very sharp in her pressed white uniform. Though her face said she was maybe twenty, she had enough stripes on her sleeve that Cassidy felt a little stupid being served by her. However, the woman appeared glad for the company on a windy day, enjoying the chance to serve cocoa to a windblown tourist.

Cassidy was warm, except perhaps her cheeks and nose. She'd stood out in the howling wind and, oddly enough, not hated it. She was becoming quite the outdoorsy type, something she'd done her best to leave on Bainbridge Island along with her youth.

She'd stood out there for an hour, thrilled by the power of it all, and then, right on cue, her sailboat had appeared. Only one person aboard this time, thrashing about in the waves. She didn't know what sort of a death-wish sailor would be out in such weather. Much of the red bottom of the blue boat showed as it strove upward as if launching to sail across the sky, spray showering in every direction and catching the sunlight like a thousand dazzling diamonds. Whoever he was, he would soon be enshrined on her wall.

Her GPS device had shown her that there was no longer a lighthouse, but she'd come anyway because it didn't feel right to open her father's letter while sitting in a Seattle condo. But no matter how she'd turned, the high wind had threatened to shred the paper out near the point. This office would have to be close enough. After all, the lighthouse keepers had lived here for almost a hundred years before the Coast Guard moved in its offices.

Yeoman First Class Natalie was on the phone and seemed quite involved.

Cassidy pulled the letter out of her coat pocket. It was much the worse for wear, beaten by the wind into a thousand wrinkles from her attempts to open it in the wind. She tried to imagine what was inside, what had her father thought to say to his thirty-year-old daughter as he lay there dying.

In the last letter, he'd been working the vines and met her mother. It had also included his stupid suggestion that she'd find the right man.

Well, it had taken her a week to call Jack James. She might not have if Jo and Perrin hadn't pushed her. They met for drinks at the Metropolitan Grill in the center of downtown. He had his ridiculous martini "stirred, not shaken." His idea of high humor; it was the opposite of James Bond. He had no idea how true that was. She'd ordered a glass of Sauvignon Blanc without even noticing the vintner. One sip told her it was a Washington white, and not one of the good ones. She'd pushed it aside.

Then she'd told the man with two first names that she was breaking it off. It was her, not him, she just wasn't meant to be in a relationship. He hadn't argued. He hadn't asked for a second chance, not even if there was another man.

"We had a good run, didn't we, Cassidy?" He was about as deep as a puddle; one that had dried up three days before.

Yeoman Natalie excused herself, "I need to get at some of the files in back. Do you need anything?"

"I'm fine, thanks." And she was. She didn't miss Jack James, not even in that moment when he kissed her cheek and they went in separate directions on the sidewalk. She'd gone around a corner and spied on him; he never looked back.

The paper crackled as she opened the letter.

Dearest Ice Sweet,

We lied to you.

Yeah, about being legitimate. But they'd married right away, and stayed together until the day Mama died. She'd forgiven them before she'd even finished the last letter. So why was the back of her neck prickling?

Your birth wasn't easy. It wasn't idyllic. Your mother went to the doctor one day, I was too busy in the fields to go with her. She came back in the doctor's car. Enforced bedrest. She was allowed to get up only twice a day. I had to hire Dale's wife to feed her and take care of the house. She lay there for two-and-a-half months to make sure you came out okay.

And colicky. Did you know they still don't know what causes that? I just asked the nurse.

In that moment she was back in the hospital room. Her father lying there, tubes running in and out of him, discussing his colicky daughter with some nurse she'd probably never met. She was far colder than she'd been minutes before standing out in the chill wind.

Twelve weeks to the day you howled like there was a knife in you. I'd walk you for hours up and down the vineyards at night just to give your mama some rest. You'd howl like there was no tomorrow. And then week thirteen you just stopped. Like hiccups suddenly gone.

How could he hide that from her? She'd always believed they had the Hallmark family. The happy child, the close couple. That's what her father always told her. That was the dream she wrapped around herself at night.

Don't get me wrong. We couldn't have loved you more. But as one part of my life made more sense, the other parts made less. The winery was growing well, but getting water for the vines was becoming harder and harder. New regulations forbade pumping from the river. I was about to dig a second well, the first wasn't nearly enough, when one of the big boys in the area drove through a new regulation, no drilling new wells unless you had a creek on your land. I didn't. Close, but not on.

The vineyard wasn't lost all at once, rather a piece at a time. I and many others lost water rights due to that one man's maneuvers. I lost hired hands to some millionaire who outbid me for my best people. Soon even my mid-level people were going.

What I learned, was that when one part of your life closes, another one opens. Your mother, our Adrianne, was the only sanity in my life at that time. When you find that person, hold on for all you're worth. And if they have half a brain, they will do their damnedest to hold onto you.

You're great, Ice Sweet, and don't forget that.

Ever!

Vic

"Are you okay?"

Cassidy nodded and wiped at her stinging eyes. Then she took a sip of the still warm cocoa to assure Yeoman Natalie that she was fine.

Just fine.

"You've got to get me out of this, Angelo." Russell wrapped both hands around his beer bottle.

"What are you talking about?"

"This blind date. I'm not coming." He scratched a fingernail on a small drip of paint that had fallen onto the settee table and hardened. It broke free and flew across the table landing on the piece of Brie in Angelo's hand. He debated mentioning it, but decided against it when he saw the look on his friend's face.

"But you are."

"But I'm not."

"Why the hell not? You fall in love in the last six days? You going back to Melanie if she's stupid enough to take you?"

Russell hands ached with how hard they were clenched.

"No." Not really. He glanced over at the laptop tucked safely on the shelf above the table.

"Can you give me a good reason?"

He wanted to, but he didn't have one. Well, he did have one, but it was too stupid to call good.

He shook his head.

Angelo pegged the piece of Brie at his face. He ducked, but not enough. It hit him in the forehead. Against all chance, the paint chip dropped into his beer bottle. He pushed it aside.

"This is important, man. Not just for you. It is important to me. I need someone who can be a half-human dinner companion. I promised to introduce her to someone who was decent."

"Find someone else."

"By tomorrow night? What the hell, Russell? This isn't like you. She beautiful. Funny. What more do you want? It was your idea anyway."

"My idea?"

"Look, Russell, if I explained it, where would be the surprise. It's a blind date. That means you go in blind. Unfair to give you an advantage. She doesn't know you either."

"You're not going to back off of this one, are you?"

"Not without a good reason." Angelo cut himself another piece of Brie, completely free of paint chips, and chomped down on it as if he were trying to hack through a tough steak rather than a soft cheese.

"Okay. There is someone."

"Since when did that stop you from having dinner with

another woman? Dinner, man. That's all. I'd bet that not even you could get a kiss on the first date from this one, even if you tried."

"Frigid?"

"Lady. Real one. Outside your realm of experience. Don't change the subject. What's your lover's name?"

Russell grabbed his beer and slugged back a big swallow. The paint chip slid down his throat before he could stop it.

He slammed the bottle back on the table. He hit it hard enough that it foamed out over his hand and dripped all over the cheese and the table. He mopped at it with a rag that he'd been using that morning to clean up the new fuel tank under the pilot berth. It still smelled of the sharp tang of diesel. Long streaks of muddy black appeared across the white rind of the cheese. He threw the cloth over the whole mess and took another pull on his beer which was now much flatter than it had been.

"Name?"

"Go to hell, Angelo."

His friend narrowed his eyes for a long moment and then he burst out laughing.

"You don't know her name. Oh, this is too rich. What's she like?"

"She likes the outdoors. Long dark hair."

"Wow. Great description, man. Thanks. I can really picture her now. Clear as mud."

"Asshole."

Angelo just grinned.

Nutcase appeared from somewhere and started sniffing at the mess on the table.

Angelo grabbed the cloth with the cheese in it and mopped up the worst of the beer puddle.

Russell ducked again, but Angelo turned and dropped it into the garbage bag full of sawdust that was drooping in the companionway. Nutcase dropped down to floor, inspected the bag carefully and then wandered back to whatever she'd been doing before.

"Tell me more."

Russell couldn't relax his fists even when he tried.

"You can't?" Angelo was getting far too much fun at Russell's expense.

Russell grabbed the laptop and dropped it onto the table with a crash. He turned it so that they could both see it.

"West Point lighthouse." He pointed her out squatting among the rocks.

"February at Alki." He pulled up the next picture. "March at Lime Kiln. Didn't even know she was in these photos until I looked at them a few weeks ago."

"She's following the same calendar I gave you."

"Duh. Figured that one out on my own, Sherlock. So, for April, I took my big telephoto with me. But the weather was really lousy. I could barely control the boat, much less make it ashore to meet her." He toggled to the last spread of photos. Six of them. Long zoom close-ups. Snapped in rapid-fire succession when the stern of the *Lady* had ridden high up in the air to give him a clear view.

Heavy hiking boots. Slender legs. Body form hidden by the trademark bulky red parka. A flag of chestnut hair streaming in the wind just begging to have fingers run through it. Coat zipped up far enough to hide the neck. Nice chin, slender without being angular. And where her face should be, two delicate hands holding a small point-and-shoot camera—aimed right at him. Almost clear enough to read the stupid brand name.

"Nice. When's the wedding?"

"Give me a goddamn break."

Angelo waved a hand at the screen. "She's not real. She a phantom who appears only on the first of each month."

"You couldn't prove otherwise by me, but she feels real. More real than…" He should never have opened his mouth.

Angelo rested a strong hand on Russell's forearm.

"Melanie was real. Is real. She just isn't headed in the same direction you are. And the girl on this screen probably has a voice like a harpy and a husband and seven kids at home. I'm offering you dinner with a flesh-and-blood lady. Nice one. Single too, though you try to touch her and I'll kill you, right at the table, and serve you your own guts over a nice bed of pasta. Eating dinner and making friendly conversation isn't cheating on some lighthouse phantom that you've never met."

Russell nodded, as much to stop Angelo's pestering him as anything else. He glanced sideways at the screen, studying how her hair appeared to move in the wind in the series of frozen moments of the photograph.

Angelo had missed two details. She was alone in every photo.

And the hands that held the little camera had no rings on them.

"How do I do this?" Cassidy knew she was losing it. Could feel her voice rising and tight. She perched on the impossibly uncomfortable green leather and stainless-steel bar stool in Perrin's dress shop.

The interior was done in retro-1950s diner. Instead of tables in the booths, there were mannequins wearing her latest designs. Instead of those chrome music players with he flip pages of songs, there were racks of clothes and accessories that would go with what the seated mannequins were wearing. Instead of a diner cashier with gums and candies and pies of towering meringue in a display case, the glass cases held hand-bags, gloves, belts. Through the swinging doors there was no cook line. Rather there was a haven of shoes, boots, coats, and from the ceiling hung an unbelievable selection of umbrellas guaranteed to stand out in any crowd.

"When was the last time you had a blind date?" Jo had her lawyer voice on, the one designed to lull the obstinate into a sense of security, the upset into a pool of calm. Cassidy felt it working on her, and fought it.

"I dunno. Freshman year. And that was plenty."

Jo glanced over at Perrin who shrugged. "How was I supposed to know Richie would take acid to get up his nerve?"

Apparently he'd been telling Perrin that he was really interested in her red-haired friend. Cassidy had finally agreed to meet him. There'd been something strange about his eyes, a glassiness she hadn't understood at the time. As a naïve freshman from an island in the Pacific Northwest, she'd been totally flattered that an upperclassman had even noticed her. They'd had a nice meal at The Atrium, her favorite campus hangout. He was bright, interesting, and definitely enamored. But the way he kept staring at her was somewhere on the line between incredibly flattering and a totally creepy.

She'd finally had to ask.

"How do I look to you?" She'd put a great deal of effort into selecting nice colors that blended well together and shapes that showed off her figure. Perrin had even done her hair and nails for her.

Richie Packer had gazed at her for a moment long enough to warm her cheeks before replying, "The body of a goddess. A neck like a great snake. Your face would scare the hounds of Hell with its slavering jaw, massive fangs. No nose. Eyes of ice and hair of a mighty, writhing inferno."

He'd tried to apologize for weeks afterward, swearing he'd never take drugs again, especially not hallucinogens. She told him it was okay, she'd sworn off ever being in his presence again.

She'd also sworn off blind dates, so how had Angelo talked her into this one? With a promise of great food and a charming man. She'd had enough of charming with Jack James. What she needed was someone with some heart and a little connection to his own emotions.

"You need more confidence. Think of it like your wine-tasting. I've seen you do that with style and panache." Perrin tossed back her head making her lime-green perm swirl about her head like a whirlpool. Impossibly ugly, except on Perrin it was so cute that it made every man under forty turn and go silent whenever she entered a room. Okay, every man of any age who still had a pulse.

"I'm not going to a man-tasting. I'm going on a blind date and I don't know what to do. You're my friends, you're supposed to be helping me."

"Send Jo. She'll wow him."

Cassidy buried her face in her hands. "I can't. I promised Angelo I'd review his restaurant this time. He's probably been preparing for a week."

"I thought they weren't supposed to do that."

"They aren't. They all do. But they've learned that I'm not above begging tastes from nearby tables. So if I get an exceptional meal, so does everyone around me."

"There," Perrin aimed the one finger not covered by her elbow-long, green gloves that precisely matched her hair. "That's the attitude. Remember that feeling, right there. Use that and you'll be invulnerable. And the man will melt and die at your feet unless he's a complete jerk."

"Clothes, Perrin." Jo spoke quietly. "She needs power-dating clothes."

"Black." Cassidy called out as Perrin started wandering around about the shop. "And no dresses."

Perrin held out a black top that had cleavage down to the navel and a swirly, pleated miniskirt.

"So not."

Perrin laughed.

By the fifth rejection Perrin had stopped laughing.

"You're tricky." She inspected Cassidy carefully. Turned back to her racks and then once more to face Cassidy. She disappeared through the swinging stainless-steel doors into the back room.

Jo met Cassidy's gaze and arched an eyebrow. Neither of them were willing to guess what Perrin would come up with next.

She reappeared in with something definitely not black. "Put this on."

Cassidy rubbed her fingers over the lush, red-and-orange fabric. "Cashmere. I love cashmere."

"Don't we all, honey. Now put it on."

Cassidy headed for the dressing room, but Perrin called her back.

"Nope. You look incredible in that black turtleneck, just pull this on over it."

She unzipped the front of the sweater and slipped it on. She zipped it partway up and moved to the triple mirror. The waist and the ends of the arms were such a dark red that they were as black as her pants. The sweater lightened upward from red, to dusky orange, and finally a dark gold the color of the inside of a pot of honey as it reached her neckline and the open zipper.

Perrin moved up behind her and looked at her in the mirror over her shoulder. She reached around and tugged the zipper a bit lower.

"I feel more naked than just the turtleneck." The fading colors and low zipper gave her a plunging cleavage, without any exposed skin.

"It works. You're fully covered, and he'll be spending the whole time trying not to look at your breasts. It's perfect. And I'll bet you another bottle of that amazing champagne we had that he won't be able to look away. Besides, you have the nicest set of the three of us; it's time you flaunted them a bit."

"I do?" She looked down, but they were just your average breasts in your average bra wrapped in a black silk turtleneck and cashmere.

"Mine are too flat, and Jo's are a bit too much, though they suit her. Yours, with your figure, they're simply great. He'll die. Trust me."

She glanced at Jo over her shoulder. Again the raised eyebrow, with a tilt of the head that indicated there was probably truth there.

Cassidy looked at herself again in the mirror. She did look good.

"On a much later date, the one you want to have sex after," Perrin pulled the zipper up halfway to her throat, "and lose the black turtleneck. He'll remember the undressed look of the first date and spend the whole second date dreaming of pulling that zipper back down."

"How did you learn this stuff?" The instant the words were out of her mouth Cassidy wanted to bite her tongue and kick herself. She met Perrin's eyes in the mirror, suddenly wide and vulnerable like a little girl. She turned and wrapped her arms around Perrin's stiff body.

"Screw them. Screw them both. They can't touch you anymore. Ever." She could feel her friend nod at last and Cassidy held her more tightly until she felt her relax a bit.

They stood back from each other but Cassidy held onto Perrin's thin arms. She felt the anger that came over her whenever she thought about her friend's parents.

"I love you just as you are, Perrin. I think you're incredible. I'm so glad you're in my life."

"Really?" She wiped at her eyes.

"Really. This sweater is perfect. I couldn't get through this without you."

Perrin finally nodded again.

Cassidy kissed her on the cheek and then clapped her hands together.

"What's next?"

"Come-fuck-me boots." Perrin laughed even though tears still trickled down her face.

"Not what I was quite after."

Jo came over, "Kick-ass boots, then."

"Kick-ass boots. Perfect."

They headed for the back room arm in arm.

Cassidy started whistling the tune.

Jo started singing the words.

Perrin laughed and joined in though her voice was still tight. "We're off to see the wizard. The wonderful Wizard—"

Cassidy stumbled to a halt after they pushed through the swinging doors. There it was.

She slipped her arms free from her friends and pulled the knee-length coat off the mannequin holding a hamburger spatula like a submachine gun.

The same length as the Michael Kors parka. The same red, but that's where the similarities stopped. The soft, red leather had been expertly tailored. She slipped it on, did up the three giant black buttons and tied the black belt of the same leather once over. Sixties retro gone high end. The broad lapels made her feel part secret agent and part superwoman.

When she turned, Perrin was nodding and the unflappable Jo made a show of dropping her jaw before starting to applaud.

"You look fantastic!"

"And," Perrin pointed, "it matches the sweater and accents her hair. You, my friend, are incandescent hot."

"THANKS FOR CLEANING UP."

"Is this good enough for your majesty?" Russell tugged once more to settle the corduroy blazer over his sport shirt. He'd even unearthed a tie with sailboats on it, but decided to go with the open neck instead. There had to be some limit.

"You look more than half human. Maybe even three-quarters. Now be nice and have fun."

"Yeah, right." He hadn't been this nervous about a date since sixth grade. Of course, it was strange having your first-ever blind date in your early thirties.

"So, Angelo, how is this my idea?"

His friend just grinned at him. "Notice the wine labels at dinner."

"I don't need wine. I need a really big scotch."

"Yeah, well forget it. I'm making you a great meal and I want you to be able to taste it."

For the next couple minutes Angelo rattled off facts about the wines he was planning to serve. Would she be tall and fair, maybe remind him too much of Melanie? Short, dark, and beautiful like his mother? Dumpy and dull like he feared no matter how much Angelo claimed otherwise?

"Got it?"

"Huh? Not a word."

Angelo punched his arm hard enough to get his attention.

"Look. The last wine. The dessert wine. Cinque Terre Sciacchetrà. It's a white: amber and flowery. Look for orange, grapefruit, and lemon tones with a dry finish. A lot of alcohol in this one. Can you remember that much?"

"Sure. Why?" He punched Angelo back just for the hell of it.

"It's your idea. Local. Local. Local. It's not just Tuscan, it's Ligurian, from my family's hometown. If you want to leave a good impression on her, knowing that much at the end may help."

"Okay."

"Get out there."

"Is it time already?" Suddenly he wanted to head for the back door and the nearest bar for that good scotch. Hell, he'd take a bad scotch right about now.

"Go." Angelo pointed. "Did you bring something for her?"

"I was supposed to bring something?" He started patting his pockets as his friend sighed. "Jewelry, clothes, what?"

Angelo went over to a huge vase of red roses, pulled one out and brought it back.

"If the girl those are for accepts her boyfriend's proposal tonight, she'll never notice that she's one shy of her two dozen roses."

Russell eyed it carefully. "I didn't do so well with the red roses with Melanie."

Angelo stuffed it in his hand and dragged him out through the swinging doors. The other patrons turned to stare as the restaurant's chef led Russell toward a table set for two and shoved him into one of the chairs.

He pulled the rose from Russell's hand and laid it across the opposite place. He leaned down to whisper.

"Stop being such a goddamn wimp."

He left before Russell could hit him again.

———

Russell missed her entrance.

He'd sipped his water, played with his fork...and started thinking about the layout of the galley. He shook out the swan or whatever the napkin was supposed to be and refolded it into the same general shape of the space he had to work with. A couple of sugar cubes became a row of cupboards. The salt-shaker where the sink would go. Pepper mill for the fridge. The knife defined the edge of the counter. More sugar cube storage below.

Stove. He smacked his forehead. He'd forgotten the stove.

Had to be in line with the keel so that it could swing when he was on a tack. He might be heeled over ten or fifteen degrees for weeks at a time. Gimbaled stove would have to go where the pepper-mill fridge was. The fridge traded places with the salt-shaker. Stove to the right or left? He plucked a petal off the rose and moved it to one side then the other of the sugar cubes.

"Some boys never outgrow their toys."

He glanced up at the woman standing before him. His eyes made it halfway back to his napkin-galley before they were drawn back.

Red coat. She wore a knee-length red coat. He opened his mouth, but closed it again as disappointment rocked him back in his seat.

This was no parka and she wasn't his Lady of the Light-houses ready for heavy weather. Instead, she'd been wrapped in red leather so tailored to the body beneath that it belonged in his studio, not out on the street.

After a moment she raised her chin and took off the coat. Only then did he realize he should have offered to take it. He started to rise, but she waved him back to his seat. Not a good start.

A waiter took the coat and he could tell that the coat hadn't lied about what was beneath.

Black leather boots with two-inch heels clung tightly up to her knees, ending just where the swirling black skirt began. Her trim waist tapered up into a sweater that started dark and ended with the colors of autumn. The black turtleneck was surprisingly sexy. The sweater brought out the reds in her brown hair, wound back into one of those painfully tight coifs and...

"I've seen you." Somewhere. He'd find it in a moment.

"And I you," she slid into her chair with a grace that was as unconscious as a model's was practiced.

"Where's your girlfriend?"

"My what?" Russell could feel his throat closing.

"The tall blonde with legs to her ears. As I recall, you were all over each other. I find it surprising that you are on a blind date after having her on your arm."

"Valentine's Day." That was it. "The woman crying in the bar."

As soon as he saw her reaction he knew it was a mistake. Her face closed. The teasing smile that had been intriguing a moment before was erased as if it'd never been.

"Sorry. Perhaps not your best moment."

"Perhaps not." She kept her gaze down as she fooled around with the rose with elegant fingers. A woman's hand, not with the daintiness of a girl's nor the sensual slenderness of Melanie's. They were a woman's hands.

"But you were beautiful in that moment." Christ. Good one, Russ. Don't know when to leave bad enough alone.

Her hands froze, but she didn't look up.

"I'm a photographer. I would have killed to have a camera to capture you."

"I'd have killed you if you had." She almost raised her gaze.

"The three of you. Like you'd been together forever. I could see you fifty years from now, the same three women. Beautiful. Close."

Under guise of rubbing his chin, he put his hand over his mouth to keep it shut before he shoved his foot in any deeper.

"Since college. Beautiful?" She lifted the rose and smelled it, looking directly at him for the first time. The clothing had shifted the hue of her hazel eyes until they were some combination of summer green and the rich gold that every autumn leaf longed to be. The rose accented the color in her cheeks as she brushed it back and forth below her nose. No detectable makeup.

"Yes," his throat was dry. "Yes, beautiful."

"Perrin maybe. The tall thin one, wild hair."

Russell shook his head barely remembering her companions as little more than positions in a composition. A waiter passed by and in his wake, he caught his date's scent. Warm, unperfumed, and heavenly.

"No. You."

She blushed and looked down again.

"I'm a... Russell. Russell Morgan."

She extended a hand. "Cassidy Knowles. Nice to meet you, a-Russell."

"Real nice." Her grip was firm and warm.

"Charm isn't one of my specialties."

"I hadn't noticed." She released his hand.

He wished she hadn't. It had felt good, that womanly hand against his rough palm and fingers. Russell tried to think up a good one-liner reply when the waiter arrived.

"Hallo, I am Giorgio. Mister Angelo has asked me to tell you that he will be choosing your dinner once again."

"Once again?" Russell aimed his question at his date who nodded so sweetly it was hard to argue.

Giorgio waited a moment, but when she didn't speak he continued.

"He has asked me to let you know this. But, also he has said, knowing your preference for a fair sample, he only will serve selections that have been ordered already this night. *Perfetto?*"

"Yes, perfect."

The waiter whisked away.

"Hey, I wanted to see a menu." He and Angelo had spent long enough redesigning the damn thing. Local cuisine, an elegant montage of Tuscany and Liguria. He'd even managed to work his sailboat into the dessert page. It was one of the best pieces he'd done in a long time—had some of the old Russell Morgan flare to it. It had been nice to know he still had it. But, as the waiter was gone and no menu was forthcoming, he turned his attention back to his date.

She'd gone quiet again. He wanted to see that smile some more. It was a hell of a good smile, even if it had been directed at the waiter.

"What's with this 'once again' stuff?"

She opened her mouth, but he cut her off.

"Wine taster. Right. I forgot."

"Did we meet before?"

He thought about the first time, as she'd thanked Angelo for a fabulous meal. He'd been, what, eating spaghetti while covered in boat dust and dirt. No. Fiberglass resin. She'd have discounted him as useless, beneath notice, no more than a blemish on Angelo's pristine kitchen. Best not to remind her.

The sommelier showed up and started chatting wines with her in a way that totally eluded him.

Listen to her, Russell; New York was all over her. Her clothes were so perfect and she probably had her hair done weekly. Her brisk way of addressing the wine steward had used short, clipped, quick words. He wouldn't have noticed if Dave and Betsy hadn't teased him about his own New York way of speaking. She was everything he didn't want. One hundred percent not his lady in the red coat. Crap! She and Melanie could be best friends.

Even her boots were a joke. Who spent four or five hundred dollars on boots except at a fashion shoot? God, his final shoot. Before the red, mid-thigh Chanel's, he'd photographed Melanie in exactly those boots. Though he'd never photographed anything like that sweater. It dipped and swelled in a splendidly provocative—

The sommelier was gone…and he was staring at her breasts. He'd stopped doing that in high school as soon as he learned what a turn-off it was. The great paradox of women: he got to see a lot more breasts unclothed as soon as he stopped staring at them clothed.

He checked her eyes. Oddly, there wasn't anger, but laughter crinkling the edges.

"What?"

She shook her head, but the smile didn't go away.

———

"THE PENNE AGLI SCAMPI, Angelo. Simply exquisite." Cassidy leaned toward Angelo and rested her chin on her palm, elbow on the table. "But wasn't that a Piedmont white rather than a Tuscan?"

Russell couldn't look away from her. She was so unaware of every motion. There was no posing. Her emotions weren't carefully considered and exhibited for the benefit of the camera or the moment. She had a natural honesty that had him mesmerized.

Angelo pulled up a chair and joined them. "I cannot fool you, Miss Knowles. I thought the Tuscan wines a little too fruity for something as delicate as the scampi. I decided that as long as the wine was Italian, I'd let it wander a little farther afield than the cuisine."

"Absolutely right. Now the heaviness of the San Rocco Barolo was the perfect choice for the Tagliata, I've never had such tender beef. What was the spicing?" She'd described the flavors for him. He could taste the sage and rosemary after she'd told him. But the juniper berry, he had no idea. He'd say she was making it up, but throughout the meal she'd kept a running commentary on flavors for each new dish and wine. When she'd asked about the other flavor in the beef, he had no idea what she'd been talking about.

"Oh no, Miss Knowles. You do not get my mother's secrets so easily."

Secret recipe. Right. He'd seen that. Time to pay back Angelo for setting him up with this New York woman, the one who snagged his attention like a harpoon.

"Anchovy paste instead of salt."

Angelo looked put out as Cassidy inspected him, then Angelo shrugged as he explained, "Sometimes it is the simple techniques that are the best."

"I've watched him rub it in."

"Watched him…" She ran the words over her tongue, the same way she rolled the wine there.

Russell really needed to learn when to shut up.

"Watched him…while you ate pasta."

"What was that?" Angelo didn't catch it, but Russell bowed his head in acknowledgement. She had an eye for detail and had finally picked him out of the mess he'd been when she was here for the wine tasting three months ago. She could probably be a decent photographer with a bit of training.

"You aren't a…" She caught her upper lip between her teeth, but he could read it on her face.

"Contractor…or a homeless person eating on Angelo's charity?"

She tilted her head to one side for a moment, made him want to run a finger down the length of neck exposed from ear to turtleneck collar. She arched her eyebrows and shrugged a yes.

He laughed, "Depends on who you ask." Melanie would say he was homeless. So would his parents and any of his New York friends for that matter. And beyond them all, this woman across the table would declare him such. No way would she be happy with the wind blowing through her hair. She might shatter if you took her anywhere rougher than the Cutters' lounge or Angelo's. She had every mark of coming from money and no trace of ever touching the great outdoors.

The shift was clear on her face. Her thoughts, so carefully guarded on her tongue, were easy to see. The slow sifting of information until she moved the smooth photographer to the possibly homeless smart-ass until she had melded the two into a perfect blend.

Angelo cleared his throat and returned his chair to the next table.

"For dessert I will be giving you Sfogliatina alla Angelo's, a puff pastry filled with a fig and cream custard. And," he bowed to Cassidy, "I hope you will approve of the wine choice."

Angelo managed to kick him under the table without Cassidy noticing before heading back to the kitchen.

It hurt.

"You like him." She aimed those hazel eyes at him.

He had to look down to think up a reply and still couldn't.

"He's a great cook."

"The best."

"How long have you two been at this?"

Russell shrugged, "I can barely heat a can of soup." For years he and Angelo had cooked together. He was a fair cook, but Angelo was in a whole other class.

"You know that wasn't what I meant."

"How long have you been with those two girlfriends of yours I saw at Cutters?" Real nice. Right back where you started the meal, Brutus. Time to stab her with it again. Dufus.

"College. Freshman year. First day." She brought that nice chin up a bit higher. She was a proud woman, who was sure enough of herself to let him know he was being a jerk.

"Right, sorry, you told me that already. Add another decade or so, that's me and Angelo. Practically from the same womb. His mom...was a friend of the family. Very close." She had been his parents' cook.

He'd learned to protect his name, to not mention that he was a part of the Morgans who ran the Morganson shipping empire. Women always got weird when they found out you had that kind of money. Melanie had been different. Maybe it influenced her in the beginning, hell, he knew it had. And he'd let it to get her in bed. But by the end it hadn't been about the money. He simply hadn't had the brains to notice the change in her feelings, because he was happy enjoying the fruits of the former not even being aware of the latter.

The dessert arrived. He jabbed at the pastry and a small geyser of cream shot out the end and smeared across the tablecloth. Before he could reach for a napkin, a small flock of waiters appeared. Without appearing to hurry, they lifted each item and replaced the tablecloth in about ten seconds flat.

"Happens all the time, sir," the waiter hurried off with his soiled cloth. It was all a fucking façade—from glossy ads to glossy women. What would his date do if faced with something that wasn't perfectly prepared? If the world weren't perfectly arranged for every step she'd taken since birth?

"So, Cassidy, what is it you want to do? Spend the rest of your life being a critic?"

"I don't know." She dragged her voice out, slowing the reply. She could obviously feel his change of attitude and she wasn't going to answer, at least not completely.

He could hear the caution as she continued.

"Hadn't really thought about the long term. I wanted to get out of New York, expand my horizons."

"Have they been expanded?"

"I think so. My syndication has grown. I'm not Robert Palmer or even close to what Craig Claiborne was, but I'm becoming known."

"And is that what you want?"

She poked at her dessert. "As I said, I hadn't really thought about long term." He could read the lie on her face. She had every minute of her perfect little life mapped out.

He could hear the note in her voice. The clipped tone that a date always used when they wanted a subject change. Well, screw that.

"Always the critic. Always a step back. A step away. You know all of these wines, but do you really know the true heart of any of them?" He'd met more real people in three months at the marina than he had in twenty-five years in the city. 'Oh, you're one of those Morgans.' And the whole fake-friendly façade would appear. Out here, no one knew but Angelo. And, now that he thought about it, Russell suspected that most of his new friends probably wouldn't have cared.

Again that stillness dropped over her. During the meal he'd learned that's when her emotions were working the hardest and was the only time they were hidden. She could be polite and funny, even, he had to admit, interesting. But whenever he'd asked a loaded question, she'd shut down and turned into zombie girl. She picked up her wine glass and eyed it carefully. Her expression unreadable, as if he suddenly didn't exist.

He needed to shut up. That's what he needed to do. He knocked back a glass of the dessert wine. It was so sweet he almost choked.

"Christ, I need a beer."

She was sipping the wine. Holding the glass just below her nose as she sucked in her breath. Her lips pursed as if ready for a kiss.

What would she look like spread out on a bed, hair undone, clothes askew or missing? All missing except for that sweater.

He really did need a beer if that's what he was thinking. If he was going to go there, he might as well go back to New York and beg Melanie's forgiveness. Melanie at least knew what she was, knew what she wanted from life. And he'd been involved in it, had helped it along now and then even before they became an item.

This woman was so proud of her perfect acuity—it showed even in her ever so careful selection of clothes. Clearly so full of herself for her achievements on something as futile as which damn wine was which.

"A lot of citrus," she spoke to herself rather than to him. "Flowers." She held the glass over the white tablecloth and looked down at it again.

"Amber. Not just gold. Amber." Her tone shifted from interest to puzzlement.

"I thought you knew everything."

"There are thousands of wines from nearly as many wineries." Her voice was almost as chilly as the wine. "I can tell you it's Italian, but I can't place it. Perhaps Tuscan. Or close by."

"Notice the lemon? The dry finish?" Why was he being such a jerk? She hadn't earned this but he couldn't help himself. He'd done it to Melanie without knowing, now he was fully aware he was doing it, but that didn't stop the next words.

"Did you miss the high alcohol perhaps?" He couldn't stop, even though he was being an asshole. He'd made Melanie think he loved her and then tossed her aside, practically called her whore with how he'd lavished gifts on her and then used her for sex.

"Not Tuscan. Liguria. Very traditional. Very authentic." He felt like the old monk with the whip scourging his own back until it bled. He had to strike out. Rake his claws against the pain within.

"Obvious marks of a Cinque Terre Sciacchetrà." He was a fucking mess. He knocked back the rest of the oversweet wine.

Staggering to his feet, he turned to see the look of horror on Angelo's face as he stood looking out from the swinging door to the kitchen.

Turned back to the woman frozen with the wine glass an inch from her pursed lips.

"Hope you enjoyed the damn meal. Don't bother to give me your number, you wouldn't want me to call anyway." He slapped a couple of hundred-dollar bills on the table to pay for the meal and walked out before he could throw himself on his butter knife in atonement.

"THE" Ristorante Italiano

There are moments in our lives that stand out. Moments when mother and daughter recognize the woman in each other. When the son finally throws the ball the father can catch. Those moments when a thousand different trivial things come together into a single event of perfection. When the symphony of musicians truly masters the composition and the composer's intent is revealed, when the dancer disappears into the ballet.

"Angelo's Tuscan Hearth" Italian restaurant has brought such finesse to the apparently simple task of a meal. Seattle has long been synonymous with salmon and other Northwest seafood. No longer. Now there is a restaurant that harkens us back to the Old World, when chefs were vied for by kings and cardinals alike. Their master is tucked away in Seattle's Pike Place Market on Post Alley.

Cassidy described the meal easily and quickly. Reliving each taste as it had occurred. Making sidebars for tasting notes on the wines as she went. It was all part of her style, the "friendly, close, personal touch" that many column reviewers had so praised and more than a few had tried to copy. She explained the meal in simple terms that let the owner of an untrained palate imagine they were indeed a master of spice and flavor, of ambience and composition.

However, one must be careful to choose one's dinner companions as carefully as one's meal or you'll end up with a jerk like Russell Morgan.

She glared at the screen, that wasn't what she'd intended to write at all.

A couple of keystrokes deleted the sentence.

A fine meal can be destroyed as easily by...

Delete.

Then she was stuck.

The ending wouldn't come. She scrolled back up and read

down the page again hoping that when she hit her stopping point, the flow of words would carry her to the end.

Nope.

She looked out the window of her tenth-floor condo at Queen Anne hill, the top of a partially submerged mountain rising hundreds of feet right out of Elliot Bay. Seattle's finest homes perched along its cliff edges. She could also see northern Puget Sound; rough water beneath a glittering sun and clouds zipping by as if they wanted to be anywhere but here. And straight-ahead lay Bainbridge Island—no longer her home.

Her column was due by midnight. Seven hours to go and she could find no inspiration in her mind, on the screen, or out the window.

Her hand was halfway to the bookcase before she stopped it. She didn't want to pull out her old columns. They'd just make her feel even less competent at the moment if that was possible. All those fun, enjoyable meals. Meals where a stupid blind date hadn't slapped at her so hard she could still feel the sting across her face.

The door buzzer jolted her out of the chair as if she'd been electrocuted. The only friends with the passcode to the street door were Jo and Perrin. She really didn't want to face either of them. Through the front door peephole she could see it was worse, it was *both* of them—Perrin with a happy smile and waving a bottle of wine.

She did her best to put on a cheerful expression before she let them in.

"Oooo, sad face," Perrin threw her arms around Cassidy's shoulders. "Didn't go well last night. In that case we come with consolation rather than cheers."

"Hi, Jo." Her hug was less fierce, but lasted a moment longer. The consolation of a good friend who understood.

"Well, come on. Give us the worst of it. Mr. Ugly, huh? Boy, doesn't that just suck the big one. Why do we say 'boy?' If I said,

'Girl, doesn't that just suck the big one' it wouldn't work as well at all." Perrin shed her yellow, woolen coat onto the hall chair.

Her outfit was '20s flapper, bright yellow with tassels. It looked perfect on her long, slender form. She didn't remove the beaded hat that was nearly a skull cap and hid all but a few wisps of the bright green hair, that still managed to look cute. Even her perfume was a light lemony scent smelling like a blossoming tree rather than furniture polish. For a moment, Cassidy wished that she had a flat, lean figure like Perrin so she could wear such an outfit and look even half as beautiful.

"Remember that fashion model the last time we were at Cutters?"

Jo fetched a corkscrew and glasses from the small kitchen and continued into the living room. Perrin dug around for cheese in the fridge as Cassidy pulled out a selection of crackers and spread them around the edges of a cutting board. Jo sat down on one of the stools on the far side of the maple butcher block counter that separated the rooms, and opened the wine.

Cassidy poured the Lindeman's Shiraz. A bit tannic, but one of the most drinkable wines at the price. Fresh and a bit spicy, placing no real demands on the palate. Exactly what she needed right now.

"The one dressed like a centerfold?" Jo twirled her glass without really looking at it.

"That's the one."

"She was your date?" Perrin slapped her palm against her forehead. "Wow, Cassie, didn't know you were walking both sides. If I'd only known, we could have had a whole different kind of fun in school. You remember Patty Jones? Ooo-wow did she have the hots for you."

"Perrin!" Jo rolled her eyes.

"What?" Cassidy did her best not to laugh. "No. She wasn't my date. And Patty Jones wasn't my type either. Patty? Really? Anyway, remember the guy who was with her?"

Perrin shook her head. Jo thought a moment and shrugged.

"I don't know how you missed him. He was incredible in a broad-shouldered, rough-and-rugged sort of way. Not so much handsome as solid, able to take the weight of the world on his shoulders and amble along as easy as sunshine. And eyes, ocean-deep eyes."

"Damn!" Perrin stamped her stocking-clad foot on the oak parquet and her tassels shimmered about her hemline. "I knew I should have gone and sat in the corner last night. Jo, next time Cassidy goes on a date with him, you and I are going double to spy."

Cassidy cut Jo off before she could reply. "There won't be another. Not with this guy. Not ever."

"Ouch! That bad? Let's go to the living room and you can tell us all. I want every sordid detail. I love the sordid details and it's always me who ends up providing them. Much less fun for poor Perrin. Old Miss Boring Lawyer over there hasn't been laid in over a year—unless she's hiding someone in her closet when she could be sharing all the good bits with poor Perrin."

Actually, Cassidy knew Jo had been on a few first dates since she'd finished the lawsuit that had consumed two years of her life. But none of them had led anywhere.

They took the wine and cheese into the living room and settled, she and Jo on the heavily pillowed couch, Perrin sitting in the matching, oversized chair. The warmth of the decorative swirls in the mahogany brown cloth and the near-black wood of the overstuffed arms made her bright yellow attire stand out even more. Cassidy had always thought of them as hobbit couches, but Perrin was no hobbit. Perhaps a slender, shining elf come to visit Cassidy's cozy cave on the tenth floor.

"Hey, those are new. They're so cute. Like a set or something."

Jo turned to see where Perrin was pointing over their heads.

Cassidy's four lighthouse and sailboat pictures. The boat's red-and-blue colors shone strong against the egg-cream walls.

"Where did you get those?"

"I took them." The second she spoke she wished she'd said they were from a flea market.

"You did? They're great. Who's on the sailboat? Some hunky guy I hope. Most sailboat guys are hunky. Egos the size of the Space Needle, but hunky."

"I, um, don't know. He just shows up."

Jo stood up to look at the pictures more closely. "But they were taken at different locations."

She sighed. Leave it to the lawyer to catch the details. Cassidy pointed to the calendar hanging where next month's photo would go. Moving the calendar slowly across the wall made it more of a journey.

"My theory is that we're both following the same calendar. The first of each month, he's there."

"Following the same calendar? Is that like having the same period?" Perrin was giggling at her own joke. She really did look like a twenty-year old flapper talking about something terribly improper.

"Yes. Sort of. I guess. Not really."

"Why are *you* there?" Jo took down the calendar and flipped through it for a moment as she settled back onto the couch. Then Jo focused on her.

Cassidy couldn't look away from Jo's dark eyes. Even the first day of school she hadn't managed the slightest evasion once Jo focused that lawyer-to-be gaze on her.

"Look at the first day of each month." Jo and Perrin did.

" 'Date with Ice Sweet'?" Perrin glared at her in mock anger. "Are you seeing some hottie and not telling us? I tell you, you and Jo were always a quiet pair. It's a good thing I found you or you both would've graduated after four years without anyone knowing you were there. And you'd probably both still be virgins. Even today. You are both—"

"Dad's nickname for me," Cassidy cut her off. "Icewine, the sweetest and rarest wine."

"So, you're going even though he isn't around anymore? That is sweet." Perrin curled back into her chair and tucked her legs under her. "That's really sweet. You and your dad were real close. I always envied that you are still. Um, now that he's gone."

Cassidy was well used to Perrin having to catch up with her own words and gave her the space to do so.

Perrin grimaced. "That came out all wrong as usual, but you know what I mean."

"Yes I do. And thanks, Perrin. We really were. He left letters too." She opened the drawer under the coffee table and pulled out the slim stack of envelopes. "They aren't long, he wrote them in those last weeks when he was barely alive. One for each lighthouse."

"Why didn't you tell us? We'd have gone with you. Three women voyaging to the wilds of the Pacific Northwest. We'd be like the three Musketeers when they traveled with Lewis and Clark on the voyage of discovery."

"Perhaps, Perrin, she wanted to do it on her own," Jo did her placating tone that never slowed Perrin down more than a few seconds. But typical Jo, she'd struck right at the truth.

"Jo's right. Though your adventuring sounds like fun, I want it to be just Dad and me. His first letter said that he wanted to go to these places with me, bring us closer together. He's telling me stuff about the past I didn't know."

Perrin waved her glass of wine at the photos, came danger-ously close to spilling the red shiraz on the white carpet. "So, there's this sailor guy in each photo. Maybe you should forget Mr. Wrong and track down Mr. Hunky Sailor. It's easy to test if he's for real. Poke his sailor's ego with a pin and if he explodes, you know he's for real."

Cassidy turned to look at the photos over her shoulder. West Point, Alki, Lime Kiln, Slip Point. There was a continuity to their relationship, even if whoever he was had no way of knowing about it. She'd never been out on a sailboat, only her dad's fishing skiff. What would it be like to go where the wind wanted to take you? To have so little control? Your life changing from one moment to the next due to the slightest whim of the winds?

She shook her head. "No, I'll do as I've always done and leave the wild ones to their own devices."

"Wimp!" Perrin waved her glass at her in a mock toast.

"Sensible," Jo nodded her approval before turning to Perrin. "Have you had so much luck with the wild ones?"

Perrin grimaced. "Not much. Hell of a lot of fun while the ride is on its way up. A mess when it comes crashing back down on me. You remember Jeffie, he was so cute and I was so gone on him. Do you think I'm the reason he went to India to follow that Swami somebody?"

"And now who is it this month?" She always had the best stories.

"No one worth even telling about. But," Perrin pointed a long finger at her. "You never told us about Mr. Wrong. Illegal change of subject. Five-yard penalty."

Cassidy grimaced, the last sip of wine distinctly sour.

"Did the sweater work? Did he," Perrin leaned in and dropped her voice to a throaty whisper, "ravish you with his eyes?"

"Yes. The sweater was perfect, just like you said. I guess I owe you some champagne. He was pretty decent about it once he realized what he was doing, but that sweater certainly gave him trouble more than once."

"Kept him off balance, I bet."

"Yeah. Right until the end when he hit me."

"Hit you?" Jo and Perrin both jerked forward.

145

She raised her hands. "No, not that. Just metaphorically. A punch right to my gut."

Cassidy hunched forward and rubbed her face with her hands but it did nothing to ease the pain.

"It wasn't good." Her gut twisted once again, just as it had last night. Just as it had when she'd been trying to finish the article. The date had been going so well. A bit awkward now and then, but a pleasant change from the boring sameness of Jack James. She'd discussed the tastes of the food and wine to cover the silences. He'd really liked her, or so she'd thought. And she'd definitely started to think he had possibility.

"Turns out he's from New York. For ten years we'd lived in the same city, me down by Greenwich, him on the Upper West Side. We saw some of the same plays, ate in a lot of the same restaurants." They'd both been gentle with each other as they recalled the day the world changed when the Twin Towers fell, but folks outside of New York would never really understand what that day had been like. Even Perrin and Jo had only been able to give sympathy, rather than true understanding, when she'd finally been able to get a call out that she was okay.

"It was all going at least reasonably well—better than a lot of my dates. Then over dessert he attacked my career. When I couldn't figure out the last wine, one I'd never had before, he practically threw it in my face. Tossed money on the table and stormed out."

"He threw money on the table?" Jo asked quietly and Perrin covered her mouth, her eyes wide.

She could only nod.

"Asshole." Jo rarely swore. "What did you do?" She rubbed a soothing hand up Cassidy's back.

She had to gulp for air in her aching lungs. By force of will alone she sat up straight, but couldn't shake off how used she'd felt.

"I paid for the meal in full. Told the owner to return the

money to the bastard, or give it to the poor. Then I left. Thank god for that power coat. Perrin, you're the best. It was the only thing that held me together until I got home." And then she'd wept in the shower until she'd nearly drowned. Wept like she hadn't in years. Wept for her loneliness and the gap left in her life by her father's death. Her gut was still sore from the purge.

Perrin moved to the couch and her two best friends hugged her from either side.

"He doesn't deserve you. You are so much better than him."

She wrapped her hands around her friends' arms.

"I am, aren't I?"

"You is," Perrin whispered in one ear. She could feel Jo's nod. She was. Way better.

"You don't need him. Who cares what a jerk thinks anyway. If he doesn't like our Cassidy, we won't like him either, will we, Jo? Not ever. No matter how nice the restaurant was. Never. Never. Never."

"Ha!" She sat upright and nearly clipped Perrin's chin with her shoulder.

"What?"

"You're brilliant, Perrin. I know exactly how to finish my review of Angelo's."

"I am? How?"

Jo squinted her eyes for a moment and then smiled a smile that would look good on an angel. A wicked angel. "Oh yes, Cassidy. National. Oh my, yes."

Perrin finally got it as well. She jumped to her feet, clapped her hands in what might be an African dance rhythm or a drunken flamenco, and started to dance, her tassels swirling about her thighs and shimmering about her hips.

In moments, the three of them were dancing together in the middle of the living room.

RUSSELL SWUNG THE SLEDGEHAMMER AGAIN. The plywood cracked. Again and again he pounded against the counter the previous owner had installed as a galley. He'd used so much glue and near enough a thousand screws that a sledge was the only way to take it out.

He slammed it again and the right side finally broke free.

Demolition. It felt good. Exactly what he needed.

The left side was finally looser. His muscles burned as he drove the hammer repeatedly against the stubborn plywood.

Without warning the whole counter broke free and fell. Twisted as it bounced off the curve of the hull.

He jumped back, slammed his head on an open porthole, his legs were stopped by the pilot berth and the counter clipped his shins so sharply that he collapsed onto the bunk. He tried to kick the counter free, but it was wedged into place and had him pinned.

"Shit!" He managed to grab the edge of it and lift it just enough to pull his legs free. He dropped the counter to the companionway floor with a bang.

He pulled up his pantlegs, doing his best not to hiss at the pain. Blood. On both shins. He touched the back of his head where he'd clipped the porthole. No blood at least, but a painful bump was already rising.

"Double shit!"

He lay down on the pilot berth and held his breath until the searing pain subsided a little. Then he pounded his heels against the boards that would be covered with cushions at some later date. He was ten years old and pounding out his frustration in his final-ever temper tantrum. Everything had gone wrong.

"Triple shit!" He'd really liked the lady despite herself and despite her New York past and her fancy ways. Cassidy was the most attractive woman he'd met since...since he didn't know when. It wasn't that she was beautiful, though she certainly was. She was also intelligent, funny, and fantastic to look at. He could close his eyes and see her—every shape of her face fit together into a unified whole. Not the studied and genetic elegance of Melanie, but what beauty really was about.

And her body was womanly rather than model gaunt. That sweater had almost killed him. Every few minutes his attention was dragged down from her face by that deepening fade of russet toward black and the hidden promise of the black turtle-neck beneath. He'd give a pretty penny to know why she smiled rather than snarled each time he couldn't stop his eyes from drifting. She certainly wasn't a tramp. Angelo had been right about that, a real lady.

Nutcase crawled out of wherever she'd been hiding from all his pounding. Seeing him lying on his back, she leapt onto his chest, settled herself in a little ball, and, now in her favorite position, set into purring like a pint-sized buzzsaw.

"But it isn't just her beauty that makes her attractive," he explained to the cat as his shins finally downgraded from excru-ciating to merely annoying. "See, there's a difference between pretty and attractive that a lot of guys don't understand." Of course, neither had he until he'd started the inevitable compar-ison of Melanie and Cassidy Knowles.

The cat buzzed a little louder. She loved when he talked and she was curled on his chest.

"Beauty is like stop-you-in-the-street 'Wow!' Attractive, that's something different." He slid a finger along Nutcase's jaw and she closed her eyes with pleasure.

"It's when everything combines in a certain way. She doesn't have to be a knockout, though she is. But you add that on top of funny, a real brain, and all that other stuff and you get a killer combination."

Killer.

He pounded the back of his head against the boards, right where he'd hit his head on the porthole, and he briefly saw stars again.

And then you blow it by going out of your way to insult her.

He reached back to rub his aching head and his fingers caught in papers. The mail. He'd stopped by the post office box and grabbed it on his way home from the hardware store and then tossed it on the bench so he could try out his new sledge.

Bill. Bill. Junk mail. Victoria's Secret catalog, toss that aside for later. Nah, chuck it. Just more vapid fantasy women. He gave it a quick flip before tossing it aside.

Melanie. She got the center spread, good for her. Damn, she looked really fine with that long body and the red teddy. Shit! If she looked this good on the page, she must have been incredible in real life. And those eyes. He'd never captured that emotion on her. If he had, he would have used her face in some of the ads. But he'd never seen in the camera that wealth of calmness with the alluring dash of pity. Mere mortals couldn't know the joy of wearing scarlet teddies for your man.

But he had seen it on her face—once. Though not on the camera. It was how she'd looked at him at the airport before turning away and leaving him behind. Calm and pity.

He chucked the catalog toward the garbage bag and missed. It flopped over the open floorboard exposing the bilge where it teetered for a long moment. The corner drooped. It disappeared below with a sodden splat. Crap. He really needed to fix that missing board in the floor.

The last envelope had Angelo's writing on it. His friend hadn't come by in a week and Russell couldn't face going to see him.

Mail, though. That was a bad sign. Angelo had occasionally sent postcards when they'd lived on opposite coasts. Neither of them was much at writing. He tore off the end.

Nutcase appeared to have slipped into another of her mid-afternoon naps.

A newspaper clipping and two, hundred-dollar bills wrapped in a sheet of white paper. One word across the paper.

"Jerk!"

Two hundred dollars. They were for...what? Then he remembered. He'd tossed them on the table, as if paying for...

"Idiot!" He jerked up to a sitting position and banged his head on the low overhead above the pilot berth. He fell back prone as Nutcase growled and dug her claws into his chest at the unannounced change of position. His T-shirt was no defense against her talons. He extracted her claws and tossed her onto the table. He sat up more carefully this time.

Idiot! He'd treated her like...like a babe from 1-900-Dial-a-Babe. "Nice dinner conversation, honey. Here's a couple of bills for your time." Damn! He'd meant to pay for the meal he'd ruined. Well, here it was back in his face once again. He jammed the bills in the pocket of his jeans.

He unfolded the clipping.

A Restaurant for Romance
by Cassidy Knowles

Oh shit! Angelo was going to bloody murder him. He forgotten that she'd been there to review the restaurant—the good and the bad. Her article would play from New York to San Francisco. She couldn't break the restaurant, but she could certainly ding it. Ding it bad. He hadn't told her, but he used to follow her columns when he was looking for the hot new restaurant to charm someone into his bed. Usually worked too. The lady had taste and people listened.

He scanned the article.

A good review. Thank God!

No, a *great* review. It sounded so good, he wouldn't have credited it except that he'd shared the meal with her. The Baby Scallop Kebob had been incredible. He could feel his mouth water again as he read about it. It had also been the high point of the meal right before he...

The chef made exquisite choices. Even the dessert wine, previously unknown to this reviewer, so complemented the fig-custard, puff pastry that this diner was transported back to the chef's hometown of Monterosso al Mare. The narrow beaches, the high cliffs, the home cooking, and the strong wines of the Ligurian region of Italy.

A little side column described the wine exactly as he'd tasted it. Only he hadn't. He'd been far too grouchy to notice even half that. But she made him think that he had. She was really good at this.

A fine meal can be destroyed as easily by poor company as a poor chef.

Ouch! Okay, here it comes. Here's where she slaughters Angelo's. And it was all his fault. Angelo was never going to forgive him. The thin paper was crumpling in his hands.

Whether making a marriage proposal, as was done and joyously accepted by a bride-to-be, or looking to celebrate fifty glorious years together, there can be no better place than Angelo's Tuscan Hearth. Bring the person you love to this restaurant and you'll never be forgotten for it. Ever.

There it was. Published. Syndicated into over two hundred markets.

Cassidy Knowles was going to forgive him…never!

CAPE FLATTERY LIGHTHOUSE

Cape Flattery, Makah Bay
First lit: 1857
Automated: 1977
48.3717 -124.7366

*C*ape Flattery was so named by Captain Cook in 1778 when he arrived at the Northwesternmost point of what would eventually become Washington State. "In this very latitude geographers have placed the pretended Strait of Juan de Fuca. Nothing of that kind presented itself to our view." And so he dubbed the cape a "flatterer."

Cook erred. The nearby Strait of San Juan de Fuca leads to the massive Puget Sound which now hosts such cities as Seattle, Tacoma, and Vancouver, British Columbia.

The lighthouse was built with the light tower itself incorporated into the building so that the keepers did not have to risk the hostile natives to maintain the light. The natives were hostile because their tribes had been decimated a few years before by a smallpox epidemic brought in by the light's construction workers.

MAY 1

*a*ccording to the GPS, Cassidy was about halfway to the viewpoint for the offshore Tatoosh Island Lighthouse. It was such a beautiful day she was practically dancing along the three-quarter-mile long trail. Spring was finally here; the winter rains had eased off and the sun shimmered down from a crystalline sky. These were the moments she was glad she'd returned to the Pacific Northwest. The buds were opening in the vineyards she'd driven past, the flowers edging forth and filling the air with their sweet scent—battling the cherry trees for her nose's attention.

The trail was a bit rough, but an easy traverse in her hiking boots. Actually, according to the GPS, they were overkill, but she wanted to get some use from them. They made her feel solid, standing square upon the earth.

"Is that what men feel like when they do that thumbs-hooked-in-their-pockets thing?" A passing bumblebee was too busy about his task to answer.

The trail had started in a huge empty parking lot. If that lot were filled in the summer, the trail would be nuts. This weekday mid-morning was a far better time to be here. The dirt path descended down through trees, twisting down to simple, split log footbridges over muddy passages.

Despite the groomed trail, it was as wild a place as she'd ever been. Twenty or so miles from the nearest town, at the end of the road, at the end of the country for that matter. She was presently the northwesternmost person in the continental U.S. Possibly by that entire twenty miles.

It reminded her of growing up in the country and how much she'd enjoyed it as a child and not enjoyed it as a teen. When had that change taken place? She shrugged. No reason to care today. Today the world consisted of little Cassidy Knowles, a mucky trail made fun by stout boots, and a new lighthouse.

She followed a side branch to a small viewing platform. A heavy rail was all that separated her from an impossibly long drop. The water lay a hundred or more feet below. Sheer islands plunged upward from the ocean into the air, their heads covered in tall caps of fir trees looking like a teen's moused doo while the Pacific Ocean rolled and splashed unheeded about their rocky bases.

If she raised her arms, she could fly. If she were to sing, her voice could be heard around the world.

Cassidy returned to the trail and headed for the next lookout, taking the exhilarating floatiness down the trail with her.

"Hey! Wait!"

She looked back to see who was calling. Her foot came down hard on a rock, the shock jarred her whole body.

Russell Morgan. She turned away before he could recognize her, but there was nowhere to go. No escape along the open trail.

She could hear his feet pounding as he ran up the trail.

"Hey! You in the red coat. Wait!"

Resigned, she stopped and turned.

Russell stumbled to a halt, a fancy camera banging against his hip. "I've been looking for... Oh, it's you."

He had the decency to blush bright red at her continued silence.

"Sorry, that came out wrong. Let me start again. Hi, Cassidy. I didn't expect to see you here." He looked down the length of her body as if he were inspecting a mannequin.

Glancing down she saw her red leather coat; it was too warm for the parka. Black leggings and her new, barely dirty, hiking boots. They now appeared as ungainly clown feet at the end of overly skinny, pogo-stick legs. Ridiculous with the high-fashion coat, but she liked the way the soft leather felt no matter how inappropriate it was for the setting.

His gaze returned to her face. "Your hair."

She reached up to check it, but it was still up in the clip that should keep it out of her face even in the wind that every light-house apparently cultivated.

"What?"

"It, uh," he shook himself as if coming awake from a dream, "looks nice."

"Thanks." If he thought a lame compliment was going to begin to make up for...

"I'm really sorry for some of things I said the other night."

"You mean a month ago?"

His expression blanked for a moment.

"A month ago? Really?"

Just how dense was he?

"Twenty-six days." *Ugh, really ultra lame, Cassidy Knowles.* She sounded like a pining female who counted the days, hours, minutes, and seconds. It was easy. Today was May first and their date, if one could call it that, had been on April fourth. Thirty days hath September, April, June, and...

He flashed one of his killer smiles and she did her best to resist its power. It was a really good smile.

"That makes this a mighty belated apology, doesn't it? Perhaps if I got down on my knees?"

"How about a kowtow?"

With the light breeze ruffling his brown hair, a worn denim jacket that outlined his wonderful upper body, he dropped to his knees and pounded his forehead three times against a patch of sand.

"Please forgive me, O Great Goddess of the Wines."

He rocked back on his heels and grinned up at her. "Better?"

"That's not fair."

"What?" He stood once again and she noticed that her eyes were about level with his chin. His shoulder was just the right height to lay her head on if they were slow dancing. Stupid image. She definitely didn't want to be around Russell Morgan for a moment longer than she had to—absolutely not long enough for a dance. Her brain had clearly taken a holiday.

"Jerks aren't supposed to make me smile. Especially ones I'm mad at."

"Cheating, huh?" He hooked his thumbs into his jeans pockets as if he were Harrison Ford and he'd just defeated the entire German Army on his own.

"Definitely."

"Well, can I walk with you a bit, if I promise to be less jerky?"

"Is that possible?"

He shrugged eloquently, "I can try, but no guarantees."

It would be tempting to blast him with some witty remark and walk away, but she could never think of them when she most needed them.

"Okay," as if she had a lot of choice in the matter, there was only the one trail and not another soul to be seen.

He bowed slightly and indicated she should walk ahead. They moved toward the point in silence until one of them had to speak or she'd go stark raving mad.

"Do you—"

"Isn't it—"

"You first."

"No, you."

He looked grumpy, but she waited him out.

"Do you come out here often?"

She shook her head. "My first time."

"Me, too. Do you, ah, go to many lighthouses?"

Her foot caught on a rock and she stumbled forward. He reached out a hand to steady her, but she didn't take it.

"Seemed like a lovely day for a drive. I wasn't really going for the lighthouse. I thought the northwest point of the U.S. might be amusing." She was babbling like an idiot. But she'd be damned before she'd tell him that she'd been collecting lighthouses for the last five months.

"What about Alaska?"

"Continental U.S." You jerk.

"That always bothered me. 'Continental U.S.' Like Alaska is on some other continent."

"Contiguous U.S. Does that make you happier?"

"Immensely." He started whistling as if he hadn't a care in the world.

"Is this your first time?"

She glanced over in time to see a wolfish grin cross his face for a moment. That definitely hadn't come out right, but she was not going to blush. Her cheeks didn't appear to be paying attention to her orders and were heating up abruptly.

"I meant—"

"Yes and no," he saved her with a casual drawl that might still have a bit of the grinning male ego. "First time here."

She focused on the trail ahead and continued placing one foot in front of the other.

"How about you? Are you a lighthouse virgin?" He said it with every sexual insinuation possible dripping from his tongue. She'd obviously given him too much credit. What were they, in high school?

"Jesus. Do you go out of your way to be insulting?"

He stopped his damn whistling. Actually, he was no longer beside her and she had to backtrack to where he halted.

"No." He shook his head, his voice as soft as the breeze wending its way through the green moss. "No. I'd have to say that you bring out the worst in me."

"I'm honored."

He bit his upper lip and inspected the sky for a moment.

"Can we try this again?"

"You already started twice."

"Third time's the charm?"

If he'd made it a statement, she'd have left him and to hell with the ferry ride, the three-hour drive, and the stupid lighthouse. But he looked pitiable. How a handsome, broad-shouldered man over six feet tall could look so lost was a wonder. Did he know that she had a weak spot for lost souls?

She looped her hand through the crook of his arm and tugged him along the trail. Once they were walking together, he unwound a bit. De-stiffened enough to bend his legs in some semblance of normalcy.

"Hi, I'm Cassidy Knowles. Yes, I'm a lighthouse virgin. This is my first one." She'd be nice to him for Angelo's sake, but that didn't mean she was about to let him one single inch into her life.

"Russell Morgan, pleased to— I really was pleased to meet you. You seemed like a nice lady at dinner, no matter how I mangled it."

"I have rarely been attacked quite so thoroughly."

"Well, you didn't deserve it."

She'd thought a lot about what he'd said. Hard not too.

"I'm less sure of that now than I was then."

Where the trail narrowed, he walked awkwardly with one foot in the mud so that she could stay well on the trail. It did make her think a little better of him.

"You made your feelings for me quite clear in your review."

She had, hadn't she. "I was…"

"Irritated? Hurt?"

"Really, really pissed," but was becoming less so with each step they took together. How was he doing that to her?

"Ah, well. I'd wager that isn't something your average date achieves quite so thoroughly."

"No, Mr. Morgan. You're a first. Though there was this one guy." She told him the story about Richie who had hallucinated her as hell-spawn.

He told a story about a horrid double-date he'd had with Angelo when they were in high school. Twins that Angelo could keep straight with no problem, but not him. "I kept trying to kiss the wrong one. Managed to piss off all three of them because they dumped Angelo along with me."

He was actually charming when he wasn't in a vicious back-biting mood. Apparently without thinking, he offered his arm as they navigated over a rough patch. She didn't need the help, but it was so unexpected that she took the offer.

Cassidy could feel the muscles under her hand. His strong bicep flexing easily as they moved over the last of the rocks, an unconscious strength easily shifted to aid her balance. She enjoyed holding a man's arm—of feeling, even for an instant, that they belonged side-by-side. A warmth ran through her that had nothing to do with the May sunshine.

Rounding the last bend in the trail, they came upon a small viewing platform raised a half-dozen steep steps above the rocky clifftop. She waved him forward, though he tried to insist that she proceed first. There was chivalry and there was climbing a half-dozen ladder-steep steps—that would place her behind right in his face.

"Jerks before ladies."

"Even redeemed ones?"

"You aren't redeemed yet, go."

He ascended, like most males, using only every other step.

Good butt, she couldn't help noticing. And grinned. Turnabout was sometimes fair play. She followed him up the ladder.

Then she stopped noticing Russell Morgan at all.

The sweep of the Cape Flattery shore spread before them. Three-quarters of the horizon was water. To the right was the Straits of San Juan de Fuca. To the left was the endless expanse of the Pacific Ocean. And straight ahead was a rocky, sprawling island, the last land before Alaska and Japan.

A few hundred yards offshore, Tatoosh Island popped from the water like the bottom of a cooking pot—flat-topped and sheer-sided. The green grass and few firs did little to mitigate the desperate isolation of the lighthouse perched on the edge of the cliff. It was no wonder that a lighthouse keeper and his assistant had attempted a duel to the death over some imagined insult. Both had been saved by another assistant who had removed the lead from the bullets before the three shots were fired.

Its beacon winked at her across the narrow passage. The light called out, offering guidance...or was it seeking aid?

Perhaps it was both. She scanned the water, right and left. The only thing that was missing was the sailboat.

RUSSELL HAD FINALLY LEFT to amble along the edges of the high cliff. Even now Cassidy could see him poking along inspecting every nook and cranny of the narrow point, as if he'd lost something. Occasionally he'd snap a picture with that fancy camera of his but even that looked less like inspiration and more like habit. At long last he headed down a side trail that appeared to lead to the bottom of the cliff.

She took the moment alone to pull out her father's letter.

Dearest Ice Sweet,

You can hold onto something so tightly that your nerves go numb and you no longer notice your death grip on it. Not until it is too late, or near enough.

Adrianne and I spent three years trying to save the vineyard. We sunk every penny we had into it until every personal belonging was sold and we'd spent almost every ounce of our life's blood. We often lived on beans and rice to stretch the money. By the time you were two, the last threads were unraveling.

Adrianne was too busy raising you to ever take to the fields again for those grueling sixteen-hour days. When her parents took ill, she went home to Bainbridge Island, Washington to take care of them. I struggled to save that which was past saving. I stayed on. Sheer damn stubbornness, I guess. Or maybe just blinders.

April 7th. That was the day. With the lack of water the last harvest had been miserable. I'd spent the winter trying to work the wine, but without your mother's help and wisdom, it failed miserably. Your mother was gone and I didn't think she'd be coming back. I had to choose between my vineyard or her and you. It was the hardest thing I've ever done. Thank all the gods, I made the right choice. I sold out and I moved to the Kitsap Peninsula and started living over your grandparents' garage.

Beware getting so locked in that you don't see what you most need to look at.

Love you, Ice Sweet.

Vic

He'd lost a vineyard and she'd never known, a Napa Valley vineyard. That would be worth a fortune now and it sounded as if he lost it for pennies. He'd taken a body blow to the heart because of her. Then he not only lost his vineyard, but his parents-in-law and then his wife. No wonder he didn't speak much of his past; the pain had run its roots deep into his life.

Russell was heading back toward her.

She crumpled the letter and shoved it into her pocket. A quick wipe at her eyes and her wet fingers cooled in the offshore breeze. She turned her face into that light breeze; she'd blame her eyes on the wind if he said anything.

He stopped and scanned the area once more, not even bothering to glance at her. Mr. Sensitive he wasn't.

She checked the ocean again, especially back down the Straits toward Seattle, but no blue sailboat braved the waters. No boat at all had appeared in the last hour except for a pair of container ships and a tanker that looked big enough to carry all the oil of an entire country. Okay, a small country.

She photographed the lighthouse out on the island, but without her sailboat, it looked empty. Felt pointless. It wouldn't really belong in the series on her wall.

Each step he took closer to her was followed by a quick glance around.

"You look as if you've lost something."

He shrugged.

"Stood up by your blonde girlfriend?"

He aimed a scathing glance in her direction.

"Sorry." She bit the edge of her tongue. "Now I'm the one being bitchy. I'm sorry."

His gaze didn't soften, but he did manage a jerky nod of acknowledgement. Tit-for-tat. The lowest form of revenge. She wanted to crawl away and hide until he was gone.

He headed back for the parking lot without offering his arm.

She was a little ashamed that she missed it; not that she actually needed any support along the well-groomed trail. His silence was becoming oppressive. She could just fade back and let him disappear ahead. Maybe she could even pretend she had to go back for something she'd dropped and check one more time for her sailboat. But somehow she knew it wasn't coming.

Besides, that was the chicken's way out.

Russell strode ahead, not fast, but with hard, jarring steps. He had powerful legs and a well-formed butt that his worn jeans outlined nicely.

What was she avoiding so much? She stuffed her hands into her pockets and her father's letter crinkled. That was it. The letter had said the same thing Russell had thrown at her.

What did she want to do? She'd walked her career path head down like some kind of bulldog.

Be the best food critic.

Know all the wines.

Be hurt when you don't know about an obscure wine from a remote Italian village.

She'd dropped nearly four hundred dollars the day after their date ordering every wine she could find from the five villages of Cinque Terre. She'd cataloged over half of them, would never forget them, but most were mediocre wines you'd expect from small village wineries. Only a few surprises in the lot and the Sciacchetrà was the best of those.

"You were right," she broke the silence without quite meaning to.

He stumbled and looked back at her. "What?"

"I said, you were right."

"No, I screwed up with Melanie."

"I meant about having no long-term plan."

For a moment they blinked at each other, both lost on a straight trail with their two cars in clear sight a hundred yards away.

"Her name is Melanie?"

"I'm sorry I said that about you."

Once again they were at a stop. Both too vulnerable. Both with their hearts out on the trail. She couldn't do it. It was a cliff she just couldn't climb. Not with this man.

"I, uh, are you going to the next lighthouse?"

He looked down and kicked at the dirt. "Next lighthouse?"

"There's one a couple of hours south, called Destruction Island. It's—" She almost said, "not on the calendar," but caught herself.

He didn't look at her, still hadn't since rejoining her at the lookout.

"It's offshore a couple miles. They say it should be visible… on a clear day…like today," she finally ran down to a stop.

He looked about the parking lot. Stared for a long moment at Jo's car. Hers was in the shop and Jo had leant her the BMW roadster.

"Nice wheels."

"Um, thanks." What was it with men and fancy cars? It was too racy for her taste, though Russell's car looked even lower and meaner than Jo's. Porsche maybe? Jo had always been the fan of sports cars, the only weakness she'd admit to.

"I think I'll head home. You?" He didn't meet her gaze but continued to be fascinated by the dirt.

"Don't know really. They say a bull lived there who hated the new foghorn. It kept charging the lighthouse whenever it went off—thought it was a competing bull." Why was she trying to talk him into coming?

He finally looked at her; his narrowed eyes indicated that he was certainly asking himself the same question. After a long moment, during which she forgot to breathe, he shrugged.

"Nah. I'm not really feeling up to it." He turned toward his little black car, but turned back and returned to stand in front of her.

He held out a hand.

She took it out of instinct rather than any desire to share contact with him.

Rather than shaking it, he covered it with his other hand. Big, powerful, warm hands enfolded hers, warming away a chill she hadn't noticed.

His sea-dark eyes looked down at her for a long moment. She could feel her knees going weak. Was he going to kiss her? What would she do if he did?

"Thanks. It was nice to spend some time with you. Perhaps

we can do this again sometime. I mean that. I'm lousy company, but you're nice."

She nodded. He let go and walked back to his car. It started with a dull roar, but he didn't disappear in a flurry of gravel as she'd expected. Instead he waited. Waited while she fished out first her keys, then Jo's, got in and started the engine.

As soon as it came to life, he did roar off, fishtailing so wildly on the gravel parking lot that for a moment she thought he'd crash into the trees. Then he regained control and put his foot down—hard. His engine roared loudly over the quiet purr of the BMW's engine even after he was out of sight.

RUSSELL LET the miles flow through him. He wasn't even really aware of where he was until he pulled into Port Angeles.

"Good job, Russ. Real safe way to drive." Eighty miles had rolled by since he'd left Cassidy in the parking lot without really saying goodbye.

He got off Highway 101 and threaded his way through town until he hit the waterfront in a pot-holed gravel parking lot. He stopped with the car's nose pointed toward the water and Canada. He thumped his forehead against the steering wheel.

"Stood up by Melanie?"

Not even close.

"Right about Cassidy Knowles?"

Not a bit closer. She had more class in her little pinky than he'd had in his whole life. She'd forgiven him slashing at her yet again. Forgiven him being there to meet another woman and being so damn obvious about his disappointment that he totally shut her out.

He flopped back in his seat and looked at his hands. He could still feel the outline of her strong fingers imprinted on both his palms. Could still see all of the colors of autumn in her eyes. Had seen those lips, those lips that he longed to kiss since the first moment he saw them pursed above a glass of wine.

And that was a path right down the wrong road. Right back into a woman enveloped in a New York state of mind. She wanted to be Craig Claiborne reborn as a woman.

She was so wrong for him.

So why hadn't he been able to stop thinking about her for the last twenty-six days?

"YOU REALLY LOOK LIKE SHIT!" Angelo shouted over the serious cranking of the R&B band in the corner of the bar and everyone else shouting to be heard by their companions.

"Thanks, buddy. Big help." Russell looked up at the mirror behind the broad, wooden bar. Bottles of liquor were lined up along the whole mirror's length. He could see only one eye reflected between the silver spouts of a bottle of Johnny Red and the next of Jack Daniels Black. The dark rings beneath the eye made it look more a ghost's than his own.

"I'm serious, man. You look even worse than the night I told you what you did to Melanie."

"Can't you just drink in silence?"

"Nope, I'm a chatty drunk. You know that." Angelo licked the salt off the back of his hand, knocked back the Cuervo Reserva shooter, and sucked on a piece of lime.

Which usually made them so compatible. Tonight Russell wanted to just... He stared at the one eye in the mirror. He wanted... He didn't know what. Knocking back his tequila, he reached for a chaser but his beer was gone.

Angelo was leaning back against the bar, checking out the crowd, and taking a slug from Russell's pint. He reached for it just as Angelo looked at him and whispered in a quiet shout.

"Target acquired!"

Russell glanced over his shoulder. Sure enough, a pair of women were sitting alone at a tiny table. Long dark hair, thin but in a Seattle-healthy way rather than a New York-anorexic fashion. She wore a halter top that revealed a nice expanse of shoulder and belly, and enough curve beneath to be very pleasing. Her friend was a perky Japanese with denim shorts cut incredibly short. Her hair barely reached her ears—flat and cute as could be in her clingy tube top. They'd noted Angelo's and his attention and were very carefully not looking in their direction, but it was clear he and Angelo were being assessed in sidelong glances that included nice smiles.

Russell turned back to the bar for another tequila, catching their disappointment as he did so.

"Oh shit," Angelo knocked back the rest of Russell's beer. "It's going to be one of those nights?"

Russell punched Angelo's arm but didn't feel much better for it.

SEVERAL DRINKS LATER, Angelo had battered down Russell's defenses and was now giving him worldly advice. Exactly what he didn't need.

"You can no go sailing away from me, my friend. You are no ready. You boat, she is no ready either." The drunker Angelo got, the thicker his accent grew. Half his mother's Italian, half Brooklyn. It would be about three more drinks until he wouldn't understand a word Angelo said. And that would be fine with him.

In fact, he couldn't wait.

"Look, *vecchio mio*. Sailing off into the unknown, it is a plan. Maybe good. Maybe bad. But it is only sailing off into the unknown. You gonna take you problems with you. Youself, he is gon' be dere."

Russell's one eye in the mirror was blearier, but he could still pick it out among the bottles. He definitely wasn't drunk enough yet.

"Melanie is in the past, man. There isn't shit you can do about that one. You go back, you open the studio, you go down on one knee, but even if she say yes, your heart, she fold up and die. I'm Italian. I know this things."

Down on two knees and bowing his head into the sand at Tatoosh. He hadn't been thinking of Melanie. He was thinking of the way Cassidy Knowles looked, standing tall above him, scowling downward as the smile tugged at the corners of her generous mouth. Again, the line of jaw to neck, of cheek to eye made him want to caress, stroke, feel. The wind picking at her tightly controlled hair, but not breaking it free—not a single strand out of control. She didn't have the New York model look. But it was certainly what New York should want.

"Hey! You no listening to me."

He wasn't. "What?"

"I tell you how to fix your whole life and make a million dollars and you not even listening?"

"I already have a million, it's just my life that's fucked up."

"Does that mean I should or shouldn't give you my number?" The long dark one was standing beside him paying her tab.

"Shouldn't."

"Should!" Angelo insisted at the same moment.

"He's really an okay guy when he isn't drunk."

"You know we've been waiting over an hour for you two to come over." She looked him up and down, predator trying to decide if the meat was worth dealing with the brain.

"Lady, if you want my advice—"

"She don't!"

He elbowed Angelo in the sternum, who gasped as he lost his breath.

"If the two of you want to jump someone's bones tonight—"

Angelo smacked him hard on the back of the head, "—you should both take him home."

He nodded at Angelo.

"He's a much nicer guy than me."

The woman signed her credit slip, with a nice tip he noted, and studied the pen for a long moment before returning it to the bartender without scrawling a phone number on a napkin. She brushed past him, her perfume like a cat in heat.

"You," she whispered loudly to Angelo, "can smack him again."

Angelo did and the woman was gone.

RUSSELL COULD BREATHE. Okay. That was a good sign.

He could open one eye. It was mostly dark except for street-lights reflecting off the ceiling. He placed his little imaginary sailboat among the shadow-shaped ceiling continents and began wending it around to distant shores, shadows with mysterious ports of call. There'd be tropical dark women, towering men, and exotic foods. Leaving the beams of light rising from the dark streets, he sailed toward the great round continent of the ceiling lamp.

Just as his boat arrived, the light blazed on and drove twin balls of fire down his optic nerves and into his brain. Which then exploded as if the sun had gone nova within the confines of his skull.

He dragged a pillow over his face and cursed roundly. The afterimage on his retina included an outline of Angelo.

"I'm gonna kill you, you turkey."

Angelo started throwing some extra sofa cushions on top of him. Each made his body shudder with pain.

"You've got fifteen minutes."

"Until I die? Fine. That'll be fourteen minutes after I've killed you." His pulse was pounding against the inside of his skull—hard enough to crack the fragile bone.

"Oh, you really scare me, big man. All talk. No fight."

Russell sat up, thinking he'd lunge at Angelo. It hurt so much that he let his momentum carry him right over to lie the other way around on the sofa.

"Just leave me in peace to die."

"No, you made me promise."

"Promise what? I was drunk. I release you from whatever foul deed I swore you to achieve."

Angelo left him alone for a moment. He was almost back to sleep when a cold, wet towel was slapped against his face.

He let out a roar as he sat up but Angelo dodged back.

"You're going to die, Angelo."

"Someday, probably not today though. I doubt if a fly would be much scared of you in your present state. Here, drink this." He shoved a glass into Russell's hand.

"What is it?" He kept his eyes closed against the painful light. He could still see every outline of Angelo's living room from the tan walls and the vast array of family photographs, to the yellow and blue pottery, and the wall of cookbooks. The memory of every object was outlined in shimmering rings on his retina.

"Water. A tall glass of cold water."

He knocked it back and nearly threw up. Three fingers of whiskey bored their way down his throat and spilled into his stomach to lie there and burn.

"Oops. Sorry. Wrong glass. That was the hair of the dog and brother did he ever bite you hard last night. Here's an orange juice and aspirin chaser."

Russell forced open an eye to make sure it wasn't sixteen ounces of vodka or gin. He sipped it carefully to get the aspirin down before setting it aside on the teak coffee table.

He opened the other eye. The room only spun a little. Even in his present state, it was cozy and comfortable.

"So. What was this damn promise you are so set on keeping?"

Angelo lounged back against a doorway, well out of harm's reach.

"We're going shopping."

"Do you have any idea how hard this is to do with a hangover?"

"Easy as fish." Angelo was holding a three-foot long salmon and bending it back and forth.

"How fresh is this one? It feels good." He directed his question to the fish monger, a huge-armed man in his twenties. Someone Russell wouldn't mess with hungover or in top shape. The man was shoveling bucketfuls of crushed ice and spreading them over his display counter as easily as Russell had tossed back shot glasses of tequila.

Russell had seen this stocking-the-fish-stall routine on one of those cute little news clips, but he'd never gotten up at five in the goddamn morning to watch it. A crowd had gathered to watch, phones and cheap cameras poised to capture the upcoming Pike Place Market ritual.

"I kept it aside for you from last night's flight. Out of the water less than twenty-four hours." The fish monger slapped the side of the fish like it was an old friend.

Angelo handed it back to him to add to the growing pile.

"And it will be on my dinner table in another twelve."

He tuned them out as the other men, all equally biceped, began chucking more fish from the van. Twenty and thirty-pound salmon arced one after another through the air, so fast there was little room between them. They flew out of the back of the truck, arced high over the sidewalk, just skimming below the open eaves of the market. At the far end they were snatched from the air and dropped onto the ice in neat rows, sorted by type, slid deep into the waiting ice in a single smooth motion. Mesh bags of oysters, clams, squid, and worse followed, rapidly filling the iced tables. A four-foot shark flew by and the small crowd of hearty tourists who had braved the early morning air applauded. The sharp stench of raw fish not yet turning bad filled the air faster than the morning breeze could clear it.

Angelo was in position and took first pick of everything that landed.

Russell had seen enough and then some. If he'd had breakfast, he'd have lost it by now.

Angelo finally rescued him from the post he was slowly sliding down and shoved him farther into the market.

"And I made you promise to abuse me this morning for what reason?" His head felt a little better, but his body felt as if he'd been in a brawl. Several brawls and all on the inside of his skin.

"You insisted that you wanted to change your life. See how the other half lived. Whatever that meant."

"Sounds like a crock to me."

"Me too. But you kept insisting you were a boat without a rudder. By the hundredth repetition I promised just to get you to shut up."

He found a stool to sit on as Angelo attacked the produce stand. Clearly he was well known here, as once again the proprietor brought out a special stash.

"All organic. All fresh within the last two days." Angelo sorted through the offering quickly and kept most of it. The few items he rejected were placed in the prime display spots of the lesser produce.

The market was starting to buzz. More restaurateurs were showing up and picking things over, but Angelo already had the best of it. The tourists, now that all the fish were thrown and their final flights to their ice beds were videoed for the neighbors back in Wichita, had retreated to small cantinas perched on the outer edge of the market. There, they'd gather close around their lattes and cinnamon rolls to stare out at the rising sun that lit up the Seattle waterfront a hundred feet below.

All that were left were people living their lives.

Fish and produce bought, they visited a butcher next—then the baker across the street who promised fresh bread that evening. Each going about their own life.

Finally done, Angelo led him down the block and they wended their way between the vans and hurrying morning people. Later the slower tourists would reemerge and clog the market until it was faster to walk in the narrow street.

The funny thing was that among all these sellers and buyers and observers, he couldn't tell who was a mess and who had their life together. They all looked so certain and purposeful in their wandering roles. Russell was half tempted to take a poll.

Was the young woman setting up the ice-cream stand looking tired because of a long night of amazing sex or because her two-year old had a toothache? Did the family in the Greek restaurant that filled the corner of a narrow, brick building always start the day with coffee so strong that the airborne caffeine was enough to wake him up? Did the young Chinese couple know how odd their Mandarin sounded on American ears, pointing with long fingers at the end of outstretched arms to indicate each topic of interest and being a pedestrian hazard? What had drawn them here from whatever land they lived in, China, Taiwan, or San Francisco?

Angelo dragged him to a small cluster of tables along Post Alley not far from the restaurant. They were the only ones outdoors—the morning was still cool and fresh though the day would be warm. Tourists were perched at tables inside. Early-start businesspeople were streaming by in suits and skirts in a frantic pattern that they probably repeated every day, five days a week.

Some goddess, by the name of Jonas, set a double espresso, a huge cup of steaming, black coffee, and a gigantic muffin in front of him with a swish and a bat of the eyelids. He ignored the flirt and the muffin, scorched his mouth when he chugged the espresso, and felt much better for it.

"Okay."

"He's back, folks," Angelo announced to no one in particular. "The man is back. Consciousness has returned."

"Let's not get carried away."

"No, let's. After you go out of your way to insult a beautiful woman who had the hots for you last night and, by the way, chasing away her terribly cute girlfriend who'd been eyeing me, I say let's go wild."

Russell searched around in his brain. A vague memory of long, dark hair swam through, but he couldn't be sure who or what it was attached to. For some reason, his brain kept connecting it to a smack on the back of his head, but he couldn't imagine making a stranger angry enough that she'd do that. Though lately, maybe he could.

"So," Angelo sipped his café leche, "what is it with you and women now? They used to trail around behind you and melt into fluttery little puddles when you actually noticed one of them. Now, you're toxic."

His blood was toxic. It still hurt each time his heart tried to force some to circulate through his brain. He couldn't seem to get the hang of Seattle women.

"Mr. Morgan," Angelo held up his croissant like a micro-phone, "when did you decide to become a misogynist?" He aimed the pastry at Russell.

"Oh, I've always hated women. That's why they can make me feel like such a shmuck." Russell bit the end off the croissant. The act of chewing stung the side of his face right up into his temple. He sipped some coffee to soften it.

Angelo pulled his shortened breakfast back.

"Is that because you truly are a shmuck and they recognize

that?" He took a bite himself and continued around a mouthful. "Honestly, what is it with you lately, buddy?"

"I wish I knew, Angelo. I wish..." He'd been idly watching the world go by on the street at the end of the alley.

People were moseying down the hill on their way to the market. Or hurrying up the steep slope with briefcase in one hand and a triple-shot latte in white, carry-out cups of immense size clutched in the other.

—And there she was!

He'd know her anywhere!

A long red-brown ponytail slapping one side to the other. Tight Lycra that followed every curve of her runner's figure exactly as he'd imagined. Better.

She was glancing over her opposite shoulder, checking to cross the street. He saw nothing of her face, nothing but the swinging ponytail. An armband held a music player and thin wires trailed from arm to ears.

Two strides. Three. Then gone. Past the end of the alley.

He stared for a moment, trying to register her in this reality. She was his lighthouse lady and she was here in Seattle. No one else had hair quite like that. And her body: outdoorsy, athletic, and totally stunning.

"Hey!" Angelo grabbed for his coffee as Russell scrambled from the table and bolted to the end of the alley. He heard Angelo curse loudly but kept going.

No one. Not one sign of her.

He sprinted up the street, so steep they actually built lumps into the sidewalk for traction. He made it to First Avenue and nearly stumbled in front of a Metro bus.

Right. Left. Across the street.

Gone!

Gone as if she'd never existed.

He stood for ten minutes, watching and waiting. Just in case she magically reappeared. She didn't, of course.

Had he fallen for a ghost? Did she exist only in photographs of lighthouses and in Lycra among a crowd of suits?

The first he was aware of Angelo was a smack on the back of his head.

"You!" he turned. Of course. It hadn't been the long, dark, stranger lady he'd insulted last night; it was Angelo who had smacked him.

Angelo pointed at his khakis. A long coffee stain ran down one leg.

"What's wrong?" Russell offered his best smirk. "Pee your pants again? Thought you outgrew that in high school."

"WHAT IS IT WITH MEN?" Cassidy pulled the pin on the weight machine and shoved it back in ten pounds heavier. The weight machines were mostly vacant at the moment. That was one reason she and Jo worked out on Sunday mornings. Perrin, not a morning person at the best of times, wouldn't be awake for hours. The rowing machines were moderately busy, the spinning cycles were the hottest new craze and there was actually a line of men and women jogging in place waiting their turns.

Jo was huffing and puffing her way through her pecs workout. She did her raise-an-eyebrow thing to show she was listening.

"You'd never guess who's taken to standing outside my condo every morning about the time I get back from my run."

"Bradley, huff, Cooper, puff?"

Cassidy sat on the bench, hooked her ankle behind the padded bar and swung her leg forward. It was heavier, but she didn't feel any strain in the knee, just on every muscle around it. About right.

"Guess again. For real."

"The man, huff, with two first names, puff?"

Cassidy started kicking her leg out.

"I don't think that Jack James even noticed I broke up with him. Not a single phone calls or note since, nothing. No. It's Mr. date-from-hell, Mr. showing-up-at-my-lighthouse-thank-you-very-much, Russell the-jerk Morgan."

Jo let the arm pads slap back against the stops and the weights slammed home with a sharp clang. She leaned her head down between her knees for a moment to catch her breath.

"You must be kidding me?"

"I wish. He was just there one morning when I came running up the hill. Almost ran square into his back. He was like one of those children's crossing guards, manning the corner, checking everyone who went by."

"What did you do? And stop kicking that way. You are going to hurt yourself."

Cassidy dropped the kick bar back under the bench and then her knee started to complain. If she'd hurt herself because of Russell, she'd…she'd…she didn't know, but he'd regret it.

"I turned around faster than Picabo Street doing a gold medal slalom run in the winter Olympics and went in through the garage entrance."

"Maybe it was just a coincidence."

"Every day for a week?" Cassidy grabbed a towel and tossed it at Jo, the sweat was forming below her white Nike headband.

"What are you going to do? I could have a restraining order drawn up for you by nine a.m. tomorrow."

"But he hasn't done anything."

Jo threw the towel back at Cassidy's face.

"That doesn't mean he won't do so in the future." Jo was using her implacable lawyer voice.

Cassidy considered it. But it wasn't scary. It was just…weird. "It's not about me."

"Oh, and how does Detective Knowles know that? Can her fine nose now scent a man's true intentions?"

179

It wasn't like Jo. She didn't usually resort to sarcasm. Cassidy swung her leg over the bench so that she and Jo were sitting knee-to-knee on the machine's two benches.

"It was like when we were out at the lighthouse. He was looking for something. Someone. He was harmless. He just looked lost…and disappointed." By week's end, he had added sullen to that look.

"I still shiver when I think about the two of you being out there alone together."

Cassidy didn't. She remembered his smile as he knelt before her, stray bits of sand still stuck to his forehead. Holding his arm as they walked out to the point. The absolute safety and peace that had washed through her as his hands wrapped around hers the moment before he drove off like a maniac.

"No. I was fine. It was simply weird."

"Hi, Ms. Knowles."

She looked up the dark muscular legs, bright blue gym shorts and matching tank top, and finally the powerful shoulders before she found Angelo's face smiling down at her. A sheen of sweat covered his face and he dabbed at it with the ends of the towel hanging around his neck.

"You know better, it's Cassidy to you."

"Thank you, Cassidy. I didn't want to stop your conversation, but I haven't had a chance to say thanks for that wonderful review you gave me. Bookings are up." He laughed with a flash of white teeth. "That's an understatement. I was going to stop serving lunches, now I'm over half full. Dinners are booked out as often as not. It's wonderful."

"It was my pleasure, Angelo, every mouthful. And I think your success has to do with more than my review. I've seen your new ads, they're great." He'd taken the Tuscan Hearth concept and run it heavily in the tourist magazines. Several clips from her review had appeared in the most recent set.

"I got the best man on it. Russell is a-number-one."

"Russell, as in Russell Morgan?" Why didn't she know this about him? She'd spent a whole meal with the man and a couple hours more in his company out at Cape Flattery. He'd never mentioned a single word about his past, his family, or what he did for a living. That was odd—not a single word.

Angelo's smile froze into a cautious look, then a reluctant nod. Suddenly aware of the dangers of mentioning his name in her presence. He'd couldn't have missed the slash at Russell she'd put in the end of the review.

How could a man with so much skill hide it so damn well? A useless bum, who drove a very fancy sports car and was an advertising wizard.

There was something not right about him.

"He's not the most forthcoming person."

Angelo squinted his eyes for a moment. He opened his mouth to say something, then apparently thought better of it and closed it again.

She rested a hand on his arm. "He's your friend, I understand. Topic closed."

He took a deep breath and covered it with a gentle laugh that spoke volumes about the challenges of being Russell's friend.

That's when she caught Jo's expression. She widened her eyes and nodded ever so slightly toward Angelo.

"Oh, where is my head? Angelo Parrano," she turned to Jo. "I told you about his restaurant. Jo Thompson, best lawyer alive and best friend ever."

Angelo bowed low keeping his hands on either end of his towel.

"You two must come to the restaurant. I will promise more civilized company and as wonderful a meal. I will tr—"

Cassidy held up a hand to cut him off. "No. No treats. We'll bring a third and we'll have a merry time of it."

"Deal!" He stuck out his hand and she shook it. When Jo offered her hand, he bent over it with a bow. He'd have clicked his heels if he hadn't been wearing sneakers. "It shall be an honor. And don't worry about the reservations. Let me know when and there will always be a table for you."

He turned and sauntered toward the locker rooms, his shorts hanging interestingly from his hip bones. He wasn't as broad-shouldered as Russell, nor as tall, but was just as handsome in his own way. He pushed through the door and she turned to meet Jo's eyes.

"I think he likes you."

"No, you."

Cassidy shrugged, "He likes the review I wrote of his restaurant, but it wasn't my hand he bowed over. And he wasn't really looking at me when he promised a table would always be waiting."

Jo actually blushed. A most uncommon occurrence. "He was just being charming." Sliding back on the bench, she continued her pec workout with renewed vigor.

Cassidy cleared her throat significantly, but Jo didn't turn, though it looked as if more color rose in her cheeks. Cassidy hooked her other leg on the kick bar and began her reps. Maybe tomorrow she'd go ask Russell who he was waiting for.

RUSSELL SAT in the cockpit and watched the marina come awake as he ate breakfast. Perry had been first up. Stopped by the boat to give Nutcase a good morning scritch before heading off without a word—though the old man had been smiling at him like a crazy leprechaun. Whatever the joke was, he was keeping it to himself.

He spotted Dave and Betsy farther down the pier, sipping coffee in their own cockpit. They waved him over, but he was too lazily comfortable where he was so he casually waved back. The sun was reaching over the high bluff which made the west end of Ballard one of the best places to live in Seattle. The views from up there were incredible. But the lifestyle down here among the boats was the best.

The sun was splashing down on Shilshole Marina. Hundreds of masts etched their sharp lines against the sky, cutting it up into brilliant blue patches of heavenly steel. The constant companionship of the water's soft lapping against the various hulls lulled him like a cradle.

He crumbled up the last bit of bacon, sprinkled it over the remaining forkful of eggs; it was the first meal on his new stove and he needed to share it with the rest of the crew. At his whistle, Nutcase hustled over from the bow and began wolfing it down. No, that was canine origin. Began, um, saber-toothing it down? Nutcase. The ultimate fluffy, tangle-haired descendant of the saber-tooth tiger. That was a laugh.

Just like posting guard on that stupid street corner for a week. What had he been thinking? There were a million people in Seattle not counting transients, commuters, and tourists. And he was expecting to meet a specific unknown person on a specific street corner.

She hadn't been at the last lighthouse, so why would she be on the same street corner? She could have moved, given up, come at a different time, or gotten married. Or could she have been a mirage as Angelo kept insisting?

Was he now hallucinating the perfect woman? It halfway wouldn't surprise him—and with his rotten imagination she probably had a voice like a troll and would despise him on sight.

It was all so stupid. He couldn't get the lady of the lights out of his head any more than he could eradicate Cassidy Knowles.

Out at Cape Flattery it had been hard to keep his eyes off her. She looked like every sea captain's wife as she stood and scanned the horizon. Every incredibly beautiful sea captain's wife. Why did she have to be so stiff and stuck up?

For a while he'd worried that by some cosmic joke, she'd

been his lighthouse companion. But when they'd reached the parking lot, she drove a very unexpected BMW roadster, more high-end New York nonsense. It was also a car that had not been one of the three he'd photographed in the Slip Point lighthouse parking lot.

He couldn't find the Lady of the Lights and he couldn't not find Cassidy. This was really getting ridiculous.

Nutcase crawled onto his lap to clean herself. This was late May, that meant Perry had given him the kitten five months ago. Almost half a year together. Born Thanksgiving Day according to Perry. The day that had changed his life.

But was it for the better? That was the thing he couldn't be sure of.

He'd barely spoken to his parents since then. He could feel their shame even if they never said it. Every conversation was beyond awkward. He could just imagine the dinner parties. "We had such hopes for the boy." "We had no idea you could do so little with such an expensive education." "We did our best not to spoil him, but what are you going to do. He grew up with money."

He *had* grown up with money—and he'd earned every cent he spent since the day he'd graduated from college. He'd busted his ass every summer of college, too, to pay for his room and board the rest of the year. They'd paid tuition and books, but he hadn't let his parents pay for anything else any more than Angelo had.

He wasn't spoiled, he just wanted what he wanted.

And that was half Cassidy Knowles and half his Lady of the Lights.

Stupid pipe dream.

He settled lower on the bench and pulled his cap down over his eyes. Nutcase curled up on his stomach for a nap.

Maybe while he was sleeping, one woman would come out of his dreams into reality, and the other one would just go away.

HE WASN'T THERE the next morning, no longer stationed at her street corner. Seattle information didn't have a listing for Russell Morgan. Cassidy didn't want to talk to him on the phone anyway; she wasn't really sure that she wanted to talk to him at all. Definitely not enough to call Angelo for his phone number. It would be unfair to put him in the middle anyway.

There were a lot of Russell Morgans on Google, thirty-five thousand hits. There was an American painter, a 1930s jazz trombonist, a UK drum teacher, a millionaire's son on someone's most-eligible bachelors list, a Santa Barbara algebra teacher, and finally an advertising photographer. Russell Morgan Studios in New York—but the link was broken, the website gone. She tried the phone number and got a Chinese dry cleaners.

She did find some credits to a car ad. When she opened it up, there was Jo's car against a mottled steel background. It looked fast and sexy. It had the inevitable cool dashboard shots and it also had a single red rose across the seat—just like the rose he'd given her at Angelo's, now safely pressed in her favorite North Italian cookbook. Even if it was from a jerk, she couldn't stop herself from keeping it. It had been a long time since anyone had given her a rose.

He also had shots of watches, suits, her own boots on someone's exceptionally long legs. Maybe Melanie's. It took her awhile to notice the pattern: no faces. An Armani ad with a very sexy woman in a man's suit, with clearly nothing else on, but the hat was pulled low, the model looking down toward her hands ready to pull apart the lapels. All that showed was her neck and a hint of the cascading blonde hair behind.

Every ad was a gut punch. Each offered high emotional impact of sex, status, comfort, and class. He had an amazing eye, as acute in composition as Perrin's in fashion.

There it was.

Some connection had been working its way through her consciousness, reaching for the light, and it had finally made it to the surface.

She was dialing Angelo before she had a chance to second guess herself. He was surprised, but willing enough once she promised it wasn't to gut Russell and string him out on a line as fish bait. Whatever Angelo might imply, he was a staunch friend.

Russell's phone was at the third ring before she realized what door she was opening. She should hang up, but he answered before she could act. His deep-voiced hello was even mellower on the phone.

"Hi, Russell?"

"Cassidy? Didn't expect to hear from you."

She didn't either, but here she was. And he'd recognized her voice. That unnerved her so she spoke quickly before she could give up.

"I was wondering if you would meet with me. I have a business proposition for you."

"I'm not in business." His voice was gruff, even harsh.

"I saw Angelo's ads. They were... I saw your old ones, too. Armani, BMW, they were...are breathtaking." She was babbling. What had been such a simple thought a moment before was becoming muddled.

She shut up and tried looking at something that would relax her. Five lighthouse pictures, four with sailboats. She moved to the sliding glass door and out onto the deck. There wasn't a single blue-hulled sailboat in Seattle's harbor.

The silence was getting long. Too long.

"Hello, Russell. Are you still there?"

Another pause, long enough for her to look at the phone's screen, it said it was still connected.

"I'm here." It was quiet.

"Look, I don't know if you need the money, but I've got a friend whose business needs help."

"One of those college friends?"

"Yes. You remembered."

"I'm not an idiot." The words were abrupt, then he burst out with a laugh. "Okay, except around you."

"So, do you want to meet? Are you interested?"

Another of those pauses. She'd give a pretty penny to know what he was thinking.

"You know where the Chittendon Locks are?"

CASSIDY MANAGED to find a spot in the crowded parking lot, no sign of his little brown sports car. She took her time wandering through the gardens and over to the boat locks.

It was a busy day. A whole flock of boats were jostling for position above and below the locks. This was the connection from Lake Washington and all of its multimillion-dollar homes to the ocean, making it a very busy thoroughfare. There was also a large haven of steel commercial fishing boats from Fisherman's Wharf that added to the mayhem.

Boats jostled about waiting their turns to be raised or lowered from one to the other. Tourists wandered along the concrete walls on either side as the Army Corps of Engineers did their best to escort the boats through safely.

Cassidy leaned on one of the steel rails to watch.

An eighty-foot fishing boat dominated the group, but the fisherman made the easiest work of it. Little speed boats got in the way of sailboats. Sailboats bumped against the big cruisers. The big cruisers couldn't muster enough sober hands to catch and throw lines and they drifted about the lock as if bobbing in a giant bathtub.

"Idiots."

Russell leaned against the railing beside her. Even as he said it, one of the big cruisers turned completely sideways, scraping the bow along one concrete wall and the stern across the other and getting stuck that way. The lock attendants started swearing to themselves as they hurried over to help. The guys on the fishing boat, covered in clothes that had seen far more fish guts than laundry soap, were all lined up at their railing to watch the show. Not one of them lifted a finger.

"Shouldn't they be helping?"

"No. They know enough to keep out of the attendants' way. To let them do their job."

She inspected the man beside her. Dark jeans, practically new, a polo shirt that hugged his shape tucked in tightly at the waistband. Was it knowing that he was a New York professional that changed how he looked? She couldn't be sure.

"What?" He caught her inspection.

"You clean up nice."

His smile lit up and she felt a warmth that might have been a February frost just moments before.

"So Angelo keeps telling me."

"You two are close." Not a question. She knew it as fact. "One of those long-term, can-screw-up-and-still-get-help kind of friends. Those are few and far between."

"He's the best. Closer than blood."

"I've got a friend—"

"The lawyer or the clothes designer?"

He was right, he wasn't an idiot. She'd mentioned them once at their dinner nearly two months ago and he had that information right on tap.

"The lawyer doesn't need that kind of help, she's already at the top of her field."

He nodded and stared out at the boats. They'd gotten the front end tied off though the steel railing was pretty chewed up. Now they were trying to lever the stern free.

"Fashion. I know a bit about that."

"Perrin's really brilliant, but she has no direction. She won't accept help from her friends, but she might from you."

He shook his head.

"Why not?" Perrin really was struggling and she and Jo hadn't found a way to help her.

"How is it going to work?" He turned to face her and his dark eyes weren't distant or closed, but looking right at her from an arm's-length away. "I waltz in and announce that you sent me, that's sure not going to go over big. No bigger than you doing it yourself."

She hadn't really thought that part through.

"Perhaps you could 'waltz in' and, hell, I don't know. This is your specialty." She was at a loss. It had sounded good when she thought it up, but, he was right, there was no way for it to work.

"You trying to set me up with her?"

"No! I—" She wasn't. Hadn't even thought of that. But what about it? Russell and Perrin, she liked macho and he might be just the stable influence... But Cassidy didn't want to see them together. She didn't know why. Couldn't go there, not with him standing so close that she could smell the ocean and sky on him. So close she could move against that wonderful chest with just the smallest step forward.

"No." She shook her head to clear it. "No. I wasn't going there."

He kept looking at her for a long moment with an intensity that was almost scary. Maybe Jo was right and she wasn't wholly safe this close to him. But was that his doing or hers? She shook her head and he eased back without moving away.

"Okay," he slouched back against the rail. "As long as we have that clear. I assume you've told her all about me." There was a touch of chagrin in his voice.

He clearly had a very good idea of exactly what she'd said.

"So, she'll know my name. You'll need to introduce me, and I'll need to make her pay."

"But she—"

He held up a hand to stop her.

"It'll be something she can afford. Maybe even barter, though I don't have much need for women's clothes. You can pay my real fees."

Cassidy swallowed hard. She was well off, but how much was a New York professional worth? Especially one of Russell's caliber?

"I don't know if I can afford you either."

He shrugged easily, "I'm not sure what it will be, but money has little value to me. Deal?" He smiled for a moment, but didn't do the expected rake of his eyes down her body. So, sex wasn't the deal either. Something else. Something he wouldn't want to do. Certainly not judging a wine contest.

"I think I'd rather pay."

He stayed serious a moment longer then burst out laughing. So hard that she started to smile despite herself. He turned back to watch the boats still chuckling under his breath.

They'd finally straightened out the big cruiser, much the worse for the wear, and were filling in the lock with sailboats.

"You're a tough lady, it's hard to make you squirm. Don't even know why I enjoy doing that to you, but I seem to. Hell, your friend, I'd probably help her out just for the fun of it. But I just thought up something better."

"Better?" her voice cracked, her throat was so dry.

This time he did look her up and down. His grin was wicked.

"You're going to hate it."

NEW DUNGENESS LIGHTHOUSE

Dungeness Spit
First lit: 1857
Automated: 1994
48.18174 -123.10962

The New Dungeness Lighthouse was one of the first built in Puget Sound. It stands at the very end of a sand spit that sticks five miles out into the treacherous Straits of San Juan de Fuca.

Also known as Shipwreck Spit, the narrow bit of land had a history long before the arrival of the Europeans as a battleground between the various local tribes. Once established, the light often guided warring tribes to its base for their bloody battles. Though the lightkeepers were never harmed, they were often living in a lighthouse surrounded by corpses.

JUNE 1

*I*t was a five-mile walk out Dungeness Spit to the lighthouse. There wasn't much of a view, a chilly fog limited Cassidy's sightlines to a few hundred feet, but there was plenty to see.

Thousands of birds joined her for her walk along the nature sanctuary: gulls fishing close ashore, cormorants standing out on logs with the wings spread to dry, and grebes diving deep whenever she drew too close. Even a couple of seals followed her from just off the beach, looking like dogs paddling happily through the waves until the moment they dove in a sinuous roll.

Her favorite were the sandpipers racing up and down the beach following the leading edge of the lazy waves, occasionally pecking at the sand. She couldn't see what they caught, but they intently followed each wave down the long beach, then raced madly back to keep their feet dry. They always made her laugh.

The GPS showed her making steady progress toward the lighthouse despite being in the dense, unrevealing fog. An endless loop of land rolled through the bubble of visibility around her. She moved her feet, but it felt as if she and the fog never moved. The land slid into her fog bubble from some unknowable place ahead and disappeared behind taking its wildlife with it. Her hair was soaked by the cool moisture, she'd let it down to keep her neck warm. If not for the parka and the red watch cap she'd be freezing despite the calendar insisting it was June.

The GPS claimed the lighthouse was only two hundred and fifty-four feet away when the fog ended like a curtain. The sunlight glittered off the white lighthouse so that it shone incandescent against the blue sky. The little outbuildings were clustered about its base including an oversized Cape Cod cottage in the now-predictable U.S. Coast Guard paint job of white with a red roof. The actual lighthouse jumped out of the cottage's midsection like a giant spear shot down from the heavens. The seagulls, who had stayed low and flew little in the fog, were soaring about the sunlit sky.

The old Indian battleground was now a pleasant park surrounded on all sides by the ocean and populated by thousands of birds. A bald eagle swooped low out of the fog, pulled up sharply, and cried in surprise at finding a human in its hunting ground. It passed barely a dozen feet away as she ducked—she'd forgotten how huge they were up close.

Cassidy checked quickly before the fog moved in, no sailboat. At least not yet. She had a feeling it would be back this month, not that she could possibly know. Whether it showed up or not, she was going to enjoy the day.

The volunteer keepers at the lighthouse were thrilled to have a guest, the fog had kept away the usual June crowds. But she'd had a date to keep with her father and, like him, possessed a bit more stubbornness than common sense.

They showed her both upstairs and down of the lighthouse and the cozy buildings. The Coast Guard had stopped staffing it in 1994. A local group had taken over management of the buildings and rented it out to people willing to spend a week at the far end of a five-mile spit of land. It sounded like heaven to her: a stack of books, a few interesting wines, and no city craziness. She could go for runs on the beach. She promised to keep it in mind. Maybe in the winter months when few would venture out here and she'd truly have it to herself.

She turned down the keepers' invitation to join them for lunch. It was awkward, but she'd wanted a little picnic by herself at one of the scattered picnic tables. She set up a meal of a small container of Asian noodle salad, half a roast beef sandwich smeared with fat-free mayonnaise and just a touch of Dijon mustard, a small bottle of Pellegrino Limonata, and a humungous chocolate chip cookie. Perfect.

The air was still cool, especially now that she'd stopped moving and the ocean lay only a few hundred feet away all around her. She kept her parka on, though unzipped, as she ate. Several large ships moved along the Straits, slipping quickly and silently along the sparkling water.

As she nibbled on the last of the cookie, she pulled out her father's letter and spread it before her.

Dearest Ice Sweet,

I'm sure now that I will never walk to any lighthouses with you. I probably won't live to hear your adventure to the first one. For that, I am truly sorry.

Regret is a funny thing. I'm lying here dying and I regret having so few years with your mother. I regret how little you knew her or her parents, truly kind people who welcomed me in when I had nothing. Yet I do not regret selling my vineyard to Mondavi.

Cassidy closed her eyes. Pretty much the most respected vintner of the Napa and Sonoma valleys. She'd walked their vineyards on the wine tours. Admired the rolling hills and drunk in the dry smell of grass and oak. The earth there was so rich and built-in layers so deep that even the oldest and hardiest of vines could not plumb their depths.

She'd been allowed to walk more of their fields than the

average tourist because of her background. She'd even spent a long leisurely afternoon with their horticulturist.

Oh God. She gazed out at the water but instead saw the rolling Napa hills. She might have walked across her father's own soil, strolled where he had poured so much blood and sweat and dreams—and never known.

My future lay in the rugged soils of the Kitsap Peninsula, tending vines that grew so slowly and a daughter who grew so fast. I missed my chance with the wine, which I don't regret. I am thankful for every day that I didn't miss with my daughter. Adrianne taught me what was important, and watching you launch yourself against the world was definitely the best part of that.

I loved you then, Ice Sweet, the best I knew how. So, don't waste your time on regrets, for I take too many to my grave.

Love you,

Vic

She lay her head down on her arms and tried to picture Victor Knowles. Not as the dying man with tubes running into his body and his eyes blurry with morphine. Nor as the bent man, old before his time with arduous work.

The father she remembered most clearly was sitting in his armchair, a book in his hand and his half-glasses sliding bit by bit toward the end of his nose, only to be pushed back at the last second before escape. A cup of tea, long since cold with forget-fulness, waiting on the small table at his elbow.

She tried to picture Vic Knowles as the young-old man he'd once been. Young, new to his Napa vineyard, but old from Vietnam. Standing where he belonged among the California hills while filled with the hopes of a new season wrapped up in the vines. The first of June thirty years ago. Then the grapes would be small, tight, and dusty green—an entire cluster would fit easily in his cupped palm. His nerves, shattered from war would now be soothed by the new growth reaching down into the deep earth and seeking upward into the sky.

To lose all that was impossible.

She could hear in his letter the regret that he claimed not to have. It had been one of the greatest losses in his life. Last month he had described the heart-wrenching decision to stay with his failing vines or go and follow his wife to a land of failing soil. It would have been so easy for him to be angry at his wife for forcing the choice upon him. Just as easy as it would be for Cassidy to be angry at herself for bringing hardship to her mother and to the poor man who had given up so much.

But he had chosen a different path.

Cassidy looked at the lighthouse built on the old Indian battleground. The temporary keepers had told her of one particularly horrid slaughter where one tribe had slain every member of another. A single pregnant woman had crawled to the keeper's residence riddled with twenty stab wounds. They had saved her from the return of the marauding band—a choice that had nearly made them the next target.

What had she herself sacrificed?

What had Russell said? She thought back to their one date for the hundredth time.

Always the critic. Always a step back. A step away. You know all of these wines, but do you really know the true heart of any of them?

The words were burned into her memory and that couldn't have happened if there wasn't some truth there. Her father had known every square foot of his land, even how the light lay upon it at every time of day. He had cherished each vine as if it they were Cassidy's brothers and sisters—a part of the family.

Russell had been right. Damn him! She didn't know the true heart of any one wine. Never mind a whole vineyard.

She raised her head to prop her chin on her forearms and opened her eyes.

And there it was.

Her sailboat!

Sliding up from Puget Sound, her burgundy sails looking

like a cutout of magnificent triangles against the crystalline waters and the far-off Canadian shore.

Letter shoved into pocket, lunch trash crammed into her daypack—Cassidy sprinted to the far side of the lighthouse, near the fog's edge, to get the boat and lighthouse in the same picture. It took forever to emerge from the other side. She was about to go back, see if she was mistaken, when the boat slid clear of the lighthouse just a few hundred yards out.

A couple of quick shots, then she exchanged the camera for the binoculars she'd purchased for just for this moment. "Compact," "high-power," "light-weight," and "weather-resistant" had combined properly at the REI counter. She quickly slid them free and focused on the sailboat.

The boat's bow slipped through the low waves as if they were clouds and air, sliding along as if it were a special effect. It was unreal how smoothly it moved and how tidy it looked.

The rich blue of the hull, the dark red of the sails, and the cheerful yellow-and-white of the decking and cabin were truly picture perfect. She tracked the view toward the back until she saw the skipper.

One man. Bent down and pulling on a line. Then he stood and faced the shore.

She dropped the binoculars. Only the salesman's insistence that she put the strap over her head every time saved them from the rocks and sand beneath her feet.

Russell Morgan.

He hadn't mentioned he was a sailor. He certainly hadn't mentioned he went to lighthouses regularly.

But where had he been last month at Cape Flattery?

Duh! Beside her. On foot rather than under sail.

And he'd been looking for someone, someone he wouldn't admit to.

She grabbed the binoculars again.

He was reaching down for something. His hand came back

into view holding a camera with a long lens, a massive telephoto.

He hadn't seen her yet.

Cassidy didn't think.

She turned and sprinted for the fog with the binoculars clutched in her fist. A wave of birds rose before her in a flurry.

The fog was like a cool slap on her burning cheeks. She didn't stop, but kept up the pace for nearly a mile until the pounding of the pack against her back and the desperate pant of her breathing ground her to a halt.

She dropped onto the sandy beach, shedding the pack and the parka because she was burning up and covered in sweat despite the chill air. She flopped back on the coat and lay like one dead while her breath and her heart pounded.

Cape Flattery. He could have sailed there as easily as he had to the New Dungeness lighthouse.

But he'd come ashore.

Which meant he'd come ashore looking for someone he'd only seen through his camera lens. And he'd been disappointed when he'd found...*her,* almost as disappointed as she'd been to be chased by *him.*

Hey, you in the red coat!

That's what he'd yelled. He'd seen a woman in a red coat. She looked down at the coat she sat on, a woman in a red parka.

But Cape Flattery had been too warm. She'd worn...her red leather coat. And he'd thought that she was...herself.

Her cheeks warmed abruptly.

She'd lied about not being...herself.

This was beyond weird. Jo was going to laugh her ass off.

And maybe that finally explained his week-long vigil outside of her apartment. He must have seen her going by in her red parka and was looking for her. Looking for her, but thoroughly convinced that whoever he was looking for wasn't the evil, snooty Cassidy Knowles.

A smile started tugging at one corner of her mouth. She fought it back, but the other side soon joined in.

Oh brother, was Mr. Russell Morgan ever in for a shock.

And she couldn't wait to be the one to give it to him.

HAD HE SEEN HER, or not?

For a moment she'd been a spot of red just the other side of the lighthouse.

He'd tied off the jib sheet as quickly as he could and grabbed for his camera. But by the time he had the tiller trapped between his knees and the camera aimed, the red coat was disappearing into the fog bank.

He had snapped an image, but it was inconclusive—no more than a fading blur in the fog.

There one moment and then gone the next.

Twenty minutes. It took twenty minutes to anchor safely behind the spit of land, dowse the sails, lower his dinghy over the side, and get ashore.

He was the only one there. There was no one at the picnic tables and no one wandering around the narrow end of Dungeness Spit.

An elderly man and his wife came out of the house at the base of the lighthouse. For lack of any better options, he wandered over to them doing his best to look casual. But no matter how many times he checked over his shoulder, there was no Lady of the Lights.

"Welcome to New Dungeness lighthouse, young man."

"Hi," he shook their hands. "Did you see a woman in a red coat? A long, red coat?"

They both took a step back. Good one, Russell.

"She's a...friend. A friend I was hoping to meet here."

The man was about to say something when his wife cut him off. "What is your friend's name?"

Shit!

"I don't know that."

The man's face closed and they both backed away a bit farther.

"Has there been..." They weren't going to answer that. "I'm..." Crap!

They must think he was insane. Dead right!

The man pulled his wife closer and squared his aging shoulders, ready to leap to his wife's defense.

Russell spread his hands to show they were empty.

"I'm really not a nut." The old man wasn't buying it. "There's this lady. She keeps showing up at lighthouses."

By the time he was done with his story, they invited him into the cottage. Betty served him tea from a porcelain teapot decorated with sailboats and sat him down in the decent but utilitarian couch in the whitewashed living room. Barney was retired Navy and they'd been high school sweethearts and still looked to be.

Over a plate of oatmeal cookies, they admitted that a young woman had been there and indeed had worn a long, red coat.

"Quite pretty," had earned Barney a loving scowl from his wife. "Very friendly, though I don't think she gave us her name."

Betty stared down into her tea for a long moment. "She did. But I didn't hear it clearly. It was unusual and she was soft-spoken. Didn't seem polite to ask again."

"Perhaps she signed the guest register." Barney led him over to the leather-bound book laid open on the sloped table just inside the front door. The last entry was three days earlier, Betty and Barney's arrival.

"I'm sorry we're of so little help."

Russell bit his tongue against any sharp reply. "At least now I know she's real. I was starting to doubt that as well."

"But she showed up in your photographs."

He nodded his head. He knew the photos didn't lie, but he'd spent his whole career making them do just that. Some part of him would never trust images, especially not digital ones.

At least his Lady of the Lights was real. Angelo might insist that he was nuts…

But she was real.

PHILLIPE, a darkly handsome Latino who apparently had no last name, met Cassidy at the San Francisco airport in a wine-red Miata with the top down. In moments, they were leaving the city behind and zipping up toward the Sonoma Valley. She had tucked Mondavi's two books as well as the coffee table book about Mondavi by Katz into her carry-on and devoured them on the way down. She'd also brought along Fassbender's definitive book on Cabernet Sauvignons, but her German was quite rusty and it was heavy going.

Mondavi might not be the most expensive in the valley—too many little boutique vineyards existed that made a profession of being outrageously priced—but they were far and away the biggest high-quality vintner. Wines of high quality that sold at affordable prices.

She'd called to find out where her father's old vineyard lay. Once they realized who she was, she'd been quickly passed to one of the assistant vintners who'd promised to give her the personal tour. Now, here she was cruising up the length of the Sonoma Valley in a sports car and chatting about the finest details of their vintnering process.

"We're really excited this year. Of course, there was that late cold snap, thirty-four degrees, which scared the daylights out of us. It came in right after the set. But then it warmed up at just the perfect pace. And Daryl, you'll meet her later, she's a magician. She knows what the roots are doing better than the vines do. What she does with water and fertilizers is staggering. She's been fooling with some of the organics and they're really playing out. It's only May, so the grapes are still tiny, but we haven't seen better since the '92 set. Boy, was that a year. As I'm sure you know. First year I worked the fields, I was a cutter then. Worked my way up."

He must have started in the fields when he was ten. Maybe he had, after school, weekends, and summers.

She saw signs for the vineyard off to the left, but he kept driving. At her look he offered her a low shout over the wind noise.

"Thought you might want to see the land first."

All she could do was nod; her throat wasn't trustworthy at the moment. A few minutes later he turned right and roared up into the hills. They left behind the busy valley floor; slipped away from the clusters of boutique towns. The masses of tourists didn't venture up here; they were all too busy traveling the valley hunting for that perfect case of prestigious wine to slumber in their basement so they felt like real wine connoisseurs.

The hills were covered in vines and orchards. Apple trees were used as wind breaks, sun breaks, and bee attractors for pollination—the tiny cubes of honeybee hives dotted the fields. Every now and then a mansion of obscene proportions thrust its head above the vines, but it was the vines that formed the texture of the hills.

Carefully tended hillsides lay awash with verdant green and soil so black it looked painted. Not a stray weed was allowed to take any nourishment away from the all-important grape. Here each plant was nurtured individually, each vine coaxed to its greatest potential.

"You picked the perfect time to come." He whipped the car onto a narrow gravel road and sped north with no concern for his undercarriage. "We're just starting the drop on that field."

"I've never seen a big one." As a girl, she'd helped her dad with "the drop." They went vine by vine, cutting off all but the finest of the bunches so that the plant would pump more juice and flavor into the remaining grapes. At the same time, they trimmed back most of the leaves to let the sun soak into the remaining bunches. But in the Northwest, vines grew slowly and weren't treated with the harshness of the California vines.

Another turn and he skidded to a gravel-spewing halt by a closed gate and leapt from the car. He moved like he drove—fast and with a nervous energy vibrating over his body like a new vine in a chilly wind.

He led her through the gate and over the first rise. There he stopped and waved his hand before him.

"I looked it up in the records. Your father's property was bounded by those two fence lines there and that row of pear trees. Twenty-nine point three acres. Four point nine seven tons per acre last year. Total yield last year was a hundred and forty-three tons. All Cab-Sauv. When I started, there was still a five-acre section of Merlot on it from the original owner, but that was finally pulled in '02. You can see the lighter stance of the new vines."

Suddenly he colored.

"Sorry, your dad had a Merlot grape planted that just didn't grow very well here. We nursed it, played with it, and phased it out. We've had great luck with the Cab-Sauv on this slope and finally converted the whole field."

He looked as if he wished to erase those last sentences and finally moved away to check the vines and the workers proceeding methodically down the rows doing the drop.

Cassidy moved slowly forward among the vines. The view across the valley revealed a massive patchwork of fields. Some fields stretched long and narrow, others square, and everywhere rows of vines traced the topography like a map—every rise and dip revealed. This field, this one small field, a quarter-mile square, was barely an afterthought in the valley's total production.

The air was thick with the smell of sap. The drop. The rows between the vines were covered in great mats of green grapes and leaves spread across the dark soil. Tons of grapes, literally. Thousands and thousands of bunches lay scattered to rot and return to the soil. The grapes that remained, they were the ones that held this year's hope. This small bunch kept and not the next—which now lay beneath her feet. On the survivors were banked the fortunes of the vineyard.

She stepped out on the soil her mother and father had labored to preserve and expand, had nearly buried their hearts and souls to save. She stood now at the core of their greatest failure.

Cassidy knelt and gathered a handful of the mud-dark earth. The vine's roots could go down thirty feet and still not hit rock. Fertile soil piled so thickly that it might as well go down forever. So different from the Pacific Northwest. Bainbridge Island had offered her father two to three feet of rocky soil to plant his roots before hardpan or rock ledge blocked the way.

Every inch of that ground had been painstakingly cleared and set by hand. Here, nascent weeds were scalped back into the soil by the most modern machinery, not a balky old rototiller that she'd never once successfully started on her own. There they battled blackberries that towered above her head after a mere week's inattention. Nothing here but the soil and the grapes.

She'd had Mondavi Merlots several times before they replanted this field in 2002. She'd drunk her family's wine without knowing, or at least a blend of it.

No matter what Mondavi had done to this soil, her father's tears were still here.

TRUE TO HIS WORD, Angelo promised them a table for three at eight o'clock on just a few hours notice. At six they hit the Virginia Inn for a couple of drinks in the cozy bar. By seven, they'd decided to go raid Perrin's store for dinner attire.

Perrin was into a sixties mode. Her hair streaked, part flapper platinum blonde, but with darker lines of oak that made her the very authentic sun-bleached gal. No sign at all of the brilliant green. Two months seemed to be the longest she could tolerate a hair color.

She flaunted a generous tie-dye skirt, that showed every bit of difference from the classic, dyed-in-Kool-Aid versus professionally done with the best of dyes on the fine-weave of quality cotton. Her peasant blouse was loose, airy, and kept slipping off one shoulder. The outfit invited you to imagine the slender, vibrant woman within.

Jo refused Perrin's insistence that she go without a bra. Instead, she selected a bright red dress that might have been worn by a flamenco dancer. Her shoulders and dark skin revealed by thin straps, and her legs by the knee-length pleated skirt and a minor bell of red petticoats. Hot was the key word to describe the result.

They fussed over Cassidy until she finally agreed to wear the slinkiest of blue dresses—one shoulder bare and her hair up. She'd had just enough to drink that she agreed to go without when Perrin couldn't find a strapless in her size. The perfect tailoring of the top was all that kept her from being indecent. The long skirt had a slit up to mid-thigh that she would do her best to keep closed. The high heels were ridiculous, but her legs did look great in the mirror.

She wore a gold chain with a tiny sailboat dangling at the end—that she'd spotted in a San Francisco airport shop while waiting for her flight home. She hadn't explained it to her friends yet.

Perrin put one of those leather friendship bracelets around each of their wrists. Jo decided to go without further adornment which was exactly right—her long, black hair pushed back over her shoulders was decoration enough.

Perrin had reached for the perfumes, but she and Jo declined. Perrin went for just a touch of lavender, behind one ear only.

Cassidy spotted a poster on Perrin's wall that had a familiar feel. She went up closer to inspect it. Russell's work; it had to be. "Perrin's Glorious Garb –the home of stand-out style." Perrin in her flapper outfit, sitting on a couch that looked homey and made for two like an invitation.

"He's great, Cassie. I can't believe you found him. Or that he's so reasonable. You're the best."

Jo inspected the poster, raised one eyebrow at Cassidy, and didn't say a thing. Well, the smokescreen was aimed at Perrin; she shouldn't have expected it to fool Jo for long.

How had the time gone by so fast? She'd meant to call him the day she'd gotten home from Dungeness Spit lighthouse, but researching the vineyard had gotten in the way. That was part of tonight's celebration—actually walking her father's land.

She'd call Russell tomorrow or the next day, once she caught up on her columns.

By the time they reached Angelo's they were in a very merry mood and men were stopping on the street to watch them walk by arm in arm. Sixties chic, flamenco red, and slinky blue sapphire. Even Jo was laughing and whispering about the one who walked squarely into a newspaper box as they went by.

The sun was near setting when they arrived. Long streaks of gold slid up the street between the buildings and a soft breeze slipped up from the Sound. They might regret not having wraps by the time they were done, but for the moment it was too warm to consider them.

Angelo came out of the kitchen personally to seat them. His exclamations over their attire made them giggle, at least she and Perrin. Jo simply blushed crimson and slipped quickly into an inside chair against a wall. Cassidy sat beside her and Perrin took the other side of the table.

"Josh Harper is coming tonight as well."

"Oh, you must seat him with us, Angelo. Set another place." Cassidy turned to her friends. "He's this great guy from *Gourmet Week*. A good friend; we started at about the same time in New York."

When he arrived, Angelo led him over.

"Way cute," Perrin whispered to her.

"Married," she whispered back. "Happily," she added before turning to welcome him. He kissed both her cheeks and smiled all around the table at introductions.

"Angelo. For seating me with three such impossibly lovely ladies, I will promise you gold, dancing women, and great reviews. Whatever you need." They shook hands in a very manly-looking clasp. He took the seat by Perrin just as the bruschetta arrived: fresh mozzarella cheese, perfect little squares of roasted red pepper, and a sprinkling of minced fresh basil on tiny slices of toast smeared with olive oil and rubbed with garlic.

"So, Josh. Cassidy says you're happily married." He nodded as he bit into one of the appetizers. She smiled in her most dangerous and charming way.

She leaned her bare shoulder against his.

"How do you feel about polygamy?"

He practically passed the cheese through his nose.

"As always, Angelo," Cassidy raised her tiny cup of decaf espresso.

He doffed his hat and sipped from his own cup, most certainly the leaded variety. "Yes, I make a mean espresso."

They all laughed knowing she'd meant the meal and that he'd known it as well. The restaurant had quieted and slowly emptied as the hours slid by. Now they were the last table that hadn't been cleaned and prepped for the next day. Of course they also had been the noisiest table the whole night.

Perrin's latest exploits and Cassidy's behind-the-label tales of the Mondavi system had kept the conversation lively—egged on my Jo's wry interjections. Cassidy hadn't yet told them about Russell, not with Josh sitting there and especially not now with Angelo joining them. It would be unfair for him to know before Russell did.

The food and wine had flowed almost as lavishly as the laughter. Perrin had flirted wildly with Josh as well as their waitress—a comely Italian girl who sassed her right back—and Angelo every time he came near. Angelo had flirted with Perrin and taken the opportunity to spread his charm to her and Jo.

Especially to Jo, though she claimed not to notice, or be interested in a scruffy Italian. But the more wine Jo drank, the deeper her blush became each time Angelo served them personally.

Now only espresso, tiny wedges of an exquisite, richly chocolate-and-hazelnut *pan forte*, and crumpled napkins remained of the meal. Cassidy could feel the electric current passing from Jo on her left to where Angelo had joined them on her right seated at the end of the table. Everyone was talking to everyone, except the two of them. Perhaps she should take Jo to the bathroom and insist that they switch places when they returned. It was the best plan she—

"Hey Angelo, where are you?" Russell Morgan burst through the kitchen doors, his voice overloud in the empty restaurant. "There you..." He stumbled to a halt as his eyes met hers. He looked ready to beat a hasty retreat even as his eyes slid from her face to inspect her bare shoulders and form-fitting dress.

She couldn't help smiling at him. The man seeking the lady in the red parka. Her. Knowing nothing about her except she wore a red coat and went to lighthouses and that was enough to make him desperate to find her. Her: the lovely princess in the tower. He: Prince Charming, who hadn't a clue how he despised his Princess in real life. Perhaps Prince Uncharming, but Cassidy realized that she liked that honest forthrightness of his more and more with time.

His eyes returned to her face as he moved slowly forward. Once again he was as she'd first met him: jeans covered with streaks of dirt and paint, both knees long gone. A blue T-shirt that showed every muscle from belt to shoulder was torn high on one arm. Even his arms had splotches of blue paint on them —the shade of which she now knew the source. He matched his hull perfectly. His hair was a tumble with flecks of sawdust—if it had been combed, it was with his fingers. Her fingers itched to do the same.

"Won't you join us, Mr. Morgan?"

It was a good thing that Angelo had his back to Russell, because his face was definitely laughing at the refined invitation for his scruffy friend.

"Oh, Mr. Morgan. You have to join us." Perrin leaned right into Josh's lap as she reached out a hand toward him. "I love that poster you made. It so captures what I want to do. I've already had three customers who came in just because they saw it."

"Um, you're welcome."

Angelo glanced in Cassidy's direction and started to scoot his chair her way so he'd be between them. She shook her head infinitesimally and Angelo scooted closer to Josh though he did arch his eyebrows in her direction. She wasn't going to say anything—no way, no how. But she didn't want Angelo between them. She was just drunk enough to feel brave.

"Are these your clothes as well?" He nodded toward Jo and Cassidy keeping his attention on Perrin. He grabbed a chair from another table.

When Perrin nodded, he smiled a bit. He still hadn't looked in her direction after his initial inspection and she was starting to feel a bit peaked about it.

"I'd like to get a series of shots with the three of you."

"Us?" Cassidy managed to choke out.

Jo was shaking her head.

"Yes."

There was no way she was getting in front of Mr. Testosterone's camera.

Russell spun the chair backwards and straddled it, his exposed knee ending up so close to her thigh she could feel the heat through her thin dress. She glanced down. The slit of her skirt had opened wide exposing her horribly. She pulled it closed before Russell noticed. Though he couldn't have missed it on his arrival, but she held it closed anyway.

"You are three classic, beautiful archetypes. And there is a synergy between you that would work well on camera. You also have the benefit of being free models, at least I assume so. Budget is important in this case." He finally looked at Cassidy. She was well aware they hadn't worked out a payment yet, but he didn't have to rub it in.

Russell leaned in close and whispered for her ears alone, "Told you that you'd hate the price."

He was right; she did. And she was well and truly trapped. She'd definitely rather pay the money.

Perrin was so excited by the prospect that she won Jo over with only a minimum of arm-twisting from Cassidy.

Russell was in a thoroughly cheerful mood about having trapped her, albeit for a worthy cause. He knocked down a large gulp from a beer bottle still covered in beads of condensation. He must have liberated it on his way through the kitchen.

His motion sent a waft of his smell her direction. Beneath the bright tang of teak wood shavings and the bite of paint, there was a raw scent like the musk of the finest red—whole, complete in itself, strong without being overwhelming.

She opened her eyes and he was inspecting her closely. She didn't remember closing them as she'd reveled in his scent. Reveled? She'd have to be careful. Russell Morgan was trouble and she really didn't need the complication.

His eyes were so close. Blue-grey eyes. Ones that would be amazingly easy to get lost in.

She scrambled around in her brain for some way to break his intent study of her face. For a way to change what was occurring in her own mind.

"Um, been to any lighthouses lately, Mr. Morgan?"

Perrin's laugh climbed quickly up the scale toward a giggle, but a quick glance across the table revealed that the others were still discussing the modeling photo shoot.

"Yes, actually," he studied his beer and picked at the corner of the label. "I sailed to one just a couple of weeks ago."

"Which one?" As if she didn't know.

"New Dungeness lighthouse up in the Straits," his tone said that he had no hint that she'd been there.

"Did you find whoever you were looking for at Cape Flattery?"

He startled and his attention snapped from his beer to her face, his eyes wide like a deer in the headlights.

"You were obviously looking for someone at the cape."

He turned back to his label, though he didn't pick at it anymore.

"I, uh... No, I didn't."

Angelo leaned over. "He's been chasing a phantom for six months now."

"Three. I didn't see her in the photos at first. And she's not a phantom."

Angelo shrugged his doubts.

Cassidy took another sip of her espresso. This was simply delicious. He'd taken photos of every lighthouse and she'd been in every photo. Had he taken one of her at Cape Flattery? She couldn't remember, but she hoped so. That way his collection would be complete, even if he didn't know it...yet. She'd replaced her own shot of the lighthouse to include one with him in it. But she hadn't yet figured out how to tell him that he was sitting next to his phantom.

"I believe in phantoms." She'd been chasing one for the last six months as well. The phantom of who her father had really been. The man she'd known and loved but was turning into a stranger in the course of a dozen short notes.

"Oh no," Russell held up a hand as if to fend her off. It was callused with hard work, but didn't look heavy despite its size. "No discussions of ghosts and visitations. I've been with so many woman who were into—"

Angelo elbowed him in the ribs. He glared at Angelo, then his eyes widened and he clamped his mouth shut.

"And how many women have you been with, Mr. Morgan?" She hadn't quite meant to drop her question into the lull in conversation, but suddenly she had everyone's attention. Or rather Russell did.

He glared first at her, then at his beer.

She could feel the heat on her own cheeks. She hadn't meant to trap him or back him into a corner.

The conversation at the rest of the table slowly drifted back to life as he stubbornly refused to look up.

She rested a hand on his forearm. She was transported back to the moment she'd taken his arm at Cape Flattery. The strength and warmth were intense against her palm. Her body was reacting in ways that made her feel flush even where the dress did cover her decently.

"I'm sorry," she kept her voice soft so that no others would hear. She squeezed his arm and was about to remove it when he covered it with his other—cool from the beer bottle but warm from the inside.

His gaze met hers and there was a tinge of sadness in how his eyes closed part way.

"We were clearly never meant to have a conversation together. We're like two porcupines with all of our bristles up and all defenses to the fore."

This was a totally different man. This wasn't the abrupt and rude Mr. Russell Morgan. This wasn't the brash sailor she'd expected, nor the cool professional. Suddenly, the man she'd glimpsed in scattered moments at dinner and at the lighthouse kneeling in the sand was seated beside her and holding her hand. It took her breath away and made the pounding of her heart the only sound she could make.

"To answer your question: too many and never the right one."

Question? What question? Her mind had definitely gone else-where. "How many women?" That was it. "Too many and never the right one." What a fantastic answer. She could feel herself melting.

He patted her hand like an old friend and withdrew his arm from her grasp.

"Sorry, stupid thing to say. I meant nothing about you. I meant…"

Russell jerked to his feet like a puppet on strings.

"Sorry to be a damper on your party." He bowed to her, "Ms. Knowles." And he was gone before she could react. Before she could protest.

Jo poked her sharply in the ribs which broke the spell that had bound her in place. She startled to her feet and trotted out through the kitchen as fast as her high heels would let her. The staff was all gone. She pushed open the back door and stepped out onto the street.

A few spaces down the block, a car roared to life with a throaty rumble—his car from the Cape Flattery parking lot. She raised an arm to stop him as he dropped it into gear, but he was faced away from her and roared off into the night.

The chill air sent a shiver over her bare leg and shoulder, and up her spine.

"I didn't take it that way."

RUSSELL STARED at the phone number Angelo had given him. He must be insane. Or really, really, really desperate.

"Yea, that describes it pretty damn well, doesn't it?"

Nutcase sat on the settee table and watched him pace the length of the boat and back.

He reached out to scratch the cat's head. She shied away in time to avoid being whacked by the phone he'd forgotten he was holding.

"Well, there are two choices. I can either agonize over this for another half hour and then it will be too late to decently call, in which case I'll be truly screwed. Or I can stop being such a wimp and dial the damn phone."

Nutcase carefully licked a paw and scraped it across the fur between her ears.

"You're no help at all, are you?"

She licked the other paw and went after a spot beside her nose. Cats had it so easy; all they needed was a sucker like him. He could use a little easy right now.

Well, there was nothing for it.

He punched in the number. When it hit the third ring, he

began to hope for voicemail, though he had no idea what he'd say to a machine. He'd think of something. Fourth ring.

"Hi, this is Cassidy." Even as a recording her voice was warm, friendly.

"Hi, this is Russell. Russell Morgan. You may recall the rather unpleasant chap from Angelo's. Could you give me a call at—"

"Don't you want to speak to me in person."

"You... Crap! I thought you were a recording."

"Well, that's a new line."

He sat down on the pilot's berth. Then lay down and put his feet up on the companionway ladder.

"Wasn't meant to be." Could he sound any stupider if he tried? "A line I mean." Indeed, apparently he could. Stupider by the second. "Why did you even answer the phone?"

"You mean other than the fact that I had no idea who was calling?"

"Yes, other than that."

"Because I like you."

"You've got to be kidding me." Great. Now his hearing was failing him.

"Well, you do have a certain knack for uncharming and also jumping to conclusions. And your ability to ask me the question I didn't even know I was avoiding doesn't help matters."

She stopped. In the silence he could imagine her, sitting in some high-rise condo, all perfectly manicured. Terry cloth bathrobe and hair done up in a towering twist of towel. If she had a cat, it would certainly never be a constant mess like Nutcase. Probably an elegant Siamese with a meow that could shatter glass.

Her voice was soft when she resumed, "Remember what you said about porcupines."

"Yeah."

"Well, I apologize. I too become all bristly when I'm talking to you and I don't know why."

"I do."

"You do?"

Russell slapped his hand against his forehead, "No, I mean that I know why I do around you."

"Willing to share?"

"Not really," which sounded awful. "What the hell. This conversation is already nothing like I'd imagined anyway. You remind me too much of my past and not enough of my future."

"Is your past so vile and your future so clear?"

Nutcase clambered up onto his chest and he mussed her hair with his free hand. The silly thing purred madly.

"No. And..." Well, he had to be honest here, though for the life of him he didn't know why. "Not as much as I'd like. It's more that you are right out of my New York past."

"There's a lot you don't know about me." It was a tease—though he couldn't easily imagine Cassidy Knowles teasing. He'd flirted with hundreds of women, every model who came through the studio and every waitress who'd ever served him for starters. But picturing a taunting tease coming from Cassidy simply didn't fit. Maybe it was a statement of fact.

"A part of me isn't interested in knowing more." Great! Insult her again. "But, uh, that sounded lousy, a part of me does." It did. "Very much." Now that he'd said it, it was true.

Nutcase head-butted his chin hard enough that he bit his tongue.

"What would you like to know?" Her voice was cautious.

"Ever been on a sailboat?"

"No."

"Would you like to? I mean," and then he plunged in, "my parents are coming to town and they'd like you more than they like me and I could really use your help with them. It would pay back anything I do for Perrin a hundred times over; I'll even find a different model if you insist though you'd be great. My parents like Angelo well enough, but they have a, um, different relationship." Angelo might be best friends with their son and they might have helped to raise him and send him to college, but he was still the son of their cook.

Nothing but silence so he kept going.

"And the others in the marina, well, they're just like me. And my parents are, they're, well, you know…" He petered out. That was it. He'd hit a new low in charm. "Look, I understand. Stupid idea. I'll just crawl back into my hole again. Thanks. Sorry to bother—"

"When?"

The word hung on the wires between them.

"Tuesday?" his voice squeaked. It had never done that before. It sounded terribly desperate.

"Day after tomorrow?"

"Ten a.m. 'D' dock at Shilshole Marina?"

There was a long pause during which he couldn't hear a sound except Nutcase's buzzing as she kneaded his chest with her prickly little claws.

"Sure." The word was so small for something so momentous.

"You're kidding? Really?"

"Trying to talk me back out of it?"

"No. Uh-uh. No way. You're committed now." Russell couldn't believe it.

"I said I would come. Are your parents so scary?"

"Only to me."

Then she laughed. It was the most miraculous sound he'd ever heard. He'd never heard her laugh. It rang from her like a thousand bells on a Christmas tree. He felt as if he'd just lost a hundred pounds, the weight he'd gained the moment his mother had called to announce their pending visit.

"What can I bring?"

"Just yourself. I'll bring lunch fixings. Just dress in layers, it can be warm or cool on the water depending on the wind. You don't mind visiting another lighthouse, do you?"

"Oh, is Tuesday the first? I didn't realize."

"What was that?"

She cleared her throat in one of those delicate, feminine ways that indicated a subject change that could never be turned around.

"Tuesday. Ten a.m. 'D' dock. Shilshole," she repeated dutifully.

"Right."

"See you then."

Then he was listening to a dial tone. But what had he said to make her angry? Only she hadn't been. He'd swear she hung up just a moment before laughing aloud.

She was the damnedest woman he'd ever met.

MUKILTEO LIGHTHOUSE

Mukilteo
First lit: 1907
Automated: 1979
47.94871 -122.30453

*M*ukilteo, in the local Native American language, means "good place for camping." In 1792 Captain George Vancouver came ashore there and named it Rose Point for all the wild roses that bloomed along the grassy shore.

Later renamed Point Elliot, it became the site of the signing of the Treaty of Point Elliot. This treaty of 1855 ended the Indian wars, established the Tulalip Indian Reservation, and truly opened the area up for significant white settlement.

The picturesque lighthouse has hosted hundreds and hundreds of weddings. Not a single one of the first hundred was rained on.

JULY 1

Russell was ten minutes early when he headed for the security gate at the head of the dock. It wasn't so much that he wanted to be there for Cassidy, it was that he needed a breather from his parents.

Breakfast at the Palisades had been very civilized and polite. Perfectly friendly to all appearances, and the waitress in constant attendance with a pitcher of mimosas had certainly helped keep his nerves in line. If he'd had half a brain, he'd have invited Cassidy to breakfast as well. Though that might be too high a price, helping Perrin was being more fun than he'd expected.

Cassidy was already waiting there when he reached the head of the dock. He opened the steel gate and stood back to appreciate her as she came through. Brown Docksiders on her feet that had clearly never seen the outside of a shoebox before today. Blue slacks with a crease up the front that was so perfect they must be as new as her unblemished shoes. Her blouse was a pale blue, fitted, button-up shirt that looked immensely feminine on her shapely frame. Her smile was radiant and her hair back in a neat ponytail.

And over her arm was a red coat. A huge coat, totally inappropriate for the heat of the day...

A red parka.

"Turn around." It was barely a croak as it escaped his throat.

She obliged, doing a slow three-sixty. The runner's ponytail. The auburn hair the same length as... And then her smile came around again, beyond radiant. Mischievous.

If it hadn't been for the railing behind him, he'd have fallen backward into the ocean.

"*You?*" He clenched the steel, real and solid beneath his shaking fingers.

She nodded.

"When? How? It can't be."

She slid a hand through the crook of his arm and guided him down the ramp toward the boats.

"It can be. I figured it out at New Dungeness, saw you through my binoculars." She was just as amiable as if they were old friends chatting on a sunny afternoon about the model sailboats racing on the Conservatory Water in Central Park. As if his brain wasn't misfiring on a grand scale already.

"And then you sprinted off into the fog so fast I thought you were a mirage."

"And then I sprinted off into the fog. I didn't think; I just ran. It was a bit of a shock."

"I'm noticing that myself." It was hard to believe that he was able to form whole words. That they were in sentences made it one of the modern miracles. He should probably send a note to some bishop or cardinal if he ever recovered.

She looked from side-to-side inspecting the various boats they passed. Fishing craft, fifty-foot power boats, and a lot of big sailboats. Most of them were deserted and quiet except for the occasional weekend visit, but 'D' dock had a nice share of liveaboards as well. She was being a little obvious about not looking up at him.

"Why didn't you...? Do you know how long I've been looking for you?"

"You mean other than the week you spent camped out in front of my condo?"

"So, that *was* you. You live near there? Somehow I knew that runner was my Lady of the Lights." He looked down at her, shocked to his core that both were standing embodied in one woman right here beside him.

"My friends wanted me to call the cops on you. It was getting a little creepy."

"Sorry, I didn't mean to spook you. I was just trying to find..."

"Someone else."

He sighed. What could he do?

"Yes. Someone else." She was right, there was a lot more to her than he'd first suspected.

"Right after New Dungeness, I, uh, had to go to California, and that trip lasted a bit longer than I anticipated. I was going to tell you at Angelo's, but you left too quickly. As to the rest, let's go meet your parents. I think they'll enjoy the story as well."

He considered throwing himself on the dock to rant until he felt better. Some traitorous part of him wanted to dance a happy jig. Another part was seriously considering tossing her off the dock...now there was a tempting image.

As if she'd been reading his mind, she slipped her hand from his arm and took a couple steps ahead.

Just as it had out at Cape Flattery, and the other night at Angelo's, her touch made him feel calm, strong, and protective. The breaking of that touch left its memory. No one, not even Melanie had ever made him feel this way.

Lady of the Lights. Cassidy Knowles. A prettied-up, city girl. A runner. A good and caring friend. An outdoors woman. He couldn't reconcile it all in his brain. How much he didn't know about her was mind-boggling.

She stopped unerringly by the bow of his boat. Of course she did. She'd seen it five times over the last six months. Christ, he'd walked to Tatoosh Island with her hand on his arm and refused her invitation to Destruction Island light. The world was whacked.

Cassidy reached out a hand toward the bow of his boat. Nutcase was perched on the very end of the bowsprit that rode just a foot or so from the dock. The cat sniffed her extended hand for a second and then launched herself across the water into Cassidy's arms. Rather than withdrawing as Melanie had or simply dodging the scruffy beast, Cassidy caught her and let her snuggle right into her arms and rub her head under Cassidy's chin.

Well, she'd certainly passed the cat test. His father came down the finger pier between his boat and the next to meet the visitor.

But would she survive the parent test?

RUSSELL AIMED the bow into the wind and set the engine to idle. With the ease of a half year of practice he raised the main and cleated off the sheet. He still hadn't run the jib halyard back to the cockpit and he hurried forward to haul it up before the boat slipped off the wind. The big foresail unfurled with a loud snap.

The breeze was fresh without being strong or cool, a perfect sailing day.

Tying off the line, he hung the loose tail in a quick coil and trotted back to the cockpit. He killed the engine and kicked the tiller over with his knee.

In one smooth sweep the *Lady* slid from loud vibrations and diesel fumes into the solid, silent pull of the world's winds. She heeled over and surged forward—a tug deep in his gut that made him feel everything would be okay. He'd come a long way from his first scary solo out to the Lime Kiln light and back.

His father watched him closely. He'd always been tall and patrician, and would look completely in place as an English lord advising a Queen. His hair was grayer, the lines deeper, but it was still a commanding face.

Russell's mother was in her usual Liz Taylor mode. Blue jeans that cost more than most evening gowns and a cashmere sweater showed off the success of her personal trainer's perseverance on a body nearing sixty. A silk kerchief of royal blue kept her thick, brown hair under perfect control. Large, round-eyed sunglasses were pushed up on her forehead as she eyed Cassidy—who was the only one at ease on the whole boat. Other than Nutcase.

The fur beast had checked in with him on her way to her perch on the boom. In moments, the ball of black fur lay curled up in the foot of the sail atop the boom. Far enough out that nothing lay below except ocean waves. Did she enjoy the danger? Or not see it? They'd tried a kitty life preserver: an unsuccessful and painful experiment. The scratches on his arms had taken a week to heal from that one.

Cassidy sat across from his parents on the low side of the cockpit, a plastic tumbler of iced tea held easily in one hand. A tiny fleck of sunscreen remained on the edge of one ear that he longed to rub in, but he didn't dare. They didn't have that kind of a relationship.

Stupid. They didn't have any relationship, other than knowing and despising each other for six months. Without even knowing they knew each other. But they did know... Angelo was gonna shit. And he was also going to kill himself for not taking the day off to join them and watch.

Unless Angelo already knew but hadn't told him. Maybe he'd begged off so he wouldn't be swimming ashore right about now.

"I didn't know you were a model, though I should have guessed."

At Cassidy's words, he dropped the tiller and had to grab for it again as the boat slewed into the wind. Nutcase popped her head up and stared at him. She slowly resettled as he didn't call "helms a'lee."

"You were a model?" he blurted it out.

His mother blushed a moment.

"Miss Puerto Rico," Cassidy informed him.

His dad nodded in agreement and threw an arm around his wife's shoulders giving her a quick hug. That was news as well. They were always so formal and separate, as cold to each other as they were to him. Maybe cold wasn't quite right. Perhaps always on show was more accurate.

"Yes. I took the prize money and moved to New York. Worked the catalog pages and runways to put myself through NYU. Close your mouth, dear. You look foolish."

He clamped his mouth shut and clipped the end of his tongue.

"You didn't know?" Cassidy gave him a puzzled expression. How was he supposed to know everything about his parents' past? She probably knew every detail about her own from the moment she exited the womb until...now. He didn't even know where her parents were.

He shook his head.

She opened her mouth. This was it. He was about to be torpedoed. He really didn't need a lecture from the person who was supposed to be his buffer.

"So, John," Cassidy turned back to his parents, "how did you two meet?"

Russell had to blink. Not only had she slipped in a perfectly natural subject change, but she hadn't sold his soul either. Some day he'd stop underestimating her.

"The opera," his mother answered. There were times he

wondered if his father could even speak. She always ran every social occasion, with immaculate finesse and warmth; one he'd always thought a bit artificial.

The look she turned on her husband was electric. They actually held hands; there was another one Angelo would never believe. Russell certainly didn't.

"Well," his father's voice was gruff from lack of use. "I was at a fundraiser for the Met."

"I was in marketing."

"Damn prettiest thing I'd ever seen came walking up to me at the hors d'oeuvres table."

"I had no idea who he was," his mother said off-handedly. "I'd just finessed a million-dollar donation from a usual hundred-thousander and decided to take the rest of the evening for me."

"Walked right up to me."

"I was headed for the bar."

"Walked right by me."

Their sentences were overlapping, their voices soft. Russell glanced at Cassidy who was enraptured by the story. Her body shifting so easily as the boat slid over the waves that it was as if she'd spent her life afloat. The sun discovered the hint of red in her hair and made it warm and alive.

"Then she looked back over her shoulder at me."

She smiled up at him, "You were staring."

"She never got her drink."

"He forgot he was holding a piece of shrimp until I stole it from him."

Cassidy's hand shifted over her heart as if she were about to melt.

He ducked to peek under the sail. They were off Edmonds already, this lighthouse was so close. They'd be there in no time. Another hour to the lighthouse if the wind held off the beam. They might go the whole way up the coast on a single tack,

Nutcase would appreciate the long nap without the boom swinging about. And it was far too deep off the lighthouse to throw out an anchor. Lunch aboard would get them most of the way back to dock. He might survive the day yet.

"Did you really?" Cassidy was busy looking amazed. What had he missed?

"What else was I supposed to do with him? He had talked my ear off until the hotel kicked us out into the lobby. It was three in the morning. They'd already cleaned everything in the room except the two chairs we were sitting on."

He looked at his father who noticed his scrutiny. He shrugged and nodded with a silly smile on his face.

They'd slept together on their first date. People didn't...well, he had often enough. But parents didn't...his couldn't...had.

"Where did you find a place?"

It was a friggin' hotel, Cassidy. Lots of beds there. His own mother—the little beauty queen-social climber that she was—had climbed right into his father's lap and his fortune.

His mother reached out and touched Cassidy's hand like a best friend emphasizing a point.

"It's New York. There's always someplace to dance."

Dance?

"We found the seediest little dive," John tapped his feet on the cockpit floor. "Smoking dark jazz."

"We slow danced past sunrise."

He was so glad that Cassidy was doing the speaking. He'd have screwed up the conversation eight different ways already. Maybe he could understand some of his father's silences. Julia Morgan had clearly charmed Cassidy Knowles and he suspected that wasn't as easy as his mother made it look. Maybe his mother really was that charming and it hadn't been the act he'd assumed all these years since...

When had he decided that anyway? Anne? No, Kristi. His mother had been ever so kind to a coed named Kristi he was about to break up with later that night. His mother totally screwed that up and he'd been so pissed. He'd been stuck with her for another three months before he figured out how to let her down easy. By then he'd totally missed his chance with... Was he really that shallow?

"That first week we went out dancing every night," former Miss Puerto Rico leaned up against his father. "John, we need to take that up again when you retire."

"You're retiring?" It blurted out of him and lay there on the deck like a week-old fish.

"I've got some bright young men who are ready to move up. You were never interested in the business and they're ready for me to let it go. Finally I realized, so am I." He shrugged off forty years as if it had been a three-month gig.

"The business?" Cassidy took the conversation back before he could fumble it overboard.

"Morganson Shipping. I made up the name even before Russell came along, but the boy was never interested in the business. Perhaps you've heard of us."

Cassidy laughed, that dancing musical sound of a thousand bells. He couldn't help smiling.

"I've seen enough of your shipping containers on my daily run down along Seattle's waterfront."

"Could have bowled me over too," Julia poked a finger into his father's ribs. "He, the jerk, didn't tell me who he was, at least not until that weekend when he casually invited me over for dinner to meet his parents. Herman and Alicia Morgan. I only figured it out at the front door. I was so scared I almost fainted."

"You were magnificent and almost as beautiful as you are now. Simply amazing, Russ. She out-niced even your grandmother and that took some doing in those days."

Russell was glad for the tiller. It was the only reason he didn't collapse entirely. Not only hadn't his mother been a gold-digger as he'd finally decided she was, but they'd just told

Cassidy he was worth millions. Actually hundreds of millions. Far above and beyond his own comfortable success.

She hadn't reacted.

At least not yet.

He certainly wasn't looking forward to their next time alone. He could count on one hand, with all his fingers folded up, the number of women who hadn't gunned for him the moment they found out who he was. Even Melanie had originally been drawn by his fortune and it wasn't until after it was over that he understood that she'd moved beyond that.

Shit!

He had liked Cassidy.

Did like her.

"CATCHING UP ON YOUR READING?"

Cassidy rammed the letter in her pocket and looked up, shielding her eyes against the sun.

Russell stood over her, moving easily with the sway of the deck. He looked like the statue of Rhodes: tall, powerful, and gazing out over the harbor and the world that was his domain. One of the seven wonders of the world.

And he was, in an odd way. Once he'd relaxed a bit, he'd been funny, even charming. But there was none of the false, pickup-line smoothness that she'd heard too many times on too many first dates. Perhaps it was because of their history, it was now too late for that.

"A bit," she kept her hand on the letter—it felt as if it might jump out and bite her if she didn't keep it trapped in her pocket.

Russell glanced back at the cockpit. She did too and saw John with a leisurely hand on the tiller. Julia leaned back against him as the boat slid easily over the sparkling water.

From up here on the foredeck, Cassidy had a splendid view

of the way ahead and to the left. The big foresail blocked her view to the right. Whidbey Island towered ahead, rocky cliffs, conifer-covered headlands. There were a few small power boats anchored in a narrow cove and they passed a brightly painted buoy over a dozen feet tall that rang its deep bell with each wave that rolled by.

Russell squatted down.

"I wanted to say, thanks. You're great with them."

He didn't even reach out a hand for balance, as if he'd been born on the boat. She'd felt off balance all day. Ever since she'd woken up with her stomach in a knot of nerves that refused to be explained away.

She nodded her head; it was all she trusted herself to do.

He was so close she could easily reach out. See if his hair was truly as soft as it looked, or touch her fingers to his smile.

"I don't know how you do it. I've never seen them so comfortable." He glanced aft again. "And how did I know so little about my own mother?"

Her hand was still on her father's letter, crumpled in her slacks pocket. He'd found work as a carpenter, a field hand, and who knew what all. Odd-job man to all the Kitsap Peninsula and Bainbridge Island as well while his wife tended ailing parents and an unhappy toddler. Rebuilding the well house at a tiny, island winery had led to a job as vintner, horticulturist, and general repairman all rolled into one. When the old owner had died, he'd left the whole winery to her father. Vic Knowles had given up everything to be with his family, and gotten everything in return, just in a different form.

You never know where opportunity lies, Ice Sweet. You never know.

"Your parents are charming. I like them a lot."

"And they like you, which may be a first among the women I've brought home."

She'd never met a man with more skill at saying the wrong thing. At first it had made her angry, now she was finding it rather sweet. He was forthright with no games and no filter. His feelings turned into speech before they turned into thought and were carefully groomed and sanitized. He was a lot like his cat in that way—a sweet mess and a bit scruffy around the edges.

"Is that what I am?"

"What?" he looked worried as he reviewed his last comment in his head.

"Am I a woman you've brought home? Konked with a club and dragged to your boat like some mighty Viking?" If a Viking like this kidnapped her, maybe she'd want to go along with it.

He opened his mouth and then thought better of it and closed it again. He shook his head ruefully.

"Porcupines."

She laughed. He'd really grabbed onto that image. He was so close that she could smell him despite the sailing breeze. His sleeves rolled up to reveal powerful arms—big, safe arms to be wrapped in. Her hand reached out, of its own accord, and rested on his knee.

The muscles were shifting easily beneath the denim, working unconsciously to keep his balance on the rocking boat. His eyes were watching hers and she could feel herself melting. Would he kiss her? She finally knew the answer to her much earlier question: if he tried, she certainly wasn't going to resist.

Her body shifted as the boat thumped off a wave and she leaned a little closer to him. Her hand on his knee steadying him as well. They were so close that her head was spinning...oak— he smelled of oak and mahogany and teak and ocean waves. Of heady reds at their prime and soft, cool whites sipped late at night in front of a warm fire.

She leaned closer. If he wasn't going to kiss her, she'd kiss him.

"'I didn't realize Tuesday was the first.'"

His words didn't make sense. This was a moment for—

"You've been to every lighthouse."

"Yes," she had, but what did that have to do with a kiss under the midday sun.

"You have the same calendar."

She nodded her head and leaned forward again.

"You lied."

No she hadn't. "About what?" She didn't ever— "Oh."

"'Oh,' she says. 'Haven't been to a lighthouse before,' she said." He pushed a strong finger against her shoulder. Hard enough to tip her away.

"You lied."

"No, I evaded." Evaded the most exasperating man on the planet.

"You lied."

If he said it one more time, she was going to smack him.

"Didn't."

"You said, and I quote, 'Yes, I am a lighthouse virgin.'" He looked immensely pleased with himself. She shoved his knee hard enough that he tipped back from his squat and landed on his behind against the lifelines.

"Do you catalog everything everyone says so that you can throw it back in their face? I didn't want you of all people to know about..." There was no way she was going to explain her own father to this irritating man.

He stared off across the water for a moment. Looked up at the sails as if he might find a clue up there. His smile twisted slightly to one side and his eyes twinkled as his gaze returned to her. Deep, ocean-deep eyes.

"Nope. Just you. Just everything you've ever said. I'd bet I could repeat every word."

"There you go, doing it again." Her heart rate had definitely jumped, it was all she could hear.

"The jerk being charming?"

He was so full of himself, and he was absolutely right. It was one of the nicest, back-handed compliments she'd ever had.

"Hey, up there." John shouted to make his voice carry above the wind. "We're almost there."

Russell stood with the grace of the wind and stepped out onto the narrow bowsprit to look beyond the sail. He paused for a long moment and then turned to her with a positively wicked grin.

He offered his hand. His grip was warm and firm as he helped her to her feet, and with the slightest little tug he could pull her into his arms whether she wanted to or not. Instead of having the decency to take advantage of the moment, he turned and placed her hand on the lifeline so that they could head back to the cockpit.

His grin didn't abate in the slightest.

ALL THE WAY back to the cockpit, she could feel Julia's scrutiny. Russell's mother didn't miss a thing and it made Cassidy's cheeks burn. She'd seen how close Cassidy had come to kissing her son. John gave no indication of noticing what he'd interrupted—if indeed he had. Maybe John was where Russell had inherited his obtuse nature.

Cassidy slid shakily into the seat.

Julia glanced at her son.

Russell stood at the tiller with his Dad, both of them looking up at the sails and absorbed in some wordless guy conversation about wind and canvas.

Julia took her hand and patted it, "Don't worry, dear. The Morgan men aren't the sharpest tacks in the bunch, but they get there eventually."

If her cheeks were heated before, they were on fire now. She turned to look away from her reflection in Julia's sunglasses, vague and pale in the dark glass.

There was the Mukilteo lighthouse. It was close, very close

as John had sailed them within a few hundred feet. She could easily see the stepped Fresnel lens through the glass windows and the octagonal banister around the third story walkway.

The sun lit the lighthouse and the keeper's cottages to a near blinding white. A brilliant green-and-white state ferry pulled out from behind it. Even the "lawn" before the beacon was white, the white of crushed seashells in the sun.

Then she noticed the canopy. It was white and light as a feather, set across the front lawn for a party. People were sitting in rows of chairs facing the water. Some at the back and sides stood for a better view: a view of a wedding.

The minister was in black and white. A groom in black, right down to the tails on his tuxedo. The boat slid forward and Cassidy saw the bride in profile. She could have been Jo's twin with her straight dark hair and rounded face—and she was absolutely breathtaking in her gown, a clingy satin with a flowing sheer of chiffon to soften the edges. She wore no veil, rather a ring of white flowers worked into her black hair.

Many of the eyes in the audience were looking at Cassidy herself on the sailboat, following her. Before she could look away, she came to her senses. Not her. They were looking at the beautiful sailboat slipping along behind the bride and groom. Cameras clicked and flashed in a brilliant display that must have surprised the bride and groom, for they turned and so did, finally, the minister.

Cassidy pulled out her camera and shot a photo of sail, water, lighthouse, and wedding.

The minister and couple waved at them. Several of the audience joined in. She waved back and felt silly and touched at the same time.

As they slipped past, she caught the wedding and lighthouse in the background and Russell Morgan in the foreground, holding the tiller and looking aloft at the set of his sails. This shot would get a place of honor on her wall.

A wedding day memory. What would hers be like? Would some beautiful sailboat pass by while she looked at the man she loved?

And where the hell was he anyway? She stole a glance at Russell.

No! Not possible.

He was pointing out something to his father.

"Helm's a-lee!" He called.

He swung over the tiller and John started doing something with the ropes.

That's when she spotted Nutcase on the swinging boom.

"The cat!" Her cry simply made Russell grin all the more. He was going to flip the cat over the side out of sheer cussedness. She tried to scramble up—Russell's hand landed on her head and drove her back into her seat. The heavy boom swung by just inches above her.

There was a soft thump as Nutcase jumped onto the cabin roof. The boom swung across, Russell ducking underneath with all the grace of long experience, even slapping the massive thing with his hand as it swung by, a smack of flesh on wood, like a man greeting an old friend.

The cat sat on the cabin roof watching the boom complete its swing. Then it daintily raised one paw to its mouth and tugged on an errant nail, leaning against the new slant of the deck to keep its place.

"You jerk!" She spun to face Russell. The adrenalin was still pounding through her, making her temples hurt. "You could have..."

She didn't know what. But he could have.

"Warned me!"

Russell's smile diminished at that point. It wavered for a moment before fading entirely.

John fussed with the lines and didn't look up. Julia sipped

her iced tea. The silence in the cockpit stretched out for an overlong moment before Russell cleared his throat.

"Nutcase knows the drill."

Well she sure as hell didn't; he'd scared the daylights out of her. She faced forward feeling angry and foolish simultaneously. And the damned cat, as if nothing had happened, turned to face the sun.

Seafaring cats. They knew their place in life. They knew when to stand fast and when to jump. Why couldn't her life be that easy?

Everything in her life had made sense—right up until she'd received the phone call that her father was dying. Even after all the caregiving and the funeral was over, order had never fully returned to her life. Her career was on the upswing and she loved living near her friends again for the first time since college. It should have all made sense, but it didn't.

Then her father's letters made it worse.

And now to cap it all off, stupid, stupid Russell Morgan.

"You don't really know anything about anything, do you?" She knew she was being angry and putting words in his mouth that he hadn't meant that way. But they stung. Like stumbling on a hive of bees on her last trip to her father's vineyard when she was twelve.

Fourteen stings.

She never went back to his fields. Her father had protested that they weren't even honeybees, just some nasty ground bees. She'd dug in her pre-teenage heels and had never again enjoyed the outdoors he so loved. She'd forgotten that memory; the moment that had turned her from the vines. Such a small thing in retrospect and yet it had changed the very course of her life.

She shook herself. How did she get her head into such an awful place? Nutcase curled up for a nap on a coil of rope that looked terribly uncomfortable until she settled herself inside the center. She belonged.

Cassidy had been having fun. Right until...

She'd just been afraid for the cat.

That was all.

But Russell had laughed. No, but he'd certainly smiled. Smiled at a joke that had pumped her so full of anger she could still scream.

She glanced back at him. He was eyeing her with a look of extreme caution. As soon as she turned, he glanced away at the sails.

Damn him! If he were still laughing, it would be easier to remain angry.

She checked the action of the boom, but it appeared to be staying safely to the other side of the boat. She stood and did her best to pretend she was stretching. It placed her closer to Russell than either of his parents. She kept her voice low, hoping the wind would make it so that only Russell would hear her.

"Next time, warn me."

He nodded carefully, even had the decency to mouth, "Sorry."

For good measure she moved forward to scratch the cat, who woke up enough to purr appreciatively before going back to sleep.

THE RATTLE and cough of the engine as it started was a rude interruption to a lazy afternoon spent lolling about before a dying breeze. After the warm sun and the water, Cassidy was ready for a long nap though she never napped and her watch insisted it was barely three o'clock.

Russell and his dad moved around in an easy fashion lowering and bundling sails. They hung rubber bumpers along one side. There was lots and lots of coiling and uncoiling of ropes to no purpose that she could quite understand. Sailboats made fixing her old VW Rabbit in college look easy.

Nutcase complained when shooed from her rope coil and showed her displeasure by going below with a flick of her tail and not a backward glance.

Julia sat beside her while the men fussed about. Despite the kerchief over her hair and her sunglasses and dark skin, the bright sheen of a day in the sun flushed her cheeks.

"I believe that you are the first woman who has ever made Russell behave. I certainly was never able to."

If this was Russell behaving, what was he usually like? She had no interest in being someone else's conscience. Half the time she couldn't stand to be around him.

"He and Angelo would get together and I would lose all control."

The other half of the time Cassidy couldn't stop thinking about him.

"They'd get into trouble before they'd even left Maria's kitchen."

"Maria? Who's Maria?"

"Maria Amelia Avico Parrano. Angelo's mother has been John's cook since shortly after I came along. Practically a family member. She and I birthed our boys within weeks of each other. Angelo and Russell learned to cook at her knee. Angelo's a better cook, but not by much."

"He told me he could heat soup."

"You never saw two boys with such a passion for fine food. Or who could destroy a kitchen so fast." Julia eyed her speculatively. "It's not like Russell to understate his skills either if given the chance. You are a very interesting woman, Cassidy Knowles."

Russell was once again at the tiller, guiding the long boat through the busy traffic streaming in and out of the marina. The

Shilshole breakwater was so tall that she could only see the very tops of sailboat masts over it.

He ducked from one side of the boom to the other to keep an eye on the traffic. The clutter of boats might move slower than the commuters on I-5, but they also didn't turn as fast or stop as readily.

Russell was completely, smoothly in control, moving as if their was no hurry in the world. The *Lady* slid through a graceful curve at his slightest command. She'd always thought of him as a bumbler, some people naturally were, but not now. Nor when he'd walked through the restaurant with the blonde on his arm. Great! She really did bring out the worst in him. He was only an irritating, irrational idiot in her presence. The worst part was, she was little better around him.

The passengers of every boat that went by, some so close she could smell what they were having for lunch over the diesel exhaust, turned to watch them. At first she thought they were watching the majestic blue hull slide through the water.

Then she noticed that the women's stares weren't directed at the boat in general. Instead, most of them watched the skipper who stood tall at the helm.

Now why did that bother her?

Julia whispered in her ear, "Russell is so damn handsome, isn't he? Even more so than his father, which is not an easy thing to do."

Out here in his element, he *was* damn handsome. She could imagine him crossing the mighty ocean with the wind tousling his hair, his cat winding about his feet, and his lady at his side.

"Ha!"

"What?" Julia turned to her.

"Nothing." No way she was going to say what was going on in her mind. It was beyond ridiculous.

Julia smiled and patted her arm, as if Cassidy's thoughts had just been published across her forehead like a Times Square reader board.

"He'll get around to it eventually. He already can't live without you, it will just take him a bit longer to realize that."

"But we aren't...don't...haven't..." She sounded like a teenager trying to backpedal.

"Yet I know how it looks when I see it."

"How what looks?" She'd better not be saying what she was saying.

Julia placed a hand on one cheek and kissed her on the other.

"We're going to be great friends, Cassidy Knowles and Julia Morgan. You'll see."

Russell aimed the boat into a narrow waterway in the forest of masts and radar thingies that was so dense it obscured the hillside behind them.

"You want me to *what?*" The cordless phone was slippery in her hands, Cassidy grabbed a Kleenex from her living room sofa's side table to wipe off the sudden sheen of sweat on her palms. It was just as slippery after she did so.

"C'mon, Cassidy. You already told Mom that you didn't have plans for the 4th of July." Russell's voice was deep and soft on the phone. Not the softness of weakness, but the softness of warm fires on quiet evenings. "You were really great with them, by the way. Thanks. You were definitely the highlight of their trip out. I'd have been dead without you."

"A 4th of July boat party?" This made her far more nervous than meeting his parents. This would be a real date.

"Right! We'll cruise down to the Seattle waterfront before sunset and toss out a hook."

"We'll go fishing?"

There was a long silence.

"Toss out an anchor."

"Oh." They really had a language all their own.

"Angelo says there's great music and amazing fireworks along the beach there."

"There is. Who else will be there?" Far more nervous. Her stomach flip-flopped, unable to believe that she was even considering the idea.

"Just a couple of the other boaters. You're welcome to bring some friends. We'll go with Dave and Betsy, they have a boat that puts mine to shame. I also just ripped out my electrical."

"You need electricity on a sailboat?" She really didn't care. She just needed to buy a minute to think. Did she really want to go out on a *date* with him? *Yes,* was the surprising answer. Well, not too surprising if she was going to be truthful about it.

He was saying something about running lights and anchor lights and radios.

Did she want to have that date among other people she didn't know? It would certainly be safer. Chaperoned—not that she needed any chaperones—at least not normally. But around Russell maybe she did. Not in case he did something. More to keep herself from jumping him and really regretting it in the morning.

He was on to metering and instrumentation.

She'd beg off on the decision, call him back tomorrow when she'd had a chance to sleep on it.

"It's interesting the different types of cable and equipment that are required to survive salt air corrosion even if it's inside the cabin. Did you know that stainless steel rots in sea air? It rots fast if it gets salt spray."

Delay was definitely a good idea. Better yet, she'd tell him to expect her if she showed up, and not if she didn't.

"Yes."

"Oh, you knew about stainless? Weird, huh?"

"No, I mean, yes, I'll be there. And no, I thought stainless was, well, stainless." That wasn't what she'd meant to say. All her standoffish thoughts were careening together to make her voice silky in a way that sounded nothing like her and a lot like someone with much more confidence.

"Really?" Russell's voice practically squeaked in surprise.

"I'd love to. See you then."

She pressed the disconnect before her mouth could invite him up to the condo which had a great view of the fireworks.

Still clenching the cordless phone, like the lifeline to a woman lost overboard, she staggered up to the glass door to her balcony. The late evening waterfront was dappled with a thousand lights and beyond the water the Olympic mountains were etched against the pink sky.

Cassidy leaned her forehead against the sun-warmed glass.

Ferries plied the water. Commercial ships unloaded at the piers. Traffic hustled along the waterfront.

She reared her head back a few inches and thumped it forward against the glass.

And she was totally adrift at sea.

Perrin had already made a date with a banker she'd been seeing for a while and had been really pissed about not going along on the sailboat. "I can't believe this dream guy of yours is that same grouch who sat at dinner for thirty seconds. How can you be dating him? Though he's a hunk, I have to admit that. And makes great ads. You should see what we have picked out for you to model. It's wicked. "

"He's not my dream guy," Cassidy had insisted over the phone; Russell was too much of a pain in the behind to be anyone's dream guy. So why had she dreamt of him last night and why was she now climbing aboard Dave and Betsy's boat?

Perrin had sniggered.

"I'm not dating him; besides, he's not always a grouch. And I'm not modeling anything lurid."

"I bet deep down he's mean."

Cassidy's guess was just the opposite, but she'd kept it to herself. She was beginning to think that Russell was a really decent man, all wrapped up in being a guy.

Jo wasn't a fan of boats; her dad had been a deadbeat Alaskan fisherman and boats always reminded her of the stench of fish and too much beer. But she only made Cassidy beg a little before caving in.

Now it was the afternoon of the Fourth and they cast off from the dock and were underway even before she and Jo had a moment to stow their belongings below. Except, here on the catamaran, it wasn't "below," it was "in the salon." She glanced wistfully at the receding dock out the long, narrow windows.

"This is it, Jo; if we jump now, we might still make it."

Her friend shook her head, "You got me on this damned thing, you don't get off the hook so easily. It doesn't look so bad anyway."

And it didn't. Russell's boat below had been a combination of beautiful mahogany shaped into pleasing curves, items neatly stowed in custom cubby holes, and a complete mayhem of sawdust, tools, and half-ripped out sections.

There had been a hole right in the middle of the floor that opened to concrete a few inches down. Being in a boat on the water and seeing that it was filled with concrete hadn't made her feel all warm and fuzzy. When Russell had answered her question that it wasn't just concrete, but rather about six tons of concrete and iron boiler punchings, whatever they were, she'd considered swimming ashore. Through the hole in the floor, she'd seen a thin film of water washing back and forth over the concrete. It had been mesmerizing and left her feeling a bit ill.

She'd spent very little time below during the sail with his parents.

Dave and Betsy's salon was like a warm living room. Everything was neatly stowed. There were a hundred homey touches: a quilt throw on a settee, a small group of pictures along the only bit of open wall, even tiny curtains for each window. Water stains on the table and fraying on two chairs in particular added to the lived-in and cozy feel.

The others were on deck: Russell, the owners, and an old man with more white beard than face. Cassidy glanced at Jo and they both moved farther into the boat. At the end of the salon there was a set of a half-dozen stairs to either side, leading down into each hull of the catamaran.

They tip-toed down the set to the left. A tiny kitchen—a galley —wrapped ingeniously around the steps. Forward lay a small bedroom, barely bigger than the double bed stuffed in it. More quilts and pictures, though definitely a guest room. It even had a tiny bathroom with a toilet and shower tucked behind the door.

At the other end of the hull was a floating office. A laptop sat on a cubbyholed desk. There were several bookshelves, mostly filled with novels, but there were three books, all with similar titles, grouped off to one side. They were by Betsy and Dave Howard.

She slipped the first book free of the elastic bungee cord that ran across the front of the bookshelf and showed the cover to Jo.

"Cruising Over Fifty." Jo read aloud.

Their hosts smiled from the cover, looking much as they did now, wearing a tiny bikini and a Speedo respectively.

"If I look that good at fifty, I've won the lottery and gone to heaven."

Cassidy flipped to the copyright page. Ten years ago.

"They're over sixty now. Damn!" She checked the picture

again. Fit without the harsh lines of gym machines and definitely no cosmetic surgery. She slid the book back into place.

They returned to the salon. Jo turned for the cockpit, but Cassidy crossed the salon and descended into the other hull.

A couple of seats were built into the hull at the foot of the steps. To the stern was the master bedroom. A sweater was tossed on the made bed and the pillows still showed the dents of their owners' heads. Cassidy could move in here in a heartbeat. Toward the bow was a small sink and a closed door.

Jo plucked her sleeve. "Enough, Miss Snoopy. There is a line between curious and nosy."

"I'm nosy."

"Right," Jo headed up the short flight of steps and Cassidy turned to follow. Behind the door was the unmistakable pumping sound of a marine toilet being flushed. Clank, gurgle, clank, gurgle. It was the first thing Russell had taught her about his boat, this one sounded exactly the same. Someone else was aboard, maybe old, white-beard's wife.

The girl who popped out of the door knocked Cassidy back onto the settee at the base of the stairs. Her bikini revealed far more than it covered. She had blonde hair, the casual fitness of being in her early twenties, and the serious curves of someone quite dangerous.

She inspected Cassidy with a quick glance from boat shoes and creased navy pants to her silk blouse. She'd never been assessed and discounted so quickly.

Then the woman's face broke out into such a large smile that Cassidy almost doubted the expression that had been there moments before. Dangerous like a shark this one.

"You must be Cassidy. Hi, I'm Teri." She held out a hand and grabbed Cassidy's with a grip that would have fit better in one of those mano-a-mano guy moments. "Russ said you'd be coming."

"He didn't mention you." Nice, Cass, real nice. But it didn't phase her new acquaintance a moment.

"Yea. Well, with Tommy gone, I was at sorta loose ends. Kinda invited myself aboard, you know."

"Tommy?"

"My ex. I kicked him overboard. He wanted me to go climb this stupid rock, El Capitan or something, and after all this training, he like wouldn't take me with him. I was, you know, really pissed."

"Ex-boyfriend? I'm sorry."

"Ex-husband—just got the papers so we're done. Two years, three months or some such. At least that's what he said. Fun, but what a waste. He was so, you know, protective. There are times when a girl needs someone to watch over her, it's kinda charming, but not all the time fer crying out loud." She shrugged in a way designed to lift her generous bosom and make it look as if her breasts were about to spring from their tiny bits of cloth.

Jo stuck her head back down, "You coming? Oh, hello."

Jo got the introduction, without the attacking handshake.

They didn't even have to glance at each other to share the thought. This girl was as wild as Perrin had been in college, with none of the class or intelligence. Teri was a disaster waiting to happen.

Back on deck, the dance began, and Cassidy started to feel far worse than a bit of seasickness. She looked longingly back at the marina, now just a tiny cluster of masts disappearing rapidly behind. This boat was much faster than Russell's and had opened the gap quickly. They'd raised sail while she was below, but the wide catamaran had stayed so level she hadn't noticed when they got underway.

Dave stood at the wheel. Instead of a narrow cockpit where everyone's knees were always bumping together in a friendly little circle, here you could spread out. There were two couch-sized places to sit with a small table bolted to the deck between

249

them. They didn't need the wide-bottomed, heavy mugs to avoid spilling drinks, just a good solid glass.

Russell stood by Dave and chatted about the "set of the sails" and "monohull vs. twin-hull leeway." While Cassidy was congratulating Betsy on her beautiful boat, Teri joined the other sailors. In moments she was cranking a handle on a winch and talking about the "lie of the wind."

Lie indeed. Cassidy couldn't believe she'd swallowed Russell's invitation—hook and all.

Cassidy and Jo joined Betsy and Perry for iced tea. It was bitter on her tongue as she watched Teri bend and flex while she worked with the ropes.

And Russell didn't stop watching Teri for a moment.

CASSIDY MOVED to the bow once they'd anchored, wishing she'd had the foresight to bring a book. It was an idyllic setting. Night was falling and Seattle was a shining backdrop as the last of the daylight was replaced by sparkling office and apartment lights. Myrtle Edwards Park was a throbbing mass of people—half the population of Seattle must be jammed in there to watch the fireworks. A band cranked out some serious dance tunes that made her feet twitch despite how she was feeling.

A hundred or more boats clustered as close to the fireworks barge as the police would allow. There were power yachts that must be over a hundred feet long and three stories tall. In between them ski boats, fishing skiffs, and two-person sailboats scuttled around while a massive three-masted sailboat cruised by in deeper water. She wanted to ask about it, but that would mean facing Russell and the permanent attachment to his hip. Teri had staked her territory and Russell played along as if everything was completely normal.

How had she so misjudged him? Perrin had been right. Jo

had simply shaken her head sadly, even before Cassidy could ask the question. It wasn't her imagination. At some point, she'd have to return to the cockpit and watch Teri continue to work at seducing Russell. For all she knew, Russell had been consoling her in the night since her ex had departed. She could easily imagine the woman producing big rolling tears that would drip down onto her heaving bosom, all on cue.

At least she hadn't invited him to the condo. There it was, she looked shoreward, not a dozen blocks away. A dozen blocks to safety and a hundred yards of freezing water she couldn't cross. It might as well be a hundred miles. She was good and surely trapped.

"Pretty boat."

The voice came from a canoe close beside the catamaran. A pair of boys in their teens were looking at the boat the same way Teri was tracking Russell.

"Thanks. Um, but it's not mine."

"Still, it's cool."

"Yeah, cool."

She'd rather be anywhere than here.

"Where are you guys from?"

"Wenatchee, you know, east of the mountains."

She did; it was a huge grape-growing area. "Did you paddle the whole way?"

The one in front rolled his eyes, but the one in the stern laughed.

"Nah, just the last little bit. We parked pretty close this morning." He nodded toward the beach.

There was a flash and a thump from the barge. A thin trail of sparks soared upward. She followed it and was rewarded by a huge flash. A moment later the bang arrived so loud and hard she could feel it as much against her chest as her eardrums.

Sometimes the answer was so obvious, it was hard to believe she hadn't had it earlier in the long, weary evening. She looked over her shoulder and saw Jo look her direction. Dave, Betsy, and Perry were chatting quietly. Russell and Teri were nowhere to be seen. They must be down below together, doing *what* she didn't want to know.

Cassidy rocked her head toward the canoe.

Jo glanced over, paused for a moment, and nodded. She made a shooing motion with one hand that none of the others noticed.

Cassidy tilted her head in a question.

Jo nodded again. She was sure.

"Hey, guys." They were both still staring upward like frogs dazzled by a flashlight.

"Yeah?"

"I'm not feeling real well. Could you give me a lift to the beach?"

"Now?"

"Uh-huh."

They both shrugged. "Sure, climb on in, lady."

Moments later, as the second warning boomed overhead, she stepped onto terra firma and felt much better.

"Thanks, guys, you're great." She kissed each on the cheek. The one in front groaned, but the one in the stern leaned into the kiss for a moment.

"Any time, lady, any—"

The first big firework cut off his sentence as it soared aloft and burst like a huge chrysanthemum.

She was the only one moving away from the beach as flecks of colored light flew through the sky and lit the upturned faces before her. She didn't turn back to look for the sailboat.

"HI, THIS IS CASSIDY."

"Hi, Cassidy. This is Russell. Look, I feel—"

"I'll be out of town for the next couple weeks, but I will be checking for messages. Thanks."

There was a nasty little beep.

"Shit!"

Nutcase scrambled away from where he'd thumped his hand on the table.

"No, that isn't what I meant. Look, um, could you give me a call?"

Stupid! Stupid! Stupid!

"No, you won't, will you."

He wouldn't either if he was her.

"Look, your friend Jo, she read me the riot act. I had no idea. Every time I tried to get near you, you ran off."

Good trick on a sailboat. He'd stopped chasing as soon as he got the message that she wanted nothing to do with him.

Jo had actually laughed in his face when he'd said that.

"I didn't even notice Teri. She isn't anywhere near your league. She's just a lonely kid."

He was sounding really pathetic. There had to be some way to cancel this message.

"Cassidy, I didn't…" but he had. "I wanted to…shit!…I wanted to spend some time with you when I wasn't being freaked out by my parents. I wanted—"

A beep cut him off.

He heard the click as his cell phone disconnected the dead call.

———

"Miss Knowles."

"Cassidy."

"Cassidy, thanks. You said that there are wines that aren't real types of wine? I don't understand that."

Thirty-five students of the Culinary Institute of America

eagerly awaited her answer. She always had a great time at the CIA summer-series classes. About the end of the first week, she couldn't imagine why she didn't move back to New York to live along the Hudson River and teach oenology. Invariably, by the end of the second week, she remembered why she never did. But this was the first week and her session had been booked out within hours of the class announcement. At least a dozen of the staff stood along the back wall to listen in.

She'd once sat in those chairs and listened just as eagerly to Craig Claiborne when he'd deigned to lecture. She was standing where Craig had stood and Palmer and Prudhomme and a host of other greats before her. She was either really good or fooling everyone.

"There are new wines all the time. Traditionally, the types of wine were based on grape and region. Bordeaux still only comes from Bordeaux, France. So, here you are, a new wine producer. You want to make your mark. What do you call your wine?"

"You just make up a name?" He was perhaps twenty years old, way too young. Sitting in the first row. Over the phone the night before, she'd bet Jo fifty cents that he'd chat her up afterward. He was damn cute and he knew it.

"They're called varietals. They have some of this grape, a bit of that. No one knows exactly what, except their vintner of course, and she'll know to the nearest thousand pounds what grapes are used. Nearest hundred if they're really good." Not that she could tell.

Damn Russell for being right. She didn't really know what happened behind the scenes. Didn't know the life of any wine at the level a vintner did. She'd spent an entire career in wine always a step back, a step away from the heart of the process. Even worse, away from the process that had been so important to her father.

"So, the vintner declares their wine by the grape, or doesn't. I recently tasted a Sangiovese from a cliffside winery in Cinque

Terre. The grape wasn't labeled because Sangiovese is not much help to separate the winery from the herd—it makes up over ten percent of the total Italian grape crop, a quarter of a million acres. Instead the winery labeled it, 'Pizza Wine.' It was simple, clear, and to-the-point marketing."

Cassidy didn't want a "pizza wine" fling anyway, and that's all the cute student would be, but still it was flattering.

"Suddenly we have the 'pizza wine' grape. Or the 'Fume Blanc,' which sounds grander. But in either case it means whatever the vintner wants it to mean. Marketing. The higher end wines are generally true to their grape, cabernet sauvignon for example. Note that I said higher end, not necessarily better. Wine is matched to meal, occasion, and palate. A $28,000 magnum of Romanee Conti '85 probably won't be nearly as good a match for pizza as that twelve-dollar varietal. But you don't often compare a burgundy *grand cru* with a bit of Sangiovese marketing."

Was that what Russell was doing with his daily phone messages? A bit of cheap marketing. Or had he really misread the situation?

Jo, even patient Jo, was getting tired of her long-distance second-guessing.

Russell's first message had been desperate. Then he'd left three more trying to explain he hadn't noticed what Teri was doing before giving it up as a bad cause. She'd thought that was the last of him.

The next day, a new message. One deliberately lighter, much less assertive, but also less unsure. The history of the Mukilteo lighthouse. He'd done some digging. One hundred and fourteen weddings there since it was decommissioned. An admiral who couldn't sleep at night because a foghorn sensor went off whenever the moonlight reflected off the white seawall. He had the wall painted black so he could get his sleep.

The next day, no call from him. Instead an invitation from

his mom to drop down to New York for the weekend, a quick two-hour train ride.

The day after that, a poem that had nothing to do with wine, boat, or lighthouse, but rather flowers, hummingbirds, and wings beating with love—all read in his wonderful deep voice. Way over the top, but so charming she was still weak in the knees. Or maybe in the head.

She didn't want to call him back and have to tell him to stop. *Admit it Cassidy, you don't want him to stop.*

She didn't notice when, at the end of class, the young questioner did indeed try to engage her attention. She walked away and left him talking to empty air.

Even before she was clear of the building, she'd pulled out her cell phone to see what Russell's next message might be.

"ONE MORE CHANCE."

There was a silence on the phone to Cassidy's opening salvo.

"Are you there?"

"Yes, just trying to catch my breath." The sound of reprieve in Russell's voice couldn't have been greater if a firing squad had just been ordered back to barracks.

"Your mom was great by the way. They took me to the Four Seasons and completely spoiled me."

"She's good at that."

"So?" She'd waited until she was home to call. Waited until his messages repeated themselves in her head so much she couldn't sleep. Messages about the success and closing of his business. Of his childhood dreams to go sailing. Of the progress of his cat on her never-ending quest for the perfect nap. All passed on in two-minute clips allowed by her voicemail.

At first he'd stumbled, been cutoff, beeped out in mid-word. By the end of two weeks of silence on her part, he had the timing down. Each message ended with a hook that made her want to start the next. A winding "tale" as soft and comfortable as his cat's.

"Well," his voice was soft and deep. He had the most amazing phone voice which certainly hadn't hurt his cause.

"There's this lighthouse. You can only get there by boat…"

She glanced at the calendar over her sofa.

"Patos Island."

PATOS ISLAND LIGHTHOUSE

Patos Island
First lit: 1893
Automated: 1974
48.789 -122.9715

The Isla de Patos, "Island of Ducks" is 210 acres of trees, rock, and sea caves making it a great favorite of smugglers over the years. In the early 1900s the lighthouse keeper and his family made a once per month trip across twenty-six miles of water to Bellingham, Washington for supplies. His nearest neighbor? The Canadian lighthouse keeper on Saturna Island over five miles in the other direction.

When smallpox struck his family, he flew the lighthouse flag upside down as a distress sign to passing ships. By the time help arrived, three of his thirteen children had died.

AUGUST 1

Mt. Baker rose like a beacon, soaring up into the heat of the summer day. Russell's boat slid up to the public pier in Anacortes. He'd told her it was a two-day trip to sail from Seattle to Patos Island and back. Cassidy had covered most of the distance in the two-hour drive north in order to avoid sleeping aboard. He'd promised she could be as safe as she wanted, which was sweet. But since they'd never been together for more than an hour without ticking each other off, she chose to meet him at the closest port.

His boat looked sharp, graceful, prettier than it had before. He'd finally repainted it. The bowsprit now had copper handrails wrapped around it. The dinghy was upside down on the top of the cabin. Everything looked shipshape, even elegant. His grin of pride was infectious.

The boat slid up to the dock and, with a brief, low rumble from her engine, came to a halt in front of Cassidy. He dropped the lifeline and helped her aboard with an extended hand—warm, strong hand.

He retreated to the cockpit and moments later, the dock was sliding away. She didn't feel the pull of the dock as she had before. This time she was glad to be aboard. Some part of her, a wild part, the one that didn't always want to do the precisely the right and cautious thing, had won out, perhaps for the first time in her life. She'd driven here with the windows down, the sunroof open, and the oldies station blasting.

"Here, take the tiller."

She stared at the stick of polished wood, longer than her arm. "I don't know how to steer a boat."

Even as she spoke, he grabbed her daypack and lowered it through the hatch. In moments, she was sitting as she'd seen him sit, the wood smooth and warm beneath her hand.

"Just choose a point and aim for it." He pointed over his shoulder. "Mt. Baker should be fine for the moment."

He moved off and began working with the ropes.

"But I don't know…" He probably couldn't hear her over the dull throb of the engine.

She stared at the mountain. It was a little off to the right, starboard. She pulled the tiller that way…and the mountain got further away. Maybe there was a current pushing them the opposite way. She pulled the tiller harder, right into her lap. The situation just got worse.

"Russell!"

He called over his shoulder, without even turning around to help her.

"It's opposite. Steer left to go right."

"Steer left to go right. What kind of a silly system is that?"

Well, right wasn't helping so she pushed the tiller the wrong way—away from her to port.

The boat swung obligingly until its bowsprit was aimed right at the mountain. And then it kept going past the other side.

She pulled it back into her lap. Russell stumbled toward the right rail, she shoved it to the left.

He didn't say anything, just steadied himself and started untying a rope from around the sail.

Smaller corrections. A little pull, a little push, and she finally had it centered on the mountain. As the boat lifted over the small waves, the bow went to the right and as it settled back into the water it went to left, but it was the best she could do. The average was about right and it wasn't as if there were highway lanes on the water she had to stay in. The only other traffic around were two small sailboats, a water skier, and off in the distance a pair of monstrous oil tankers anchored in the broad bay.

Russell pulled up the sails with an easy hand-over-hand motion. As the great flaps of red mainsail slid upward, she expected that there was more muscle to the process than it appeared. He made it look easy.

He tied off the first one and raised the one up front—the jib.

"Turn off the key."

There was one at the end of the cockpit, right next to some dials and meters. Who knew sailboats had keys? With a click, the rumble ceased and the world was suddenly quiet. Several of the dials flopped over to zero.

"Aim for Lummi," he pointed negligently off the left side. Port side. Four letters in port and left, more letters in starboard and right.

"Which one's Lummi?"

"The third island." He returned to the bow, ending the conversation.

Stupid man. Third island? She didn't see any islands, just a line of green hills. Maybe the third hill was the third island. She pulled the tiller toward her and the bow moved the wrong way. She caught it quickly and pushed it away.

Russell didn't stumble this time. Maybe she was getting smoother control—or he'd prepared himself now that he knew she didn't have a clue.

The boat had been coasting since she'd turned off the motor...then the wind caught the sails. In moments they were sliding ahead. The meter labeled in knots slid upward four, five, six and the boat heeled over.

It took some pressure to keep the tiller straight, but not a lot, just enough to know she was steering the boat. Russell took his time tidying up various ropes along the deck. He even stopped to play with his cat. When they were done, he tossed the cat at the sail; it slid down to the boom and settled quickly for a nap.

Damn them both.

By the time he finally returned to the cockpit, she was getting the hang of steering. It was the most powerful feeling she'd ever had—the great craft answered her whim and the force of the wind drove them forward with a happy splashing of the waves down the side. She didn't really want to give it up, but it was his boat.

Russell slid into the cockpit and sat on the bench seat, but made no move to take the tiller.

"Hi, Cassidy. Thanks for coming." He set his feet on the opposite bench and rested his elbows along the back. "Not much wind in August, but it's nice not to be fighting some gale to get to a lighthouse."

He looked great. Cutoff shorts, still showing some of the stains that matched his boat's deck, revealed muscular legs. His dark T-shirt was a perfect match for his dark eyes. The wind tugged at the curls of hair. Bare feet.

"Pirate."

"What?"

"You look like a pirate. Well, a modern pirate."

"I seem to have misplaced my sword. And you seem to have misplaced your heading."

She was aiming square at the second hill, island. She shoved the tiller over. The sails snapped loudly at the sudden change.

He pulled on one of the lines and the boom swung closer over the deck.

There was a loud mew from the top of the boom.

"It's okay, girl. Just a newbie on the crew. We pirates can't be too choosy, just have to scavenge what we can find on the high seas."

A man who talked to his cat in whole sentences.

"I must have a thousand photos of that silly beast. I'm thinking of producing a book of cat photos. You know, the cute little things by cash registers."

"Cats of the world?"

"Cats of the world?" He rolled the sound over his tongue. "That's perfect. A whole little series. Cats of the South Seas."

"Caribbean Cats."

"Mediterranean Cats."

"Coy Cats of Cancun."

He grinned at her. For the first time since she'd boarded, he really looked at her. And she totally lost her heading. The sails flapped. Nutcase mewed loudly and thumped down onto the deck. But she couldn't look away.

He'd sent her roses on the last day of her class. Not a little bouquet, he'd sent an armful. Dozens of long reds, yellows, and whites delivered in the middle of class right in front of everyone. She hadn't been able to speak over the applause and good-natured laughter.

He slid a hand over hers on the tiller. With a gentle pressure, he eased them back onto course.

She was trapped, the tiller across her lap and Russell Morgan across the only way out from under.

He didn't lean toward her. Wouldn't hear her heart crashing away but sending no blood at all to her brain. He merely held her gaze with those eyes.

Once they were back on course, he released his hold on her and sat back.

He stared over the side at the water for a long time before he spoke.

"Do you want me to take you back to the dock?"

She could see that the words cost him deeply. He didn't turn to face her—which was good, because if he had, she'd have been lost. She was pretty lost anyway. His offer was perhaps the nicest compliment she'd ever had—it was also about the sexiest.

She'd given little thought to what might happen aboard the boat with Russell and only a cat for a chaperone, beyond choosing to drive to Anacortes rather than sail. However, now that she was here, there was little question of what might well happen if she remained. Even if common sense said run, she couldn't deny how it felt to be sitting so closely beside him.

She managed to shake her head. He didn't see because he wasn't looking.

"Let's…" her voice was barely a whisper. If they had been traveling by engine instead of wind, he wouldn't have heard her.

But he did and turned.

His eyes weren't begging…not quite.

Unable to speak, she shook her head once more.

They both smiled carefully.

He turned back to watch the water.

"WE'RE NEARLY THERE."

Cassidy didn't awake with a start as he'd expected. She woke slow, like a cat stretching and considering her next action carefully. Perhaps a yawn, perhaps another stretch. She'd napped for several hours in the shade of the cockpit bench. He'd managed not to stare too much. Part of him was amazed that she felt safe enough to sleep in his presence. He'd take that as a plus.

She wandered below and was a while coming back up.

She'd changed into shorts and a halter top that nearly blew

his blood pressure. Her light blouse was now open, worn more as a shawl against the sun than a cover. It revealed and hid her figure with every motion and breath of the wind. Her hair, let down from its tight bun, cascaded about her shoulders. Her face still had that sleepy look of freshly wakened and washed with cool water.

"Christ! You are so far beyond Teri's league."

The warm-and-washed look turned icy so fast it knocked the air out of his lungs.

"You're gorgeous!" She was.

The chill frost was replaced by a charming blush.

She was beyond that. Teri was shapely, Melanie was beautiful, but Cassidy Knowles, while not centerfold beautiful, was incredibly attractive. You couldn't not look at her.

"Uh, thanks."

He shook himself. "Sorry, I, that didn't, but you're..." He slapped a hand over his mouth.

She leaned down and kissed him on the forehead. Her hair slid along either side of his face. He had a view right down her neck and into her halter top. But it was her smell that got him. Warmth, home, and the open ocean with no perfume, not even scented soap. There had never been any woman who smelled like that. Ever.

Taking the seat opposite, she stretched her long legs across to his side. So close, he could reach out and stroke them if he dared. Cassidy had runner's legs, every curve just perfect—unpainted toes. Now why did he find that sexy? He was being ridiculous.

Look up, Russell. Look at the island. Check the chart. Reef along the east point. Shoals in close on the north. You'll rip off your keel if you don't pay more attention.

He swung to the south, into deeper water. Sailing around the western point, they slid around into Active Cove. There were two state-run mooring buoys, both open, which was rare for a

Friday in August. He did his best to concentrate only on swinging into the wind. He hooked the buoy on the first try and cleated it off, letting the sails back him away until they were at rest.

He had the sails part way down before he noticed Cassidy was standing across the boom, looking lost.

Without speaking, he showed her how to flake the sail into neat folds atop the boom. When it was lying neatly between the lazy jacks, he snapped the bungee cord in place. The jib was dropped and flaked in record time. Her hands were agile and strong once she knew what to do. They didn't have to talk, it was so easy and so natural.

Don't go there, Russell. She's just this incredibly desirable woman who has agreed to come out sailing with you. And only for the day at that.

The sails were set and the boat was well-tied. They were standing on the foredeck, a space barely three by five feet between the cabin and the forehatch.

For the life of him, he didn't know what to do, didn't know what to say. Should he reach for her or turn away before his pounding blood blew his brainpan into a puddle of mush?

"I loved the roses." Her voice was deep and throaty, hoarse on a lesser woman. Sexy as hell on Cassidy Knowles.

She stepped into his arms and their lips met with an electric shock that nearly knocked his knees out from under him.

They hadn't even looked at the damn lighthouse yet.

"I, UH..."

"Don't!" Cassidy was glaring up at him, just a few inches shorter, just a breath away.

"What?"

"You were going to apologize."

He nodded.

"Well, don't."

"But..."

She held up her hand to silence him, but he ignored her.

"I promised safe passage. I promised that you'd be as safe as you want to be aboard my boat." And now he'd gone and kissed her. Kissed her long and hard with a need that had surprised them both—well, it had shocked the hell out of him anyway. And it had been fantastic.

"I said, 'Safe'."

"You did."

She raised an eyebrow, a smile tickled the corner of her mouth. That soft, strong mouth. He wanted to kiss her again and feel how it changed as that smile took shape.

"And?"

"I took advantage." Stupid. Stupid. Stupid. Angelo would smack him but good.

"Russell?"

"Yeah?"

"Don't you think I'm old enough to know my own mind?"

"You're old enough to—"

"Careful there, big boy."

He bit his tongue and looked away from that maddening smile. The lighthouse was perched a few hundred yards away, on the northernmost San Juan Island. Next stop was Canada. They were out at the limits.

"Old enough to...make me completely insane."

"Nice save."

"Weak, but best I've got on a moment's notice. Did you really like the roses?"

"It'll do. And I loved the flowers. How did you know where to send them? And two weeks of poetry and stories and sea chanties. Gads!" She rested her hand on her heart. Somehow he had touched her, rather than scaring her off. *Duh, she was here, wasn't she?*

He needed to get some distance or he wouldn't be able to control himself. He let her go and moved to the dinghy and began to untie it from the deck cleats.

"I Googled you and your class popped up. I called the dean to find out when your last class was."

"You called the dean?" Cassidy undid the other ends of the lines. She started to untie the rope on the bow of the dinghy until he stopped her.

"We'll need that. Couldn't reach him, so I talked to some chef, Clara somebody." Together they lifted the little boat over the lifelines and dropped it bottom down into the water. He should have cleaned it. There were a thousand paint splotches. Globs of epoxy that probably wouldn't let go without taking some of the boat with them.

"You talked to Master Chef Clara Nichols? I barely got to talk to her."

"Nice lady. She helped me find a good florist, too. They want to talk to you about a Christmas class down at the California center as well."

She stood with her fists on her hips. Her eyes snapped with a fire that came out of nowhere—goddamn he loved when she did that. Cassidy Knowles was feisty and strongheaded, which suited him right down to his toes. He was torn between throwing her overboard or dragging her down to his bunk below. To buy himself a moment of equilibrium, he pulled the oars out of their cradle and tossed them down into the dinghy instead.

Then he turned to face her and matched her stance, fists on hips.

Finally she blew at her bangs.

He blew at his even though he didn't have any.

"What am I supposed to do with you?"

"Either climb into my bed or my boat."

She didn't laugh in his face; she didn't get angry and slap him either. Both were good signs.

Instead, that smile opened up its thousand-watt brilliance on him and he had to restrain himself to not lean across and taste it.

"There's no bed here," she made a show of looking up and down the rocky beach. "I'll take the boat."

They both knew there was one down below, but he managed to keep his mouth shut. Instead, he nodded and untied the painter, using it to lead the dinghy back toward the break in the lifelines.

"Yes, I'll take the boat," her voice behind him little louder than the lapping of the water on the hull. "For now."

The painter slipped from his fingers and he almost lost the whole mess into the sea.

CASSIDY HAD a terrible time hiding her smile as she lay back in the stern of the tiny rowboat. Russell pulled stoutly on the oars, making the dinghy nearly launch with each stroke. His eagerness to return to the sailboat was showing. She did her best to look Victorian and swooning as the pirate dragged her to his lair.

He showed the effects of their afternoon. His shirt had grass stains, a couple of leaves and a bit of branch perched in his hair—right where she'd tucked them in while he kissed her. And now she knew how wonderfully soft his hair truly was.

They had run about the island like a couple of teenagers. Grabbing a kiss at the very westernmost tip of the island. Slapping her hand against those tight jeans of his and discovering a few things about that butt of his. One, his body was just a firm as it looked. Two, it was good that she was fleet of foot, because he was a very fast runner when motivated.

The dinghy thudded into the side of his boat so hard she almost flew forward into his arms. In seconds, the boat was tied off and the oars had been tossed aboard.

He climbed up first and offered her a hand. She stepped straight into his arms and probably bruised her lips they came together so hard. They both leaned into it: tasting, touching, groaning. He dragged her blouse open to attack her throat, her neck, the top of her breasts. Everywhere he went was a new adventure.

He definitely wasn't a useless man who didn't know what he wanted. He clearly wasn't thinking about the latest stock deal or sporting event. Russell was completely here with her, wholly present in her arms, and she sure as hell wasn't going to let go.

Russell moved down to his knees to nuzzle her exposed belly.

Clawing at his shirt, she dragged it over his head. Ran her hands down that broad, strong back. He smelled of sea salt and man. There was no other word for it.

She pulled at his arms until he rose back to his feet so they could once again feast on each other's mouths. He suddenly bent down and put his shoulder into her waist, lifted her from her feet as if she weighed little more than his cat. She pounded his back, hard enough to make him grunt, not hard enough to make him put her down.

Her ears were buzzing loudly as he turned for the cabin.

No, it wasn't her ears. It was a speedboat filled with teenagers, roaring by less than a dozen feet away. A moment later their wake caught the sailboat.

The deck tilted.

She grabbed for what she could and latched onto the back of his belt and the waistband of his jeans.

He staggered one way. Staggered back.

And then she was flying free—soaring through the air in a moment of weightlessness.

They she hit the ocean with a splash.

The water was freezing. She kicked for the surface and gasped for air. The water was so cold it was hard to think.

More water sprayed in her face.

"Goddamn it, Morgan!"

He'd surfaced next to her. "This water is bloody cold."

"No shit!" She palmed a big spray of seawater into his face. While he spluttered, she looked up at the moored sailboat. Even in the few moments they'd been in the water, the current had drifted them away from it. They both swam, but didn't make any headway at first. She dug in deeper, kicked harder; it was slow work against the ocean current. She was getting colder and weaker with each passing moment.

They finally reached the boat where she grabbed onto the stern of the dinghy but couldn't pull herself up. The deck of the boat was far out of reach; what had been an easy step up from the dinghy was now a vast wall of wood. She lunged, but couldn't get close to the edge of the deck. And the cold was making her joints ache.

Russell dove.

"Don't you leave me!" she shouted down at the water.

Then he shot out of the water, half his body shooting into the air. A thousand drops of water sparkled all over him like a merman emerging from the deep. One hand caught the edge of the deck. Biceps flexed, shoulders rippled, and in moments he was aboard.

A hand reached down from above. She grabbed it.

He heaved, practically pulled her arm out of its socket.

Moments later she was sitting in the cockpit, the remains of her blouse wrapped around her as the shivers began to set in. There remained no sign of the kids in the speed boat, not even a wake.

"Come on. We have to get out of these clothes."

She shuddered. "That was the original idea. Now I'm n-n-not so motivated. How can water be so cold?" Her hands wouldn't stop shaking.

He pulled her to her feet and guided her below. The ladder was a major challenge.

"Puget Sound has a huge tide," Russell finally grabbed her by the waist and simply plucked her off the ladder and set her down inside the cabin. "Fresh sea water from Alaska pumps in here every day. Good thing it's summer; it means that you have a life expectancy of about twelve minutes in this water. In the winter, it's more like four before hypothermia sets in."

"Great!" The cool shade inside the boat only chilled her more deeply.

"Can we sue them or something?"

"They're long gone. The little shits."

He peeled off her blouse and halter top, but had the decency to leave the bikini top she'd put on as a bra. She'd never felt so unromantic before in her life. Going to the doctor was more exciting than this. She tried to undo her shorts, but couldn't control her fingers. He undid them and shucked them off her legs.

"You are one big goosebump."

"That's because I'm freezing to death, you big hunk of meat. I don't have all the insulation you do."

He grabbed a blanket and wrapped it around her. He held her close and scrubbed his hands up and down her back to warm her up. His chest was cold and wet, but she leaned into it. She didn't want to admit to being scared, but watching the boat drift away in that moment before they'd started swimming had been terrifying. Her life had suddenly gone out of control as she was ripped from everything safe.

He smelled so good. She hid her face against his chest and luxuriated in the warmth of his scrubbing hands. Her very joints hurt with the cold. Moments ago she'd wanted to throw herself against his body, now she wanted to cower there.

Another shiver shook her so hard she couldn't even hold onto the blanket which slipped off her shoulders.

"You really took a chill. Come on," he dragged her forward.

She managed to step around the missing floorboard despite the silly putty that had replaced her knees. Moments later he'd removed the last of her wet clothes and had her tucked into the bed. She pulled the covers over her head and gave in to the shakes.

Moments later he slid in beside her and wrapped his arms around her.

It was the safest place she'd ever been.

If only it wasn't so damn cold.

CASSIDY DIDN'T REMEMBER when the shivers stopped. She didn't remember falling asleep. She didn't remember it getting dark.

There was a loud purring in her ear.

She rolled toward it and was rewarded with a faceful of fur. Nutcase's purr rose to an active buzz.

Then she became aware of two things simultaneously.

First, she wasn't the only human in this bed.

Second, she had no clothes on.

She lifted the cover and started to slip out of the bunk. A strong arm came from behind, looped around her waist, and pulled her back. In moments she was spooned back against Russell's chest, his arm a powerful rope around her waist.

Third, she discovered, he wore no clothes either. Despite that, she didn't feel trapped.

"Feeling better?" His voice was thick with sleep.

She nodded. Was this what she really wanted? If she didn't, she'd better move soon. Her body chose for her as she shifted closer against the heat of him. She'd never take being warm for granted again.

His arm slid farther around until it encircled her waist and tucked under her rib cage. Then she felt the growing pressure against her behind. Russell loosened his grip and shifted away.

He really was a gentleman. Well, mostly.

"You had to take off all of your clothes, too?" She wrapped her arm over his and pulled it back around her waist to let him know she was teasing.

"They were wet. It seemed like a good idea at the time." The last was said so close to her ear that his breath tickled.

Again he offered to back off. She wondered what it cost him to lean back so a tiny gap of warm air filled the space where his chest had been.

She rolled in his embrace and pushed on his shoulder until he lay on his back and she straddled him.

"Watch the overhead."

Raising her head slowly, she just brushed the underside of the decking. The boat was rocking gently with the rhythm of the sea. It felt so natural that her body followed it as easily as a leaf finding the breeze.

Russell's hands, those big rough hands she'd admired so often, wrapped ever so gently around her waist practically encircling her.

They slid upward, traced the line of her ribcage. Rather than latching onto her breasts in a typical he-man crush, his callused thumbs traced the side of her breasts with the softest of touches. He supported her as she leaned down for a kiss.

His mouth, so eager and forceful before, was a soft welcome. He ran one hand into her hair and the other over her behind.

She rubbed up the length of him and he groaned into her mouth. Lip to lip, chest to chest, every curve of him felt wonderful.

And his shoulders were amazing. She slid her arms beneath

them and grasped them from behind. Shoulders big enough to carry the world.

Traveling in the upper tiers of the wine and restaurant circles she'd met her share of rich heirs. But Russell played none of their games—showed none of the ego about the wealth he had. His touch didn't assume or demand, rather it coaxed and asked—a question that her own body was more than happy to reply to in the affirmative. He had a body that had been custom made for her. She worked her way down, planting kisses on his throat and chest.

His hands played with her hair.

His groan returned with a gasp as she slid him between her breasts. A little farther and she was able to make him groan and arch with his need. When she returned him to her cleavage, he grabbed at her shoulders and dragged her upward.

When they were once again even, she whispered in his ear, "Do you have...?" Christ she was being forward, wasn't she.

He reached somewhere to the side in the dark of the boat. There was a slight crinkle. It repeated with a little more energy. Then a frantic rattling of foil.

"Shit. My fingers, they aren't..."

She silenced him with a kiss and slid her hand along his arm until she found the condom. She sat back up as she unwrapped it. He was nervous. It was so charming that she'd have made the decision now, if she hadn't already.

He moaned again as she unrolled it slowly over him. The delicious contrast of soft and hard made her fingertips want to explore. He was writhing by the time she braced her hands on his chest and lowered herself over him.

When he was finally inside her, they sighed in unison. And they both laughed as Nutcase abandoned the bed in disgust with a loud thump of paws on the floor.

All of the heady need built over months had mellowed and sweetened with a little aging. He traced his hands down from her face, over her breasts, finally cupping her buttocks hard. He thrust up as she thrust down.

It was too much. Some part of her, some part she didn't know, let forth a throaty growl like a lioness taking down its kill. Her senses closed into the rocking of the boat and the perfect rhythm as he filled her deeper and deeper. It was a heady swirl of heat and sea salt. Of wave after wave after wave pounding up through her and making her release over and over again.

When her body had hit its limit, when she could climb no farther, Russell launched himself upward, thrusting so far inside her they could have been the same body. She could feel each pulse of his release, each separate moment, triggering her own body into one last mind-numbing, soul-crashing wave.

When he finished, she slid down against his chest. His hands, soft as kitten fur, brushed against her face and over her hair. He stroked over the bridge of her nose and traced the arc of her eyebrows.

"Oh. My." His voice husked out about an octave lower than usual.

She couldn't agree more.

IT WAS late morning when Russell dragged on shorts and wandered down the companionway. Spotting Cassidy on the port bench of the cockpit made his world shift. It wasn't anything she did. She was simply sitting there, her back to him as she faced the stern. One of his dress shirts riding loose on her shoulders, the sleeves rolled up to her elbows.

He hung back in the shadows and watched her. Her head was tilted down as she read something in her lap and her hair hung like a shawl over her shoulders. She wasn't a stranger out of place. She'd taken to the boat as naturally as if she'd always been there—had always been in his life. Nutcase was curled up by her toes, asleep in the sun. In a single day, Cassidy had already become a fixture in the cat's life.

For the first time, ever, Russell could imagine his sea voyage with two. He could see spending time with this incredible woman, a lot of time. *You can't fall in love with someone overnight.* He could almost feel Angelo smacking him on the back of the head. But it wasn't overnight. He'd never known so much about a woman before bedding her.

Even that was wrong. He hadn't bedded her. They'd made love. Repeatedly. Wonderfully. Deliciously. Until exhaustion had finally dragged them back under.

He stepped onto the companionway ladder, which groaned as always.

Cassidy spun to stare at him.

For a single instant he saw the red-rimmed eyes. The tear-stained cheeks, then she turned away.

He froze on the step. Shit! So that's how the morning after was going to be. What had he screwed up this time? Angelo could probably tell him, but he was a hundred miles and a two-day sail away.

Russell turned back into the cabin and strode back toward the stateroom. He was there in five steps. No space on a goddamn boat. What was he thinking? Two people couldn't live on something this small, not even for one night. It wasn't humanly possible. He needed to punch something.

Punch it really hard.

And what was he supposed to do with her now? They were hours from the nearest port. More than half a day from her car, even with the motor.

Shit!

Why had he gotten his hopes up? Stupid-ass dream about finding the right woman. Instead, he'd found something new to screw up. And there was no guide on what it was this time, or what it would be next time. He pounded the side of his fist against the butt of the mast where it came through the deck. Hitting it felt good. He raised his fist to hit it again.

A cool hand touched the middle of his back and he froze.

He turned slowly, his fist still above his head.

Cassidy didn't look up at it.

Didn't even look at him.

She leaned against his T-shirt and he heard a gasp for breath.

He lowered his arms slowly. She began to shake. Her arms tucked between them just as when she'd been so cold yesterday. With her head tucked under his chin, he could feel her body shudder.

A tentative hand on her back released some unknown dam. In moments she was sobbing against him, long, racking, gasping sobs.

He pulled her closer.

Now he had even less of a clue what to do than before.

"I'm sorry, Cassidy." It would help if he knew what he was apologizing for. "You tell me what to do and I'll make it better."

She rocked her head back and forth keeping her face planted against his sternum and cried harder. That was a clear no.

"I'll go away, if that's what you need." God, how could he say that? Even as he held her he felt more powerful than ever before in his life, as if he could somehow protect her from the world. Unfortunately, what he needed to protect her from was himself.

He took a deep breath. If that's what she needed...

"You won't even need to see me again." Christ! The words ripped his throat as he offered them up.

One of her hands slid from between them and slid around his neck. She again shook her head and held on tighter.

At a complete loss, he decided to just keep his mouth shut. Powerful was replaced by helpless between one breath and the next and it felt lousy.

If he felt this way about her already...

Just shut up, Russell. Your brain is made of undercooked tapioca. One of Angelo's favorite insults. Small, hard nuggets in a slimy matrix of useless goo.

He managed to settle back on the bed with her sitting in his lap. He kissed the top of her head and stroked her hair.

"It'll be okay. Somehow it'll be okay."

In response she pulled her other hand free and shoved a crumpled piece of paper into his hand. He unfolded it as well as he could with one hand. It was a short letter, covered in a spidery scrawl that might have belonged to a child. Actually, it reminded him of one of the funniest letters he'd ever gotten. Angelo had written to him once as he was going under the drugs to have his impacted wisdom teeth removed. The letter had started clear, concise, a little complaining, mixed with some gossip about a pretty nurse. As the handwriting decayed, so had the train of conscious thought. The end of the letter had been an illegible blur—Angelo's pen had actually dragged all the way across the page in a fading line that they'd never been able to translate.

Cassidy's letter was mostly readable. Someone who called her "Ice Sweet." Not a name he'd use, fire and ice maybe, with a lot more fire than he'd ever met before. Cassidy was a deep banked, hot fire; the kind that would burn forever. He glanced at the bottom. Vic somebody.

Dearest Ice Sweet,

I thought about never telling you this part of our past. About letting the truth die with me. But finally decided that taking it to the grave wasn't fair to you. Maybe the drugs have clouded my judgment and your father is wrong, in which case, I'm sorry.

Her father was dead. Russell flipped the page over, one side only. Cassidy had gone quiet. Her head resting on his shoulder, her hand on his chest, like a little girl going to sleep.

Your birth was harder on your mother than she ever let on. I was preoccupied with the loss of one vineyard, which nearly broke my heart, and the start of the next. The work was just as brutal, and your mother wasn't able to help. Her parents were failing fast, your grandfather had a massive stroke and your grandmother just gave up. She caught pneumonia the day before he died and was gone within the week.

And he'd asked Cassidy to help protect him from his parents. His wealthy, healthy, loving parents. Shit!

You were born by C-section. There was an infection. Then other things went wrong. We thought they were treated, but some damage was done, something not removed entirely or... We never knew. When the ovarian cancer struck, it took her so fast I barely had a chance to say goodbye.

I always told you she was called to the hospital and killed on the way. It was almost that fast, but that wasn't what happened.

She wasn't a nurse, though she nursed my heart after Vietnam, and you and her parents. She was a nurse of the heart, the gentlest soul I've ever known. I didn't know she'd never come home when I took her away that last time. Truth of truths, maybe I didn't ever really say goodbye. I still miss her so much that every day it is a hole in my heart.

I feel as if I really did get a chance to say goodbye to you. I'm so glad you moved back to Seattle to spend my last six months with me. It is the greatest gift you could have ever given me.

Love you, Ice Sweet

Vic

He turned the page over again. Still blank. He folded it carefully and tucked it back into her hand. She clenched it slowly into a fist, the paper's crinkling the only sound other than the gentle slap of waves against the hull.

"When did he die?"

"Christmas Day." Her voice was hoarse, barely a whisper. She found a Kleenex and blew her nose with a very unwomanly honk. She was really a mess.

"I hate crying. I haven't wept like that since, I don't know, ever. Maybe since Mama didn't come home."

"But it's August. How...the letter?" She'd been reading a letter on the bow of the boat when his parents were there. And he'd noticed her reading one out at Cape Flattery while he poked around the rocks looking for his Lady of the Lights.

For Cassidy.

"He gave you the calendar of lighthouses."

She nodded against his chest.

"And...a series of letters."

Again the smooth slickness of her hair rubbing back and forth under his chin.

"He's taking a whole year to say goodbye."

This time she was quiet, though he could feel the gentle warmth of her tears soak once more into his T-shirt.

"He sounds like a wonderful man."

"The best."

It took her a while, but she told him about the letters. About his sunny California vineyard followed by the one in rainy Bainbridge Island. Cassidy told him of her trip there and what it had felt like to stand on the soil that had once been his—knowing the vines were gone, but still able to feel his spirit there in that soil.

"You were right." She was sitting on the floorboards, leaning back against the mast now. Her feet propped against his thigh as he sat sideways with his feet against the stove and his lying partially under the settee's tabletop, against the inside curve of the hull. He'd never have guessed that it was so easy to be casual and relaxed around Cassidy Knowles.

"I was right?" Wouldn't that just shock the shit out of Angelo. "About what?"

"About my not really knowing a wine."

"It was a stupid-ass remark made to a woman I didn't even know. I thought you were—"

"What?"

He shook his head. It would make him sound even dumber than he was.

She poked one of her toes into his ribs. He tried to scoot away but there was nowhere to scoot. She started to wiggle them and he had to shove her leg away. She slid the other foot up the leg of his shorts and wiggled them there. He sat bolt upright and cracked his head on the underside of the table.

Her laugh spilled out between her fingers even as she mumbled an apology and tried to reach for his head to check for bumps.

An attempt to push her away achieved nothing. Once she ascertained there was no bump, she kissed the spot.

"All better," she declared.

He turned his head and kissed her. Time slowed, nearly ground to a halt as his blood hammered in his head. Without even thinking about it, he had one hand on her breast, no bra beneath the light dress shirt. She crawled into his lap and in moments they were sprawled back on the narrow strip of the passageway floor.

She pulled his T-shirt out of his shorts and slid a cool hand across his chest.

"Oh. My."

"You said that before," she didn't stop.

He had and it was just as true now. How could anything feel so wonderful? Then she teased his nipples.

"Give."

"Anything."

"What were you going to say?"

He clamped his mouth shut. She ground her hips against him almost painfully hard.

"Give."

Give? He could barely remember how to breathe.

"Give."

"Okay," he gasped for breath, but there wasn't any air on the boat. "Okay, just stop that for a second so I can uncross my eyes."

She stopped. Mostly. As if the slow motion of her hips in perfect rhythm with the ocean was one bit less distracting. "Give. You thought I was…"

"A stuck-up, Upper East Side, rich bitch, spoiled brat."

Her smile was beatific. "Not a self-made, Northwest island girl, who busted her ass for every inch she ever gained?"

"Uh. No." He couldn't believe this was the same woman who had frozen him out on that first date.

"Not one of the country's leading wine tasters who studied how to be Upper East Side because she didn't have the lazy-ass, Upper West Side fortune?"

With a quick grab at the back pocket of her shorts, he managed to get the leverage to flip her onto her back.

"I busted my ass too. I've earned every damn cent I've ever spent since junior year of high school." Where did the sudden anger come from? It had soared like a flame inside of him. And now here he was pinning her to his floor, taking advantage of his strength. He shoved away—stood and moved off to the galley.

She caught up with him after he'd climbed into the cockpit.

The boat was just too damned small.

"Sorry. I was just teasing. I know you earned it. Your dad told me about it when we had dinner in New York. About how proud he was of you for finding your own way."

He stared aft. Looking at the sea, the sky, the island, trying to focus on anything.

"You wouldn't joke about that?" Had he misjudged every single event in his life?

She slid her hands around his waist from behind and rested her head on his shoulder. Together they looked out at the lighthouse.

The day was fading. They'd made love all night, and slept most of the day. The sun was already westering, though the long Northwest evening was far from over.

"We make a pretty sad pair of porcupines." Her voice was kind, her hands strong and gentle.

She pulled one of his hands free from where he'd jammed them into his pockets.

He opened his mouth. To explain. To apologize. To thank her for perhaps being the first woman in his life to not care about his money, or his past, or what he might do in the future. The first to like him as he was: a god-awful mortal mess.

She rested a finger gently across his lips to silence him.

Not releasing his hand, she guided him down onto the cockpit bench where they made love until the stars ruled the sky.

IN SOME WAYS it was the trickiest shoot Russell had ever done.

Perrin had loaded most of the contents of her store into his boat and he'd anchored off the Seattle waterfront. By the second or third clothing change, the three women had gotten over the self-consciousness that usually caused amateur shoots to look so stiff and miserable.

They laughed more than any group he'd ever been with. They teased him mercilessly, starting with "hubba-hubba" noises and rapidly degenerating to incredibly raunchy—with Perrin definitely taking the lead there. When, in an unthinking moment, Russell had stripped off his shirt because of the sun's heat, Perrin had started a series of catcalls and whistles that could be heard over most of Elliot Bay.

The technical challenges of lighting, background, and a shooting platform that was in constant motion occupied most of his mind. The sun would be right, but the background wrong.

The background and light right, but the proper shooting position was five yards off the beam. Some of Perrin's more classic designs wanted the older part of Seattle in the background. The more outrageous outfits were accented, more vivid, alive with the mid-town skyscrapers as a setting.

Several times he clambered out onto the boom and swung himself over the side, snapping half-a-dozen images before he swung back inboard. He'd tried standing in the dinghy, but the water was a little too lively for him to keep his balance.

Then Cassidy got him. He was sitting in the dinghy, shooting up at the women on the boat. She was dressed in a skimpy summer beach outfit. His white dress shirt, the one she'd never returned, open and blowing in the gentle breeze. She grabbed one of the shrouds that soared up to hold up the mast.

Leaning out over the water and, with a siren-like beauty used to tease sailors onto the rocks of despair, flashed one of her killer smiles.

His heart stumbled. His hands wielded the camera more out of habit than intent. He didn't need the camera, smiling Cassidy was forever burned into his mind. Moments later Perrin and Jo were with her.

The Three Sirens.

The Three Fates.

Three Sisters.

Jo, Perrin, and Cassidy.

Truth, Joy, and Beauty.

At some point they fed him a sandwich which he'd eaten without tasting. He had to change out the memory card in his camera three times.

As the sun set, he began to wish he'd rented the flash umbrellas. The changing light—with just a few elegant accents —would set the stage for Perrin's collection of eveningwear.

"Cassidy. Grab the storm sail," he called down. He'd been banished from below, the women's changing room.

Moments later, she tossed it out of the hatchway.

"You sure you never sailed before?"

All that answered was her bright laugh and it definitely did something racy to his heart. In the short last month, she'd inhaled sailing knowledge as if she'd been born to it. They'd anchored in quiet coves up in the Canadian Queen Charlottes, ridden out a forty-knot storm in the Straits when they'd decided to visit Destruction Island lighthouse by sail. And love. Holy Christ they'd made incredible love.

He hung the white storm sail from the main boom and the lifelines, then tied the excess off to the boom.

Jo came up first. A black sheath that followed every curve perfectly. It rode low enough to reveal the bounty of her breasts, but high enough to be pure class. Her long black hair was swept forward over one shoulder. As she turned, she revealed the bit of magic that was Perrin's trademark—every piece had some surprise: often subtle, occasionally blatant.

Jo's dress didn't reveal her whole back as might be expected. Rather, only a small, open area revealed her beautiful olive skin. Exactly the spot a man's hand would rest during an intimate waltz or... He had to smile.

He had Jo swing back as if in the throes of tango, the reserved woman released by the dress and his request. Her hair swept back along the deck and her body arched in pleasure, passion, and joy. The flash reflected off the sail covered her in a ballroom's soft lighting, etching her against the oranges and golds of the sunset beyond the water and the sharply outlined peaks of the Olympic Mountains.

Perrin slid into the picture, taking the man's position in the dance. A pantsuit, but like none he'd ever seen in a dozen years of New York fashion. The slacks had seams that climbed in an iridescent spectrum from ankle to hip. The triple-layered jacket lapels shifted from traditional black to the shades of the rainbow depending on how she moved. But they weren't heavy, rather they accented the plunging cleavage of the single-buttoned front. The cleavage of a woman wearing nothing but the jacket and pants. A perky hat that might have fit a sixties secret agent if not for the single peacock feather above the right ear. She was at once in control, powerful, and incredibly erotic.

She and Jo danced about the narrow deck, posed at the edge of the dance so that he could capture each alone, and then whirled together in a flurry of laughter and sensuality. Yet there was never a moment, despite all their fooling around, that there could be a doubt about the orientation of these two women. They were friends dancing together, to make the men wild.

Perrin had been very strict about that. She didn't care what others thought about her, but she didn't want to embarrass her two friends. Her love for them went so deep.

In their various meetings preparing for this shoot, she'd revealed tiny glimpses of how they had saved her from her parents' past. The abuser and the whore who had no compunction about using their own daughter, selling her. How she'd surely have gotten herself killed, or killed herself, many times over if it hadn't been for Cassidy and Jo. Her wild experiments with drugs, alcohol, and men had all been tempered by them. She loved her life and she attributed it entirely to her two best friends.

He'd fallen further in love with Cassidy as he heard of the interventions, sometimes in the middle of Vassar campus. Cassidy had brought Perrin home for every vacation so she'd never be alone where her parents could get at her, or even alone with her own originally self-destructive tendencies.

Then Cassidy came up from below and he forgot about everything. She moved slowly, her dress shimmering in the golden light. No sequins. Nor glitter. The threads of the material caught, reflected, and refracted light but appeared as plain and simple as a red evening gown. Not the red of a wild woman, but the dusky red of her chestnut hair. The dress wasn't blatant, it wasn't a slap in the face like Perrin's pantsuit, or a sensual masterpiece like Jo's. It spoke as much of the observer as of the wearer. High-necked, long-sleeved, her cascading hair the only adornment other than a small sailboat on a thin gold neck chain.

It was a look that invited him into the warm circle of the woman within. Almost of its own will, his camera raised to his eye. They moved in slow motion. Step, click, flash. Shift, click, flash. This time Russell and Cassidy were the two dancing.

The images of Cassidy shifted about him. The color rising to her cheeks made her that much more alive. The sparkle in her eyes as she relaxed made her that much more desirable.

He moved about the deck to capture different angles, heights, backgrounds, and still her smile dazzled him.

She bent out of one frame giving him a shot of the top of her head. When she stood straight once more, Nutcase, in all her fuzzy disarray, cuddled against Cassidy's chin. He came in closer. The camera never ceased its whirr-click, flash.

Nutcase looking at Cassidy, Cassidy looking directly at him. Whirr-click, flash. Beauty.

Cassidy looked down at the cat. Whirr-click, flash. The nurturer.

Cassidy and the cat both looking at him. Totally self-contained. Whirr-click, flash.

He stopped. Dropped the camera to his side. How could he not want to be with this woman when she looked at him that way? He wanted her in his life.

A loud pop startled him from his reverie.

Perrin laughed aloud and began pouring champagne into small glass tumblers.

He looked back at Cassidy, but she was facing away. Dropping Nutcase onto the cockpit cushions.

"I thought that last outfit would get you." Perrin pushed a glass into his free hand and extracted the camera from his limp fingers, unwinding the strap from behind his elbow. She slid his camera into its case then dropped onto the bench seat next to Jo. She planted a big, sloppy kiss on her friend's cheek.

His knees finally buckled and he landed on the bench across from them. He'd never worked as hard or enjoyed himself so much. He knocked back the glass of bubbly and it scorched his throat as sharply as scalding coffee.

Cassidy still stood by the tiller. Her floor-length dress made her look like some fantasy being, inviting him to be with her forever.

"God, you are so beautiful."

That smile of hers lit the night more brightly than any flash. She slid down beside him, pulled his arm over her shoulders, cuddled in close against his side. The blood hammered so loudly in his ears he couldn't hear a single word being said though he could see Perrin and Jo laughing at something Cassidy said.

They teased Nutcase and drank champagne. He sat outside. They didn't shut him out and it wasn't that he didn't belong.

No. He sat outside himself, observing and amazed. The shock was that he truly did belong.

ADMIRALTY HEAD LIGHTHOUSE

Whidbey Island
First lit: 1861
Extinguished: 1922
48.15702 -122.67943

*H*igh on the towering cliffs of Whidbey Island, this lighthouse didn't survive the transition from sailing ships to those driven by steam. The lighthouse marked the farthest side of a wide channel, and ships powered by steam did not need to cross Puget Sound before turning South for Seattle or north for Vancouver. They simply exited the Straits and turned at the Point Wilson light.

The dormant light served as a medical clinic and barracks for the Fort Casey gun emplacements during WWII. At that time it was painted olive drab and the light room was removed. The Island County Historical Society eventually repainted it white and red and rebuilt a light room.

SEPTEMBER 1

Dearest Ice Sweet,

It's funny. By the time you're reading this, I'll have been dead for most of a year. Time is a strange thing. Life speeds up and slows down-maddeningly slowly when there is pain and sorrow. And it's a blur through the good times. It should be the other way around.

With your mother gone, I thought my life was over. Knowles Valley Vines was lost, and both parents-in-law and my wife were gone. Yet those years were so busy that they'd be hard to remember if they also hadn't been so full. The daughter I'd left in my wife's care needed a father.

I'd thought about moving, you were young enough, it probably wouldn't have mattered. But where? There had been so much heartbreak in the California soil, that I couldn't drag you or myself back there. I didn't want to work for someone else on "my" land and I had no family on either side, so I stayed where I was as much by default as anything else.

The Bainbridge vineyard needed my attention because the vines were finally producing. I mixed in Northwest flavors: strawberry, blackberry, huckleberry. I did some of the marketing your mother had suggested: Eagle White, Dugout Rose, and Olympics Red were all hers.

They were hectic, wonderful years; watching you grow was an education in itself. Your mother had left behind a huge collection of books. You started devouring them thinking they were mine, but that was your dead mother passing on her greatest joy to you. To us. I read like mad to keep up with you. I'm glad that we were able to share that part of your mother's past.

If I could wish anything, it was that you had stayed in the vine-yards with me. I think we could have had such a rich life there. I wanted to leave the vineyards to you, but you had your own plans. I sold them for a lot of money, from struggling my whole life to very comfortable in a single moment—a shock to an old man. Enough to set you up for many years to come, but you know that by now, assuming my medical bills don't wipe it out.

We've walked together a long way, let's not stop just yet.

Love you, Ice Sweet

Vic

Cassidy folded the letter and slipped it back into her pocket.

"A long way, Daddy." This year had been both slow and fast. It had been such a mix that she barely knew what to make of it. The loss of her father, enough money to live off for a decade without any other income, her increasing fame as a columnist, and Russell.

Dear Russell. He sat a dozen yards away facing Puget Sound, carefully not looking in her direction. The water stretched from Admiralty Head here to the Port Townsend light ten miles away on the Olympic Peninsula. His unease showed in the way he plucked strands of grass from the high bluff edge, then worried them into thin strips with his fingernails before pitching them off the edge. Did he even notice that the sea breeze up the cliff face was lifting his offerings and dumping them behind him?

"Hey there."

He jerked around at her call. Hustling over he almost sat,

then stood again. She patted the grass and he thudded down beside her.

"You okay?" His first thought was always for her and she still wasn't used to it.

"Yeah, no gut wrencher this time. Just about my growing up and how much he enjoyed those years."

He pulled her over and kissed the top of her head. "I'm glad. You didn't need another like the last one. I'm still angry about that. Hell of a bomb to leave in a letter; he took the coward's way out."

That was her Russell. He was all straight-ahead and forthright, as strong and straight as the lighthouse that rose three-stories high behind them. Her father's choice had made perfect sense to her, but she'd never been able to explain it to Russell's satisfaction.

Her father was gentle and considerate. He wouldn't risk their last weeks together with a fight. If he'd blamed her or been angry, he'd have put it in the first letter—not waited until August. She was glad she'd opened the letters one a month. If she'd read some of this right after his death, she'd have been hurt much more. And really pissed her off.

"I hear that you've got more business." Some things it was simply better not to talk about.

He pulled another grass blade and started his inattentive dissection.

"The head of a small consortium of stores was eating at Angelo's—attracted there by my ads. He told her about Perrin's. Turns out she shops there...because of the ads." He shrugged, those big shoulders rising unevenly then settling only part way back.

"Then why did you say yes?"

Again the shrug. "Well, I'm still a month or so from getting the boat ready. And I want to take another navigation class or two. Gives me something to do."

She nodded, not wanting to push. She had enough worries of her own. But she was worried about that hunch as he sat. And she was worried about him sailing off into the sunset and what that might mean to them, though they'd agreed to not discuss such things.

"I got an interesting phone call this morning."

He half turned his head to show he was listening, but he didn't stop his botanical experiments. The scent of new-mown grass escaped from his little cuttings.

"From Italy."

Another blade went flying only to be grabbed by the breeze up the face of the eighty-foot cliff and tossed behind him. Another tiny offering at the base of the lighthouse.

"Sienna."

"What's there?"

"Montalcino wines."

"And this means?" He still wasn't looking at her.

"The Italians heard I was talking to Mondavi and they want a shot at me." It was kind of nice to be wanted. Even though her mind was made up, at least if she were going to make the change. She'd thought Mondavi's stellar treatment of her in June had been nothing more than them wooing a wine reviewer.

Last week they called with a much more serious offer. They offered to create a new position specifically for her, wine director. She was invited to bring her palate to the vintner's aid, her writing to marketing's aid, and her insights to the winery's aid. A hand in shaping one of the finest wineries in America. They even had invited her down for the harvest as a "get to know each other"—first class, all expenses paid, of course.

The wine-column world was great, but it was limited. She saw that now. Russell had been onto it way back at the beginning and her dad agreed with him. Wine reviewers lived on the outside looking in and—now that she was aware of it—she hated that feeling. She wanted to be in the game, affecting decisions, shaping flavors, accentuating the superb, and casting out the ordinary.

"Sienna?" His attention shifted at last to her face.

"I'm not really interested, but they were very persuasive. I'm going to California during the harvest in a couple of weeks, so I'll just fly to Italy from there, maybe catch their harvest time as well."

"Sounds good."

BUT IT WASN'T. Russell couldn't think of a thing to say all the way home. Neither of them were grumpy. Cassidy had tried to start the conversation a couple of times, but it always fizzled out. As much her doing as his. It wasn't a comfortable silence, but it was a companionable one; both lost in their own thoughts.

He'd dropped her at the condo to write her next column.

She might come by the boat later.

They spent most nights together, as often as not on the boat. They both claimed it was to keep Nutcase company, but he didn't sleep well in high-rise condos—though being with Cassidy in that big bed or sitting before that amazing view had already gone a long way toward changing his mind.

California. Italy. Even if she stayed in Seattle or went back to New York, her life was on the land, attached to root and vine.

His future was on the ocean.

The more he thought about that though, the less comfortable it was. He enjoyed the photography. He'd really liked working with Angelo and Perrin. They'd been fun and made him feel good about himself and about what he could do. The boat would be done soon, as done as wooden sailboats ever were. And he liked knowing the local waters. They too were becoming familiar and comfortable without any sign of growing dull.

The consortium of little stores might be fun. But he hadn't told her about the Seattle City Trade Association that had approached him about a national campaign. He'd turned them down cold despite the vast sums in their advertising budget. He didn't do the ads for Angelo or Perrin for the money. The SCTA was maybe a little more personal than a BMW or a Rolex, but maybe not. Maybe it was the same thing, just wrapped up in the softer, kinder style of the Pacific Northwest.

Was the sailing just another escape? Another way to not have to truly decide about his life? But that didn't feel right either. He was far happier on the boat than he'd ever been on dry land.

After dropping off Cassidy, he wandered down the dock, and the moment he stepped aboard he felt...home. He fed Nutcase out in the cockpit, grabbed at a beer, and cracked open a fresh tube of Ritz crackers.

Perry strolled by and Russell called him over. "Got something I've been meaning to give you."

He ducked below and grabbed the small album and another beer.

Perry came aboard and was trying to feed a cracker to Nutcase.

"Don't get her started on my private stash."

"Not interested." He ate the cracker himself and opened the beer with a nod of thanks.

"Finally figured out what you were talking about. Made this for you to say thanks." He handed the album to him. It was a small one, one picture on each facing page, forty photos in all.

Perry opened to the first page. A photo of Nutcase, curled up in her cardboard box, not much bigger than the lens cap he'd tucked beside her for scale.

The next pages were her discovering the boat...and him

discovering his companion. He knew the rest by heart as Perry paged through the book.

Nutcase sleeping on the boom, another looking out at the lighthouses. A look of fascination, then of terror at a breaching orca. Arguing with a seagull twice her size at close enough range that Russell hadn't been sure whether or not to run to her aid. But she'd won handily, protecting their boat like a hissing hellcat, the seagull flapping off his bowsprit perch in disgust.

The final picture hadn't been his, but it was arguably the best of the lot. Cassidy had been behind the camera. He'd been asleep on the deck with Nutcase asleep on his chest. The high cliffs and towering Destruction Island lighthouse were visible as a soft background. A blow-up of that one hung down below on, right next to the one of Cassidy and Nutcase from Perrin's photo shoot.

Perry stood and went below without asking permission. It was just the way the old man was. He was harmless, so it was easy to ignore his eccentricities. Maybe he needed to use the head.

He came back on deck and held the closed book with both hands for a moment. Then he returned it to Russell.

"No, it's yours. I made it for you."

The old man shook his head. Took a couple of the Ritz crackers, raised his beer in a salute, and stepped off the boat. When he was even with Russell, standing on the finger pier, he took a long swallow of his beer. His old blue eyes wrinkled in what Russell had learned was a smile.

"The Sailing Cat. First in a series. Big hit." Then he was gone.

———

RUSSELL PLAYED WITH NUTCASE A LITTLE, finished his beer, and idly flipped through the album in the failing light of the day. Perry was right. New York would eat it up. He'd send it to Arnie and she'd have it sitting next to every bookstore cash register in the country by Christmas.

At the second to last page, there was the photo of Nutcase sleeping on his chest. He could have sworn he'd put that one at the end. He turned to the final page.

There she was. Cassidy, in that incredible evening gown with the boat and the city a soft backdrop, and Nutcase curled up in her arms. The look on her face still blew him away. He thought he'd photographed love before, but it was as if he'd only photographed the word itself and here was the true emotion. There was love, humor, passion, and...something indescribable. Whatever it was, it made him feel incredible that for even that instant of time it had been aimed at him.

Perry had nailed it; her entry into his life was what made the book complete and personal—it told the story. The collection would go ballistic.

Stowing the crackers, he locked the cabin and headed for Cassidy's. He couldn't lose her to some status-seeking California winery. Couldn't lose her to a bunch of high-rolling Italians. Screw their tacit agreement not to discuss the future. There had to be a way to keep her and he was going to do something about it now.

He punched in her keycode at the lobby entry and made it all the way to her door, had even raised his hand to knock, before the absurdity of the situation sunk in.

Since when had he ever said the right thing? He should go consult with Angelo. Or should he? His friend had talked about Jo enough, but hadn't done anything about his attraction to her. Granted, his restaurant was taking off. Really taking off. Cassidy had done another write-up and this one had caught the attention of the magazines. Suddenly *Sunset, Conde Nast,* and *Cigar* were coming out to write up "Angelo's Tuscan Hearth" above and beyond Cassidy's column. Maybe now wasn't the best time to get advice on how to handle his girlfriend.

Girlfriend.

He'd had lovers, but never a girlfriend—at least not since high school. Natasha Beckworth, senior prom—though she'd been a lover, too. Maybe she'd been more lover and less girlfriend. They'd had great sex, but he couldn't remember a thing about what she did or didn't like.

Cassidy had been the one to teach him the difference between lover and loving someone. He didn't need Angelo's advice; Russell knew what woman he wanted.

He knocked on Cassidy's door.

No answer.

Harder.

Still nothing. But he heard a clink of glass, or something from inside.

Harder still.

Now there was an echoing silence.

Then he heard it. A long, low moan. A moan of someone in pain.

He threw his shoulder into the door—there was a loud crackling of wood.

He hit it again—with all the force of his college linebacker days—and the door blew inward.

She wasn't in the kitchen or the bedroom-office. He raced into the living room and stumbled to a halt.

The table was littered with wine bottles and half-empty wine glasses, but no Cassidy. A bottle of red had fallen to the floor and a long red stain spread across the white rug.

No one was in the bathroom...nor the master bedroom.

He heard the moan again and dashed into the bedroom she'd converted into a wine cellar.

There she sat, still dressed in the jeans and shirt she'd worn to the lighthouse this morning, but they no longer looked so pristine. Red stains were dribbled all down her front. Her legs were splayed before her like a little girl and another twenty or more wine bottles were open around her. Most had a matching glass, some part full—but most of the glasses stood empty.

She moaned again, struggling to uncork yet another bottle. In no condition to do so, the corkscrew kept slipping from her fingers. The moan was part growl of frustration and part wounded animal.

He squatted down in front of her. Russell considered removing the bottle from her hands, but decided that discretion was the better part of valor as she was wielding the corkscrew as much like a sword as a kitchen tool.

"What are you doing, Cass?"

"I've lost it, Daddy. I've lost it somewhere." She looked about the room for a moment, ceasing her efforts to uncork the bottle. She didn't turn his direction.

"Lost what?"

She bowed her head down over the bottle and stopped struggling with it.

"I can't taste it. I can't. I tried. Just like you taught me. But I can't taste it."

He slid the corkscrew and the bottle with its mangled cork from her fingers and set them carefully aside.

"That must have been a hell of a letter." Her dad was really starting to piss him off. Next one, he wouldn't leave until he was sure she really *was* fine.

He did his best to lift her clear of the nest of glasses. A couple fell onto the hardwood floor and rolled away as he shifted her into his arms; he'd have to deal with those later. Hopefully, none of it would leak down into the ceiling of the ninth floor below before he could mop it up.

She kept complaining as he moved her.

"My life is over. Can't taste anyting. All doze years. So mussh work. Gone. Wasshted. Down the drain. Corked. Thas it. I'm corked. Just like a bad shwine."

Their first stop was the bathroom floor. She wasn't steady

enough to stand while he stripped her. Russell looked at the stains all down her front and decided to settle for expediency. He set her in the tub clothes and all, then cranked up the shower.

"Cassidy Knowles. Corked. Spoiled-ed in the bottle. So sad."

Too drunk to even protest, she sputtered at the water as it ran down her face, but that was all. He did his best to clean her up with a washcloth as the water ran over her. He aimed the spray off her face and trotted back to the other room. Four of the bottles she'd knocked over had corks partly rammed into them, thankfully the bulk uncorked horde of bottles had remained upright. The three fallen glasses looked as if they been mostly empty. Either she'd been pouring less as she went, or drinking more—he'd bet on the latter. He threw a towel on the worst patch and decided he'd come back later.

The glasses in the living room were much fuller. She'd still been just tasting in here. The red in the living room was going to be a different cleanup problem. He righted the bottle and saw that it was a 1969 Mouton Rothschild Bordeaux. That stain on her carpet was worth hundreds of dollars. He let his eye range over the dozens of others open on the table, the coffee table, the side table... Thousands of dollars of wine. Damn! And he thought his studio parties had been extravagant.

A curse sounded from the bathroom and the sound of splashing.

He hustled back to the more immediate problem.

RUSSELL SAT on the balcony off Cassidy's bedroom and watched the stars slowly turn over Puget Sound. Once she'd finished emptying the contents of her stomach into the toilet, he'd showered her as well as he could and managed to get her to spit after he brushed her teeth for her. He'd tucked her into bed after forcing her to drink some water and take a B12 vitamin he found in her medicine cabinet. It was the best hangover cure he had to offer, though she was still going to have a doozy.

The cleanup had taken a while—handwashing thirty-seven glasses. Hard to believe she even had that many or the room to store them in the small kitchen. Dinner for eight and four wines for a meal; maybe not that hard to imagine, but it was still a lot of washing. The red wine stain answered fairly well to the old trick of club soda and salt, but she'd still need a professional carpet cleaner.

Now he sat with a glass of the Bordeaux and some crackers and cheese. It was somewhere before dawn. Stars could still be seen, despite the waterfront lights below and some vague twinkling on the distant shore that was Bainbridge Island. What perversity had led her to get a condo facing what her father had lost?

Well, nothing to do but wait.

Wait for what? He must be more tired than he thought. He rubbed a hand over his face. There'd been something so urgent that he'd rushed over.

The future. Their future. Right.

Well, it was hard to go a whole lot further without knowing what Cassidy was thinking. That in itself was kind of funny. He'd done a lot of growing this last year. His mom had pointed it out when he went back to New York for a visit last week; Julia Morgan approved of Cassidy with all her heart—that much was clear.

Russell had walked out on Melanie with little thought for her and no awareness of her feelings. When their intensity surprised him, he'd gone to the West Coast anyway. Now? Now he was in limbo while Cassidy considered her destiny in California and Italy for Christ's sake.

For the hundredth time he looked at the waterlogged letter

on the little wrought iron table. He had found it crammed into her jean's pocket.

If I could wish anything, it was that you had stayed in the vineyards with me. Then I wouldn't have had to sell my life's work to strangers.

"Good thing you're dead, old man. Or we'd be having some words right about now." Hell of a burden for a dead man to place on his living daughter. *As if we don't have enough problems making our own decisions.*

"Russell?" Cassidy's voice trembled out into the darkness. He hadn't heard her get up, even though he'd left the sliding glass door open for that purpose. The late-night lull was past and the first sounds of the waking city had begun: street cleaners, service trucks, crazy, hyper-driven corporates, and restaurant owners. It probably wasn't all that long until Angelo would be awake and down at the market for his daily visit to the fish, produce, and meat vendors.

"Right here, Cassie."

She came to him in the faint glow of the city lights. She lowered herself into the chair beside him with a hesitancy of movement that he knew well from past experience. Once she was settled, she took his hand. He held it lightly, knowing that everything must be hurting.

"I feel..."

"Shh. I know."

"I don't remember you coming in."

"Good. Then you won't remember that I splintered the frame of your door as I did so. My shoulder appreciates that you locked only the handle and not the dead bolt."

"You busted down my door?"

"I panicked when you wouldn't answer, but I could hear you groan. Sorry, I'll fix it tomorrow." He looked up at the sky. There was no light yet, but there soon would be. "Later today."

"I don't remember."

"Don't remember my tossing you in the tub? Helping you puke? Brushing your teeth for you?"

"I didn't! Not really?"

"How I had my wanton way with you?"

"While I was drunk?" She sat up at that, though she froze and he felt sorry for what the sudden motion must have done to the inside of her head.

"Well, not the last, but all the other stuff, yes. I did shower you and towel you down. Though it wasn't as much fun as usual."

He reached his hand to stroke her cheek, marveling as he did every time how soft it was and how personal it felt. To be so close to someone he wanted to touch so much ranked beyond marvelous.

"What do you remember?"

"I sat down to write my column. It was going fine. I was working on a little section about the effect of climate between California temperate, Washington temperate, and the new Piedmont vineyards that are opening up in the foothills of the Italian Alps. But I couldn't remember the taste of a Bainbridge Island Pinot Noir. I grew up with that wine, probably the first one I ever tasted."

She was rubbing her forehead as if she could pull the memory out with her fingertips.

"I checked my notes, but I never wrote it down. Who could forget their first wine?"

Russell didn't even remember his last wine the way she did though the dregs were still in the glass. It was far and away the best Bordeaux he'd ever had.

"So I opened a bottle—and I couldn't taste it," her hand started to shake in his hand as the memory returned.

"My palate is gone," her voice grew shaky. "I opened a California Pinot, then a French Chardonnay. Nothing. None of them…" Her voice trailed off on a catch of breath. Her thoughts had finally caught up with her words.

"My palate is gone," her silence was echoing, punctuated by the sound of a Metro bus' diesel roaring far below.

"Kiss me."

"What?"

"Kiss me."

"I'm telling you my life is ruined. That it's over. My gift is gone after twenty painstaking years of study and practice and you want me to kiss you?"

Russell nodded, knowing she could see the outlines of his face in the growing light.

She huffed a few times and finally leaned forward to give him a quick peck on the lips.

"Um, thanks for helping me out."

"You're welcome. Now kiss me."

She practically growled when she did so. She leaned in and really kissed him—kissed him so hard that his body went electric. What had started as an attack quickly turned so sensual that it was hard not to drag her through the doors to the bed waiting only a few feet away.

He broke it off before she did.

"Now. Tell me what you tasted."

"The ocean and the sky. You always taste like that." News to him. He considered a moment and decided he could live with that, especially if Cassidy liked it.

"What else?"

She tipped her head sideways, in the way she always did when analyzing a flavor, whether a wine or a chocolate truffle. It was the moment when she was most quiet and most stunning.

"Plum and eucalyptus. Bitter cherry…You inveterate bastard!" She punched his arm hard enough to hurt. To really hurt because she found the nerve cluster.

"Am not," he rubbed at his wound as she shook her hand in pain.

"Are too. You didn't ravage me. You ravaged my 1969 Bordeaux. That was a graduation gift from my dad. I was saving it."

"Yup. You were. For last night."

That dropped her back in her chair. "Last night?"

"Most of it was in your carpet when I arrived. I got out the worst of the stain, so I guess it's in your sink now. I had a half glass while watching over you. I saved the last half glass for you."

Her voice was ridiculously small. "I don't think I could drink any wine now if my life depended on it."

"How about kissing me again? To make up for punching my arm so hard."

She leaned over just far enough to kiss him on the arm. "What else did I open?"

"I don't know. I lost track somewhere after thirty bottles."

"Thirty?" Little more than a squeak.

"Kiss me again."

"Why?"

"Because," he rose and helped her to her feet. He swung her up into his arms and headed back into the bedroom.

"I like proving that your palate is still just fine."

POINT ROBINSON LIGHTHOUSE

Maury Island
First lit: 1887
Automated: 1978
47.3881 -122.3746

*T*he Point Robinson light and foghorn is the principle guiding beacon between Seattle and Tacoma. Fog is an especial problem on this point of Maury Island. In 1897, the sole keeper, who had been asking for an assistant for years, had to run the whistle for 528 straight hours on his own. In those twenty-two long days he shoveled thirty-five tons of coal by hand to power the whistle.

His request for assistance was granted. But it was 1903, six years later, before one was assigned to the light.

OCTOBER 1

"*Y*ou didn't ask her? Mama mia, you're an *idiota!*"

Russell was, but that didn't mean Angelo was going to get away with it. He dug around in the boat's fridge for a couple Cokes.

"And have you called Jo Thompson yet?" He called out the hatchway to Angelo up at the tiller.

"Low blow, my man. Low blow."

"Have you?"

"Shit, no. What's a classy, hot-shot lawyer gonna see in a lousy, Eye-talian servant's son?"

Russell came on deck and shook the bottle hard before handing it to Angelo. Angelo groaned and slipped it into a cup holder unopened.

"She may be a big-time lawyer, but you're a big-time restaurateur."

"Oh, yeah. One whole restaurant. That'll really impress a lady like that."

"Got news for you, buddy boy."

Angelo just glared at him.

"Fisherman's daughter." Russell turned away and peeked under the sail as the light finally dawned over Angelo's face.

"Lighthouse ho."

There it was, right on cue. Point Robinson was a windy, god-forsaken spot known for its shrouds of fog and today didn't disappoint. They'd spent much of the morning creeping through fog banks and dead reckoning from one channel buoy to the next. A little sunlight broke through around the light-house itself, enough to make a pretty picture of the light wrapped in a foggy, surreal landscape of mystery.

He pulled out his camera and starting snapping photos for Cassidy. It didn't feel right though. Without her here, the purpose was gone. He wanted to see the lady on the beach in her ridiculous, knee-length parka. Or spend a lazy afternoon teasing the sassy wine-connoisseur lying back in his dinghy. Hell, he'd be glad just watch her as she cranked on a winch or played with the cat. Even Nutcase seemed despondent without her, curled up in the cockpit rather than out on the boom.

"Did you know that some poor chump shoveled thirty-five tons of coal in three weeks to run the fog whistle here." He ran the telephoto out and searched the beach. Not a single woman walked on the beach.

No point in even looking; Cassidy was at thirty-five thousand feet zooming from California to Italy. The wineries were really courting her hard. She'd had a half dozen offers in the last fifteen days, sight unseen. They both knew that she was going to end up in California; the Italy trip was only because she'd committed to go in the initial flush of excitement.

Angelo steered up into the wind a bit making him reset the sails. "Why are you changing the subject?"

"What subject?" Russell didn't want to talk about this with Angelo.

"Why didn't you ask her to marry you?"

He really, really didn't want to talk about this.

CASSIDY HELD the letter in her lap.

She'd promised Russell that she wouldn't read it without him, but it was the first of the month and here it was in her lap. He'd insisted that she wait a week. He would come over after her interviews were done and they'd go and play along the Amalfi coast for a week. He'd bring photos of the lighthouse and be there while she read the letter.

She knew he wanted to protect her from whatever the next letter held. And he'd been kind enough to insist *without* throwing her last debacle in her face—forty-three bottles, almost six thousand dollars in wine, some of it irreplaceable. Worst of all, it had been over a week before she could face drinking any wine at all. By the time she could, everything she'd opened that night had started to turn. Even with vacuum corks, they were clearly off.

No, she was strong enough to do this on her own. She didn't need to depend on Mr. Russell Morgan for strength, no matter how sweet he was about it.

She checked her watch—ten a.m. west coast time. Just about right for Russell to be sailing by the lighthouse.

She tore open the letter. The scrawled hand was weaker and her heart twisted to imagine her father's efforts to scribe even these few words. It was shorter than any prior letter. Even the sentences were shorter. As if he had to rest between each thought.

Dearest Ice Sweet,

There is a truth that I have learned. Be true to your passion. Your mother was true to her great love for family. I loved the vines. Each of us had full, complete lives. We were true to our passion, in whatever form it took.

Your passion isn't the vine, it's the wine. And the writing. Look at why you like it. That is the passion. I thought my passion was Knowles

315

Valley. But it wasn't. It was the vines. I was never happier than when I was walking the rows. California or Bainbridge. For me, it was the vines and you.

Love you Ice Sweet,

Vic

"I know what's important, Daddy. Truly I do." She would listen to what the Italians had to say, but she knew what was important.

RUSSELL TOOK his bottle of Coke and rolled it slowly back and forth between his palms. The cool glass felt good despite the fall day.

"She's over the Atlantic somewhere right now. That's a bit out of reach. I'll ask her when I see her next week."

"You know where you're going yet?"

She was going to meet his plane at Sienna airport with a rental car. They'd poke along the Amalfi coast, or slide over to Monaco and the French Riviera. A whole week, just the two of them and Italy—that's all he cared about.

"I'll know when the time is right. When the mood is right."

Angelo swore loudly, waved for him to take the tiller, and went below. The *Lady* slipped along the shore and Russell fell back to watching the lighthouse slip slowly by. It was a sweet one—all alone at the foot of the hill, guarding the far end of a long, lonely beach road.

Angelo came back on deck after several minutes and shoved a cell phone into his hand.

It was active. He put it to his ear and it was ringing. He looked to his friend, but Angelo just took the tiller and focused on the way ahead.

"Uh, hello?"

"Hi, who is this?"

"You called *me*." The voice was crackly and there was a funny lag.

"Cassidy?"

"How did you call me?"

"I didn't."

"Yes, you did. I was just sitting here and the phone that's mounted on the headrest in front of me rang."

"Uh," Angelo was one sneaky, spectacularly good friend. "I miss you. Guess I just wanted to hear your voice. Ange..." Angelo kicked his shin. "Uh, I figured if you could call out from a plane, you could probably call back the other way."

"It's nice to hear your voice, too. I'll be on the ground pretty soon, we're over Sardinia now."

"Cassidy, I was wondering..." He wanted to do this when she was sitting across from him, holding his hand or playing footsie under the tablecloth. Something.

"What?"

"If, ah..."

"You're still coming next week?" The worry in her voice gave him confidence.

"Of course. Can't wait."

"I've picked some lovely places to go."

"Wonderful." Come on, Russell. Get your shit together. This was probably costing dollars per second. Of course it was Angelo's phone, so why should he care.

"I—"

"We'll be landing shortly," a heavily accented voice cut across the airwaves. "Please shut down all electronic devices and return your seat backs and tray tables to the upright position."

He could just hear her as they repeated the instructions in Italian. "Thanks for the call. I'll talk to you as soon as I'm settled. Bye."

She was gone before he could respond.

"Wimp."

"We were cut off. They're landing. Thanks, Buddy. Thanks for the try." He went to toss the phone back to Angelo, then noticed it was his, as were any call charges.

He pulled out a pocketknife and pried the cap off his soda. It exploded in his hands spraying foam and sugar all down his shorts and legs, dribbling into his shoes. Nutcase scrambled for cover, splashes of sticky foam all over her coat.

Angelo pulled his own bottle from the cup holder and, with an over-pleased grin, opened it with a small "phsst."

———

THE PORSCHE ROARED up to the airport terminal. Angelo had promised to treat it nicely while he was gone. Angelo hadn't even bothered to buy a car and Russell sure wasn't going to travel with a bunch of smelly fish in the restaurant van right before climbing on a plane for a fifteen hours. Perry was going to take care of his boat and Nutcase. He really had nothing to worry about, so why was he such a nervous wreck?

Angelo whipped up to the curb missing an old lady by inches; probably scared a decade off her life.

Russell started to climb out, but Angelo grabbed his arm.

"You gonna ask her?"

"Yes."

"You promise?"

"I promise."

"Okay, cause if you come back from the most romantic country in the world, and you haven't, I'm a gonna whip your behind."

"You and what army?" Russell went for the sneer, but couldn't find it anywhere handy.

"Me and Cassidy, that's who. You ain't gonna mess with her, are you?"

Russell shook him off, climbed out of the car, and signaled

for Angelo to pop the trunk lid. He grabbed the duffle and his camera bag, then slammed the lid back into place.

Angelo pushed up in his seat and looked at him over the windshield.

"And you remember what I told you."

"Cinque Terre. Get idea photos for your next restaurant, 'Angelo's Home Hearth.' It ain't your home, buddy. I keep telling you, 'Umbrian Hearth,' but hey, why listen to me."

"It was home for a thousand years before Mama came to America."

"She was sixteen, pregnant, and ran away to the land of opportunity. You're a born-and-buttered Brooklynite. As in New York, America, the United States of."

"Fine. That'll be my third restaurant. Just get me some good photos. Hokay?"

Russell slung the bags over his shoulder.

Crap! Some romantic getaway. Now he was supposed to work, too.

Angelo dropped the Porsche into gear and would have removed Russell's kneecap if he hadn't dodged quickly. His car and his best friend roared off into the distance.

Crap again!

Now this was class. Russell punched the accelerator and the car leapt ahead on the Autostrada.

What woman would have thought to rent a Ferrari Spider rather than a lousy sedan? Cassidy would. He could kiss her, had kissed her. And it had been even more incredible than the first time. She was more confident and more sure of herself than ever before and that was about the sexiest thing he'd ever seen. She'd even rented them a hotel room at the airport so they didn't have to wait more than the time it took to cross the terminal and go up two stories in the elevator. They'd almost done it in the elevator like a couple of teens—might have if they'd been on the third floor instead of the second.

She now lay back in her seat, a kerchief over her hair and large Italian sunglasses hiding those luscious hazel eyes. Her hand rested on his thigh as he ripped along, heading north out of Sienna. He was on top of the world, it just couldn't get any better than this.

At Lucca she aimed him south toward Pisa. It was the wrong direction for Cinque Terre but—screw Angelo—Russell just didn't give a damn.

That's when it hit him: he really didn't give a damn. For a month he'd been worrying himself sick about the Seattle City Trade Association contract and then the new offer from the Pioneer Square Association. He just didn't care. That was the old him.

It was Russell Morgan the studio photographer who worried about contracts and sweated over jobs until they were perfect and then some. The new Russell didn't give a damn about Pioneer Square or Seattle City. And he sure as hell didn't need the money, so from now on he'd only do what was fun.

If he took a big contract, it would be the next step on the road to personal oblivion. He knew the old networking routine, had turned it into a highly profitable, multi-million-dollar business with dozens of employees once already. Hell, he'd had three people whose sole job was to hunt weird props that no one had ever used before: from trained tree frogs to the Smithsonian's collection of every Medal of Honor left at the Wall of the Vietnam Memorial. Then he'd had: office manager, accountant, lighting grip, camera assistant, makeup artist...the list went on and on.

Done and done—never again would he go there. If it wasn't something he could do himself, in his leisure time, then from now on his automatic answer would be "no."

Cassidy pointed him to exit at Livorno.

He'd had fun doing the ads for Angelo, but that was for his best friend. The ones for Perrin were a blast, but that had far more to do with the three women than the work itself. Perrin had a sharp intelligence hidden behind her frivolous façade. And Jo had a wicked sense of wry humor masked with reserve and sophistication. Cassidy was just plain lovable.

There it was. She was plain lovable.

He raised her hand from his thigh to his lips and kissed the back of her hand. When he released it to shift, she stroked his cheek just as he had hers. The tingle made him settle deeper into the seat, more aware than ever of the precious cargo he carried.

More directions now, Cassidy led him down smaller streets. Italian drivers really were crazy, but they made some extra space for the slick, black Ferrari. Italians respected sports cars the way the French respected bicycles. He used the extra space to slip through the knotted midday traffic.

She led him past the scenic old city and past rows of businesses. They ran out to the beach, turned left…and there it was.

"Oh. My." He pulled the car to the side of the road and shut off the engine.

"Hey, you're only supposed to say that about me."

He leaned over and kissed her until his lips felt bruised and the catcalls of passing drivers made his ears ring. But he had to look back.

"This is incredible! It must be ten stories high."

"Eleven. The Germans blasted the old lighthouse to smithereens when they were retreating, but the Italians rebuilt it to the original plan using all the original stone they could salvage."

The Livorno lighthouse rose from the edge of the busy shipyard. Cargo ships, loading cranes, and railcars scuttled about its base, but the stepped cylinder soared above them all.

"Boy, these Italians really know how to build a lighthouse."

"Isn't it great? And the best part..."

He turned to her. She'd pushed her sunglasses up on her forehead, just as his mother had worn them. In that moment he could see the woman who would make Julia Morgan a grand-mother. Cassidy Knowles-Morgan someday going for a sail on their own child's boat. She was the woman he wanted in his life more than was possible.

The woman he loved.

He never said that before. Not to her and not to himself. Not to anyone, ever. Yes, he'd talk to Angelo about how to propose to Cassidy, but the L-word was completely unexplored territory —that had remained impossibly foreign until he'd arrived in it. Now that he was here, it made perfect sense.

He *loved* Cassidy Knowles.

"The best part," she bubbled on, "is that it was built in 1304, almost two hundred years before Columbus. The oldest we've visited was 1857, Cape Flattery and New Dungeness."

"I'm sorry, Cassidy. I know you're incredible and I love you, but that rates an 'Oh. My.' There's just no way around it."

He watched her closely, it took a moment for it to register. Then he saw it hit, like someone had thumped her in the solar plexus. Her jaw dropped and he heard a gasp. The next moment she swarmed into his lap despite the cramped cockpit and steering wheel. If he thought he'd been soundly kissed ever before, he was happily mistaken.

Being kissed by Cassidy was better than sex with most women.

Finally she whispered in his ear, "I love you, too."

He held her even tighter.

THEY DROVE up to Monterosso along narrow twisty roads that tunneled through mountains, often only a lane wide. In any lesser car than the Ferrari, it would have been a scary ride rather than scenic and fun. They laughed most of the way.

She told him about California and Montalcino. She'd already written a column about the food and wine at each, as well as several more about winemaking to intersperse over the next year.

"I don't give away any company secrets, but it is amazing how similar and how different the processes are. It's like the lighthouses. California is so new and slick. They have their gravity feeds between stainless-steel tanks, and everything is temperature controlled to the degree and staged to the hour— so long in steel then so long in oak. All scientific and you could eat off the floor in any of the mechanical rooms."

"Exactly what I'd want to do."

She thumped his arm playfully and he laughed for the sheer joy of teasing her. He downshifted for another hairpin turn as they climbed then descended then climbed again through the coastal range. The jagged hills broke the vistas into sharp chunks of sky, hill, and tree. Far lower than the mountains of the Cascade Range, but more dramatic in their own way.

"In California they're actually boring caves—carving vast cavities into the mountainsides that don't belong there geologically—just for show. The "caves" come complete with carpeting, furniture, a wine bar, even huge casks that are just for show and aren't really used. All because caves are the 'in thing' now."

To Russell's way of thinking it meant too many New York advertising agencies had opened branches in Napa.

"The Montalcino wineries are done with casks that are older than the vintner's great-grandparents. Wine is processed, tanked, purified through the same steps, but nature has a bigger part in it. The same care but less technologic frenzy. And instead of fabricated caves they have real ones that have been there forever. Some of them date back to the Etruscans—they're the ones who helped the Romans get started."

Her excitement was so high—she was so thrilled by what she'd seen—that he couldn't ask her now. At first he hadn't because he didn't want to spoil her wonderful welcome, then because the drive was so fun. And he was still trying to process that she loved him.

And that he loved her.

Had he said it to anyone other than his mother? Ever? And even that had become dutiful, until their last visit. Until he'd realized that she had put up with, for the last double-fistful of years, his jumping to wrong conclusions about her. And Cassidy had dispelled them all with a few casual questions. Their last visit had been the best ever and it was all Cassidy's doing. How could he spoil this for her?

He'd wait just a little longer.

IT WAS ALL TOO perfect to be true. Cassidy had been transported by the magic of her father's letters and the man beside her into a new world, and it was a world of possibilities. She'd aspired to be the next Robert Parker—the first female megastar of the wine-tasting firmament. To become the top of an exceedingly small world.

But the vineyards were breathtaking; that's where it all happened. On their third day in Cinque Terre they found the winery in small village of Corniglia where the Sciacchetrà was made—the wine that had fooled her at their disastrous first date. It was made underneath Carla Parrano's home, a distant cousin of Angelo's. They entered the winery itself through a narrow oak door at street level that had long since grown dark with age and been polished smooth by human hands.

They descended into the mountainside: to an Italian cave

turned into a wine cellar over six hundred years before. The air was cool, the floor and walls stone. The casks were packed so tightly together that there was barely room to get around them. And the wine tasted so sweet and light with a gentleness from the vat that didn't, couldn't survive the ten-thousand-mile journey by boat and rail in bottles. This wine wasn't intended for export. To make this wine work, you had to bring the wine tasters to the wine and she could think of a dozen different ways to do that—just a part of her newly expanded view of the big picture.

She led Russell up into the rock-wall terraced vineyards of Cinque Terre. The terraces were barely ten feet wide, each supporting a couple dozen vines in a few feet of soil. For a thousand years, grapes had been cultivated here. Cultivated just this way, in tiny little patches by hard labor. Ingenious, hip-wide monorail cars climbed from one terrace to another transporting the grapes and the more daring tourists.

Russell's camera snapped away, taking pictures of cliff-edge vineyards, restaurants, and fishing boats dragged up onto the miniature beaches.

In Manarola, the fourth of the five little towns of Cinque Terre, they found a hidden *ristorante*—a true locals' place. They were the only tourists there despite the warm October. Russell's Italian was rusty, but he'd learned it at his cook's knee and it came back quickly. Hers was much worse, just enough of it left from college to make it fun rather than a struggle.

The owner bustled to their table in the middle of the meal and rattled off a flurry of Italian she had no chance of following.

"What did he say?"

"I dropped Angelo's name; they know about him."

"Really? That's great. Local boy made good, huh?"

More Italian rattled back and forth, and then the owner jerked to stare at her, slapped his hands to his heart and ran back into the restaurant.

"What? What did you do to him?"

Russell just shook his head and shrugged. No grin. He didn't appear to know. She looked away and checked again, still no grin. Okay, he was as mystified as she was.

The owner came running back, the waiter and waitress, and a woman who had to be his wife in tow. He was also waving a worn newspaper over his head.

He thumped it down on table, pointed his finger at an article then brought his fingertips to his lips and tossed the kiss into the air.

They both leaned in. It was titled "Angelo's Tuscan Hearth" and her picture sat at the head of the column. The rest was in Italian, definitely her writing though. Her agent had told her about Italy, she'd just never imagined the translation. It was the second of her three reviews. Down at the bottom, there it was.

She wasn't going to point it out.

She didn't need to.

Russell's groan filled the air much to the consternation of the owner who she quickly reassured. She couldn't quite read the translation, but she didn't need to. She'd written the words herself.

Bring the person you love to this restaurant and you'll never be forgotten for it. Ever.

"In every language," Russell moaned.

"WHY THAT'S TERRIBLY FLATTERING."

Cassidy had been saying that a lot lately. California and Italy were in a bidding war for her expertise. Even hiding away on vacation, news of increased offers trickled her direction. Germany and France had both left lengthy voice messages, or rather a lengthy series of messages in two-minute chunks that Russell was painfully familiar with.

He leaned against the stone parapet of the microscopic balcony. Barely big enough to stand in, but enough for him to stare down at the tiny harbor. It was just big enough to tuck the *Lady* in among the fishing boats. Nutcase would love this place.

He could hear Cassidy in the bedroom checking up on the latest flurry of offers. Cassidy Knowles was in play and the games had begun. Salaries, personal villas, cars, and personal assistants were being bandied about in a high stakes poker game that showed no sign of reaching its limit.

Even the Cinque Terre Consortium had anted up, though they'd been outbid before they even made the offer and they knew it. But they'd done it with style, closing the little Manarola restaurant and inviting a couple dozen of the local chefs, vintners, and officials to feast Italian-style around a long table. There'd been far more food and wine than business.

Russell had enjoyed the impromptu singing and a copious of laughter. By the time they were done, he'd been hugged at least twice by every person there.

The Ligurian wine industry here had suffered due to the attraction of the almighty tourist dollar. Vines on cliffs were arduous work; turning your five-hundred-year-old cellar into a quaint restaurant or gift shop was far easier. The five-town Consortium had come up with a solution: they were giving the terraces away before they fell into disrepair and slid into the ocean. To retain ownership, the new owners were required to farm them for at least four years. An ingenious and low price-of-entry way to get new blood into the industry.

Russell could already think of several different campaign ideas. And the Consortium knew that it needed a Cassidy Knowles to make it all happen. Their offer: a small house perched over the beach, with an even smaller budget to fix it up, a survival stipend, and a marketing budget that would barely pay for the rental on the car they'd left parked at Monterosso.

The chances of her throwing it all away to go sailing with

him were getting slimmer by the minute. Angelo was right. He should have asked her before she left, before they had a chance to get to her. But then he'd have trapped her and that couldn't be right either.

He could still feel the scars on his back from his own narrow escape from success' taloned claws. There were several major accounts who still called him and the ones who'd spotted his work for Angelo or Perrin were hounding his cell phone with requests for "just one more spread."

It was the road to nowhere.

It was the road back to a studio, living there because next door would be too far away. Part of the package deal would be a series of lovers who looked like Melanie, or aspired to, but didn't touch his heart.

He'd had enough of too many lovers. He now had a girl-friend, a woman he was in love with. And he wanted more of that. Wouldn't his mother laugh her ass off knowing what he was feeling right about now. Angelo sure would.

Cassidy hung up the phone.

He didn't turn when she ran her hand up his back.

"I'm sorry. It's overwhelming."

He nodded. He knew the temptation was huge. It was "The Life" all over again. Except now it was Cassidy who had set her sights on it, and he wasn't a part of the equation. He didn't want to be a part of That Life. He'd been there once and barely survived.

"Hey, lover."

He jolted beneath her touch. That's exactly what he'd called Melanie, the moment before he destroyed her life by asking her to go to Seattle with him.

He pushed past Cassidy, away from the balcony and into the *pensione*. It was so damn small. He'd been caged. He was Cassidy Knowles' captive lover while she made choices that he could never survive. He groped about the room, found the door, and was out on the streets in moments. He headed up the hill, climbing the cobbled streets, and when they gave out, the terraced fields of vines. It was only when he reached the highest terraces—those which had been abandoned first by the shrinking Cinque Terre wine industry—that he ground to a halt.

Exhausted he dropped to the earth and rested his head on his arms.

"Shit! Melanie, I'm sorry. You never deserved that." It hurt like hell to be wearing that same burden himself. He didn't want Cassidy's life. No more than she would want his. And where did that leave them?

Sure, a fish can love a bird, but where would they live? Old joke. Sad joke.

"WHAT THE HELL, RUSSELL?" Her side was killing her, the stitch dug in like a hot knife. All her morning runs through the vast vineyards of California and Italy hadn't prepared her for the vertical cliffs or the pace that Russell had set up these hills.

He raised his head from his arms and it was the saddest she'd ever seen him.

She dropped to the soil beside him and kneaded her side. She slid an arm around his waist but he shrugged her off.

"What did I do?" Damn it. They were in this incredibly beautiful, romantic wonderland of the Italian coast.

He shook his head, but didn't answer.

"Is it the phone calls? I'll stop those. I won't check another message until we get home."

"Home."

"Well, that's some response. C'mon, Russell. You know I suck at guessing games. Talk to me." He didn't even a smile a little.

"Where's home, Cassidy?" His voice was deep and rough. As if he was fighting for every word.

"I don't know. Seattle I guess. Maybe Oakville in Napa soon. How the hell should I know? Where's your home, Russell? On some damn sailboat?"

"Yes," he finally looked at her. "Yes! It's on some *damn* sailboat. My home has a cat. It has belongings. It is a place where I like myself. It is a place where I'm at my best. How about you, Cassidy? Where are you at your best?"

"In your arms." She'd said it flippantly, but once said, it was true. It was the one place she could be where the world made sense. When the mad jangle in her head went quiet.

"C'mon, Cassie. I'm not talking about sex."

She hadn't been, at least not once she thought about it. But she couldn't answer his scorn—couldn't face his anger.

He closed his eyes. He just sat there with his eyes closed. His arms—those nice, strong, safe arms—crossed over his own knees.

The shining blue of the Mediterranean lay spread out before them. Somewhere over that way lay Sardinia, then France, Spain, the Atlantic, and the entire width of the U.S. So many miles away. But it didn't feel so distant when she sat here with Russell.

She reached for him again, but hesitated with her fingers a scant inch from his shoulder. Finally she withdrew and dropped her hand into her lap.

Everything had been going so perfectly. California had a wonderful offer on the table; they were offering her access to every aspect of the organization. Italy had a nice Old World feel that could be fun, but not as exciting. The U.S. companies, and now there were four of them, exhibited an energy and a vibrancy that egged her on. The French offers were more about status and, she had to admit, a chance to work with *grand crus* was tempting. The Germans were all about money—a lot of money.

"Why can't you just be happy for me?"

He shuddered. He actually shuddered.

"What? Come on, Russell. Talk to me."

He didn't turn to her as he spoke. "Where is home, Cassidy Knowles?"

HE DIDN'T SPEAK AGAIN EXCEPT to repeat his question. No matter what she did or said.

"Where is home, Cassidy Knowles?"

When the evening settled in with a foggy chill, that raised goosebumps over her whole body, she deserted him and descended back to the hotel. Though she waited all night, there was no sign of Russell.

Some romantic vacation.

She dialed for her messages. Seventeen. She hung up without listening to a one of them.

At dawn there was a knock on the door and she rushed over to open it.

Instead of Russell...instead of throwing their arms around each other and both being sorry...a maid held out a note.

The paper crackled as she opened it. Russell's writing, not her father's. But it was as if they were both speaking from the same page.

Cassidy,

You are really going places. I'm happy for you. Unfortunately, they aren't places I want to go. The car is in your name and the keys are on the bureau. I've taken the 6:30 train to the airport. I've left money and instructions with the front desk to ship my belongings. Just leave them in the room and they'll take care of it. Though if you'd hand carry my camera to Angelo, I'd appreciate it. Don't if it's too weird for you.

Best of luck with your future,
Russell

The first thing she noticed was the clock. 6:45. Gone! He was gone. How could that be? What had she said? She'd gone over it a hundred times in the night. And she still didn't know.

Maybe one of the seventeen phone messages was from him. But she knew none of them would be. He'd spent a cold, lonely night in an abandoned vineyard, come down the hill with the dawn, and left town.

"Where is home, Cassidy Knowles?" As if he were questioning a complete stranger.

Well, to hell with him. She wasn't going to ruin her vacation because of some jerk of a man. Breakfast. That was it. She'd eat breakfast, take a walk, and then she'd feel better. She was just dizzy from the cold and the long night awake in the chair.

Cassidy didn't like leaving his camera in the room. She slung it over her shoulder as she went out.

THE CAMERA WAS heavy and dragged at her shoulder. She pulled it into her hand, wrapping the strap as a brace behind her elbow just as he'd taught her.

With the camera in her hand, she started to see pictures to take. A pot with a single red geranium on a narrow set of stone steps, the very stone worn by a thousand years of footsteps. A neon-bright purple door beckoned her to photograph a stone house so old it might have been quarried by Noah's sons. A Dalmatian stuck her nose out between forest-green, wooden shutters to watch her go by. A black and dapple-gray cat impossibly asleep on the narrow keel of an up-turned fishing dinghy.

It was different seeing a village through a camera. Each image she took became a memory of its own. A man who would have passed for an aging hippie back home sat in the sun beneath a shingle advertising his surgery. He offered her a nod and a smile before returning to the novel in his lap. A butcher skinning a lamb. A baker totting a huge basket of crusty breads into one restaurant after another, his load lightening with each stop.

Where is home, Cassidy Knowles?

She'd be damned if she knew.

BROWN'S POINT LIGHTHOUSE

Tacoma
First lit: 1887
Extinguished: 1963
47.3059 -122.444

*O*scar Brown was the station's first keeper in the early 1900s. He moved his wife, a horse and a cow, and a piano onto this remote point. He often rowed the three or four miles to Tacoma to attend concerts. An accomplished musician, when the roads finally reached the lighthouse he became a noted piano teacher when he was not tending the light.

The concrete block lighthouse, though less than a hundred yards from the keeper's cottage, was often inaccessible when major storms flooded the swampy ground. Brown would take a rowing dory out through the mud to add oil or trim the wick.

The striking mechanism for the fog bell had to be wound every 45 minutes. Brown slept little during the long spells of dense fog that frequently plague the point. When the mechanism broke, his wife would count out the twenty-second interval between his strikes. Brown had served thirty years before the fog bell was replaced by a powered horn. The bell traveled to a church for some years but has returned to the old lighthouse, with a bowling ball for a clacker.

The keeper's cottage is now the centerpiece of a city park. The dwelling's gardens are filled with rare, heritage plants maintained by the local horticultural society.

NOVEMBER 1

*C*assidy was right back where she'd started.

Alone and huddled behind a lighthouse in a blinding rain and a roaring wind.

Better equipped, Cassidy wasn't likely to freeze to death, but that didn't make her any happier to be here than at West Point lighthouse last January.

Damn you, Russell. Not one message. Not a single note. When she'd handed his duffle and his camera to Angelo it had been so awkward she'd had to run out of the restaurant not knowing if she would speak or cry had she opened her mouth. Russell had ruined everything.

Jo and Perrin had tried to cheer her up. But neither could explain his final question. They agreed that "in your arms" was a good answer. Light and funny, yet romantic and cozy, too. It had the added benefit of being more than a little bit true. Now her condo felt like a foreign land—with Shilshole Marina and Angelo's wholly out of bounds.

Yesterday she'd finally tried to call him, but his phone was disconnected. He hadn't even left a forwarding number. Russell had gone into hiding. Well, good riddance. She didn't want to talk to him anyway—which was a complete and total lie.

After tomorrow it wouldn't matter anyway. She'd set aside three days to drive down the coast. Professional movers would empty the condo after she left, and they'd have her house in Napa set up before she got there. A decorator would be there on day four to help her turn it into a home.

So there, Russell Morgan. My home is in the hills above St. Helena, California. In the true heart of American wine country. Is that good enough for you?

She knew it wasn't. Some part of her knew it wasn't, but she was at a loss over why or what to do about it.

Get it done...and get out of the rain before her fingers turned to icicles.

She pulled the last two envelopes from her pocket. She wouldn't be here for December, so she'd brought both. And chosen the closer lighthouse. Besides, she'd visited December's lighthouse at Ediz Hook twice already, on her way to two of the others. She'd even seen it from the water with Russell when they'd sailed out to Destruction Island. There wasn't even a lighthouse at Ediz Hook anymore, just a flasher atop the Coast Guard station.

Leaving Puget Sound was going to be a major advantage of moving to Mondavi. There was no part of the Sound or Seattle that had escaped Russell's touch—no part of it that could be just hers. Napa would give her a chance to purge her soul of him.

Damn porcupine!

She tore open the first letter and huddled over it to shield it from the rain. The writing was so uneven that she had to construct each word a letter at a time. Her heart clenched with sympathetic pain for the effort he'd taken to write it.

Dearest I. S.,

Too sick to even write out her nickname.

I followed my destiny north. I left behind my dreams. I discovered new ones. The most important discovery, the one that made my whole life worthwhile, was the love of my dear Adrianne and for my lovely Cassie. There is ice in your veins, a cold determination to put your head down and battle it out. That you got from me.

From your mother, you got the largest, most loving, sweetest heart there ever was. Listen to that. It is your heart that will make you happy, not your head. And I now know, that is what counts.

You are the Ice and the Sweet,

Vic

"But I followed my heart. I'm following it to the land you loved."

And yet all she felt was misery.

All those years "Ice Sweet" had more meanings and she hadn't known. Her curse and her legacy had become her nickname, always wanting more and always feeling the pain.

Was there any point in even opening the last letter? She already knew the last words of a dying man.

"You would have loved Knowles Valley." Vic Knowles had spoken his last words to his daughter just minutes before he died. His one great regret and she now had the chance to set it straight. A Knowles would once again walk that land—and she would love it with every *ounce* of willpower in her soul.

She turned the last letter over and over. He'd left off the GPS coordinates. Misspelled the name of the lighthouse. But, if they'd come this far together, she might as well finish the journey.

Dearest I.S.,

Remember, above all else. Home is neither a place nor a state of mind. It is family.

Thank you for being my family. For being my home.

All my love,

Daddy

Daddy.

In the end, he'd finally felt worthy to name his role in her life. And that was his final word, ever. The wonderful father he'd always been. Always believing in her and—just as strongly —always doubting himself.

Home was family.

No.

It couldn't be.

Had Russell been asking that of her?

Had he proposed and she hadn't even noticed?

The realization burned behind her eyes, in her head and in her heart. Like an oak barrel being charred by fire on the inside; it made the oak accessible to the wine while it also mellowed and aged the wine in the process. The precious oak, used for its own flavor.

But there was a second reason they used oak, for both wine and whiskey. Steel trapped the wine, suffocated it. Even the giants of the ultra-modern Napa Valley spent time in oak. And while there, one or maybe two percent of the alcohol and other aromatics leaked out through the porous wood. They slid from the wine and disappeared. It was a tiny loss, but enough to transform a mediocre wine into a wonder.

Giving up so little gained so much.

Could she let go of that precious percent? And what would it be? Or was it too late? Had she missed her chance, locked up in the steel vat of her own icy stubbornness?

Her father's words were washing off the page of his last ever letter to her. He was gone, taking his past with him. Vic Knowles had left her alone to face her future. Yet another piece for Cassidy to let go of—shed one layer at a time.

She looked at the lighthouse: perched on the rock, a concrete tower surrounded by a barbed wire-topped fence. The old bell was in a small shed at the back of the park. The rowing dory, long gone, replaced with a replica that would never again leave the boat house to be dragged, pushed, and prodded, through the mud flats. The remote keeper's dwelling now in the midst of a posh neighborhood, rentable by the day, and tended by the Points Horticultural Society. All of the history had escaped; no sign remained of the remote corner of Puget Sound where the first keeper had managed to land a piano in 1903.

She stood alone.

The only sign of life she could see through the drenching rain was a blue-hulled sailboat with red sails.

She blinked.

But it was still there slicing through the rain.

Russell, coming to their lighthouse.

Coming to her!

She ran from her partial shelter behind the lighthouse and clambered up onto the rocks.

The *Lady* continued straight toward her for a long moment, then it jibbed abruptly, awkwardly, shearing off to the west, away from the lighthouse. No—away from her.

She'd hurt him. Not because she'd meant to, but because she didn't understand.

"Russell," her voice was little more than a croak. She tried again. It was no better.

He was glancing over his shoulder, but he wasn't turning back.

She waved her arms to no effect.

Her coat. She was wearing her red parka, for the first time in six months it was cold and wet enough.

Unable to fight her way out of the zipper with her frozen fingers, she dragged the coat off over her head.

"Russell." She waved it against the wind and rain. "See the coat, damn you. See the coat. Red coat, Russell. Don't leave me behind. Red coat. Red! *Coat!*" She cried it out into the storm.

The boat continued away from her, until it was barely a shadow in the pounding rain. She was soaked to the bone, but wasn't willing to turn for her car. There was no way she could give up while there was even the slightest hint of a chance. Not even after that.

He *had* to come back.

She waved the coat once more, but knew it was too little too late. The horizon remained empty. Cassidy let the coat slap wetly against her leg and lie on the sea-spattered rocks.

Then off to the north, in a direction she hadn't been watching, the *Lady* once again emerged out of the driving rain.

Cassidy frantically waved the coat again. He was coming back...for her? Please, let him be coming back for her.

The boat pulled close in, a few dozen yards offshore. With one single, emphatic point, Russell indicated the boat launch on the other side of the park.

She ran. She sprinted. She leaned into the rain and flew across the muddy lawn and the rough rocks. She skidded as she leapt onto the wet wood and raced down the dock.

He was there before her. Floating a dozen feet off the end, just a little too far to jump. She considered it anyway, but knew of the bone-aching cold that waited there. The rain pounded off his incandescent yellow slicks like a parade of snare drummers gone mad.

One more time she waved the sopping red coat at him. She didn't know what else to do.

"What?"

She didn't know. How was she supposed to know what to say? She had no idea. His hostility was so open that it pushed her back hard enough to nearly make her stumble and go swimming off the dock's other side. His angry pain lay so sharp and clear, that it made a scar on the face that had once looked at her with such love. It was an ugly scar and she had been the one to put it there.

"Where were you? I tried calling."

"I disconnected the damn thing."

"Why?" As if she didn't know. To avoid her.

"I'm leaving."

"When?" He couldn't. He wouldn't. Not without a goodbye. Not without...

He pointed north. He had the same calendar she did. Ediz Hook Lighthouse was the December lighthouse—one of the very last in Puget Sound on the way to the open ocean.

"Now?" She choked out the word.

He nodded without softening. He kept the boat away from the dock with practiced nudges of the controls and the tiller.

She had to think of what to say. Had to get it right. Had to let him know that...

"I'm giving up the angels' share."

"What's that, some special condo deal they offered you on the beach?"

"It's the second reason they use oak barrels in making wine. The first is flavor. The second—the angels' share—is what they call the part that escapes through the porous wood. The extra that is lost, let go of, to make the wine that remains behind even better."

"And what have you let go of?"

How should she know? She didn't have all the answers on tap. She was making this up as she went. She flapped her arms and let them drop to her side. Then wrapped them about herself because she was rapidly turning into a human popsicle. Maybe not sweet, but certainly icy and soaked through to the skin.

"How about this? Crazy idea." And she'd think of it in a second. "Hear me out. Okay?"

"I won't live in Napa."

"I'm not asking you to."

"Or Sienna."

"Will you shut up for a second?"

"Amazing pictures by the way. You have a great eye."

"I have two of them. Now, be quiet."

He bit his upper lip and nodded.

He'd noticed the pictures. She'd loved taking them; loved that connection to place and time. Maybe, just maybe that was a part the answer. Anything was better than the bitter dregs that had chewed up her life these last three weeks.

"You're leaving now because you can't stand to see all of the places we were happy together."

He didn't speak, but she knew now. She knew how to read the pain in his eyes. The wound to his heart shot across his face and he looked away. But he didn't hit the throttle. He didn't leave. Russell simply hung his head against the pain.

She raised her voice, to make sure he could hear her over the rain.

"I have an offer. It's a crazy offer. They don't even know what they need, but I do. I haven't told you about it yet. *They* don't even know about it yet." Neither did she, but an idea, or the idea of an idea was forming. If she could think fast enough, maybe she'd find it.

"I'll make them an offer they can't refuse." Please, Russell, you made the offer once, make it again? Please.

"Who? China? India?"

"I told you to shut up." But the words came gently from her throat. She imagined, hoped that they sounded like the caress they were.

"It's got a lot of great sailing and great people. I know you'll feel connection there. I know it. They need help. They need my help."

He didn't react.

Think, Cassidy. Think harder.

"And, uh, they need an advertising specialist, too. Not some high-end New York studio godlike grunt who doesn't really care. They need someone who is only happy when he connects with his heart. With his really loving heart."

He stopped fussing with the controls. The boat began to twist a bit in the protected waters along the dock. He still looked away, but she could see the shift in his shoulders, in his stance, and read her first signs of hope there.

The stark anger was gone. She had a chance.

She hopped on one foot and then the other hoping to jog some words loose from her freezing body. Standing out in the November rain just might be colder than falling overboard, but she wasn't about to jump into the water to find out.

The chance that Russell would freeze her out was many times scarier than merely being dragged out to sea.

"It would give me a chance to really be involved in the entire process. Cultivation to viticulture to marketing. Not control, but involved, understanding. Like you said on our first date, I'd get to know the whole story of the wine. And I'll, I'll make it a cooperative of some sort. I'm sure they'll do it. They're really good people. They could be world class with my help. With *our* help"—there it was—"but it only works with the two of us."

He turned to face her.

"They have just a dozen or so wineries but with amazing potential. If they could work together, we could make them into the next great wine region. It's a little place, probably less total acreage than Mondavi, never mind Napa. It's called Puget Sound. Maybe you've heard of it?" Maybe, just maybe you'll remember that you proposed to me among the Italian vineyards and forget that I was too wrapped up in my own world to hear it.

The boat drifted a few feet closer to the dock.

"So I was thinking. We could, um, sail all over the Sound, up the Inside Passage to Alaska on occasion and... Then, you know, we'd..."

What, Cassidy?

"...together we'd..."

What is it you really want?

Help me, Daddy.

That was it. He already had.

345

She stood up straight, moved to the edge of the dock until her toes hung over the ocean, raised her arm, and pointed a finger at his heart now so close as the *Lady* drifted near.

"As long as we're together, that's all that matters."

The stern bumped against the dock, closing the last of the gap between them, her finger actually came to rest against the center of his slicker-covered chest. He looked at her with the eyes she remembered, the ocean-deep eyes that she'd gotten lost in the first time she'd seen them.

In his arms. Her flippant answer had somehow been the truth.

This time she knew what to say and how to say it.

"*You* are my home."

END NOTES

My apologies to Brown Point Lighthouse for the addition of a dock. The original, much larger dock, installed to service the logging on the hills beyond, was removed in the 1930s.

My joy, to take a year and travel with my wife to the dozen lighthouses pictured on a calendar that she gave me for Christmas. She is my home.

Keep reading for an excerpt from book #2:
Where Dreams Reside
And reviews are a HUGE help.
Thanks for joining my journey, Matt.

IF YOU ENJOYED THIS, YOU MIGHT
ALSO ENJOY:

WHERE DREAMS RESIDE (EXCERPT)

NUMBER 2 IN THE WHERE DREAMS SERIES

*J*o Thompson prided herself on her practicality and calm demeanor. It had humbled opposing counsel and convinced even the most reluctant judges and juries. It was a weapon she could wield with the elegance a chef plied her knife.

So why was she standing here feeling...mushy?

Definitely not her norm. Even a sip of the exceptional champagne, that sparkled across her tongue with the same joy as the June evening, only helped her focus a little.

The setting was glorious, a broad white canopy fluttering in the light evening breeze that drifted over the lawn. Through its open sides she could see the Mukilteo lighthouse and, sliding out from behind the brickwork tower, a large green-and-white Whidbey Island ferry nosing out onto the waters of Washington State's Puget Sound. Sunset—a path of gold on the saves—straight to her. As if it was trying to lead her away from her so-clear route through life.

The whole thing was so romantic that even contemplating it choked Jo up all over again. She turned back to the goings-on under the canopy.

Cassidy was positively radiant. Her best friend wore a cream-and-ivory lace sheath wedding dress that clung to her shape like a caress. Every time she even breathed, hidden threads of metallic silver glinted and sparkled. On a more provocative woman, or even a lesser one, it would have been indecent. On Cassidy all it did was smolder, which was clearly giving her new husband something to think about.

The first dance hadn't been a tango, but she and Russell had certainly danced it like one, as if they were the only man and woman alive in the whole world. The reception might now be winding down, but they still moved together, constantly teetering on the edge of a tangle of fiery passion.

Jo searched out the third member of their self-proclaimed "Terrific Trio." Perrin was flirting with the father of the groom, who was almost as handsome as his son. And, with her typical effervescence that exceeded even the champagne's, was doing so despite Russell's mother happily draped on his arm. Julia Morgan took Jo's arrival as an opportunity to return to the dance floor with her husband.

"They're such a beautiful couple," Perrin sighed happily as she and Jo leaned their shoulders together.

"They are." It was clear that they'd been dancing together for years. Jo had never learned, but they made it look so intimate and fun that maybe she'd have to find the time.

Someday.

In her copious spare minutes between lawsuits.

Perhaps not.

She only really managed to carve out time with Cassidy this week because she was in between cases. A situation that would be ending first thing tomorrow morning.

Lanterns warmed the scene as the summer evening slowly faded in the background. A live duo were knocking out songs that you couldn't help at least tapping your foot to. Above them, the Mukilteo lighthouse spun and cast its beam upon the June waters.

"We done good!" Perrin jarred Jo's shoulder with a sharp nudge.

"No, you did. The dress you designed for her is a marvel."

"It does make her look pretty marvelous, not that she doesn't normally. Still wish Russell had let me do something with his outfit." He stood with his best man taking a momentary breather from the dance floor.

Jo arched an eyebrow at her, "Do you think you could make him look even better than that?"

Perrin offered her a bit of a grimace. "Probably not. He's sooo hunky in that tux, but it would have been fun to try."

"He doesn't just look that hunky," Cassidy slammed into them from behind and draped her arms over Perrin and Jo's shoulders, the sweet peas laced into her hair scenting the first-night-of-summer air. "He *is* that hunky! I can't wait to rip his tux off." Then she blushed bright red and grinned at the same time.

Jo pulled her in, "You done good, Cassie. Exactly what you're supposed to be doing and who with."

Cassidy laughed. A laugh she'd rarely displayed even when they were college roommates over a decade before, but she had discovered it with Russell Morgan.

"When do you fly out?"

Cassidy grabbed a piece of prosciutto-wrapped shrimp from a passing waiter. She tried to eat it, speak, and chortle all at the same time and nearly choked herself.

Jo handed over her glass of champagne from which Cassidy took several swallows and then released a loud hiccup.

"Tomorrow morning."

"Wellll," Perrin drawled out the word. "I'm sure he'll let you finally sleep on the flight, unless you're going for an entry in the mile-high club."

Cassidy's smile and blush definitely grew. "Russell might have mentioned something about that."

"Damn," Perrin stamped her foot. "I am so jealous. I want reports. Perrin wants reports." She began counting on her fingers. "Is married sex better than single sex? Does high altitude make it, well, better somehow? Pluses and minuses of doing it in four-star hotels, Italian villas, and sailboats on the Mediterranean. Take notes. You'll be graded afterward."

"Yes, Perrin. I promise a report. When I get back from three weeks of sailing the Amalfi coast with the man of my dreams, we'll all go out, get drunk, and I'll tell you every little sordid detail about my most private sex life."

"Good." Perrin nodded emphatically. Her hair, presently dyed as black as Jo's, swirled about her pale face. As usual, she'd missed the sarcasm in Cassidy's voice.

Jo also knew from experience that Perrin would indeed be wheedling at least some of the juicier details out of their friend in due time. This allowed Jo to, without parsimony, both share Cassidy's present amusement at Perrin's expense and later enjoy the results of Perrin's somewhat voyeuristic but highly effective curiosity.

Cassidy hugged them both close, "Best friends ever."

"Best friends ever," she and Perrin repeated.

While Perrin was both more tipsy and much more emphatic, Jo could feel the truth of it once more softening her heart.

"Where's my goddamn camera?"

"Let it go, *mio amico.* You're the best man, Russell. No, wait. You're the groom, I'm the best man, though with how Cassidy is looking in that dress, the groom really oughta be someone handsome and Italian like me." Angelo Parrano slapped Russell on the back hard enough that the groom almost snorted his beer.

"But just look at them." Russell insisted.

There was no question who "them" was.

It was almost impossible to look away from the three women friends, but he managed because he knew he'd been staring.

Russell's friends from the dock where his sailboat was moored in Seattle were mostly dressed for the Northwest, clean jeans and button-down shirts. They clustered together by the buffet table Angelo had spent most of last night putting together, eating the gourmet food with as much attention as they'd eat a bucket of chicken. He'd bet money they were talking about sailing. It was a topic they never tired of.

Near the bar stood a group of Russell's New York friends. They were dressed far more fashionably, looking dark, edgy, and wholly out of place at a Pacific Northwest wedding reception—outdoors at that, held beside a picturesque lighthouse. Clearly, in their opinions, the wedding of one of America's wealthiest bachelors and an internationally known food-and-wine critic shouldn't be in a setting more rustic than the ballroom at the Carlyle in Manhattan.

A dozen or so of the Northwest's top vintners from Cassidy's new Northwest Wines venture were in attendance.

She'd also invited a daunting slice of the restaurant world—Michelin-starred chefs and food critics with a global voice.

It shouldn't be surprising who Cassidy's friends were. Still, it was his restaurant, Angelo's Tuscan Hearth, where they'd held the rehearsal dinner. And now it was his buffet they were presently tasting and judging.

He looked away because he couldn't bear to watch, even from a distance.

Yet out of the whole crowd, there was no question which "them" Russell was referring to or why, as a professional photographer, he was desperate for his camera. The three women laughing together made an amazing picture.

Cassidy was right out of a magazine shoot. As a matter of fact, she soon would be. Angelo knew Russell was planning to use her in that dress for the next ad campaign for Perrin's Glorious Garb. Not just a boutique for edgy clothes, but now astonishing wedding dresses as well.

Actually he'd be an idiot if he didn't use all three of them in exactly these dresses. Perrin had done one of her fashion-design numbers on herself and Jo Thompson as well. Courtesy of a dye job, Perrin's hair matched Jo's, a straight fall almost as black as night to the middle of their backs. Their dresses were cut from the same cloth, but that's where the similarity ended.

Perrin's pale skin and blue eyes were offset against the light celery-green fabric by severe lines in the dress' tailoring that accented the slender lines of her body and revealed unexpected flashes of that creamy skin. She looked long and dangerous, like a racing sailboat or a Miyabi chef's knife.

Jo's darker skin, revealing her part-Alaskan heritage, was kissed by the gentle green curves of her dress. Each swoop and swirl accented her full figure and the fitness he knew she earned through hard sweat at the gym. A man could become lost while navigating among those curves until there was no hope for his return.

The three women had their foreheads together and their arms around each other's waists.

"Truth, beauty, and joy. Jo, Cassidy, and Perrin." Josh Harper observed over Angelo's shoulder even as Perrin burst forth with one of her bubbling laughs. The reviewer from *Gourmet Week* had come up between Angelo and Russell. He knew Josh from a couple of stellar reviews of Angelo's Tuscan Hearth and his habit of coming there to eat when he was in town, even when he wasn't researching for a review.

"Guess it wasn't hard to tell what was grabbing our attention." Russell noted. "You're good with words, Josh. Maybe you should write for a living or something. No, wait. Those are my words."

"I only steal from the best," Josh sighed as he watched the three women. "There are moments when being happily married really sucks."

"And moments when it's damn good." Russell took a swallow from his bottle of beer. "So what's your excuse, Angelo?"

He tried to speak, he really did. But Jo Thompson had just raised her head and was looking at him from beside the other two women. Her dark eyes inspected him as only a top corporate lawyer could, slowly taking him apart like a fine chiffonade, one sliver-thin slice at a time.

Russell's punch on his arm sent him staggering to the side. His wine, thankfully a white Oregon Viognier, spilled down the leg of his gray suit pants, and perfumed him with its warm floral components.

"Shit, Russell!"

"Sorry buddy. I'd feel bad, but I have to go dance with the most beautiful woman here." He finished his beer, handed Angelo the empty before going to fetch his wife. Having his hands full was the only thing that kept him from smacking the groom a good one.

Angelo stood there, empty wine glass in one hand, a drained beer bottle in the other, and a stain down his tuxedo pant that made it look as if he'd just peed himself. Like a lush on display. He shook his leg to try and shake loose the wet pant leg clinging to his skin. It didn't work.

Then he looked up and saw that Jo was still watching him. A soft smile, the kind that came the instant before a laugh, lit her face.

Josh clapped Angelo on the shoulder as Russell and Cassidy hit the dance floor, appearing to float several feet above it in their happiness.

"Yep! A good woman has definite perks." Josh said moments before his own wife swept him up to join the dance. All of the happily married couples dancing beneath the emerging stars was an amazing spectacle.

But Angelo couldn't stop watching Jo Thompson.

Keep reading.
Available at fine retailers everywhere:
Where Dreams Reside

ABOUT THE AUTHOR

USA Today and Amazon #1 Bestseller M. L. "Matt" Buchman has 70+ contemporary and military romance novels, and action-adventure thrillers. Also 100 short stories and lotsa audiobooks.

Booklist says: 3x "Top 10 Romance of the Year" and among "The 20 Best Romantic Suspense Novels: Modern Master-pieces." NPR and B&N say: "Best 5 Romance of the Year." PW declares: "Tom Clancy fans open to a strong female lead will clamor for more."

A project manager with a geophysics degree, he's designed and built houses, flown and jumped out of planes, solo-sailed a 50' sailboat, and bicycled solo around the world...and he quilts. More at: www.mlbuchman.com.

Other works by M. L. Buchman: *(* - also in audio)*

Action-Adventure Thrillers

Dead Chef
One Chef!
Two Chef!

Miranda Chase
*Drone**
*Thunderbolt**
*Condor**
*Ghostrider**
*Raider**
*Chinook**
*Havoc**
*White Top**

Romantic Suspense

Delta Force
*Target Engaged**
*Heart Strike**
*Wild Justice**
*Midnight Trust**

Firehawks
MAIN FLIGHT
Pure Heat
Full Blaze
*Hot Point**
*Flash of Fire**
Wild Fire

SMOKEJUMPERS
*Wildfire at Dawn**
*Wildfire at Larch Creek**
*Wildfire on the Skagit**

The Night Stalkers
MAIN FLIGHT
The Night Is Mine
I Own the Dawn
Wait Until Dark
Take Over at Midnight

Light Up the Night
Bring On the Dusk
By Break of Day
AND THE NAVY
Christmas at Steel Beach
Christmas at Peleliu Cove
WHITE HOUSE HOLIDAY
*Daniel's Christmas**
*Frank's Independence Day**
*Peter's Christmas**
*Zachary's Christmas**
*Roy's Independence Day**
*Damien's Christmas**
5E
Target of the Heart
Target Lock on Love
Target of Mine
Target of One's Own

Shadow Force: Psi
*At the Slightest Sound**
*At the Quietest Word**
*At the Merest Glance**
*At the Clearest Sensation**

White House Protection Force
*Off the Leash**
*On Your Mark**
*In the Weeds**

Contemporary Romance

Eagle Cove
Return to Eagle Cove
Recipe for Eagle Cove
Longing for Eagle Cove
Keepsake for Eagle Cove

Henderson's Ranch
*Nathan's Big Sky**
*Big Sky, Loyal Heart**
*Big Sky Dog Whisperer**

Other works by M. L. Buchman:

Contemporary Romance (cont)

Love Abroad
Heart of the Cotswolds: England
Path of Love: Cinque Terre, Italy

Where Dreams
Where Dreams are Born
Where Dreams Reside
Where Dreams Are of Christmas*
Where Dreams Unfold
Where Dreams Are Written
Where Dreams Continue

Science Fiction / Fantasy

Deities Anonymous
Cookbook from Hell: Reheated
Saviors 101

Single Titles
The Nara Reaction
Monk's Maze
the Me and Elsie Chronicles

Non-Fiction

Strategies for Success
Managing Your Inner Artist/Writer
Estate Planning for Authors*
Character Voice
Narrate and Record Your Own Audiobook*

Short Story Series by M. L. Buchman:

Romantic Suspense

Antarctic Ice Fliers

Delta Force
Th Delta Force Shooters
The Delta Force Warriors

Firehawks
The Firehawks Lookouts
The Firehawks Hotshots
The Firebirds

The Night Stalkers
The Night Stalkers 5D Stories
The Night Stalkers 5E Stories
The Night Stalkers CSAR
The Night Stalkers Wedding Stories

US Coast Guard

White House Protection Force

Contemporary Romance

Eagle Cove

Henderson's Ranch*

Where Dreams

Action-Adventure Thrillers

Dead Chef

Miranda Chase Origin Stories

Science Fiction / Fantasy

Deities Anonymous

Other
The Future Night Stalkers
Single Titles

SIGN UP FOR M. L. BUCHMAN'S NEWSLETTER TODAY

www.ingramcontent.com/pod-product-compliance
Lightning Source LLC
Chambersburg PA
CBHW050615110726
47899CB00001B/115